NANCY
DREW
FILES
VOL. I

Don't miss more mystery:

Nancy Drew Files Vol. II

NANCY DREW FILES

VOL. I

Secrets Can Kill
Deadly Intent
Murder on Ice

CAROLYN KEENE

SIMON PULSE

NEW YORK LONDON TORONTO SYDNEY NEW DELHI

SIMON PULSE
An imprint of Simon & Schuster Children's Publishing Division
1230 Avenue of the Americas, New York, New York 10020
This Simon Pulse paperback edition September 2019
Secrets Can Kill copyright © 1986 by Simon & Schuster, Inc.
Deadly Intent copyright © 1986 by Simon & Schuster, Inc.
Murder on Ice copyright © 1986 by Simon & Schuster, Inc.
Produced individually in 1986 by Mega-Books of New York, Inc.
Published separately in 1986 by Pocket, an imprint of Simon & Schuster, Inc.
Cover illustration copyright © 2019 by Fernanda Suarez
All rights reserved, including the right of reproduction
in whole or in part in any form.
SIMON PULSE and colophon are registered trademarks of Simon & Schuster, Inc.
NANCY DREW, AN ARCHWAY PAPERBACK and colophon are registered
trademarks of Simon & Schuster, Inc.
THE NANCY DREW FILES is a trademark of Simon & Schuster, Inc.
For information about special discounts for bulk purchases, please contact
Simon & Schuster Special Sales at 1-866-506-1949 or business@simonandschuster.com.
The Simon & Schuster Speakers Bureau can bring authors to your live event.
For more information or to book an event contact the Simon & Schuster Speakers
Bureau at 1-866-248-3049 or visit our website at www.simonspeakers.com.
Cover designed by Sarah Creech
Interior designed by Hilary Zarycky
The text of this book was set in Electra LT Std.
Manufactured in the United States of America
2 4 6 8 10 9 7 5 3 1
Library of Congress Control Number 2019944459
ISBN 9781534463127 (pbk)
ISBN 9781481414456 (*Secrets Can Kill* eBook)
ISBN 9781481414463 (*Deadly Intent* eBook)
ISBN 9781481414470 (*Murder on Ice* eBook)
These titles were previously published individually.

CONTENTS

SECRETS CAN KILL

CHAPTER ONE

Hands on her hips, Nancy Drew stood in the middle of her bedroom and surveyed the situation. New clothes lay everywhere—strewn across the bed, draped over the backs of chairs, and spilling out of shopping bags.

Laughing at the mess, Nancy reached for a just-bought pair of designer jeans. "How do you like the new look in private detectives?" she said, slipping the jeans on. "Undercover and overdressed!"

"I'd give anything to have a job like yours." Bess Marvin studied the label on an oversized green sweater that would be perfect with Nancy's reddish-blond hair. "Not only did you get to buy a whole closetful of clothes for it, but you'll probably be asked out by every good-looking boy at Bedford High."

George Fayne swallowed the last of her frozen yogurt and asked, "What's going on at that school, anyway?"

"I don't know all the details yet, but it doesn't sound too terrible," Nancy said. "Lockers broken into, a few files and some digital equipment missing, stuff like that." She zipped up the jeans and took the sweater Bess was holding out. "The principal, Mr. Parton, said he'd tell me more tomorrow. I won't say the case is going to be a piece of cake," Nancy said with a grin, "but it doesn't exactly sound like the hardest sleuthing I've ever done, either."

At eighteen, Nancy Drew already had a reputation in her hometown of River Heights as one of the brightest, hottest young detectives around. And she'd earned every bit of that reputation the hard way—by tracking down clues and solving mysteries that ranged from arson to kidnapping.

Nancy took every case seriously, of course, but somehow, going undercover as a high-school student to find a small-time vandal just didn't seem very heavy. After all, she'd been up against some really tough characters in the past, like armed robbers and blackmailers.

Nancy studied herself in the mirror. She liked what she saw. The tight jeans looked great on her long, slim legs and the green sweater complemented her strawberry-blond hair. Her eyes flashed with the excitement of a new case. She was counting on solving the little mystery fairly easily. In fact, Nancy thought it would probably be fun! "Right now," she said to her two friends, "the hardest part of this case is deciding what to wear."

"That outfit, definitely," Bess said. "You'll make the guys absolutely drool."

"That's all she needs," George joked. "A bunch of freshmen following her around like underage puppies."

"Oh, yeah? Have you seen the captain of the Bedford football team?" Bess rolled her eyes. "They don't call him 'Hunk' Hogan for nothing!"

Bess and George were Nancy's best friends, and they were cousins, but that was about all they had in common. Blond-haired Bess was bubbly and easygoing. She loved romance, and she fell in and out of love every other month.

George, with curly dark hair and a shy smile, was quiet, with a dry sense of humor and the toned body of an athlete. George liked boys as much as Bess did, but she was more serious about love. "When I fall," she'd say, "it's going to be for real."

Both girls had helped Nancy to solve cases in the past, and they'd just spent the entire day with her at the shopping mall, helping Bedford High's "new girl" choose her new wardrobe.

"Anyway," Bess went on, "Nancy will be completely immune to the charms of Hunk Hogan. She's got Ned, right, Nan?"

"Right." Nancy glanced at the mirror above her dresser, where she'd stuck a snapshot of Ned Nickerson, and her grin changed to a soft smile as she thought of the first boy she'd ever loved.

Nancy and Ned had a very special relationship. They'd known each other since they were kids, and when they'd first realized they loved each other, they'd thought it would last forever. But neither one was ready yet for a "forever" commitment, so occasionally they drifted apart, dating other people. Yet somehow, Nancy always found herself coming back to Ned. They were so in tune with each other that no matter what they were doing—whether it was tracking down the clues to a mystery or planning a private party for two—it seemed that they could read each other's thoughts.

Nancy smiled to herself and wondered if Ned knew what she was thinking at that moment, which was: that as good as he looked in a photograph, with his light brown hair, soft dark eyes, and gently curving mouth, Ned was a hundred times better in the flesh.

Shivering as she remembered the feel of his arms around her, Nancy promised herself that when she solved the Bedford High case, she would definitely join him for a long weekend with his family at their cabin in the mountains.

"You're right," she said again. "In my eyes, no guy can compete with Ned. But if I meet some really gorgeous senior, I'll be sure to get his number for you."

"Great!" Bess fingered the gold locket she always wore around her neck. When she was in love, the locket carried a picture of the lucky boy. At the moment it was empty. "But I don't want to be a complete hog," she said with a laugh. "Get a number for George, too."

George blushed and tossed a pillow at her cousin. "No, thanks. I'll find my own guy."

"I've heard that before," Bess joked. "Come on, Nancy's in a perfect position to fix us up. Who knows when we'll have a chance like this again?"

George tossed a second pillow, but by then she was laughing, too. "Nancy's supposed to be solving a crime, not setting us up."

"Who cares? She can do both! Right, Nan?"

Bess tossed one of the pillows at Nancy, Nancy tossed it back, and in a few seconds, the girls were in the middle of a full-fledged pillow fight. Soon the room was a bigger mess than ever, as feathers flew from the pillows and slowly drifted down onto the piles of clothes and shopping bags.

The free-for-all was still going strong when the Drews' housekeeper stuck her head around the door and good-naturedly dodged a flying pillow.

Hannah Gruen had been with the Drews since Nancy was born. After Mrs. Drew died, when Nancy was still a baby, Hannah's role had grown way beyond that of housekeeper. Mrs. Gruen had hugged and scolded Nancy through childhood, bandaging scraped knees and kissing away tears. As the years went by, she was always ready with encouragement and advice. And, of course, the hugging and scolding had continued, too. In time Hannah had become almost a second mother to Nancy. She was always there when Nancy's father's work as a lawyer took him away from his daughter. Carson Drew trusted Hannah implicitly, and Nancy loved her without question.

"Hannah!" Nancy giggled when she saw Mrs. Gruen in the doorway. "I know what you're going to say—it's a school night, and I'd better clean up my room fast and get to bed early!"

"Well, I couldn't help thinking that you *are* starting a new assignment tomorrow, and you *should* probably get a good night's rest," Hannah said. "But the real reason I'm here is to give you this." She handed Nancy a manila envelope.

Nancy took it and saw her name printed in black marker. There was no return address, no stamp, no postmark. "Where did this come from?" she asked.

"I haven't the vaguest idea," Hannah replied. "I went out to sweep the front porch about five minutes ago and there it was, poking out of the mailbox."

Nancy fingered the package, then held it up to her ear. "Well, it's not ticking," she joked.

She ripped open the envelope and pulled out a disc labeled WATCH.

"Oh, terrific," Bess said. "A movie. I've been dying to see a good movie lately."

"Too bad we don't have any popcorn," George said as they trooped down the hall toward the den.

"I just bought a bag," Hannah said, heading for the kitchen. "Come help yourselves if you get hungry."

In the den Nancy turned on the television and then opened the cabinet that held the DVD player. "I wish I knew where this came from," she said. "Who goes around leaving DVDs on people's doorsteps?"

"Maybe it's some advertising gimmick," Bess suggested.

"No, I've got it!" George began laughing. "It's that fitness program Bess was so interested in—the one with all the gorgeous guys."

Nancy grinned. "Yeah, I had the feeling she was more interested in the boys than the exercises." She slipped the disc in and pushed the play button. "Okay," she said, joining Bess and George on the couch, "get ready."

The girls were still laughing as the movie started, but after the first few seconds, the laughter stopped.

"What is this, anyway?" George asked.

Leaning forward from her corner of the couch, Bess gave a little cry of surprise. "It's *us*," she said. "Look!"

In silence the girls watched themselves doing exactly what they'd done six hours earlier: entering the shopping mall and arguing about which store to go to first.

But after that the camera stayed almost exclusively on Nancy. There she was, studying the mannequins in the window of a fashionable boutique; there she was again, coming out of a store called Ups & Downs, checking her wallet.

"You were afraid you'd left your credit card in the store," Bess said. "Remember?"

"I remember." Nancy didn't take her eyes off the screen. "But I don't remember anybody hanging around filming the whole thing."

The camera stayed on Nancy: riding the escalator, going in and out of stores, sipping a Coke. Then it showed the three friends eating hot dogs by the fountain in the center of the mall.

George shook her head. "This has to be some kind of weird joke."

"It's weird, all right," Nancy agreed. "But if it's a joke, I'm not laughing."

"There can't be much more," Bess said. "Panache was the last store we went into."

Sure enough, as they watched themselves come out of Panache, the camera zoomed in on Nancy. The last frame froze in a close-up of her smiling face.

Nancy was reaching out to turn off the TV when a screeching, whining sound made her stop, her hand in midair.

Then a high-pitched, hideously shrieking voice invaded the Drews' cozy den. "Stick with shopping, Nancy Drew. It's a lot safer than snooping at Bedford High!"

CHAPTER TWO

Early the next morning, as Nancy was pulling her red Mustang out of the Drews' driveway, the sound of the frightening voice came back to her once again. "Stick to shopping, huh?" Nancy muttered under her breath. "Fat chance." She shifted her car into drive and was just stepping on the gas when she saw Hannah hurrying out the front door.

"You almost forgot this," Hannah said, handing Nancy an orange canvas duffel bag that held notebooks, pens, and makeup—everything Nancy had packed for her "first day" at school.

"Thanks, Hannah." Nancy stifled a yawn and smiled as she took the bag. "I almost forgot my most important prop for this job."

"You don't look very alert this morning, I must say," Hannah commented. "In fact, you look downright sleepy."

"I'm fine, Hannah, really. See you later!" Nancy waved cheerfully as she drove from her house, but Hannah had been right. Nancy was definitely less than bright-eyed and bushy–tailed.

No wonder, Nancy thought. Getting to sleep the night before had been next to impossible. She was always a little edgy before she started a new case, but the past night had been worse than usual. She'd lain awake, running the mysterious video through her mind over and over again.

The creepiest part was that horrible voice. The sound of it had echoed in Nancy's head all night and into the morning. It had obviously been electronically distorted, but realizing that didn't make it any less scary. And knowing that someone had been following her all day was definitely frightening. Nancy couldn't help thinking about the equipment that had been taken from Bedford High. Could there be any link between the two? Nancy wondered.

Who was responsible? And why? Why would some high school kid who was into rifling lockers and stealing a few files go to such trouble to scare her off? And how did whoever it was know about Nancy's assignment? That was the question that had kept the young detective awake the longest.

Nancy had tried not to think about those pieces to the Bedford High puzzle. She knew she wouldn't figure them out until she actually got to the school campus and did some on-the-spot research. Still, she hadn't been able to keep her mind off the troubling questions. And there she was on the first day of a case, nervous and droopy-eyed!

As she drove the fifteen miles from River Heights to the town of Bedford, Nancy tuned the car radio to a random station, hoping the music would clear her head. She slowed, passing the local Ford dealer. The new Mustang GT Convertible she'd been drooling over was still inside. Be cool, Nancy, she said to herself with a half smile, trying to keep her heart from pounding. Then, pressing her foot to the accelerator, she zoomed toward town.

Bedford was beautiful, small, but with large homes surrounded by lush lawns, and, no doubt, swimming pools tucked away in the back somewhere. On the outskirts of town, along the road to the high school, Nancy passed several houses that could only be described as mansions.

Bedford was obviously a place where a lot of rich people lived, Nancy thought as she pulled up to a stoplight near the high school. At just that moment a sleek, expensive black Porsche 911 eased up beside her in the next lane.

Nancy glanced over, admiring the car, and its owner gently revved the engine. The powerful motor gave a soft, throaty rumble, then another. Nancy smiled at the obvious come-on and lifted her gaze to the driver.

The guy in the Porsche was one of the most gorgeous boys Nancy had ever seen. He looked about seventeen. He'd probably been a towhead when he was little, but now his blond hair was highlighted with streaks of honey-brown. And his eyes— were they brown or black?—were full of light and laughter as he gave Nancy a playful grin and revved the engine once more.

Suddenly Nancy was wide awake. She grinned back and fluttered the gas pedal on the Mustang. Two can play this game, she thought.

Out of the corner of her eye, Nancy saw the turn arrow change to green. Still looking at the boy, she smoothly shifted gears. Then she peeled out ahead of the Porsche, swinging wide into his lane so that he had to follow her all the way down Bedford Road. She was definitely back in high school!

Nancy lost sight of the Porsche somewhere in Bedford High's student parking lot, and as she joined the crowd of kids swarming up the school's front steps, she stopped thinking about it. Of course, its driver wasn't quite so easy to forget.

Bedford High wasn't big, with a total enrollment of about six hundred students. But it seemed to Nancy as if every one of those students was milling around in the building's front hall. They looked like a typical bunch of kids. While they waited for the final bell, they laughed together, calling to each other, talking about dates and upcoming tests.

For a moment Nancy felt exactly like what she was pretending to be—a transfer student coming into a new school in the middle of fall semester. There she was, facing a bunch of strangers who already knew each other and were checking her out, trying to figure out who the new girl was. She felt exposed and self-conscious, and like all new kids, she wished she had a friend nearby. That's the way you're supposed to feel, Nancy told herself. At least it was a good cover.

Nancy was standing alone, trying to remember the directions to the principal's office that she had been given, when a snatch of conversation caught her attention.

"You know I can't give you a ride," a boy's voice said. Nancy could detect the frantic pleading in it. "I just *can't*. If I miss practice, I'll be kicked off the team!"

Then came a second boy's voice, calm and slow and coldly self-assured. "Miss practice . . . or else," it ordered.

Nancy craned her neck, trying to locate the source of that unpleasant little exchange. There was no way, however, to match the voices to any of the faces in the mass of chattering students around her.

I guess there's at least one super-creep in every high school, Nancy thought to herself. But as she headed for the principal's office, she kept hearing the harsh sound of that calm, cold voice. There was an intimidating power in it. And obviously, whomever it belonged to had someone scared.

Nancy turned down one of Bedford High's drab green hallways. No matter how much high schools changed, she decided, the paint jobs never seemed to. Nancy found the principal's office and told the secretary that she had an appointment with Mr. Parton. The principal didn't keep Nancy waiting five seconds.

Stepping into the office, Nancy took one look at Mr. Parton and decided to try to solve this case in record time. Not only did she want that weekend with Ned, but Mr. Parton looked like he was on the verge of a nervous breakdown. For the sake of his health, she'd better work fast!

"It's driving me insane!" Mr. Parton declared, dramatically pounding his fists against his temples. "And are the police any help? Noooo. Beef up security, they say. Ha! Try getting the salary for another guard out of the school board. A patrol car drives around the school every night. We can't be bothered with a little file-filching. It's your problem, they say."

Mr. Parton paused for breath and then chuckled to himself, shaking his bald head and smiling at Nancy with worried brown eyes. "Thank heavens I know your father. If he hadn't suggested that I hire you, I don't know what I'd have done."

Probably collapsed, Nancy told herself, but she kept her thoughts silent. She smiled. "I'm glad you did call me, Mr. Parton. I'm ready to get started, but first I just want to make sure I've got the facts straight. You mentioned files being taken. What files?"

"Actually, we're not sure." Mr. Parton shook his head again. "But my file cabinet and the senior guidance counselor's—both of which are kept locked, by the way—have been tampered with several times. We don't know if anything's missing because everything's always put back in the wrong place.

"Then there are the lockers," Mr. Parton went on, rubbing one hand over his shiny head. "We know that at least four lockers have been broken into. Our maintenance man reported them." He leaned forward, hands clasped. "But no students complained."

"It could have something to do with drugs," Nancy suggested. "That would explain why the kids kept their mouths shut."

"True. And I won't say that Bedford High is drug-free. But I do know for sure that there aren't any drugs in my file cabinet. And what about the digital equipment?"

Right, Nancy thought, remembering the "movie" she'd received.

"Whoever's taking the stuff is very selective," the principal said. "We lose a lens here, a charging cable there, then a couple of blank discs and flash drives. Some of it's even turned up mysteriously a few days after disappearing."

"And you're sure whoever's pulling all these stunts is one person?" Nancy asked.

"I'm not sure of anything," Mr. Parton said, frustration mounting in his voice. "But I'm almost certain that a student, or more than one student, is behind it all."

"Why couldn't it be a teacher?"

"Well, the police, much as I'm disappointed in them, did do me one favor. They questioned the faculty, checked them out, and came up with zilch, except for the bio teacher, who turned out to be a scofflaw. Two hundred dollars in unpaid parking tickets."

Nancy laughed. "Well, having me pose as a student was a good idea." She stood up and reached for her canvas bag. "I'd like to get started, but first I need to know if I have your permission to check things out my own way. I mean, I may have to break a few rules to get to the bottom of this."

"Whatever it takes. I'll clear it with the police," Mr. Parton said emphatically. "And don't go yet." He motioned for Nancy to sit again. "I may not be thinking too clearly these days, but I do know that you'll need a contact while you're here, somebody you can talk to freely. Someone who can introduce you to a lot of kids. The principal isn't going to help any student fit in. Even I know that."

"Your thinking's not all that fuzzy, Mr. Parton." Nancy laughed again. "So. Who's my contact?"

"One of our seniors. A good student, completely trustworthy. And very popular, president of the class, which is why I chose him. He can introduce you to other students."

"You mean he knows about me already?" Nancy asked, once again thinking about the disc.

"No, I thought I'd introduce you two and let him in on the plan at the same time." Mr. Parton checked his watch. "He should be here any minute."

At that moment there was a knock at the door. Mr. Parton opened it, and Nancy looked up and found herself face-to-face with the beautiful driver of the black Porsche!

"Nancy Drew," the principal said, "meet Daryl Gray."

His eyes weren't brown or black, Nancy noticed immediately. They were the dark, dusky color of ripe blueberries, and they were rimmed with lashes that had to be at least half an inch long. Nancy had never seen eyes like that in her life.

Some contact! she thought.

Daryl Gray listened politely and with interest as Mr. Parton explained the entire situation. If he was surprised at Nancy's role, he didn't show it.

Instead, Daryl's incredible eyes kept straying to Nancy each time Mr. Parton mentioned her name. And when the principal said something about Daryl showing Nancy the ropes, Daryl's mouth curved into a slow, teasing grin. Nancy couldn't help returning it.

The attraction between them crackled like electricity. Nancy wondered how Mr. Parton could possibly miss the sparks, but he seemed oblivious to everything but his problem. He went on and on. As Nancy tuned out the principal's voice, she tuned into the beautiful face before her.

Finally the harried principal said something that brought Nancy back to reality. "Nancy, the school is counting on you. I've done what I can. Now it's up to you. At this moment Daryl is the only one, aside from me, who knows who you are and what you're doing here. The rest is in your hands."

And Nancy, remembering that hideous voice on the video, finally tore her eyes away from Daryl.

You're wrong, Mr. Parton, she thought. Somebody else knows who I am. And that's the person I have to find.

CHAPTER THREE

The warning bell rang just as Nancy and Daryl left Mr. Parton's office. Together they fell into step with the crowd of kids hurrying to their homeroom classes. Out of the corner of her eye Nancy caught Daryl looking at her, a strange little smile on his lips. "What's funny?" she asked.

"Nothing." Daryl laughed softly and shook his head. "It's just that I've never met a detective, especially a beautiful redhead who drives a Mustang."

Nancy laughed too. "Well, I've never met a senior who drives a Porsche."

"It's my favorite toy." They rounded a corner and Daryl casually put his hand on Nancy's shoulder to guide her out of the way of a group of kids coming in the opposite direction. "I'll have to give you a ride sometime, show you what it can do."

At the touch of Daryl's hand, Nancy felt a delicious tingling sensation, and suddenly she found herself wondering what it would be like to have Daryl's arms around her. Daryl Gray was powerfully attractive.

"Do you think it would be good for making fast getaways?" Nancy went on in the same teasing manner.

"Sure," Daryl replied, leaving his hand where it was, "but I hope you're not planning to make a getaway real soon. After all, we just met."

"And besides, I have a mystery to solve, remember?"

"Right. And I hope it takes a long, long time."

They were both laughing, looking into each other's eyes as they turned another corner and bumped into what felt to Nancy like a rock wall.

"Sorry," the wall said.

Nancy touched her nose to make sure it wasn't broken, and then smiled at the guy, who was big and handsome, and built like a truck.

"Walt, meet Nancy Drew. She's a transfer student," Daryl said smoothly. "Nancy, Walt Hogan."

Nancy smiled again, remembering what Bess had said about Bedford's football captain. "Hunk" fit him perfectly.

"Yeah," Walt said, not returning her smile, "nice to meet you."

Walt strode off, and Nancy turned to Daryl. "He seemed a little angry," she commented.

"Yeah, he hasn't been Mr. Friendly lately," Daryl agreed. "And you should see him in action on the field. He's like a bear just out of hibernation—mean and hungry."

"I don't suppose he's interested in cinematography, by any chance?"

"I thought detectives were supposed to be more subtle than that."

"Why should I be subtle with you?" Nancy teased. "You're my contact, aren't you?"

21

Daryl's hand tightened on Nancy's shoulder. "I sure am," he said softly.

Nancy and Daryl were standing in front of Nancy's homeroom class, waiting for the final bell to ring. About ten other kids were waiting, too, and as Nancy laughed at Daryl's last remark, she caught a girl staring at them.

The girl was blond, pretty in a tough, hard-edged kind of way, but she didn't look too friendly, Nancy thought. She was watching Daryl intently. Then as someone called out "Carla!" she moved her eyes to Nancy's face for just a second before turning away. In that brief instant she gave Nancy the strangest look. It wasn't a look of dislike, Nancy thought, it was more like a challenge. She wondered how much this Carla knew about her.

The final bell rang, and Daryl gave Nancy's shoulder another squeeze. "I guess this is it for now," he said. He leaned so close that Nancy felt his breath on her ear. "You're on your own, detective."

Actually, Nancy didn't expect to do much detecting on her first day. She was new in school; she had to find her way around, get used to the rhythm of the place, and meet a few people before she could start asking questions.

Part of Nancy's cover was to act like a new girl—lost and a little out of it—which was easy, since that was how she felt. Daryl wasn't in any of her classes and she didn't know anyone else.

Most of the kids ignored Nancy. The first really friendly girl she met was a pretty blond with aquamarine eyes, who waylaid Nancy after English.

22

"Hi, I'm Sara Ames," she said. "You're new here, aren't you?"

"My name's Nancy Drew, and you're right, I'm brand-new."

"Well, don't worry, you'll fit in fast," Sara said. "But I wanted to get to you before anybody else did."

"Oh?" Nancy wondered if Sara might have some secret information.

"I'm editor of the *Bedford Sentinel*," Sara went on, "and we're desperate for people to work on the paper. I noticed in English that you can at least read and write," she joked. "And I bet you're going to be popular, so you'll have lots of good contacts. The *Sentinel*'s fun. What do you think?"

Nancy smiled to herself at the thought of her "contact." She smiled at Sara, too, for making her feel welcomed. "Thanks for asking," she said. "Let me feel my way around a little more, okay? Then I'll let you know."

"Great! There's a staff meeting tonight, room 215. I hope you can make it." With a friendly wave, Sara dashed down the hall.

Nancy's next class was American history. She'd almost forgotten just how boring a bad teacher could be, but the droning voice, the intimidating looks, all of it reminded her why she'd been happy to leave high school behind. She'd certainly be happy to leave history behind! The forty-five-minute period dragged on and on. Halfway through, Nancy let her mind wander. Anything was better than the teacher's monotone.

Purposely putting Bedford High's mystery out of her mind, Nancy thought about Sara Ames's offer to join the newspaper staff. She was tempted to accept it. Maybe she could have a double cover—new girl and student reporter, investigating the vandal of Bedford High. It might work, she thought. But once she solved the case, she'd be leaving the school, and that would leave Sara minus one reporter. It didn't seem fair.

When American history was finally over, Nancy heaved a sigh of relief along with the rest of the students. "Class," the teacher called over the noise of the final bell, "read the next two chapters in your textbook for homework."

"Great," Nancy groaned to herself. "Boring homework, too." The Bedford High mystery was turning out to have hidden liabilities!

On the way to lunch Nancy spotted Sara Ames at the entrance to the cafeteria and decided to tell her she wouldn't be joining the newspaper. That way Sara wouldn't feel hurt when Nancy didn't show up at the staff meeting.

"Hi," Nancy said. "Listen, thanks for asking me to join the paper, but I think I'd better make sure my grades are in good enough shape before I do anything else, you know?"

"Okay," said Sara. "I understand. Just let me know whenever you're ready."

"Thanks," said Nancy.

Sara rushed off, and Nancy entered the cafeteria. She looked around uncertainly. Where should she sit?

At that moment she heard someone call her name. Turning, she saw Connie Watson waiting in the cafeteria line.

Nancy knew Connie's name because the teacher had called

on her in French class. Connie's face had turned the color of a ripe tomato as she'd given her answer, and after class Nancy had noticed that no one walked out of the room with her. Connie seemed anxious, though her eyes were friendly. She smiled shyly and said, "Hey, would you like to eat lunch with me?"

"I wish I could," Nancy said sincerely, "but I've got to talk to the counselor about my schedule—I've been stuck with two gym classes, can you believe it? I'm just going to grab a yogurt and keep going!"

What Nancy really wanted was a chance to snoop around the media room, provided it was empty. If it wasn't, maybe she could ask a few "innocent" questions.

After promising Connie that she'd sit with her the next day, Nancy paid for her yogurt, headed down the hall, turned a corner, and stopped. Some detective you are, she told herself. You didn't even bother to find out where the media room is!

Nancy was about ready to go back to the cafeteria and ask Connie when she saw Carla walking toward her. Nancy hadn't forgotten the challenging look Carla had given her that morning, but she put on a bright smile anyway. "Hi. This is embarrassing, but I'm lost. Could you point me in the direction of the media room?"

"Oh, it's easy to get lost in this place," Carla said with a friendly smile. "Just go to the end of this hall, turn left and follow the hall to the end. Then go through the door on your right and down the stairs. You can't miss it."

"Thanks," Nancy said, just as nicely. "I appreciate it."

Maybe I was just being paranoid this morning, she thought

as she walked along. Nancy turned left and went down the second hall. She pushed open the door, started down the steps, and stopped. The staircase obviously wasn't going to take her to the media room. From the look of things, it would probably lead straight to the boiler room.

On the other hand, she thought, maybe Carla really is a prime pain in the you-know-what.

Or maybe Carla had something to do with the anonymous disc. That might explain why she would go out of her way to steer Nancy away from the media room.

Nancy was moving back up the stairs when she heard scuffling sounds from below. She stopped, listening, then heard a muffled shout.

"Just lay off, Jake Webb," a voice said. "You're a nobody, a waste of space." The voice grew angrier. "I've given you what you want, so get off my back."

Footsteps pounded up the stairs. Before Nancy could move, Walt Hogan, the surly star of the football team, was beside her. He wasn't just surly, though. He was furious, his face flushed with anger. Walt shouldered Nancy roughly aside. Then his fury exploded and he rammed his clenched fists into the door before shoving it open and storming through.

While Nancy tried to decide whether to run after Walt, she heard a soft laugh. Looking down, she saw another boy, one she hadn't met before, staring up at her.

"Well, if it isn't Bedford High's newest scholar, Nancy Drew," the boy sneered. "I'm Jake Webb."

Jake smiled as he began climbing the stairs toward Nancy, but the look in his eyes was cold. "Do you always go around poking your nose into other people's business?" he asked. "Not too nice, Nancy Drew. Maybe I ought to explain a few rules to you. Otherwise, you won't get very far at Bedford High."

Nancy recognized the voice. It was the same one she'd heard in the main hall that morning, coolly ordering some desperate kid to "miss practice—or else." Jake's face went with his voice, Nancy thought—lean and bony, with a tight-lipped smile under sharp, ice-blue eyes.

Nancy felt an overwhelming urge to tell the creep to buzz off. But Jake wasn't acting like the average high-school egomaniac, and she was curious to see what he was up to.

Jake climbed the stairs until his eyes were level with Nancy's. Still smiling, he ran one finger lazily up her arm, across her neck, and to her lips.

"Rule One," Jake said softly. "Keep your mouth shut about what you just heard. If you don't, you'll never learn Rule Two."

CHAPTER FOUR

Nancy was tempted to bite Jake's finger and see what happened, but instead she forced herself to push his hand away calmly. She was so furious, she didn't even think about being frightened. Who did this guy think he was, anyway?

"Who makes these rules?" she asked. "You, I suppose?"

"Clever Nancy," Jake said with a laugh. "Go to the head of the class."

The longer Nancy stood there, the stronger the urge she had to push Jake Webb down the stairs. She'd already decided that he was a prime candidate for the Bedford High vandal (not to mention the Bedford town jail), but at the moment all she wanted was to get rid of him.

"Look," she said, "I don't know what you're trying to do, but I think I ought to tell you that I don't scare easily." She put her hand on the door. "Why don't you just crawl back under your rock?"

Without waiting for Jake's reaction, Nancy pulled the door open and almost bumped into Daryl Gray.

"Well, well," Jake scoffed. "It's 'King Cool.'"

Completely ignoring Jake, Daryl smiled at Nancy. "Hi. I expected to see you in the cafeteria."

"She couldn't make it," Jake said. "She had more important things to do than eat."

"You okay?" Daryl asked Nancy.

"I was getting a little bored with the company, but I'm fine now," she said. "How'd you know I was here?"

"Are you kidding?" Jake leaned against the doorjamb and grinned. "King Cool has the inside track on everything—girls, cars, clever ways to make money. Right, King?"

Quickly Daryl shifted his glance to Jake. "You talk too much, Webb," he said sharply. "I'm tired of the sound of your voice. Do everybody a favor and give your mouth a rest."

"Anything you say, King." Jake held Daryl's gaze for a second. "But my eyes'll still be open—you can count on that." Then he slouched off down the hall.

Nancy let out her breath. "What was all that business about your money and keeping his eyes open?"

"Hard to tell with that guy," Daryl said. "How'd you run into him, anyway?"

Nancy explained, and noticed a funny look on Daryl's face when she mentioned Carla, but she decided not to ask about it. "Anyway, I'm glad you came along," she said. "I was just about ready to blow my cover with that creep."

"Jake Webb's personality fits his name," Daryl said with a grimace. "He's just like a spider waiting for a fly to come along. I can't believe he actually works in the principal's office. But most of us here are pretty all right. I'll prove it to you if you'll come to the dance with me this weekend."

"That's a pretty intriguing invitation," Nancy said with a smile. "I'm too curious to turn you down."

"It's a date, then."

Daryl touched her arm in a familiar gesture before walking away. Once again, Nancy thrilled to the feel of his hand. As she hurried to her next class, she pictured the two of them dancing together, arms around each other. The picture brought a smile to her face. As long as she was at Bedford High, she thought, she might as well have some fun.

By the time her last class of the day was over, Nancy's head was a blur of names and faces, a jumble of bells and pounding feet. As she'd expected, she hadn't done much detecting at all. Only two people—Carla and Jake—stood out in her mind as possibly connected to the vandalism and to the disc she'd received.

She wanted to find out more about both of them, but first she wanted to take a look around the media room to see if she could discover any connection between the missing equipment and the mysterious recording.

She wasn't taking any chances on getting lost a second time—she asked a teacher for directions and, after stashing some books in her locker, made her way to room 235.

The door was locked. Probably only the teacher had a key. Well, Mr. Parton *had* given her permission to do "whatever it takes," she thought. She reached into her duffel bag and pulled out an extremely handy little device—a credit card—and took a careful look down the hall.

SECRETS CAN KILL

Connie Watson was walking straight toward her.

"Hi, Nancy!" Connie called. "I've been looking for you. The football team's got practice this afternoon and I thought you might want to go to it with me." Connie blushed and bit her lip. "You don't have to, though. I mean, if you're too busy, that's okay," she said quickly, as if she were used to being rejected.

"No, I think I'd like that," Nancy said, pocketing the credit card. Maybe she'd get a chance to talk to Walt Hogan. She was very curious about the cryptic conversation she'd overheard on the stairs. "Let's go."

The weather was warm for early October, and several dozen kids were sitting in the bleachers watching the players and the cheerleading squad. Nancy and Connie arrived just in time to see Hunk Hogan getting chewed out royally by the coach. Nancy couldn't hear what was being said, but she wondered if Walt was in trouble because he'd arrived late. If that was it, then it was probably his voice she'd heard in the main hall that morning, pleading with Jake. She hadn't recognized it when she met him, but if it *was* Walt, then she had more reason than ever to talk to him.

The cheerleaders were energetic and colorful in their bright orange and white uniforms. Nancy admired their routines and even had to admit that Carla, who seemed to be the captain, was very good.

Beside her, Connie sighed. "I'd give anything to be a cheerleader," she confided. "Of course, I'm too shy, so it's not worth

31

thinking about. Besides, even if I were more outgoing, I'd never make it. Not with Carla Dalton in charge. She can't stand me."

Nancy nodded sympathetically. "She's not too enthusiastic about me, either, but I don't have a clue why."

"Oh, that's easy," Connie said. "Ever since you arrived at Bedford High, Daryl Gray hasn't taken his eyes off you, and Carla can't stand competition." She put her hand over her mouth and giggled. "Personally, I love seeing Carla get what she deserves."

"You mean Carla and Daryl have a thing going?" Nancy asked. That explained the funny look on Daryl's face when Carla's name had been mentioned. Nancy couldn't picture Daryl being interested in someone like that, but she really didn't know him all that well.

"Off and on," Connie told her. "It's been off for a couple of weeks, but when you showed up, I guess Carla decided you were invading her territory."

So Carla's jealous, Nancy thought. That might make her nasty, but it didn't make her a criminal.

"Actually, I'm surprised she still wants Daryl," Connie went on. "Carla's only interested in one thing—money."

"Well, Daryl can't be heading for the poorhouse," Nancy remarked. "Not if he drives around in a Porsche."

"It is a little weird," Connie agreed, "especially since his father lost practically all his money a few months ago in some big business fiasco. For a while the Grays were one of the richest families in Bedford, but now . . ."

Connie's voice trailed off as she shook her head in sympathy. Nancy was sympathetic, too, but she was also curious. Not about the Grays' money problems—that was simply none of her business—but about what other tidbits of information Connie might have. She was something of a gossip, Nancy thought, and gossips could be a big help. Connie was chattering away again, pointing out various kids on the field, when Nancy noticed the bracelet on her right wrist. "That's beautiful," she said, touching it. "What is it, art deco?"

"I . . . I don't know," Connie said, nervously fingering the intricately patterned gold. "It was a present . . . I don't know anything about jewelry."

"I love it. It looks like an antique," Nancy told her. A little flattery never hurt when you wanted information, and besides, she really liked Connie. "So, tell me more about Bedford High," she prompted. "Hey, I hear there're some weird things going on—stuff getting stolen and lockers broken into."

"You must mean the 'phantom,'" Connie said, seeming relieved at the change in subject. "That's what I call him, since no one knows who he is."

"Got any ideas?"

"No. And most kids don't really care. I mean, it's all so juvenile."

So much for inside information. Then Nancy had to sit on the hard bleachers for an hour as Connie proceeded to give her a detailed account of everyone's love life, grades, family, and friends. Nancy learned a lot, but nothing that was going to help. One day down, she thought. How many more to go?

• • •

Nancy arrived at school the next day, determined to start putting the puzzle together, or at least to gather a few of the pieces.

Instead of study hall she had gym during second period, and stretching her muscles and limbering up felt good. Maybe the exercise would limber her mind up, too, so she could solve the case.

Two minutes into gym, though, her mind was on something else.

"Excuse me," a voice said.

Nancy stopped in the middle of a sit-up and smiled at Carla Dalton, who was standing over her. Who knows, she thought, maybe a smile would help.

"I'd really appreciate it," Carla said, "if you'd keep your problems to yourself."

"What are you talking about?"

Carla put a hand on her cocked hip. "I'm talking about the way you ran and tattled to Daryl yesterday," she said nastily. "He chewed me out about it this morning. I mean, can't you fight your own battles?"

"Let's get something straight," Nancy said calmly. "I didn't 'tattle' to Daryl. He asked me how I got lost, and I told him. I don't want to fight with you, Carla," she went on, "but since you asked, yes, I can fight my own battles—and I usually win."

Nancy went back to her sit-ups, still smiling, but inside she was seething. This is all I need, she thought.

A few minutes later, though, she wondered just how petty

Carla was going to be. It was her turn on the trampoline, and as she prepared to go into a high flip, she noticed that the girl spotting her had changed places—with Carla Dalton.

It threw her concentration off. It shouldn't have, but it did. And as she sprung high into the air, she knew she was off balance.

There was no time to catch herself. If she'd had a reliable person spotting her, she wouldn't have worried, but Carla's back, she noticed, was conveniently turned. Before Nancy could stop herself, she was hurtling over the end of the trampoline—heading for a major collision with the floor.

CHAPTER FIVE

At the last possible second, Nancy pushed her body to the limit, twisted desperately in midair, and hit the floor — with her rear end. Thank goodness not with her head. It wasn't the most graceful move she'd ever made, but as she sat there breathing shakily, she decided that it was better to be a klutz than a corpse.

Nancy was tempted to prove to Carla then and there that she was ready to fight the battle. But when she got to her feet, she noticed that the gym teacher was doing it for her.

"Dalton!" Miss Gibbs was livid. "This isn't the pom-pom squad. You have to use your brains in here, if you have any! Drew could have broken her neck!"

Which would not have broken Carla's heart, Nancy thought grimly. It would have made her day.

Most of the girls had rushed over to Nancy, asking if she was all right, whether she needed to see the nurse, whether she was sure nothing was broken.

"Thanks," Nancy said gratefully. "I'm still in one piece. But I think I lost something."

"What?" somebody asked.

"My hips," Nancy joked. "They're permanently embedded in the gym floor!"

Twenty minutes later, Nancy took her seat in social studies. She was still slightly rattled and was hoping for a lecture so she could just take notes and get her breath back.

"Okay," the teacher said gleefully, "clear your desks of everything but paper and pen. It's pop quiz time!"

Nancy joined the other kids in groaning, and took as long as possible finding a notebook and pen.

"Don't worry," the boy behind her said. "Mr. Warner's quizzes are so bad, nobody passes. If you flunk, you won't be alone."

"Right," the girl to her left said. "The only one with a chance is Hal Morgan."

Nancy glanced to her right and noticed that Hal Morgan was chewing his fingernails nervously.

"He doesn't look too confident," she whispered.

"Yeah, that's weird," the girl whispered back. "You know, it's funny. Hal's been the class brain forever. Always studying, you know? Never had time for anything else. But then this September, he surprised everybody by running for class president against Daryl Gray. He didn't win, but he sure did try. I can't believe how much time he spent campaigning."

"Maybe that's why he looks nervous," Nancy said. "Maybe his grades dropped during the campaign."

The girl shrugged. "Maybe. But he's been talking about going to Harvard, so he must be doing something right. And his SATs were off the top of the scale."

"Okay, scholars," Mr. Warner cackled. "Let's get this show on the road!"

By the fifth question, Nancy had decided that the boy behind her was right. There was no way she was going to pass the quiz. At least she didn't have to worry about her grade-point average, like everybody else.

She glanced at the clock, to see how much more torture she might have to go through. As she did she noticed that Hal Morgan seemed to be having trouble concentrating, too. In fact, his eyes were on *Nancy's* paper. As soon as he saw her glance at him, he looked away.

The teacher asked the next question, and Nancy wrote down her answer. Then she deliberately put her hands to her hair so her paper would be clear.

Sure enough, Hal made a pretense of stretching and yawning, and as he rolled his head around, his eyes once more zeroed in on Nancy's paper.

It was obvious, to Nancy anyway, that Hal the Brain was copying her answers. But why? Why would somebody so smart bother to cheat on a pop quiz?

Well, it sure isn't going to do him any good, she thought as they passed their papers to the front. Hal's going to get exactly what I get, which is probably a fifty.

She didn't think much more of the incident until after class. As she left the room, she saw Jake Webb lurking in the hall. Then she saw Hal walk up to him, reluctantly, the way most people walk into a dentist's office.

Wondering what those two could possibly have in common, Nancy attached herself to a group of kids who were standing around, moaning about the quiz.

It was hard to hear everything, but she caught enough to make her extremely curious.

"Listen," Hal was saying, "I've got my own essay to write before I can get to yours!"

"That's cool," Jake said. "I'll give you till tomorrow. How's that?"

"That's not enough time, and you know it." Hal sounded panicky.

"Oh, too bad," said Jake sarcastically. "Well, I guess I don't have to tell you what'll happen, right?"

Hal let out a big sigh and Nancy saw the defeated look on his face. "Okay, okay," he said. "You'll have it tomorrow."

That guy is really the pits, Nancy thought as she watched Jake walk cockily down the hall. He acts like a king, and he's got at least two lackeys—Walt and Hal—doing his bidding. How many others are hustling to follow his orders? And why? Why would anyone want to do anything for Jake Webb?

Without really thinking about it, Nancy had begun following Jake, but when she saw him turn into another hall and open his locker, she decided she might learn something about him if she could see what was inside that locker. She didn't know what she'd be looking for—money, maybe—but it was worth a try.

As she passed him she got a look at the locker number—515—and before Jake saw her, she walked quickly to the water fountain at the end of the hall. She had to drink enough to float a ship, but finally she saw Jake's scuffed sneakers pass by and out of sight.

It was lunchtime and the hall was empty. Nancy moved quickly to locker 515. A credit card wouldn't be any help this time. But a professional lock-picker's kit would. Fortunately, along with her makeup and lunch money, Nancy's canvas bag just happened to have such a kit. She found the right-size pick and had the padlock off in half a minute. She pulled the door open and was ready for a leisurely exploration when she heard a voice.

"Be back in a second," it said, "I forgot my psych book."

It was Jake Webb. Quickly Nancy raked her eyes over the inside of his locker. Only one thing caught her attention—a shoebox. Dangling from it was a beautiful gold bracelet, *exactly* like Connie Watson's.

That was all Nancy had time for. She shut the door and moved away just as she heard Jake's footsteps round the corner.

He has no way of knowing what you were up to, she told herself. Just keep on going.

Nancy kept on going, but she was sure Jake Webb's eyes were on her back every step of the way.

She was glad to get out of his sight, even though once she was, Nancy still couldn't relax. What was Connie's bracelet doing in a shoebox in Jake Webb's locker? It had to be the same bracelet; it was an antique, probably one of a kind. Maybe Connie lost it and Jake, lowlife that he was, found it and decided to stash it.

When Nancy spotted Connie in the lunch line she decided

to make sure she was right. "Hi," she said. "Guess what? I think I know where your bracelet is!"

Connie jumped as if she'd been stung. "My—my bracelet?"

Nancy pointed to Connie's bare wrist. "Right. You lost it, didn't you?"

Connie nodded, her eyes wide.

"Well," Nancy went on, "I'm pretty sure I saw it—are you ready?—in Jake Webb's locker!"

Shaking her head, Connie backed away slowly, fear in her eyes. "It—it couldn't be mine," she stammered. "I lost mine at home. I mean, I didn't lose it. I just didn't wear it today, that's all."

"Connie, what's wrong?"

"Nothing!" the frightened girl said. "Really, nothing's wrong! I have to go. There's this meeting I forgot about. I have to go," she said again, and all but ran away.

Some really weird things are going on at Bedford High, Nancy thought as she watched Connie hurry off. And so far, they all lead to one person—Jake Webb. She didn't know if Jake was the phantom vandal, or the anonymous video stalker. But she did know he was up to something. All she had to do was find out what.

By the end of the day Nancy was ready to explode. First Connie had treated her as if she had some horrible communicable disease. Then she couldn't find Walt Hogan or Hal Morgan, so she hadn't been able to question them. Plus, she still ached from that fall off the trampoline. Things were definitely not going well. What she wanted most of all was to go home and soak in a hot tub.

Instead, Nancy decided she'd better make another pass at the media room. She didn't want to leave Bedford High empty-handed, not for the second day in a row.

The room wasn't locked. When Nancy walked in, the only person there was Daryl Gray, who was peering at a shelf of discs. Suddenly she felt happy for the first time all day.

"Am I glad to see you!" she cried.

Daryl spun around, startled. Then his lips parted in his Porsche-driver's grin. "Nancy Drew, isn't it? New girl and"—he glanced around at the otherwise empty room—"private eye? How's the detecting going?"

"Don't ask," Nancy said with a groan. "Anyway, what are you doing here? I didn't know you were taking a media class."

"I don't," Daryl said. "I was just doing some detecting of my own—looking for you." He came over to Nancy. "Looks like we found each other."

The nearness of him made Nancy forget all her problems. "I'm glad we did," she said. "I'm so glad, in fact, that I'm inviting you to go for a milkshake. Right now."

"Sounds great to me."

"Good. I'll drive," Nancy said teasingly, "and let you see what my Mustang can do."

As they walked through the parking lot, Nancy spotted Jake Webb among the cars. Probably siphoning gas, she thought. Every time she saw him, she remembered how he'd threatened her on the stairs the day before. Was that his first threat? Or had he tried to scare her off before with the video?

Then Daryl put his hand casually on Nancy's shoulder and she forgot about Jake Webb and simply enjoyed the touch of Daryl Gray.

"How is it going, really?" Daryl asked again as they got into the Mustang. "Have you found any clues? Are any of the pieces fitting together yet?"

Nancy started the car with a roar. "I never thought I'd say this," she admitted with a wry smile, "but right now, the last thing on earth I want to do is solve a mystery."

Glad to be leaving, Nancy headed out of the parking lot and down Bedford Road. Daryl didn't ask any more questions about the case, and she was grateful. There'd be plenty of time to think about it later; just then, all she wanted to do was drive.

As they headed away from the high school, Bedford Road became narrow and winding. Through the trees Nancy caught glimpses of water.

"That's Bedford Lake," Daryl pointed out. "It has some nice secluded benches. Why don't you drive down there?"

Down is right, Nancy thought as the grade suddenly became steeper. She'd been doing about thirty-five and all of a sudden the needle climbed to fifty. A blind curve was coming up. Nancy put her foot on the brake. The pedal sank to the floor, and her stomach sank with it.

"Hey," Daryl said, "I don't want to sound like a driver's ed teacher, but don't you think you should slow down a little?"

Nancy couldn't answer him. The brakes were gone, and her car was shooting down the winding road, completely out of control.

CHAPTER SIX

The car picked up speed, careening wildly down the hill. Nancy downshifted to second, then to first. The Mustang slowed, but not enough.

"Sharp curve coming up." Daryl spoke quietly, but Nancy heard the quiver in his voice. She couldn't blame him—she was too terrified to speak.

Hands glued to the wheel, Nancy guided the car into the curve, praying that she wouldn't meet another car coming up. The road remained clear, but it also grew steeper. And as she came out of the bend, she could see the stop sign at the bottom of the hill. It was still fifty yards away, but in her imagination she was already on top of it, could see the Mustang tearing into the intersection and colliding with whoever was unlucky enough to be in the wrong place at the wrong time.

Amazed that her hand was steady, Nancy reached over and slowly pulled up the handbrake. It didn't work. The car was going so fast that the brakes had burned out.

The stop sign was looming up ahead. There was no time to think. Instinctively Nancy aimed her car at the soft shoulder on the opposite side of the road. With an impact that snapped their heads back, the Mustang hit the bank, went up on two wheels, and wobbled for what seemed like an eternity. But finally, with a bone-jarring thump, it landed upright.

Nancy shut her eyes and leaned her head on the steering wheel. She was breathing like a marathon runner. When she opened her eyes again, she saw Daryl pry his hand loose from the dashboard. "Well," he said with a gasp, "so that's what your Mustang can do."

Nancy reached for his hand and held on tight. She felt like crying, but when she opened her mouth, a giggle came out. It was a perfectly normal hysterical reaction, she told herself. Then she giggled again.

There was a smile in Daryl's voice as he said, "How about letting me in on the joke?"

"It's just"—Nancy tried to stop laughing and couldn't—"I remembered that my car is due for an inspection in two weeks. Now the gears are probably stripped, the front bumper has to be completely smashed, and the brakes are burned out—" This last thought brought Nancy out of her dreamworld.

Her car! What had gone wrong? True, it needed an inspection, but that was just an official thing. Besides, she'd had new brakes installed six weeks ago. Something awfully strange was going on, and whatever it was, Nancy had a definite feeling that it wasn't good. She pushed open the door and jumped out.

"Hey! Where're you going?" Daryl called, rolling down his window. He stuck his head out and saw Nancy kneeling by the left front wheel, peering underneath the fender. "What is it?" he asked.

Nancy stood up, so angry she could hardly see straight. "The brake cable," she said grimly. "It's been cut."

"What?! Are you sure? I don't get it. Who'd . . . ?"

"Wait!" Nancy held her hand up for quiet. Then she sniffed the air. Frowning, she ran to the back of the car and sniffed again.

"What's wrong now?!"

Nancy could hardly believe what she was going to say. "That rock we went over? I think it cracked the gas tank. Daryl, the car could blow! It could blow any second!" She started down the hill. "Get out of the car. Hurry up!"

There were no footsteps behind her. "Nancy!" she heard Daryl call. "Nancy, I can't open the door! It's jammed!"

Nancy didn't hesitate. She raced back to the car and fought with the door from the outside, but she couldn't get a good grip on the handle because the door was on an angle, leaning toward her.

She ran to the driver's side. The smell of gas fumes was stronger than ever.

"Get your seat belt off," she said to Daryl, finally managing to open her door. She helped him climb out. "Now let's go!" She grabbed his hand. "The car's already beginning to burn!" she said as they ran desperately down the hill.

When the car blew, they were only a few yards away from it. The force of the explosion flung them into the underbrush by the side of the road.

They clung to each other. For a moment, hardly able to speak, they stared at the burning sports car.

"Nancy, are you all right?" Daryl whispered at last. His eyes were bright with concern.

Nancy nodded. Feeling the heat of Daryl's breath against her cheek, she hardly noticed her bruised knee and scratched arms. It seemed the most natural thing in the world for them to keep their arms around each other. Nancy closed her eyes and breathed deeply. When Daryl had first touched her two days before, in the hallway, she'd wondered what his arms would feel like. Now she knew—they felt fabulous.

But with that fabulous feeling came another feeling—guilt. It wasn't Ned whose arms were holding her; it wasn't Ned whose voice was murmuring her name. And hadn't she said just three days before that nobody could compete with Ned Nickerson? Well, maybe no one could in the long run. But at the moment—in the short run—Daryl Gray was doing a pretty good job of it.

It was a dangerous moment, emotionally, and Nancy knew she wasn't ready to deal with it. Before Daryl's lips reached for hers, she eased herself gently from his arms.

"Hey," she said softly.

"Hey, yourself." Daryl's blue eyes were smiling. Looking at Nancy, he gave a long sigh. "So," he said in a throaty voice, "how about answering the question I never got a chance to ask. Who would do something crazy like this?"

"I have a pretty good idea." Anger made Nancy's voice tight. She pulled away and felt herself stiffen. "Does the name Jake Webb ring any bells?"

"Jake? Sure," Daryl said slowly, sitting up. "I can see him doing something like this. But there's no way you can prove it, is there?"

Nancy was silent for a moment. She was remembering Jake's threat on the stairs, remembering him in the parking lot half an hour ago, hearing that voice on the recording: "Stick with shopping, Nancy Drew. It's a lot safer than snooping at Bedford High."

Well, she hadn't done much "snooping" yet, but she hadn't backed off either. Had Jake, for some reason, decided to stop her before she got any further?

"You're right," she said as she and Daryl got up and brushed the leaves and dirt off their clothes. "I can't prove it. But I think Jake's the one."

"So what are you going to do?"

"Talk to him about it," Nancy said. "First thing tomorrow morning."

"Hey, Nancy, I wouldn't do that," Daryl said quickly. "Jake Webb's not the kind of guy you go around accusing of something, believe me."

"I believe you," Nancy told him. "I also think he has some explaining to do."

Daryl took her hand, sounding really worried. "You shouldn't mess with that guy, Nancy!"

"I'm not going to mess with him, I'm just going to talk to him." In a way, Nancy was almost glad that Jake had given her something to think about. It took her mind off how she felt about Daryl, which was a mystery she didn't want to solve just then. "Please don't worry. I'll be careful," she said, flagging down a car that was passing slowly. "But Jake Webb is up to something, and I'm going to find out what it is."

"I think Daryl's right," George said as she drove toward Bedford High the next morning. Until Nancy got another car, George and Bess had to play chauffeur. "I think you should steer clear of this Jake Webb and go right to the police. Show them your car. Then let them deal with Jake."

"That's what I think, too." Bess leaned over the back seat and grinned at Nancy. "Now, tell us more about Daryl Gray."

"You'll probably meet him one of these days," Nancy said. She stared out at the beautiful Bedford houses, trying to decide the best way to approach Jake. Daryl was the least of her worries at the moment, even though she couldn't help remembering the kiss he'd given her after driving her home the previous night.

Before he'd kissed her, he'd tried once again to talk her out of confronting Jake. Nancy was touched that he was so worried about her, but she was sure she could handle Jake Webb. After all, she wasn't going to meet him in some dark alley; she was going to walk right up to him in the halls of Bedford High. She couldn't wait to see the look on his face when he saw that his plan hadn't worked—that she was alive and ready to take him on.

"What's happening?" George interrupted Nancy's thoughts, pointing to the wide front steps of the high school.

Nancy looked and saw at least half the student body milling around outside. The kids were talking in little clusters, waving their arms, pointing dramatically. Then she saw the police cars, one with its red lights still flashing.

"Well, at least you'll have police protection when you talk to Jake," Bess joked. "I wonder what they're here for."

"Good question," Nancy said. Could Daryl have called them? She didn't think so. He'd tried to talk her out of dealing with Jake at least ten times, but he'd never once suggested that she go to the police, which was a little strange, when she thought about it.

She didn't think about it for long, though. As soon as she got out of the car, she joined the nearest group of kids.

"What happened?" she asked. "What's going on?"

One of the girls turned to her, fear and excitement in her eyes. "It's Jake Webb," she said breathlessly. "He's been killed!"

CHAPTER SEVEN

Nancy wondered for a moment if she'd heard right. "Did you say killed?"

"Yes, he's dead!"

"But . . . how?"

"Nobody knows for sure," the girl went on, "but somebody found him about twenty minutes ago, and they say his neck's broken." She shivered. "It's awful, isn't it? I heard the guy who found him is still throwing up. Personally, I'm sure I would have passed out. I mean, can you imagine?"

Nancy could hardly imagine any of it. All night she'd been gearing up, getting ready to face Jake Webb, to accuse him, among other things, of trying to kill her. And in spite of what she'd told Daryl and Bess and George, she *had* been scared. Well, she wouldn't have to be scared anymore, not of Jake Webb.

Still finding the whole thing unbelievable, Nancy reported the news to Bess and George. Then she climbed the front steps and went into school. As she moved through the main hall, she heard bits and pieces of conversation that told her a little more about Jake Webb's demise:

"Right next to the media room, at the bottom of the stairs—hard, cement stairs. Geez, no wonder the fall broke his neck."

"They say he's been dead for two hours—I wonder what he was doing here at six in the morning?"

"Probably planting a bomb."

"Too bad he fell first."

"Fell? The guy didn't fall, no way! Didn't you hear about his face?"

Jake's face. That's what Nancy heard most about on her walk through the hall. His face was bruised and cut. The bruises could have come from a fall down a flight of cement stairs. But not the cuts around his eyes, not his split lip.

Jake had been in a fight before he hit the hard floor in front of the room. And if that was true, Nancy thought, then he didn't fall. He was pushed. And if he was pushed, then her investigation had just taken a giant leap—from vandalism to murder.

No one she heard even pretended to feel sorry that Jake was dead, and as she thought about Hunk, Hal, Connie, and who knew how many others, she realized that a lot of people around Bedford High would have wanted Jake to vanish. But who would have wanted it badly enough to give him that push?

When Nancy reached the scene of Jake's "accident," the police and the man from the coroner's office were still gathered there. The body, thank goodness, was gone.

She knew that if she talked to the police then and there, they'd listen to her. They'd probably even ask her to join their investigation.

But if she did that, she'd blow her cover. And if she did *that*, she might as well kiss the secrets of Bedford High good-bye.

Since the police were busy at the stairwell, Nancy decided that then might be a good time to check Jake Webb's locker. She wanted to look at the contents of that shoebox before anybody else got to it. What besides Connie's bracelet had Jake stashed away?

She was so busy wondering if Jake's locker would have any clues hidden in it, that she didn't see Daryl until she bumped into him.

"Daryl, hi!" Even with everything else on her mind, Nancy felt a warm rush of feeling at the sight of him. "I guess I don't need to ask if you've heard the news."

"Hardly." Daryl took her hand, but he did it in an absent-minded way. "I just talked to Mr. Parton," he said, his voice low enough that only Nancy could hear him. "He told me to tell you it's murder, definitely."

Nancy's eyes widened, but she wasn't really surprised. "Did Mr. Parton say anything about me, about what I should do?"

"Just that he wants you to stay on the case," Daryl whispered, "and to handle it your way."

"Great! I was hoping he'd say that." Nancy breathed a sigh of relief and squeezed Daryl's hand. "Now I can really follow some leads." She started to walk away but Daryl held her back.

"Wait a second," he said. "If Jake was the vandal, then your case is solved. You're into murder now, Nancy. I think you should back off."

"You've got to be kidding!" Nancy couldn't help feeling

insulted. "Why should I back off? Do you think it's too complicated for me or something?"

"Hey, no, I didn't mean that." Daryl's violet eyes were full of worry. "It's just that it's probably going to get dangerous, Nancy. You don't have any idea what you're up against."

"No, I don't, but I'm going to find out." Nancy smiled at him. "Thanks for worrying about me, but please try not to," she said. "Really. I can take care of myself." Out of the corner of her eye, she saw Carla Dalton heading toward them, and she couldn't resist planting a kiss on Daryl's cheek. She wanted to anyway, but having Carla as a witness made it even more fun. "Gotta go now," she told Daryl. "I'll talk to you later, let you know what I've found out."

The halls were still jammed with kids discussing the morning's main event, but luckily the final bell rang as Nancy reached Jake's locker. She was surprised that everyone was still marching to the sound of bells, on that day of all days, but it was a good thing old habits died hard. The hall cleared in a matter of minutes. Nancy pulled on a pair of rubber gloves—no sense leaving fingerprints for the police—and quickly broke into locker 515.

The shoebox was still there, but something else caught her eye first. With a grim smile, she pulled a pair of wire cutters off the shelf. Turning them over in her hands, Nancy thought how easily they must have snapped her brake cable.

Underneath the wire cutters was a small black box. Nancy recognized it immediately as a battery for a video camera. She would have bet her designer jeans that Jake stole it from the media room and used it to record her and Bess and George on their shopping spree.

Finally Nancy took out the shoebox and lifted the lid, her heart beating with anticipation. Connie's bracelet was still there, along with a recent article from the school newspaper that carried a picture of Walt Hogan being brutally tackled during a game. The headline read, "The Hunk Gets Hit—He's Down but Not Out." The story went on to explain that if Walt missed the upcoming All-State Championship game because of injury, his badly needed football scholarship—and his ticket to the pros—might be in jeopardy. But Walt pooh-poohed the injury, claiming that nothing would stop him from playing in the All-State game.

At the bottom of the box, folded in half, was a wad of official-looking papers. As Nancy opened them she recognized them at once, without even reading the heading. They were SAT exams. There was just one difference between them and the ones she'd once toiled over—the set of exams in Jake's locker already had the answers marked in.

Nancy studied the curious contents of the box, trying to make sense out of them. She was positive now that Jake was the Bedford High vandal. The battery and the SATs pretty much proved that. But, looking at the bracelet, she wondered if he was also into stealing. It didn't really matter if he was, except for one thing—someone had killed him. And Nancy was determined to find out why.

The police were going to be asking the same questions, she knew, so she put the shoebox, the wire cutters, and the battery pack back where she'd found them. She closed the locker door and was trying to come up with an excuse for being late to her first class, when a voice behind her said, "Well, if it isn't Nancy Drew, girl detective. You always manage to be right in the swing of the nastiest things."

CHAPTER EIGHT

Nancy whirled around and came face-to-face with a tall, black-haired young woman whose vivid red lips were curled in a scornful smile.

Oh, great, Nancy thought. This is exactly what I need—Brenda Carlton!

As she looked at Brenda, standing there in her trendy trenchcoat, a notebook and pen in one hand, Nancy felt like laughing. Brenda had delusions of being an investigative reporter for *Today's Times*, her daddy's award-winning newspaper. But as far as Nancy was concerned, the only thing Brenda did well was mess up Nancy's investigations. She'd done that too many times for Nancy ever to trust her, and there she was again, smirking and lurking.

"Well, Brenda," Nancy said, "what are you doing here? Trying to play reporter?"

"I saw you first, girl wonder." Brenda gave Nancy a saccharine smile and flipped open her notebook. "Let's see," she said, pretending to scribble with her pen, "'When this reporter arrived at Bedford High, the first person she ran into was none other than Nancy Drew, *alleged* private detective.' How does that sound?"

If she talks any louder, Nancy thought, the whole school'll

know who I am. "Okay, Brenda, what do you *think* I'm doing here? What do sleuths usually do at the scene of the crime?"

"Scene of the crime? This looks like a high-school locker to me, not the bottom of a stairwell." Brenda's green eyes swept over Nancy in a quick, but all-seeing, glance. Pointing a red-nailed finger at Nancy's history book, she smiled. "Oh, I see! You're posing as a student. How clever of you! I'm surprised you thought of it."

Dropping the sweet voice, Brenda went on, "Now, why don't you give me a few more details about what's going on here? If you don't, all your little high school friends are going to find out real fast what you're really up to. And I have a feeling you wouldn't like that at all."

"Is that a threat, Brenda?"

"Of course it is, Nancy. So how about it? Are you going to give me the whole story?"

Nancy sighed. What choice did she have? The case was complicated and dangerous; she couldn't solve it and battle Brenda Carlton at the same time. "All right," she said, gritting her teeth, "I'll make a deal with you."

"A deal?" Brenda's silky eyebrows drew together in a frown. "What kind of deal?"

"The kind of deal that'll give you the exclusive story," Nancy told her. "Face it, Brenda, the police aren't going to give you the time of day. And right now, I know more about what's going on than they do. So when it's over, I'll be able to give you the real story, right down to the last juicy detail."

Nancy watched Brenda's frown change to a smile. Probably

seeing her byline already, she thought. "There's just one catch," she warned. "I give you the story *after* I've solved the case, not before. If you want to know everything I do, stay out of my way and keep your mouth shut about who I am. Think you can manage that?"

For about thirty seconds Brenda wavered between taking her chances with the police then, or making a deal with Nancy for later. Finally she reached a decision. "Well, all right," she said, pouting. "I'll do it your way. But," she warned, "you'd better keep your part of the bargain or the only role you'll ever play again is 'unemployed detective.'"

Nancy bit her lip to keep back any insulting remarks that might blow the deal. But as she watched Brenda stroll away, she promised herself that someday, she was going to close that reporter's notebook for good.

With the police swarming all over the school, Nancy's investigation didn't get very far. All the kids were talking about Jake, of course, but even so, Nancy wasn't able to learn much. All the kids had opinions, but they were just gossip and speculation. Nancy wanted to talk to the three people whom she knew had some connection with Jake—Walt Hogan, Hal Morgan, and Connie Watson. She didn't see Walt at all, and Hal didn't hear her call to him after American history, or maybe he didn't want to hear her. He looked extremely nervous. So did Connie, who once more acted as if Nancy had developed a sudden case of overwhelmingly bad breath.

If anyone has any answers, Nancy thought, they're not admitting it. Nancy didn't have any answers either, but she thought she might find something in the media room. Obviously, Jake had been "borrowing" the school's equipment; maybe Nancy could find some clue that would tell her why.

The door was locked again, so Nancy used her credit card. As she worked the lock, she thought she heard a noise coming from inside the room. She stopped, listening. There it was, a faint thump, as if someone had dropped something on the floor.

Could a policeman be in there? It was four o'clock in the afternoon; the halls were empty of students, and Nancy had watched the two patrol cars drive off half an hour ago. Still, they might have left one officer behind to guard the school. If they had, Nancy decided that it wouldn't help her case any to get caught.

She raised her hand and knocked loudly on the door. Then she listened again. No sound this time. After a few more loud raps, she decided that whatever she'd heard hadn't come from inside. The empty halls picked up sounds from everywhere. The noise could have come from the floor above. She worked the lock again and pushed open the door.

The room was a wreck. Cables and wires were strewn across the floor like uncoiled snakes, and at least half the discs had been pulled from the shelves and lay in scattered piles on the desk and the floor. Nancy knew the police must have searched the place after finding that battery pack in Jake's locker. Either that (and they were real slobs), or somebody else had been there. Could that someone have been Jake's murderer, after some kind of evidence?

Suddenly Nancy didn't like all the silence around her. She cleared her throat noisily and told herself that if the murderer had been there, he (or she) was probably long gone. And from the look of things, he hadn't found what he was after. Maybe she could beat him to it, she thought.

Quietly Nancy closed the door behind her and stepped over several lengths of cable to the middle of the room. Her gaze fell on a neat row of about thirty discs in cases, still on the shelf.

Nancy crossed the room to the shelf and saw that the discs were just movies. Glancing at the familiar names, Nancy thought maybe they weren't worth her attention. But then, one of the labels caught her eye. Right next to *The Great Gatsby* was a disc labeled *I Spy*.

I Spy? It wasn't anything Nancy had heard of. Nancy decided to have a quick look at it. She just hoped the actors were good.

After the first few seconds Nancy wished there *were* actors. Instead, Nancy knew she was seeing reality.

The first person on the recording was Hunk Hogan. He was sitting on a bench in what must have been the locker room. No one else was visible, and when Walt glanced cautiously around, Nancy decided that *he* had decided he was alone.

After another careful look, the star tackle reached into the duffel bag at his feet and took out a roll of white tape. Obviously in great pain, he began to wrap it around his rib cage, wincing the whole time. Nancy remembered the article in Jake's locker that told of Walt betting all his hopes for a football scholarship on the upcoming All-State game. From the look of him, he'd be lucky to get dressed for that game, much less play in it. Walt was hurt, but he'd hidden it—from everyone except Jake Webb.

The media room was stuffy and hot, but Nancy shivered as a chill ran up her spine. She'd been right—this case was much, much bigger than anyone thought. And the *I Spy* disc was an extremely hot piece of evidence. Too hot to be watching smack in the middle of Bedford High.

Quickly Nancy pushed the stop button and removed the disc. She was reaching for the monitor to shut it off when she heard a noise. Or thought she did. She snapped off the monitor and listened. For a few seconds the only sound she heard was the blood pulsing in her ears. But then came another noise, a squeak, as if someone had stopped leaning on a table. Or a door!

At the far end of the room was a door marked "Supplies," and as Nancy listened again, she heard another muffled sound. Someone was in that supply room. And it wasn't a policeman. A policeman would have been out by then, asking her what she was doing there, demanding that she turn over the disc, which was crucial evidence in a murder investigation. And who else would be interested in such crucial evidence but Jake's killer?

For an instant Nancy froze. If the killer was in that supply closet, Nancy's life was in danger. So was the evidence. She knew she had to get out fast. Noiselessly she dropped the disc into her bag. She wanted to run, but she was afraid of alerting whoever was behind the door. Slowly, quietly, she inched her way across the room to the hall door. With a sweaty hand, she eased it open and slipped out. Then she tore down the hall as fast as she could.

It was late afternoon and the hall was dark. The stairs leading to the first floor were even darker, but Nancy didn't slow down. She jumped the last four steps, skidded around a corner, and raced toward the main door. As she neared it she thought she heard footsteps on the stairs, but she didn't bother to turn around and make sure. Still moving fast, she rammed into the panic bar, expecting the door to fly open.

The door didn't budge! Nancy was certain she heard footsteps behind her. She gave the door another desperate push. Nothing.

Okay, she thought. I guess it's showdown time. Taking a deep breath, Nancy turned around, ready to face the intruder.

CHAPTER NINE

Nancy closed her eyes, waited a beat, then forced them open. The dark hall loomed ahead of her. She focused on the bottom of the staircase, held her breath, and waited again. All she saw were shadows, and all she heard was her own heartbeat. No one was there. Not now, anyway.

Letting out her breath in a sigh of relief, Nancy leaned against the door—and found herself falling backward as the door opened easily, depositing her on her rear on the stone steps outside.

Of course, she thought, picking herself up, it's a double door. You just pushed the wrong side.

Glad to be outdoors, Nancy took several deep gulps of the cool autumn air. Then she saw George's car make a slow turn around the side of the building.

"Hey!" Nancy waved her hand and ran down the front steps. "Here I am!"

The car slowed, and Bess stuck her head out the window. "We were just about to give up and go home," she said. "George has been driving around this parking lot forever, but I kept telling her you probably got a ride with Daryl."

"I wish I *had* been with Daryl," Nancy said as she climbed

into the back seat. "He's a lot more fun. And a lot safer, too."

"Why? What happened?" George wanted to know.

As they drove away from Bedford High, Nancy filled them in on everything that had happened, from the details of Jake's murder to her own scary escape from the media room. "And wait'll you see the video," she said, patting her duffel bag. "It'll never win an Oscar, but it's one of the most fascinating movies I've ever seen."

When they got back to Nancy's River Heights home and settled down to watch, they soon discovered that the tape was even more fascinating than Nancy had predicted. And Walt Hogan wasn't the only person Jake had made into a star.

Bess sighed as she watched Hunk tape his ribs. "How can he stand to play when he's in pain?"

"It's his only chance for that scholarship," George said. "If he doesn't get that, he'll never make the pros."

"Yeah, and he wasn't about to let anything stand in his way," Nancy commented. "Not the pain, and not Jake."

"Poor guy." Bess sighed again. "At least Jake Webb can't bother him anymore. Do you suppose Hunk is glad, deep down, that Jake's dead?"

"He wouldn't be human if he weren't," Nancy said. "But I have a question for you. Do you suppose Walt Hogan had anything to do with getting rid of Jake?"

Before either of her friends had a chance to answer that startling question, another face appeared on the television screen—the face of Connie Watson.

"Who's that?" Bess asked.

"A girl from Bedford High," Nancy told her, and scooted to the edge of the couch, wondering what on earth shy Connie could possibly have done to get a part in Jake Webb's "movie."

She soon found out. The "setting" was a sidewalk sale in fashionably quaint downtown Bedford. All the shopowners had brought their wares out to the sidewalks on what looked like a sunny autumn day. Crowds of shoppers strolled by, eating ice cream cones and stopping to look at paintings, handmade pottery, and furniture, and, Nancy noticed with a sense of dread, jewelry.

Nancy knew what was coming the minute she saw the jewelry display. Sure enough, the camera panned the crowd and focused on Connie Watson, a large shopping bag in her hand.

Nancy's heart sank as she watched what happened next. Connie picked up a bracelet—the one Nancy had seen her wearing—and admired it for a minute. Then she seemed to ask the shopowner the price and reluctantly put it back on the display table.

"Now just watch," Nancy told her friends. "She's about to make the biggest mistake of her life."

Hovering at the edge of the jewelry table, Connie waited until the owner was busy with about six customers at once. Then a close-up, courtesy of Jake the cameraman, showed her hook a finger under the bracelet and slide it into her conveniently waiting shopping bag. The camera pulled back then, and Connie melted into the crowds that filled the sidewalk.

But Jake wasn't through with Connie. His next shot caught her going up the front steps of the high school, the early morning sun glinting on her new gold bracelet.

"So far we've seen somebody covering up an injury and somebody shoplifting," George said. "I wonder what's next."

"I'm not sure I want to know." Bess shuddered. "This whole thing gives me the creeps."

"Oh, no!" Nancy pointed to the television screen and shook her head in amazement. "It's Hal Morgan. I should have guessed."

The next installment of Jake's horror show followed Hal, nervous nail-chewer and future Harvard scholar, straight to the door of the office of Bedford High's principal. Like Walt Hogan, Hal probably thought he was alone, because he glanced furtively around before entering the office.

The camera didn't follow him inside. It held steady on the closed door. Five seconds passed and then the door opened. Out came Hal, who stood still, obviously trying to work something out in his mind.

"You can almost hear the wheels turning," George remarked. "He's empty-handed. I wonder what he's after."

"Answers," Nancy said.

Bess looked confused. "Huh?"

"Just keep watching," Nancy told her. "You'll see what I mean."

Having worked out the problem, Hal walked quickly to another door. Without bothering to look behind him, he opened it and went inside. The camera stayed on the sign on the door, which read, "Counselors' Offices."

When Hal came out this time, he wasn't empty-handed. He didn't look worried or confused anymore, either. The camera gave Nancy and her two friends a brief glimpse of Hal's triumphant smile, but it lingered longest on what he held in his hands—answer books for the SATs.

"How could Jake record that without Hal seeing him?" George asked.

"He really knew his stuff," Nancy said. "He probably set that one up by remote control. That would explain why the offices had been broken into earlier. He must have been rigging up the camera." She thought a minute. "I wouldn't even be surprised if he gave Hal the idea for stealing those answers, just so he could tape the whole thing. After all, Jake did work in the principal's office."

When the screen went blank, Nancy turned off the television. "I'm glad that's over," she commented.

"So am I." Bess stood up and stretched. "I don't know why, but movies always make me hungry, even this one. Let's go see what's in the refrigerator."

In the refrigerator they found leftover take-out Chinese food. Sitting at the round oak kitchen table, the three friends discussed what they'd just seen between bites of lo mein and shrimp fried rice.

"Obviously, Connie didn't buy that bracelet," Nancy said. "She stole it. And after Hal lost so much ground trying to become class president, he knew the only way he'd get into Harvard was to cheat on the SAT so that he could get unusually high scores."

Bess poured herself some more soda. "And poor Hunk. It must be awful to feel so desperate!"

"Why do you think Jake did it?" George asked. "Money?"

"Maybe." Nancy crunched thoughtfully on an ice cube. "But I think it was more of a power trip. He would find someone's weak spot and dig in. Jake liked knowing everybody's secrets. That's probably how he found out about me in time to film us at the mall that day. He must have had his ear to Mr. Parton's door when Mr. Parton talked to my father. He knew my 'secret,' too. He liked being king of the mountain."

"Yeah, well, somebody finally pushed him off," Bess said. "And no wonder. He must have had things on half the kids in school."

"But he only has three people documented," George pointed out. "Nancy, do you really think one of them killed him?"

Nancy shrugged her shoulders in frustration.

Later, after George and Bess had left, she took a long hot shower, trying to come up with an answer to George's question.

Walt Hogan was strong enough to give Jake that final push, she thought, especially if he'd been angry. And Hal wasn't exactly a lightweight. If he'd been desperate enough, he might just have decided to challenge Jake.

She couldn't rule out Connie either. Sweet, gossipy Connie Watson was as strong a candidate for murderer as the two guys. Anyone could have pushed him.

Nancy turned around and let the warm, misty spray roll off her back. Jake Webb wasn't just a thief and a vandal, she thought, he was the Bedford High Blackmailer. Getting power from kids who'd made mistakes must have given him a kick, a sick, sadistic kick.

But somebody had finally kicked him back. The question was, who? Was it really one of the kids filmed—Walt or Connie or Hal? Could one of those three Bedford High students have been so determined to get out from under Jake's thumb that he or she murdered him to keep a secret safe?

CHAPTER TEN

Nancy pushed her sloppy joe aside and reached for Daryl's hand across the cafeteria table. "I need a favor."

"Just ask," Daryl said with a smile. "What? You need a ride home after school?"

"Not exactly," Nancy answered, looking mysterious. "I lucked out. This morning my dad surprised me with a new Mustang GT convertible."

Daryl rolled his eyes. "You've got to be kidding."

"The deal is I'll pay him back when the insurance money comes through." Nancy grinned sheepishly. "Plus twenty years' allowance, I've been told."

"Poor baby," Daryl teased her, leaning close enough to brush his lips against her ear. "So what's the favor? You want me to test-drive your new toy?"

Nancy didn't tease back. "No," she said, forcing herself to pull back from Daryl's handsome face. "I want to tell you something, but you have to promise not to breathe a word of it to anyone."

"I can keep a secret, Detective. Promise."

They were alone at a table in the farthest corner of the cafeteria. Any of the kids who happened to glance their way probably thought they were having a private romantic talk. But love was the farthest thing from Nancy's mind at that moment as she quietly told Daryl about Jake Webb's blackmail.

When she finished, she sat back and sipped her iced tea, waiting for Daryl's reaction.

But Daryl must have been so stunned he couldn't think of anything to say. He just stared at her with wide, dark-blue eyes, his face almost blank.

"It's okay to be shocked," Nancy said. "I was, and I'm the detective."

"Yeah, I . . ." Daryl shook his head and whistled softly. "Wow. I *am* shocked. I mean, it's unbelievable."

"It is—unless you've seen the recording."

"So what are you going to do with it?" Daryl asked. "Turn it over to the police?"

Nancy shook her head. "I guess I'll have to give it to them pretty soon. But since Mr. Parton is letting me handle this my way, I'd like to work on my own just a little longer. For now, that disc's going to stay safe at home, where I can keep an eye on it."

Daryl nodded. "I guess you think one of those kids killed Jake, huh?"

"I don't know what I think yet," Nancy admitted. "I don't want to believe it at all."

"But they're the only ones on the disc, isn't that what you said?" Daryl asked quickly.

"Yes, but somehow I just . . ." Nancy sighed.

"Jake really blew it for everybody, didn't he?" Daryl looked sympathetic and concerned, just the way Ned would have reacted, Nancy thought. Then Daryl leaned across the table and gave her one of his sexiest looks. "Don't take this wrong, Detective, but be careful, okay?"

Warmed by Daryl's concern and support, not to mention his touch, Nancy spent the rest of the afternoon—in between classes—tracking down the three "stars" of Jake's video.

She found Hal in the library, just beginning a paper that she happened to know was due in two days. "Hi," she whispered as she joined him at the study table. "I thought you'd be finished with that by now. Everybody says you're super smart."

Hal gave her a nervous smile and shrugged. "Even whizzes get behind sometimes."

"Well, I guess you don't have to worry, though," Nancy went on. "I mean, if you're smart enough to get into Harvard and write papers for Jake Webb on the side, then—"

That got Hal's attention. "What do you mean?" he interrupted in a whisper. "I don't know what you're talking about."

"Really?" Nancy was all innocence. "Gee, I was sure I heard you and Jake talking about it in the hall, right after that pop quiz, remember?"

"No. You didn't. I mean, you must have heard wrong." Hal stood up, gathering his stuff together with shaky hands. "Look, I've got to get going."

"Oh, too bad," Nancy said. "I was going to ask your advice. See, I'll be taking the SATs soon and I thought maybe you could give me some hints on how to handle them. Everybody says your scores were sky-high. How did you do it? Or is that a secret?"

Hal looked so nervous, Nancy thought he might break down right there in the library. But he managed to hold himself together long enough to mumble something about "luck." Then he rushed out of the room, but not before shooting Nancy a look of pure terror.

Nancy wasn't sure what to make of it. Was Hal scared because of the SATs he'd stolen, or had he done something much worse than stealing and cheating? She decided to try again with him, but first she wanted to talk to the other two.

Walt Hogan wasn't hard to find. He stood out like a redwood in a grove of saplings, and she spotted him right before fifth period, heading out one of the side doors. Good, she said to herself. I was looking for an excuse to cut calculus anyway.

Nancy followed Walt across the campus toward the track, where she watched him run two laps before he stopped, throwing himself down on the grass. He was gasping as if he'd just run a three-minute mile, and she figured he must still be in pain.

"Tired?" Nancy asked pleasantly as she dropped into the grass beside him.

"Yeah." Walt grunted a couple of times and then opened his eyes. "Do I know you?"

"Well, we met," Nancy said. "Monday, remember? We sort of bumped into each other in the hall and Daryl Gray introduced us. I'm Nancy Drew."

"Yeah, sure." Walt didn't look sure at all. "How's it going?"

"Fine." Nancy plucked some grass and twisted it around her finger. "I watched you at practice the other day," she said. "You really amaze me. I mean, I fell off the trampoline and I could barely walk, so I know what you're going through."

"What do you mean, what I'm going through?" Walt asked.

"The pain," Nancy said. "Jake Webb told me all about—"

"Webb?" Walt broke in. "What kind of business did you have with that guy?"

"No business," Nancy said quickly. "He just explained about your injury and I wanted you to know that I understand."

"Look!" Walt jumped to his feet and stood towering over her. "I don't know what that slime told you, but whatever it was, he was lying!"

Nancy got to her feet and faced him. "Hey, okay," she said. "Don't get excited. I just thought—"

"Don't think!" Walt shouted. He took a step toward Nancy, and for a second she thought he was going to hit her. "Just get out of my sight! There's no pain because there's no injury, you understand?"

With an angry glare, Walt turned and slowly walked toward the school. Nancy let her breath out. She'd taken a few judo classes, but not nearly enough to prepare her to face a raging, two-hundred-pound football player.

Walt was touchy, to put it mildly, but Nancy still didn't have anything more than suspicions to go on. No more hinting, she told herself. With Connie, just come right out and say what's on your mind. As horrible as the truth is, you have to confront her with it. At least you won't have to worry about being attacked. You hope.

CHAPTER ELEVEN

Nancy found Connie Watson in the gym after school, watching cheerleader practice. She climbed the bleachers to her side.

"I have to talk to you," she said quietly. "About Jake Webb. And your bracelet. And a video I found."

Connie's face flushed and then drained of color until it was white as the moon. "I . . . I don't . . . ," she stammered.

"Look," Nancy went on, ignoring the girl's panicked eyes, "the police found your bracelet in Jake's locker. And I know it's yours because I saw the video—the one Jake made of you stealing it. I haven't shown it to the police yet. But I will unless you tell me everything you know about how Jake was murdered."

Tears ran down Connie's cheeks, making them glisten under the bright gym lights. "It all started at the beginning of the school year. See, that bracelet wasn't the only thing I stole," she admitted. "I took a sweater the first time, and it was so easy I decided to try for a jacket." Connie swallowed hard. "Only that time I got caught. It's all in my school file."

"And since Jake worked in the office, he found out about it," Nancy commented.

Connie nodded and took a shaky breath. "I didn't know he knew, of course. But then, after I took the bracelet . . . Well, I know it was wrong but I wanted it so much, and there was no way I could afford it! I promised myself it was the last time. But then . . ."

She wiped her face and sniffed loudly. ". . . Then Jake came strutting along, said he had a 'movie' he wanted me to see. I nearly died when I saw it! I told him I was going to return the bracelet, but he made me wear it. When I tried to get rid of it, he stopped me and kept it himself. He said he knew all about my shoplifting record and that if he told anyone about the bracelet, I'd probably go to jail. And he was right!

"So after that, I had to do everything he asked." Connie shuddered. "Everything. I hoped that when he died, my secret would die with him."

Nancy felt terrible, but she had to keep pushing or she'd never get to the bottom of the mystery. "But Jake didn't just die," she said. "Someone killed him."

"I know, I know," Connie moaned. Then she looked at Nancy sharply. "I didn't do it! I'm not sorry he's dead, but I didn't kill him—and I can't believe you think I might have!"

With a sob, Connie ran down the bleacher steps and out of the gym. Nancy felt helpless. She wished she could have told Connie everything would be okay. But Connie had as much reason to knock off Jake as anyone else he'd blackmailed. Until Nancy found out who did it, she couldn't afford to feel sorry for anybody, not even sweet Connie Watson.

• • •

Still thinking about the answers she didn't have, Nancy left the gym and walked outside to her car. Daryl Gray was leaning against the driver's door, and Nancy's stomach did a little flip at the sight of him.

"I can tell by the look on your face that your 'interviews' didn't go too well," he said when she reached his side.

"You're right," Nancy admitted. "I'm not much further along than I was last night. But I'll figure it out eventually." She looked at him with a mock frown. "What are you doing here, anyway? I didn't think you'd ever come within fifty feet of a car of mine."

"When you want to be with somebody enough, you have to take chances." Daryl put a hand on Nancy's shoulder and brought his lips close to her ear. "Besides," he whispered, "I have an ulterior motive." He pulled open the door for her. "What I really want, aside from spending some time with you, is to see that video."

"You mean *The Secrets of Bedford High?*"

"Yeah. It sounds wild." Daryl shut the door after her and leaned down, his head in the window. "No, really, I thought maybe I could help. I know all those people better than you do. Maybe I can find some clues."

"It sounds good to me," Nancy said. "Let's go."

"You lead, I'll follow," Daryl said, and walked off toward his Porsche.

Half an hour later, the two of them were in Nancy's house, sitting close together on the beige couch in the den, sipping lemonade and looking at the Jake Webb production.

Daryl watched carefully but didn't say much, and Nancy was acutely aware of his closeness in the darkened room. As Connie Watson faded into the crowds of shoppers, Daryl brought his arm up and around Nancy's shoulder, his hand resting lightly on the back of her neck.

By the time Connie was walking up the school steps, neither Daryl nor Nancy was watching. Their eyes were on each other.

"I hate to tell you this," Daryl said softly, "but I didn't see anything that might help you out."

"That's okay," Nancy whispered. "I'm glad you came over anyway."

As if they'd both thought of it at the same time, they moved their heads closer together until their lips were touching. Nancy slid her hands up Daryl's arms, felt his thick blond hair under her fingers, felt his lips press against hers. She could hear her heart pounding in her ears, and then suddenly she heard another sound—the doorbell.

Reluctant, but almost relieved, Nancy disentangled herself from Daryl's arms and stood up. "Bad timing, huh?"

"The worst," Daryl groaned ruefully.

The doorbell chimed again and Nancy went down the hall to answer it.

"Nan, hi!" Bess's smile changed to a gape as she stared at Nancy. "Were you taking a nap or something?"

"No, why?"

"You look a little . . . wrinkled," George pointed out.

"No, I was just—" Nancy stopped when she realized that her

friends were staring at something behind her. Turning, she saw Daryl walking down the hall toward them, smoothing his hair with one hand and straightening his shirt with the other.

After a quick introduction Daryl turned to Nancy. "I think I'd better get going," he said with a warm smile. "See you tomorrow, okay?"

Bess could hardly wait until he was out the door. "Wow," she said breathily. "No wonder you look so glassy-eyed, Nancy. He's gorgeous!"

"For once I can't argue," George said.

"If I hadn't just met somebody else—" Bess went on, "and by the way, his name's Alan Wales, Nancy, wait'll you see him—I'd definitely fall in love with Daryl Gray. What were you two up to, anyway?"

Nancy was saved from explaining by another bell—the telephone. "Nancy," Hannah called from the kitchen. "It's for you. It's Ned."

"Thanks, Hannah," Nancy called back. "I'll take it in my bedroom." With a flustered smile, she turned to Bess and George. "I'll meet you in the den in a couple of minutes. Oh, turn off the TV, would you? I forgot."

"I can't imagine why," Bess teased.

Alone in her room, Nancy tried to compose herself before she picked up the extension. Would Ned hear anything in her voice that would reveal what she'd just done? She hoped not. After all, Daryl was exciting, but Ned Nickerson was the one she loved. Wasn't he?

"Ned?"

"Hey, Nancy. How're you doing? I miss you."

She could hear the smile in his voice. "I miss you, too," she told him. "How's life at the university?"

"Busy. I've got good news, but first, tell me how the case is going."

"Well, I'll put it this way—it's still going." Nancy didn't really want to get into it. She might have to mention Daryl and she wasn't ready for that. "What's your good news?"

"I'm coming down this weekend."

"To River Heights?"

"Where else? That's where *you* are, isn't it?" Ned laughed. "What's the matter, don't you want to see me?"

"Are you kidding? Of course I do!" Nancy could say that truthfully, but still, she wondered what the weekend would be like. After all, she had a date with Daryl for the dance. What would Ned think about that? "When will you get here?" she asked.

"Tomorrow, early afternoon sometime. I'll call you as soon as I get there. Nancy?" Ned lowered his voice. "I can't wait to see you. Let's do something special."

"You're on," Nancy said with a grin, although she couldn't imagine what they'd do, not if she was busy with Daryl.

After she hung up, she tried to figure out whether to tell Ned everything about the case, including her two "close encounters" with Daryl, or to keep those incidents a secret and just pass Daryl off as one of her contacts in the case.

She was staring at the phone and chewing on a fingernail when George stuck her head around the door. "Nancy? Could you come in the den? There's something you should see."

Glad to be distracted, Nancy followed George down the hall and into the den. "Bess was just about to turn the TV off when something came on," George explained. "I guess Jake had one more scene."

"Who is it?" Nancy asked. "Who else was Jake manipulating?"

"Oh, Nancy," Bess said. "Look."

George pushed the play button and a face appeared on the television screen. Nancy didn't say a word. She couldn't. The face belonged to Daryl Gray.

CHAPTER TWELVE

In disbelieving silence Nancy watched her "contact" in front of an unseen camera. She had to keep reminding herself that it wasn't a performance. It was for real.

Scene One—Daryl got into his Porsche and drove off, the camera lingering on a sign for Route 110 East.

Scene Two—The Porsche pulled into the parking lot of a tacky-looking diner called the Red Caboose. Daryl got out of the car, walked across the street, and stood waiting on the sidewalk. Jake had obviously stayed behind, hidden somewhere in the Red Caboose lot.

Scene Three—A heavyset man with thick hair and a bushy mustache joined Daryl on the sidewalk. Jake zoomed in for a closer shot. The camera zeroed in on an identification tag clipped to the man's pocket. Nancy tried desperately to read the name. She thought she could make out an M and a D, but she wasn't sure. Jake hadn't been able to get a tight enough shot. Daryl and the man exchanged a few words, and then the man handed Daryl a small envelope, which Daryl stuffed in his jeans pocket. The man walked away, revealing on the chain-link fence behind him a sign, about one foot square. The letters were unreadable.

Scene Four—Another shot of Daryl in his car, this time passing the high school on Bedford Road.

Scene Five—The Porsche turned into a drive. No house was visible from the road, just an intricately scrolled wrought-iron fence on each side of the drive.

That was it. Five short scenes that blew Nancy's world apart. Less than an hour earlier, she'd been in Daryl's arms, a victim of his warm eyes and smooth personality. Then suddenly she'd discovered that he, too, was a victim—of Jake Webb's scheming mind.

A few things began to make sense—the way Daryl had tried to talk her out of dealing with Jake, his eagerness to know how the case was going and to see the video. With a shudder, Nancy wondered what would have happened if he'd stayed long enough to see himself on the screen. Would he have killed Nancy for the disc, the way he might—just might—have killed Jake?

Pushing that awful thought from her mind, Nancy jumped up and turned the TV off. Then she started pacing around the room.

"Nancy," Bess asked, "are you okay?"

"Just totally confused." Nancy managed a laugh. "I mean, obviously Jake had something on Daryl. But what? It really doesn't show him doing anything wrong."

"It doesn't show much of anything," Bess agreed. "He just went someplace, met a man, and then went someplace else. I know!" she said. "Maybe he had a gambling thing going."

That made sense, Nancy thought. After all, with his father practically bankrupt, Daryl would want to keep up his slick lifestyle somehow. Gambling wasn't so terrible, she told herself hopefully.

"Well, we're not getting anywhere sitting around talking about it," George pointed out.

"You're right. Let's get going. I want to try to follow Daryl's route on the video." Nancy grabbed the keys to her car. "We know what the others did. Now let's find out what Daryl's secret is."

Nancy's new car sped along Route 110. "Just keep your eyes open for that diner," she reminded her friends.

"I won't miss it," Bess said. "I'm famished."

"We're not going there to eat," George told her.

"I know, but it wouldn't hurt to get a takeout order. I was so busy with Alan that I didn't even get lunch. Oh, Nancy," Bess went on, "I can't wait for you to meet Alan! He's not only good-looking, he's talented."

"At what?"

"He plays the guitar, and he's really serious about it. I'm sure he'll be a superstar someday," Bess said loyally. "Oh, I just remembered! His group's playing for the Bedford High dance tomorrow night!"

"Hey!" cried George. "Look on your right! It's the Red Caboose."

Just as Daryl had done, Nancy pulled into the parking lot, and the three girls got out. Facing away from the diner, across Route 110, they could see the chain-link fence, and now that they had a full view, they could see several of the small, square signs attached to the fence at regular intervals.

Beyond the fence was a vast complex of buildings. As Nancy and her friends crossed the street to the sidewalk where Daryl had met the man, Nancy wondered if the buildings were a factory of some kind.

Bess reached the fence first. "'Private—Authorized Personnel Only,'" she read from one of the signs. Then she was quiet as Nancy and George joined her and read what was printed below that, in smaller letters. "U.S. Government."

"I didn't know there were any government offices out here," George said. "What is it, I wonder. A research place or something?"

"Let's find out," Nancy said. "I'm sure anybody who works at the Red Caboose knows what it is." She spoke calmly, but inside she was becoming very nervous. What could Daryl possibly have to do with the U.S. Government?

"It's an Air Force defense plant, honey," the man behind the counter said, in answer to Nancy's question. "They're up to their ears in secrets over there—designs for bombs, blueprints for nifty little radar devices that'll track down a missile before it's even left the ground, stuff like that." He gave the counter a swipe with his dishcloth and shook his head. "Tell you the truth, I get scared sometimes. If the United States is ever attacked, you can bet some country's got a bomb picked out for that place. And you know what that means for the Red Caboose."

• • •

Nancy and George were reeling from the idea that Daryl might be involved in spying somehow. Bess tried to perk them up as they walked out to the car. "Look," she said hopefully, "it might not be as bad as it seems. We don't know what that man gave Daryl. Maybe Daryl started a private messenger service."

"Maybe," Nancy said. But her thoughts were whirling around madly. Jake wouldn't have bothered with Daryl if Daryl were innocent. But what exactly was he guilty of? And how big was this case going to get? It had started out as petty vandalism, then it moved up to blackmail, and then to murder. Now what? Could it really be espionage? "Let's take a ride to Bedford," she said. "I want to find out exactly where Daryl delivered that envelope. That must be what he did, even though Jake didn't get it on camera."

It was dark by the time they reached Bedford Road, and as they drove by the high school, the road became darker. This was the super-rich section of Bedford, "The Mansion Mile," as Nancy had heard someone in school call it. But from the road, with high shrubbery and thick groves of trees masking the grounds, it was hard to see any landmarks.

Finally, though, George spotted the wrought-iron fence they'd seen on the recording, and Nancy turned into what seemed like a private drive. There was no gate and no sign to tell them whose property they were on.

"What do we do now?" Bess asked. "Pretend we're lost?"

"Good idea." Nancy drove through the opening in the fence.

As soon as they were on the property, the drive curved

sharply to reveal a gate anchored to two moss-covered pillars. In the glare of the headlights the girls could easily read the sign posted on the gate: RUSSIA: PRIVATE PROPERTY.

"Russia?" Bess said.

"I think it's an estate, a kind of compound for diplomats," George told them. "I remember reading that a lot of countries buy foreign property so their officials can have someplace to go to relax. We're not all that far from the U.N., you know."

"We're not all that far from the defense plant, either," Nancy said.

Before anyone had a chance to comment on that remark, the gate swung open and searchlights flooded the area. The girls heard the sound of an engine and saw a pair of headlights round a curve in the drive in front of them. The headlights were getting closer fast, and they were heading straight for Nancy's car!

CHAPTER THIRTEEN

The floodlights lit up the Mustang, throwing everything outside it into pitch darkness, except for the two headlights. They were dancing over the bumpy drive, looming closer and closer.

"Who do you suppose that is?" Bess squinted in the glare. "It's coming awfully fast!"

George cleared her throat. "Somehow, I don't think it's a welcoming committee."

"Let's get out of here!" cried Nancy.

As the headlights approached the gate, Nancy stepped on the gas, steered the Mustang into a tire-screeching U-turn, and peeled out of the drive. Just as they neared Bedford Road, Bess let out a faint shriek and pointed to a clump of bushes at the end of the drive.

Nancy gasped. Jumping over the bushes and onto the drive directly in front of her car were two figures. In the beam of the headlights, the girls could see that they were men, dressed in black jumpsuits of some kind. One was hefting a long-barreled pistol. The other was unslinging a rifle from his shoulder.

Instinctively Nancy moved her foot onto the brake pedal.

But then she stopped. "What am I doing?" she said. "If they think I'm going to slow down and make small talk while a gun is pointed at me, they're crazy!"

Nancy moved her foot back to the gas pedal and stepped on it, mashing down on the horn at the same time. Bess put her hands over her eyes, but George and Nancy saw the two men hold their pose—legs wide apart, guns at the ready—for about two seconds. Then, as the Mustang bore down on them, they jumped aside. Wheels spinning and gravel flying, the car swerved sharply onto Bedford Road.

"Are we going to live?" Bess asked.

"Not if we don't hurry," Nancy answered. "Look."

Behind them, turning out of the private drive and coming fast, was a dark-colored, unmarked van.

"It's not over yet," Nancy said. "Let's see how far they're willing to go."

Except for Nancy's car and the van, Bedford Road was nearly deserted. Nancy raced the car past other estates, past the high school, past a solitary jogger in white. The van stayed close behind, not losing an inch.

Suddenly Nancy saw a traffic light ahead of her. It was green, and Nancy eased up on the gas pedal.

"What are you doing?" Bess cried. "They'll catch us!"

"Maybe, maybe not." Nancy slowed as much as possible, keeping her eyes on the traffic light. Behind them, the van's headlights were bright enough to read by. The light changed to amber and Nancy felt a jolt as the van rammed into the back of her car.

George's head snapped back as the van once again made contact with the Mustang. "Uh, Nancy," she said, "if you're going to do what I think you're going to do, do it now. The light's been yellow for five seconds."

"Right. Hang on!" Nancy pushed the gas pedal and raced through the intersection just after the light turned red. The van's brakes screeched, but then its driver decided to risk running a light. It tore through the intersection only a few feet behind the Mustang.

Nancy shook her head in disbelief. "Where are the police when you really need them?" she joked. Actually, she was glad that a police car hadn't been lurking at the intersection. A high-speed chase through the streets of Bedford might get the driver of the van in trouble. But when he showed his diplomatic papers or whatever he carried around with him, he'd be off the hook. Then Nancy could do one of two things—blow her cover or get arrested. Neither choice was very appealing.

Reluctantly Nancy slowed the car to a respectable speed. "Anybody got any suggestions?" she asked.

Bess spoke up immediately. "Let's eat."

"Oh, Bess," George said with a moan. "Get serious, will you?"

"I *am* serious," Bess protested. "There's a pizza place just ahead on the right, and it looks jammed. Do you really think those creeps would follow us in there?"

"I'm ready to try anything," Nancy said, and swerved sharply into the parking lot of Guido's Pizza. As she squeezed the car into the last available space, she glanced into the rearview mirror. The van slowed for a moment, then sped down the block and out of sight.

"It worked," she said, with a shaky laugh. "You were right, Bess. I guess it would have blown their image if they'd followed us to Guido's and shot us over a pepperoni pie."

"Speaking of pepperoni," Bess said, "I really am starving."

"So am I," Nancy agreed. "Let's go pig out."

Guido's was jammed, as Bess had predicted, but the three girls managed to find a table near the kitchen door. As Nancy sank into a chair, she glanced around and saw several kids from Bedford High, including Carla Dalton. Terrific, she thought, Carla's a quick way to ruin an appetite. Carla was talking to somebody whose back was to Nancy. She was so involved in whatever she was saying that she didn't notice anyone else.

When their pizza arrived, Nancy discovered that not even Carla Dalton could kill her appetite. Hungrily, she and Bess and George wolfed down slices of the big pie, not saying much of anything. When only one slice was left, Nancy leaned back in her chair and sipped her Coke. "Well, we finally know what Daryl's secret is," she said quietly, "and it's a lot worse than shoplifting."

Bess nodded. "It's really unbelievable, though. I mean, a high-school kid involved in spying? Who would ever guess?"

"That was probably the point," George said. "But Daryl's not the worst one. That man from the defense plant and probably one of the diplomats—they're the real bad guys."

"Daryl's not squeaky clean, though," Nancy remarked. "I'm

sure he knew exactly what he was doing." She wasn't really shocked anymore, just angry. And she was more angry at herself than at Daryl. If only she hadn't been so stupid. If she'd kept her mind on her job and her hands to herself, she wouldn't be feeling like such a sucker.

First things first, she told herself. Solve the case. Then you can kick yourself!

Bess broke into her thoughts. "What kind of stuff do you think Daryl was taking from the guy at the defense plant? Blueprints? Secret designs for bombs?"

"Probably," Nancy said. "And I'll bet it paid really well." Well enough, she figured, to keep gas in Daryl's Porsche and a grin on his face. "Daryl did it for the money, I'm sure, not for any political reason."

"I guess it beat bagging groceries after school," George commented. "Daryl must have thought he had it made."

"He did, until Jake found out," Nancy said. "It must have freaked him out, but he was so cool, you would never have guessed. What an actor!" Had Daryl been acting with her, too? she wondered. Coming on to her just so she wouldn't suspect him? She had to admit that that was exactly what he'd done, and she'd fallen for it! Well, she'd stopped falling, and now her eyes were wide open. "What I have to find out," she told the other two, "is who killed Jake. Was it someone from the compound or the man at the defense plant? Or was it Daryl? Or Hal or Walt or Connie?"

"Do you really think Daryl could have done something like that?" Bess asked.

"I'm just not sure," Nancy admitted. "But I have to find out. The question is how? I can't just walk up and—" she broke off suddenly.

"What is it?" George asked.

"Look who's here." Nancy pointed to Carla Dalton's table. Carla and the person she'd been with had stood up and were threading their way through the crowded room. Carla's companion was Brenda Carlton. They were headed toward Nancy.

"What's the ace reporter doing here?" George wondered.

"She'd better not be following me," Nancy said grimly. "We made a deal. If she messes me up, I'll take her reporter's notebook and burn it."

"Who's she with?" Bess asked.

"Oh, that's the famous Carla Dalton." Nancy laughed. "The one who likes to let people fall off trampolines." She giggled and then whispered, "I wonder what she'd say if she knew her ex-boyfriend was a spy?"

"She'd probably chew him out for being stupid enough to get caught," Bess joked.

As Brenda and Carla approached the girls' table, Brenda gave Nancy a sideways glance and a nasty wink. Nancy felt like throwing the last slice of pizza at her and watching the tomato sauce ooze down Brenda's black suede boots, but she held herself back.

Carla was chattering away about Bedford High's big dance as she and Brenda walked by, but she took the time to jostle the girls' table hard enough to spill Nancy's drink.

Bess took a wad of napkins out of the container and handed

them to Nancy. "Carla doesn't give up, does she?" she said, seething. "I don't understand why you haven't gotten back at her."

But Nancy had other things on her mind. Brenda, for one. *Had* she been following them? If she had, Nancy would have to be super careful. The case was at its trickiest point. She couldn't afford to let Brenda get even a whiff of what was going on.

Then there was Daryl Gray. How was she going to handle him? "Of course!" she said suddenly. "Carla just gave me the answer."

"The answer to what?" George asked.

"How to get Daryl to spill his guts," Nancy told her. "Bess, you said Alan Wales is playing at the dance tomorrow night, right? So you'll be there, won't you?"

"Of course," Bess said dreamily. "I'm his biggest fan."

"Good, I might need your help." Nancy turned to George. "Yours, too."

"But I don't have a date."

"I've got one for you."

"I don't like blind dates," George protested.

"Trust me," Nancy said with a grin. "You'll love the guy I have in mind."

"So how are you going to handle Daryl?" Bess wanted to know.

"Very carefully," Nancy said. "But no matter what, tomorrow night, I'm going to pop the question to him. Only it won't be one he's expecting."

CHAPTER FOURTEEN

Bess smoothed out the skirt of her cherry-red dress and stood on tiptoe, trying to get a glimpse of herself in the mirror. "It's no use," she said with a sigh. "I'll have to wait until this place clears out."

"I'm not in any hurry anyway," Nancy said tensely. She and George and Bess were in the girls' bathroom just outside the Bedford High gym. It was the night of the high school's first big dance. For an hour and a half Nancy had been putting on an act—first when Daryl had picked her up at home, then on the drive to Bedford, and for the past forty-five minutes while she'd been dancing with him. She'd laughed and joked and made conversation, pretending that everything was the same between them. She probably deserved an Oscar for her performance, she told herself wryly. But staying in character was growing difficult. She'd been glad when the band had finally taken a break and she could take refuge in the bathroom and just be herself.

"Well, it won't be much longer," she said with a nervous glance at her watch. "I wish my hands weren't so clammy."

"Don't worry," George told her. "Daryl will just think you're excited to be with him."

"Speaking of that," Bess said, giggling, "what do you think of Alan Wales, Nancy? Isn't he absolutely gorgeous?"

"Incredible," Nancy agreed. Actually, she hadn't paid much attention, but she didn't want to hurt her friend's feelings. "When this case is over, we'll all have to do something together."

"Oh, sure, that'll be great!" Bess said. "Of course, Alan's really serious about making it in the music business, so he's always busy. But we'll try to find a spare hour somewhere."

Nancy was glad Bess had a new boyfriend, but she just couldn't work up any enthusiasm for the subject, not at the moment, anyway. It wouldn't be long before she had to confront Daryl, and that prospect was making her heart pound so hard it almost drowned out the sound of Bess's voice.

A girl behind Nancy finally moved away from the mirror, and Nancy grabbed the space. Well, you don't look terrified, she told herself. Actually, she looked good. She was wearing a dress she'd worn the year before, at a university dance with Ned—a soft blue wraparound that hugged her waist and came to a mildly revealing V in the front.

That V had put a sparkle in Daryl's eyes, but Nancy knew that the sparkle would fade fast once she started talking to him about Jake Webb, a man at a defense plant, and a diplomatic compound. What worried her was what would happen next. If Daryl was the murderer, would he turn on her? It was hard to imagine his getting vicious, but she knew it was a chance she had to take.

Nancy leaned close to the mirror to touch up her lipstick, and just as she brought the tube to her mouth, a girl moved into the space next to her, bumping Nancy's arm with her elbow.

Nancy stared at the pale red smear on the side of her mouth, and then at the girl who'd helped put it there. Carla Dalton.

George passed Nancy a tissue. Bess raised her eyebrows and shook her head. Nancy wiped her mouth and started over again. Carla ignored everyone, brushed her hair, and then turned to leave.

Suddenly there was a loud shriek, followed by a distinct thud. Carla was sitting on the bathroom floor, legs sticking out in front of her, narrow lips pressed into a thin line of disgust.

Nancy was trying to figure out how Carla had gotten there, not that she cared, when Bess cried out, "Oh, I'm *so* sorry!" Her voice dripped with mock sympathy. "Me and my big feet! My mother always told me to be sure to keep my feet out of the way or people would trip on them, but I guess I just didn't see you coming." She shook her head and clicked her tongue. "Here, let me give you a hand up."

"Don't bother," Carla said through clenched teeth. "You've done enough!" She got clumsily to her feet and stalked out of the bathroom, but not before Nancy saw a large, soapy water stain smack on the rear of Carla's peach colored dress.

"Nice work. Thanks," Nancy whispered to Bess.

"Well, I just couldn't let her keep dumping on you," Bess giggled. "You've got enough on your mind."

George fluffed out her short dark curls and then checked her watch. "It's almost time," she said. "The band'll be back in just a couple of minutes."

Nancy took a deep breath. "You guys know what you're supposed to do, right?"

George nodded. "Don't worry. We'll be there." She grinned. "By the way, you were right about that date you got for me. He's terrific."

"I kind of like him myself," Nancy agreed with a laugh. "Okay, then," she went on. "I'll see you after the next break. Keep your fingers crossed." With another deep breath and a last look in the mirror, she walked out of the bathroom and into the Bedford High gym.

The band was just reassembling, and Nancy took a moment to try to relax before finding Daryl. The gym was decorated with hundreds of crepe-paper streamers, and colored spotlights sent shafts of red, blue, and orange to the floor. Nancy spotted Walt Hogan, looking happier than she'd ever seen him. She didn't see Hal or Connie, and she realized that Connie probably never went to dances. Maybe when this case is over, Nancy thought, Connie will straighten her life out and stop trying so desperately to be somebody she's not.

Alan Wales, the latest love of Bess's life, picked up his electric guitar and, with a frown of concentration, started in on a wild, pounding rock number that put everyone into motion.

"Okay, Daryl," Nancy said under her breath, "here I come, ready or not."

Her heart still pounding, Nancy threaded her way through the crowded gym until she reached Daryl Gray's side. Without a word, Daryl grabbed her hand and pulled her close to him.

"Hey," Nancy joked, "this is a fast dance. I don't think I can move like this."

"Who wants to move?" Daryl whispered in her ear.

"I know what you mean." Nancy traced his lips with her finger and pretended to be feeling as passionate as Daryl was. "Let's just stick around a little while longer, though, okay? If we leave now, everybody will know why."

"I don't care about everybody," Daryl said with a grin. "But all right. As long as we're here, we might as well dance."

For almost half an hour, Nancy danced with Daryl. The band was good, keeping up a steady stream of popular rock numbers, as well as a few originals. They were all loud and fast, and it was almost impossible to carry on a conversation. Nancy was just as glad. She'd have to do some fast talking soon enough.

Finally, just before the next break, the band started in on a dreamy slow dance. Daryl took Nancy in his arms and held her tight, barely moving to the music. With a sigh he said, "This has to be the best night I've ever had."

This is it, Nancy told herself. She pulled her head back

until she could look in Daryl's eyes. Touching his lips again, she whispered, "It could be a whole lot better, though, couldn't it? Especially if we spent some time alone together. I've danced enough now. How about you?"

With a slow smile Daryl laced his fingers through hers and led her through the gym, around the slow-dancing couples, and out the door.

Nancy shivered as they crossed the parking lot, but it wasn't because of the cool night air. It was because the dangerous part of the evening was coming up, when Nancy would find out who Daryl Gray really was. Was he a nice guy gone wrong, or was he a killer?

Except for a few widely spaced lampposts, the Bedford High parking lot was dark, as Nancy had expected. Daryl's Porsche loomed like a black hulk in the shadows. Nancy forced herself to smile as Daryl unlocked the car and ushered her inside. As he walked around to the driver's door, she heard strains of music coming from the gym, and wished, for a second, that she were still at the dance.

Once Daryl got in the car, though, Nancy didn't have time to think of anything but his arms. They were around her immediately, and Nancy couldn't help remembering that just a few days before, she'd loved that feeling. She didn't love it anymore, but even as Daryl held her, she felt a pang of regret that he was involved in something so twisted.

Thinking of what Daryl had done, and might have done,

made Nancy pull away. "Hey," she said breathlessly. "Not so fast, there's plenty of time."

"I know, I know." Daryl was just as breathless. "I just love the way you feel." He leaned forward to kiss her.

Nancy put her arms around his neck, and when the kiss was over, she decided it was time. Bringing her lips close to his ear, she whispered softly, "I thought you'd like to know—I found out why Jake Webb was killed."

CHAPTER FIFTEEN

For a second Daryl didn't move, and Nancy wondered if he'd even heard her. "Daryl?" she whispered again.

Finally, slowly, Daryl pulled away from her and sat back. In the faint light Nancy could see a look of surprise on his face. But fear was mixed with that surprise, and she knew that nothing was ever going to be the same between them again.

"Well," Daryl said. "Good work, Detective. How'd you do it?"

"I was lucky," Nancy admitted. "A piece of evidence was right in front of me, but I didn't see it for a while. It was on the disc."

"Jake's?" Daryl asked sharply.

"The one and only."

"Wow, you never know, do you?" Daryl gave a low whistle. "So which one did it?"

What an actor, Nancy thought. "It wasn't Hal or Connie," she told him. "It wasn't Walt Hogan, either." That was a guess on Nancy's part.

Daryl frowned. "But I thought you said you knew who killed Jake."

"No, I didn't. I said I knew *why* he was killed. There's a big difference."

Daryl shifted impatiently. "He was killed because he was blackmailing people and one of them finally stood up to him. We already know that."

"Yeah, that's true," Nancy agreed. "But it wasn't one of those three. They were all tucked in their beds when Jake took that fall." Nancy was still going on guesswork. For all she knew, Hal, Connie, and Walt could have formed a team and pushed Jake down the stairs on the count of three. But she didn't believe it, not for a minute. "So," she went on, "don't you want me to tell you what I found?"

"It's not exactly what I had in mind when we came out here," Daryl said, trying to joke, "but if you really want to talk instead of . . . doing other things, then go ahead."

"Okay, here's what I saw," Nancy said. "I call it 'The Daryl Gray Show.'" Calmly and quietly she went on to describe exactly what she and Bess and George had seen after Daryl had left her house that afternoon. "*Surprised* doesn't even come close to the way I felt," she said. "Sick is more like it."

Daryl didn't say anything, so Nancy kept talking. "But I was confused, too. I mean, I still didn't know what Jake had on you. So I decided to find out. I don't have to tell you where I went, do I? Out Route 110 to a U.S. defense plant. Then back to Bedford to a private estate where Russian diplomats hang out—relax, study a lot of top-secret plans from the defense plant, stuff like that."

Nancy shook her head and laughed softly. "I can just imagine how Jake felt when he realized what was going on. He must have thought he was sitting on a gold mine." She leaned forward slightly, and in the semi-darkness, she saw the expression on Daryl's face. He looked resigned, like a trapped animal that knows it can't get free. But like that trapped animal, he also looked angry, ready to strike out at anyone who came close.

For the first time since she'd left the dance with Daryl, Nancy felt she might be in danger. He was so close to her, physically, and she found herself wishing the Porsche were a little more roomy. Some space would be nice just then, the length of a football field, for example.

You're almost finished, she told herself. Just get it over with. "I know Jake told you that he'd found out your secret. I don't know how much of your 'salary' you had to fork over to keep him quiet, but that doesn't matter," Nancy said. "It probably didn't even matter to Jake after a while, because Jake decided to go after the bigger fish, didn't he? Which of your 'contacts' did he try to blackmail? The one at the defense plant? The one here in Bedford? Both?"

Daryl turned his head to look at her, and Nancy saw that the anger was growing stronger. "Well, it doesn't matter," she said. "I'll find out." She spoke quickly, wanting to finish before Daryl exploded. "What I really want to know—and what I think you can tell me—is who killed Jake. Was it you?"

The explosion came then. Nancy felt Daryl's hand—the touch of which had once made her quiver with excitement—

close over her wrist in a painfully tight grip. Then he was getting out of the car, dragging her roughly after him. Nancy stumbled and felt her knee scrape the parking lot pavement, but Daryl had grabbed her arms by then and was pulling her up and pushing her against the car.

"Listen," he whispered hoarsely, "Jake got in over his head, and so have you. If you think I'm a killer, what makes you think I'd stop with Jake Webb?"

Nancy saw the look of desperate fury in Daryl's eyes and knew she needed help. Fortunately she'd planned for it. As she stared back at Daryl, she saw his eyes blink suddenly as three sets of headlights were switched on in three different locations. The glare blinded both of them for a second, but Nancy heard car doors opening and knew that Bess and George were on their way. Most important, George's "blind" date—Ned Nickerson—was with them. Nancy was glad he'd come home for the weekend. Knowing he was there made her feel stronger.

Daryl heard the doors, too, and the sound of hurried footsteps on the pavement. He turned his head just in time to see the three figures moving swiftly toward the Porsche. Then he ran.

"Nan, are you all right?" Bess called out.

"I'm fine!" Nancy shouted back. She took off after Daryl, but before she'd taken even two steps, she felt someone rush past her. When she saw who it was, she stopped. Ned Nickerson could handle Daryl Gray any day of the week.

Ned's strong legs easily ate up the distance between him and Daryl. As Nancy watched he sprang into the air, landed on

Daryl's back, and brought them both crashing to the ground. Then he was up, yanking Daryl to his feet. He half-dragged him back to the Porsche and slammed him up against its side.

"Ned!" Nancy had never seen him act so rough. When he'd arrived earlier, she'd told him everything about Daryl, except for his feelings about her—and vice versa. She was saving that for later, when the case was all cleared up. But seeing the tension in Ned's face, she wondered if he suspected something. She hoped not. She definitely couldn't handle it at the moment.

But then Ned loosened his grip on Daryl's jacket and turned to Nancy with an apologetic smile. "Sorry," he said. "I tend to get carried away when some killer threatens my girlfriend."

"Girlfriend!" Daryl exclaimed. Then he cried, "I'm not a killer!"

"You could have fooled me," Ned said quietly, as he stepped away from Daryl and let Nancy take over.

"You didn't kill Jake Webb?" Nancy asked.

Daryl shook his head. "I just said that stuff to scare you off." His voice was drained of energy. He looked defeated. "The guy at the defense plant—Mitch Dillon—killed Jake. He told me so." Daryl took a shaky breath and then went on. "See, Jake wasn't satisfied with blackmailing just me. So he forced me to get him in touch with Mitch. Mitch played along with him, let Jake set up a meeting at the school. Then he told Jake to give him the disc or he'd kill him." Daryl shook his head again, as if he couldn't quite believe it. "I don't have to tell you what happened then."

"Knowing Jake, he probably laughed at the guy," Nancy said.

"Yeah, and he died laughing, the stupid jerk." Daryl was calmer now. There was no anger in his voice, just sadness. "Anyway, when Mitch didn't get the disc, he was ready to explode. He told me to get it, came on really strong with all kinds of threats."

"It was you in the media room that day, wasn't it?" Nancy asked.

Daryl nodded. "I started to chase you," he explained, "but I just couldn't go through with it. I mean, what was I supposed to do when I caught you? Beat you up?" He smiled weakly and shrugged. "Waiting until you told me about the recording was one of the hardest times I've ever been through. But then when I watched it with you, I wasn't on it. I thought I could put this whole thing behind me."

Finally Nancy had the entire story. She should have felt like celebrating, but she didn't. She felt more like crying. From the looks on Bess's and George's faces, she could tell they felt the same way. How could you celebrate when someone—even a creep like Jake Webb—had been murdered? When Daryl Gray's life was probably ruined?

Nancy glanced at Ned. As usual, he sensed how she felt before she had to tell him. He came over and put his arm around her shoulders. Nancy smiled at him and then turned back to Daryl.

"I don't think you'll ever be able to put it behind you," she told him. "Not completely, anyway. You'll have to face up to what you've done, and to what the government will want to do to you."

Daryl didn't bother to answer. He just gave a defeated shrug, not meeting her eyes.

"But I think I know a way for you to make it a whole lot easier on yourself," Nancy went on.

Daryl raised his head, a spark of interest in his beautiful eyes. "How?"

"By helping us catch the murderer."

"You've got to be kidding! Mitch has nothing to lose at this point." Daryl's eyes swept over the parking lot, as if he were trying to find an escape route. But he was trapped, and he knew it. "Don't you understand?" he screamed. "He'll kill me!"

CHAPTER SIXTEEN

Ned turned the car smoothly onto Bedford Road, heading toward the high school. Then he glanced over at Nancy, who was frowning in concentration. "Do you really think Mitch Dillon would kill Daryl?"

"I just don't know," Nancy admitted. "Who can say for sure?" She felt uncomfortable just thinking about it. On Friday night, in the parking lot, she'd spent almost forty-five minutes convincing Daryl to see things her way. By helping her put Mitch Dillon behind bars, she'd said, Daryl would be easing his conscience. And it might help him out of some of the trouble he'd gotten himself into. She'd told Daryl that *he* didn't have much to lose, either. It had been easy enough to say then, when she was persuading Daryl to go along with her plan.

But Monday was three days later, and in a few short hours, they'd be putting that plan into action. It was a good plan, Nancy knew, but no plan was foolproof. And if something went wrong, Daryl would be the one to pay the price.

Sensing her worry, Ned reached over and squeezed her hand. His class load was light for the next few days and he'd decided to stay and help out. "Hey," he said gently. "Everything's going to be fine. I'll be there. George and Bess and Alan will be there. Even the police are coming. And you're way ahead of the game, where they're concerned. You've already solved the case and they're still scratching their heads about it."

"Well, I had a head start on them, plus a very important piece of evidence." Nancy began to feel better. "Besides, I do need them. They're the only ones who can make an arrest."

Nancy giggled, remembering the look on the police captain's face when she'd told him her story. He'd never heard of Nancy Drew, girl detective, and it took two phone calls—one to her father and one to Mr. Parton—to make him stop looking angry and start looking amazed.

Once he got over his amazement, though, the captain had been more than willing to go along with Nancy's plan. It was a simple plan, really. Daryl had called Mitch Dillon, told him he had the incriminating disc, and set up a meeting with him for Monday afternoon at five-thirty. At the meeting Daryl would make sure that Mitch talked about murdering Jake Webb. The best part of the plan was that Nancy and her friends were going to record the confession, using a hidden microphone.

As Ned drove toward Bedford High, Nancy checked her watch. In a few hours the case would be over, she hoped. The thought of having to wait out the entire day in school was driving her crazy. But she wanted to keep an eye on Daryl and make sure he didn't bolt. She didn't think he would, but she couldn't take that chance.

"Now, remember," Ned joked as he pulled the car to a stop,

"don't lose your lunch money and don't cut any classes."

"Very funny," Nancy said. "How about if we trade places? You go to school and I'll scout around the meeting place?"

"No, thanks. But I will make a deal with you." Ned leaned over and put his hand on the back of her neck. "You behave in school and our trip to the mountains will be next weekend. Mom and Dad are dying to get up there. The cabin has a big stone fireplace, and it's really cozy on cold nights."

"You've got yourself a date." Nancy bent her head and kissed Ned, wondering how she'd ever thought Daryl Gray was exciting. But she had, and she was going to have to deal with that sooner or later. Later, she told herself. She gave Ned another lingering kiss, then hopped out of the car and went in to school.

If Nancy really had been a student, she would have flunked out for sure. At least ten times that day, she'd been caught staring out the window instead of taking notes, and her English teacher had come right out and asked her if she'd left her brains at home. "Where is your mind, Miss Drew?" Nancy was tempted to tell him that her mind was on blackmail, espionage, and murder, but she kept her mouth shut. He would probably have sent her straight to the school psychologist.

She saw Daryl twice—in the hallway and in the cafeteria— and he seemed fine. Nervous, but ready to go, he said. Nancy was nervous, too, and edgy with waiting, but knowing that Daryl was holding up okay made her relax a little.

The next time she saw him was at the meeting place, a public park near Bedford High. She'd joined Ned, Bess, Alan, and George there as soon as school was out. Ned had been exploring the park most of the afternoon, finding the best place to conceal the camera. He was showing Nancy some heavy shrubs that looked perfect, when Daryl came running up to them. Nancy glanced at his face and felt her heart begin to sink. Daryl looked terrified.

"It's Mitch, he . . ." Daryl gasped for breath. "He called me at school, pretended he was my father. We—we can't go through with this!"

"Why not?" Nancy asked. "What did he say?"

"He said he can't make it at five-thirty," Daryl told her. "I don't know if he suspects anything, but he's going to be here in ten minutes, and there's no time to let the police in on the change of plans!"

Nancy felt a moment of panic herself, but in just a few seconds, that panic changed to anger. "Look," she said, "maybe he does suspect something. He wouldn't be a very good spy if he didn't keep his eyes open. But he can't possibly have any idea about what we've got in store for him. We can't just give up. He could be planning to leave the country or something. This might be our last chance to get him!"

"Nancy's right," Ned said quietly. "Besides, if Daryl doesn't show, then Mitch will definitely suspect something."

It was too late to try to do any more persuading. Nancy just looked at Daryl, silently urging him to hang in. Daryl stared at the ground a few seconds, considering. Then he raised his head and nodded at Nancy. "Let's go, Detective."

As calmly as if they had an entire police force waiting in the wings, the six young people took their places. Bess and her rock-star-to-be sat close together on one of the park benches, their arms around each other. They didn't have to pretend to be in love, Nancy noticed.

Nancy, Ned, and George concealed themselves behind the shrubs, where they could film the encounter without being seen. Nancy panned the camera over the park, stopping on Daryl for a few moments.

Daryl was sitting on another bench, some distance away from Bess and Alan. Nancy had been worried about him before, but as she looked at him now, the worry vanished. He was lounging casually on the bench, idly scanning one of his school books, looking as calm and relaxed as the day she'd first seen him at the stoplight in Bedford.

"He's pretty cool," George commented softly.

Nancy nodded. "He really missed his calling. He should have been an actor." A branch was poking her in the ear; she reached up to push it away and felt Ned's hand close over hers. She smiled and started to say something, but just then Ned's eyes shifted from her face and she felt him tense. "Company," he whispered.

Through the camera lens, Nancy watched a heavyset man stroll into the park. He was wearing jeans and a dark-blue windbreaker, and as he stopped by the duck pond, he brought out a handful of popcorn from his pocket and threw it into the water. He didn't hurry or glance around. He was simply a man taking a late-afternoon walk through the park.

Just one thing set him apart and made Nancy's hands begin to sweat—his bushy mustache. It was the same mustache she'd seen in Jake's video, and he was the same man who'd met Daryl in front of the defense plant. It was Mitch Dillon, spy, killer, and soon-to-be convicted criminal, if everything went the way Nancy hoped it would.

Dillon stopped feeding the ducks, and as he walked along the curved path at the edge of the pond, Nancy could tell that he wasn't as oblivious to his surroundings as most people would have thought. His eyes roved constantly over the park, looking for signs of a trap. As he glanced over the shrubs where the camera crew was hidden, Nancy instinctively held her breath, even though she knew he couldn't see her.

Then Dillon took a drink from the water fountain, and when he straightened up, he gave the surroundings one last look. Seemingly satisfied, he wiped his mustache and began a slow amble toward Daryl.

Nancy gripped the camera tightly, holding it steady as Dillon eased himself down on the bench beside his "contact." Nancy saw Dillon's lips move; then Daryl nodded, reached into his bookbag, and pulled out an envelope. It wasn't the incriminating disc, of course; it was blank. Daryl didn't hand it over right away, though; instead, he started talking, and Nancy knew he was talking about Jake Webb.

Keep talking, she urged Daryl silently. Get that murder confession out of Dillon and onto the recording device you're wearing under your shirt.

Nancy hated being where she was, out of earshot, looking at the scene through a tiny lens. She wanted to be where the action was, hearing everything for herself. It was frustrating, being so out of it. She toyed with the idea of giving the camera to George or Ned and sneaking through the bushes until she was closer to Daryl and Dillon, but she decided it wasn't worth the chance. One false move, one too many twigs snapping under her feet, could blow it. And she couldn't afford to blow it, especially without the police to back her up.

Dillon reached for the envelope then, but Daryl didn't let go. He was still talking. That must have meant that Dillon hadn't said anything about Jake's murder. Nancy wondered why. Could something have gone wrong? Was Daryl being so obvious that Dillon suspected something?

Keeping the camera steady, Nancy looked away for a second. Maybe a "real" look would tell her something. But before she could see anything, a blinding flash of light went off in the bushes in front of the park bench. Nancy stared long enough to see Mitch Dillon leap up from the bench, the envelope in his hands. Then she dropped the camera and began running. Something had gone wrong, and Dillon was on his feet. Nancy had to stop him before he got away.

CHAPTER SEVENTEEN

As Nancy raced through the bushes a scream rang out, shattering the peaceful silence of the park. There was another scream, and then a woman's voice cried, "What are you doing? Let go of me!"

Although the shrubbery blocked Nancy's view, it didn't matter. She would have known that voice anywhere. It belonged to Brenda Carlton. The reporter had blown it for Nancy again.

Nancy was so angry she was shaking. Mostly she was angry at herself. She'd made the deal with Brenda, and she should have known better. Brenda couldn't be trusted; she was trouble, right down to the tips of her perfectly manicured nails. Thinking about Brenda made Nancy careless for a second, and a second was all it took. A thick root lay like a snake across the path; Nancy tripped on it and went sprawling facedown, right next to the bench where Daryl and Mitch Dillon had been sitting.

"Well, well, who's this?" Dillon said with a sneer. "Another member of the kiddie corps? Get up!" he ordered roughly.

Nancy stood up, quickly appraising the situation. Daryl was standing a few feet from the park bench, Brenda's camera and its flash attachment on the ground in front of him. Dillon had one arm around Brenda's neck, and in his other hand he held a gun. The gun was pointed at Brenda's head.

"Nancy, please," Brenda stammered. "I didn't mean for this to happen. If—if you'd just told me everything, I would have stayed out of your way!"

"You've been following me the whole time, haven't you?" Nancy said.

Brenda nodded and then winced as Dillon tightened his grip around her throat. Brenda's eyes were terrified, and Nancy couldn't help feeling sorry for her. There was no pity in Mitch Dillon's eyes, though. They were about as compassionate as a shark's. "That's enough chitchat, girls," he said. "It's time to stop playing games."

"This isn't a game," Nancy said.

Dillon eyed her coolly. "You're right, it's not. It's real life, and it's going to get rough if you don't do what I say." He shifted his glance to Daryl. "I want that camera," he said, eyeing Brenda's camera on the ground. "You hand it to me and nobody gets hurt. I'll walk out of the park and out of your lives. It'll be like a bad dream."

It already is, Nancy thought. Her mind was racing, trying to figure out what to do. Then suddenly she noticed something— Bess and Alan were close by, but neither Ned nor George had followed her through the shrubs. So Dillon had no way of knowing that they were even around. Nancy knew Ned and

George well enough to know that they weren't just standing by, waiting to see what happened. One of them had probably snuck out of the park already and called the police. If Nancy could keep Mitch Dillon talking, keep him from leaving somehow, then there was a chance they could get out of the mess. All she needed was time. "What happens if you don't get the camera?" she asked.

Dillon sighed wearily. "If I don't get the camera, then somebody gets hurt. Do you want to guess who?" He spoke as if Nancy were a child asking annoying questions, and Nancy decided to play along with him.

"Who?" she asked.

"Who do you think?" Brenda cried. "I'm the one he's pointing the gun at! Will you just give him the stupid camera so he'll let me go?!"

"Smart girl," Dillon said. "I suggest you follow her advice, Red."

Nancy hated to be called Red, especially by someone like Dillon. "And if I don't, then you'll kill her, just like you killed Jake Webb, right?" she asked.

"You're catching on fast," Dillon replied. "I already killed one nosy kid. I'm not afraid to kill another. You got it just right."

At least we got the confession, Nancy told herself, no thanks to Brenda.

Dillon shifted impatiently. "Now, how about the camera, Red?"

Nancy gritted her teeth. "If you want it so much, why don't

you get it yourself? Nobody's stopping you. We're all just a bunch of stupid kids, remember?"

"You may be stupid but I'm not," Dillon said. "You think I don't know what'll happen if I reach for that camera? You'll try to play hero and jump me, and even though I'd win, I just don't have time for a brawl right now."

"I'll bet," Nancy said. "Gotta catch a plane to Russia, right?"

"I'm starting to lose my patience." Dillon shook his head in disgust and turned to Daryl. "Okay, buddy. Do your partner one last favor and hand me the camera. Now!"

"Don't do it, Daryl!" Nancy shouted.

"Nancy!" Brenda squeaked. "What are you doing? He's going to kill me!"

"That's right." Dillon was staring at Daryl. "I'm going to kill her if you don't give me that camera in ten seconds. Ten . . . nine . . ."

"Hey." Daryl held out his hands. "Just keep cool, Mitch. I'll give it to you."

"Six . . . five . . ."

Brenda opened her mouth, but no sound came out.

"Four . . ."

Slowly Daryl bent down and took hold of the camera strap. As Dillon reached the count of two, Daryl straightened up and in one quick move swung the heavy camera at Dillon's face. At that same instant the gun went off.

The gunshot set Nancy into motion. She didn't know if

Dillon hit anyone, but she hurled herself at him, determined to stop him from doing any more damage. She hit him just below the knees, and as she tried to get a good grip on his jeans, Dillon reached down and took a swing at her. His fist collided with her jaw in a punch that gave her an instant headache.

You really do see stars, Nancy thought. Her ears were ringing and her vision was blurred. It was hard to tell exactly what was going on, but she sensed a lot of movement around her. Then she heard a familiar voice calling to her. "Don't worry, Nancy!" Ned shouted. "The police are on their way!"

Nancy rubbed her eyes and saw Ned and Alan racing together after Mitch Dillon, who was charging across an open field of grass, heading for the sidewalk that bordered the park. He was still clutching the fake disc in one hand, and the camera swung wildly by its strap in the other.

If Dillon had only known that neither was going to do him any good, he might have gotten away. But he was determined to take all the "evidence" with him, and it slowed him down. The heavy camera kept banging into his knees. It probably hurt, Nancy thought with satisfaction, which was why Dillon finally broke stride for a few seconds and tried to get a tight grip on the camera itself.

Those few seconds were all it took. As Dillon grappled with the camera, Ned and Alan put on a burst of speed and reached him just as he was about to take off again. First Ned, then Alan leaped on top of Dillon, the three of them rolling over and over until they came to a jarring stop against the base of a water fountain. Dillon wasn't going anywhere for the moment; they had him. Nancy closed her eyes in relief.

When she opened them again, the first person she saw was Brenda Carlton. Her butter-soft leather boots were covered with mud and grass stains, her red silk blouse was missing two buttons, and a smear of lipstick decorated her chin. She was still sitting where Dillon had tossed her; the gun was right next to her, and every time she looked at it, she sobbed hysterically.

A hundred sarcastic remarks went through Nancy's mind, but before she could decide which one to say, Bess touched her shoulder. "Nan?" Her voice was shaky. "Do you know anything about gunshot wounds?"

"What?" Nancy whirled around to face her friend. "Were you hit?!"

"No, I'm okay," Bess assured her. "It's Daryl."

Daryl Gray was sitting a few feet away from Brenda. His handsome face was pale, and his eyes were full of pain. He was clutching his right shoulder, and even as Nancy looked a bright red stream of blood seeped through his fingers.

"I don't think it's too bad," he said as Nancy crouched beside him. "But it sure does hurt."

He grinned weakly, and Nancy smiled back. "Thank you," she said. "You really came through for us."

"So did this," George said triumphantly. She emerged from

the bushes and pointed at the camera she was carrying. "I got the whole scene on video, every last bit of it!"

Nancy gave her a thumbs-up signal for victory, and at the same moment she heard a police siren, faint at first, but growing louder by the second. It was all over. They'd done it, and Nancy laughed, barely feeling the pain in her swollen jaw.

CHAPTER EIGHTEEN

When Nancy walked into Mr. Parton's office the next afternoon, the principal stood up and gave her a smile that seemed to light up the entire room. The confused, worried look had left his eyes, and there was a definite spring in his step as he came around the desk to shake her hand.

"Your father told me you were first-rate," he said, beaming at her. "I'm glad I listened to him."

"Thank you," Nancy said with a laugh. "I'm glad you did, too." She sank into a chair and took the mug of steaming tea Mr. Parton offered her.

"How do you feel?" the principal asked. "I understand you made 'direct contact' with Mitch Dillon's fist."

Nancy touched her jaw. There was a purple bruise on it that her makeup didn't quite cover, but she decided it went with the territory. "It only hurts when I laugh," she joked. "Anyway, it was worth it to see the police handcuffing Dillon." By the time the police had arrived at the park, all the fight had gone out of Mitch. He'd listened in stony silence as his rights were read to him, but Nancy could see the panic in his eyes. He was finished, and he knew it.

"Murder and espionage." Mr. Parton whistled softly. "Right here in Bedford. If not for all this, it might still be going on." He shook his head in amazement. "Well, Dillon won't be busy for a long time, that's for sure."

"What about his foreign contact?" Nancy asked.

"I don't suppose we'll ever get the whole story," Mr. Parton said, "but I heard on the news this morning that two 'diplomats' checked out of their Bedford mansion last night."

"I guess that takes care of the spy ring, for a while anyway," Nancy said. "What's going to happen to Daryl Gray?"

Mr. Parton's good spirits took a dive for a moment. "I don't know yet." He sighed. "He's in deep trouble, no doubt about that. I still can't believe he did what he did."

Nancy agreed, but she felt strongly that Daryl deserved a break. "I know you feel terrible about him," she said, "but I think if it hadn't been for Daryl, Mitch Dillon would have escaped yesterday. Daryl did the right thing in the end. He also got shot for it."

Mr. Parton nodded. "You're right. And I'm sure the government will agree with you. He'll have to pay for what he did, but maybe the price won't be so high." He sipped some tea and relaxed again. "By the way, the police are holding Jake's disc for evidence, but they've promised to keep as quiet as they can about Walt and Hal and Connie."

"That's great!" In spite of what they'd done, Nancy couldn't help feeling that those three kids had been victims as much as anyone else. "Have you talked to them?"

"To all three," Mr. Parton told her. "Hal's taking the SATs again, Walt decided to bench himself for a while, and Connie's agreed to get some help for her shoplifting problem. So there's a happy ending after all. And," he went on, "I didn't mention your part in the case, even though I wanted to."

"Good. Who knows?" Nancy said. "I might have to come here undercover again someday."

Mr. Parton winced and then shook hands with her. "Don't take this the wrong way," he said, "but I hope not."

As Nancy took a last walk through the halls of Bedford High, there was a spring in her step, too. She had solved the case, but it was more than that. She caught sight of Hal and Walt and Connie and noticed that all three of them seemed to have lightened up overnight. In fact, the whole atmosphere of the school had lightened up. Maybe since the biggest secret had been revealed, the smaller secrets—injury and cheating and shoplifting—could be forgotten.

A lot of kids were carrying copies of *Today's Times*, and Nancy noticed that Brenda Carlton had finally gotten her name on a front-page story, beneath the headline BEDFORD POLICE CRACK ESPIONAGE RING. Nancy smiled to herself as she picked a copy of the discarded paper off the hall floor. Brenda must have been very happy to keep her part of the bargain and leave Nancy's name out of the story.

As Nancy quickly scanned the article, she saw with relief that Daryl's part in helping catch Dillon got just as much play as his role of courier for spies. Brenda, naturally, didn't mention her own near-disastrous actions at all.

Daryl was still in the hospital, the story said, but was expected to recover quickly. Nancy had a feeling that he could always bounce back, and she was hopeful that in a few years he'd be able to move past the nightmare he'd been involved in.

So things were turning out okay, she thought as she pushed open the door and walked outside. She had just one loose end to tie up, and then she could put the Bedford High case behind her and move on to the next one, whatever it might be.

The loose end was Ned Nickerson, and he was waiting for her in his car. Nancy thought this was as good a time as any to tell him about Daryl. She pulled her jacket collar up against the chilly October wind and went down the steps to meet him.

"Hi!" Ned pushed open the door for her and took her hand as she slid in. "Did everything go okay?"

"Fine," Nancy said, and told him what Mr. Parton had told her.

"Great. Then it's all over, huh?"

"Almost." Nancy linked her fingers with his and took a deep breath. She wished she'd had a chance to discuss her problem with Bess, but there hadn't been time. Besides, Bess was so involved with Alan Wales that she was hardly paying attention to anything that was going on around her. She and Alan ate, slept, and breathed guitars and musicians. Nancy was on her own. After another deep breath she said, "Ned, there's something I have to talk to you about."

"I bet I can guess," Ned said softly. "It's Daryl Gray, isn't it?"

"You mean you knew?"

"Not really," Ned told her. "But I saw the way he looked at you a couple of times. And the way you looked at him."

Nancy should have guessed. Ned knew her better than anyone else. "It wasn't much, really. I mean we didn't fall in love or anything like that. I guess we were just attracted to each other. I wasn't looking for it to happen, it just did."

"You don't have to explain," Ned said. He stared ahead of him, at the entrance to Bedford High.

"But I want to." Nancy squeezed his hand and tried to get him to look at her. "I feel terrible telling you, but it's better than keeping it from you. Because I love you," she said. "No other guy could be as perfect for me as you are."

"Then it's over?" Ned asked.

"It hardly got started," Nancy said.

"So there's nothing to talk about, is there?" Ned finally looked at her, but Nancy couldn't read the expression in his eyes. She couldn't tell what he was thinking.

"I guess not," she said. "But I wanted to tell you anyway."

"I understand. I'm glad you did." Ned pulled her close and kissed her gently. "Let's get out of here, okay?"

"Okay." Nancy kissed him back and settled herself in the seat. She was glad she'd told him, too, but had she done the right thing? Ned said he understood, but did he, really? Would she have understood if he'd told her about some girl at the university?

Nancy shook her head, trying to get rid of such disturbing

thoughts. It was over. She'd done what she thought was right, and she'd just have to wait to see what happened.

As the car pulled away from the school, Nancy turned and took one last look. It was a handsome, modern building, and it appeared peaceful in the afternoon sun. It was hard to believe the things that had gone on behind its red brick walls.

Nancy turned and caught Ned's eye. He was smiling at her, and she felt a sudden urge to run her fingers through his hair. She also felt relieved that she'd told him the truth about Daryl. She didn't want any secrets between her and Ned. She'd found enough secrets at Bedford High.

DEADLY
INTENT

CHAPTER ONE

C ome on, Bess, cool it," Nancy Drew whispered. "People are starting to stare."

But Bess Marvin seemed not to hear her best friend's voice. "I just can't believe it!" she gushed. "It's all too much! New York City, Radio City Music Hall, the Bent Fender concert . . ."

"The hottest rock band around," said Alan Wales, Bess's latest boyfriend. "And they've invited us backstage!"

"Oh, George, help me with these star-struck kids," teased Nancy. "I think your cousin might lose it."

"Well, you have to admit, this *is* going to be one incredible vacation," George Fayne said, falling in step with the group.

"The best," Nancy declared, running a hand through her reddish-blond hair. "And no mysteries, just fun. This detective needs a little break."

At eighteen, Nancy had already earned a reputation as one of the nation's top young detectives, solving mysteries all across the country, and overseas as well. Her most recent one, though, *Secrets Can Kill,* had started in a high school just a few miles from her hometown of River Heights.

"Well, maybe you need a break, Nan, but *I* can think of

one mystery I wouldn't mind solving," Bess spoke up.

George threw her cousin a puzzled look. "Since when are you into detective work?"

Nancy was puzzled, too. George was always eager to jump right in and help her on a case, no matter how dangerous, but Bess usually had to be coaxed. Unraveling mysteries scared her, and she was the first to admit it.

"Yeah, what mystery do you want to solve?" Nancy asked.

Bess giggled. "The mystery in Barton Novak's big green eyes," she answered. "I wonder if he's as gorgeous in real life as he is on MTV."

"I should have figured." George let out an exasperated sigh. "You're not planning on doing anything to embarrass us in front of him and the rest of the band, are you?"

"Yeah, don't go getting any ideas," joked Alan, pulling Bess closer to him.

"Hey, guys, don't worry. One guitarist is enough for me." Bess stood on tiptoe and gave Alan a kiss.

In the few weeks since they'd met, Bess and Alan had been inseparable—joined at the lip, Nancy liked to joke. They reminded her of the way things used to be between her and Ned Nickerson.

Nancy found herself wishing for those days. But then, it had been her own choice to get involved with Daryl Gray during her last mystery. And although it was over with him almost before it started, she couldn't blame Ned for being upset. Since then, she had visited Ned once at Emerson College, and he had come to River Heights for a weekend, but things had been cooler than usual between them, and that hurt. She could only hope they could put the past behind them.

"Nancy Drew! Earth to Nancy!" Bess tapped the top of Nancy's head. "Anyone home up there?"

"Sorry, Bess. What—?"

"I said that of course Alan's my number one guitarist, but it *is* pretty incredible that we're going to meet Barton Novak in a few seconds, isn't it?"

Returning to the exhilaration of the moment, Nancy smiled. She remembered the thrill she'd felt listening to Bent Fender and how she'd followed their rise from struggling performers to top stars.

Alan echoed Bess's enthusiasm. "I've memorized practically every song Barton's ever recorded. The first thing I ever figured out how to play on my own was the lead for 'Break Down the Walls.'" He moved his hands, playing imaginary notes on an air guitar. "I'm so psyched that you guys are taking me along tonight!"

"Alan, how could we not take our favorite future rock star to meet our favorite current rock star?" Nancy smiled and gave him a light punch on the arm. "Besides, Dad said the musicians in the band were happy to have us all."

Nancy's father, a lawyer, was negotiating the band's new recording agreement. Normally, Carson Drew worked on criminal cases. But Bent Fender's drummer, Roger Gold, was the son of his old college roommate, Sy Gold, who had recently moved to a town not far from River Heights. He and Nancy's father had rekindled their old friendship, and now Carson Drew was doing Mr. Gold a favor by working on the contract for his son's band. In return, Roger and the band were letting Nancy and her friends come backstage for one of their concerts, and they were going to give them a personal guided tour of the New York rock clubs.

"What a mob scene," Nancy said as she and her friends edged through the crowd of noisy fans in front of the Music Hall. Off on one side of the building, Nancy caught sight of a polished brass door.

"This is it, the stage door!" she exclaimed, mounting a few steps and pushing the door open. Just inside, in a glass booth, sat two burly security guards in identical tan uniforms.

"Hi," Nancy said. "Roger Gold told us to come back and see him before the show."

The bearded guard frowned wearily. "Young lady, do you know how many times we've heard that one?"

"But it's true," Nancy insisted. "His father is a friend of my father's. He's expecting us."

The guards exchanged glances. "Why don't you kids give us a break?" the other one said. "There have been at least a dozen folks in here already, trying to get to see the band. We—"

"Roger said you'd page him when we arrived," Nancy interrupted, remaining polite.

The guards exchanged another glance.

"Listen," Nancy persisted, "I'll make you a deal. You let

Roger know Nancy Drew and her friends are here, and if he doesn't want to see us, we'll leave. I promise."

The guard with the beard shrugged and picked up the telephone.

"Way to go, Nan," whispered George.

A few seconds later, the guard was hanging up the receiver, an apologetic look on his face. "I really thought—I mean, so many kids come back here—"

"No problem," Nancy said. "You were just doing your job."

"He said he'll meet you downstairs."

The guard pointed to the elevators. "Jeez." He scratched his head. "I could have sworn you were just another bunch of wild fans."

"We are," Alan called back as they headed for the elevators. "But we're a lucky bunch of wild fans!"

Nancy laughed. Alan had hit the nail on the head. From the moment she'd heard Bent Fender's first single, she'd been hooked. And now she was about to get a behind-the-scenes look at one of their concerts. It wasn't just any concert, either. It was the first of Fender's Rock for Relief shows, a series of benefits to aid children with disabilities.

A wave of excitement washed over Nancy as she and her friends got into the elevator. She smoothed her hand over her short, electric-blue skirt and picked a thread off her oversized sweater. She also wore a pair of patterned tights, which looked perfect with her favorite ankle boots.

"Don't worry. You look great, as usual," Bess told her. "You too, George," she added, eyeing George in her simple black jumpsuit.

"You look pretty fabulous yourself," George returned. "I love that turquoise shirt with your blond hair."

"You look amazing, Bess," Alan said. He was wearing tight jeans and a T-shirt, the picture of a rock-and-roller. Bess reached up to tie a turquoise bandanna around his neck.

"Same color as your shirt." George grinned. "Looks like you're color-coding your boyfriend."

The elevator door slid open, and the friends stepped out. There, looking just as Nancy had pictured him, stood Roger Gold, unmistakable with his spiky black hair and single silver earring.

"Hi," he said easily.

There was an uncomfortable silence as Nancy and her friends studied the legend standing before them.

Roger smiled at each of them in turn, his gaze finally coming to rest on Alan. "Well, *you're* not Nancy," he joked.

Nancy took a step forward. "No, I am," she said, not quite believing that she was talking to a superstar like Roger Gold. "And these are Bess and George and Alan." She indicated each of her friends in turn.

"Hello," they chorused nervously. Nancy saw how tongue-tied they looked.

"Nice to meet you all," Roger responded. Then he said, "Nancy, I've been hearing stories about your father ever since I can remember. My dad claims they were the best roommate team in the history of college life."

"Yeah, my dad says the same thing." Nancy was still a bit awed by Roger's presence. Although Barton Novak's name was almost synonymous with Bent Fender, Nancy had always felt most loyal to Roger. After all, their fathers had been best buddies. Nancy had not met Roger before, since he had grown up with his mother outside of Los Angeles, but she'd known about him long before he'd become a star.

"Did your dad ever tell you about the time he and my dad got into the kitchen at the dining hall—" Roger began.

"—and colored the mashed potatoes purple," finished Nancy. She laughed, loosening up. Roger was so open and friendly that he made it easy to remember that stars were people too. "And how about when they had that ten-foot-long sub delivered to their history class?"

"Yeah. That's one of my dad's favorite stories," Roger said. "So where is your father, anyway?"

"Back at the hotel, getting ready for the opera. He's not too big on what he calls 'that music you kids listen to.'" She gave an embarrassed shrug.

"Hey, don't worry about it. Your dad told Barton and me that he wasn't into rock when we talked to him about our contract. To each his own." Roger hesitated. "Hey, listen, let me introduce you to the rest of the band. They're in the lounge having a little preshow Ping-Pong match. Linda's our resident champ. She's wasting Barton."

Nancy saw George's face light up at the mention of Linda Ferrare, Bent Fender's bass player and backup vocalist. George was a great fan of Linda's tough, powerful voice and dynamic style.

Roger led them to the lounge and pushed open the door. There, at one end of the Ping-Pong table in the center of the room, stood Barton Novak, his brow creased in concentration beneath a shock of blond hair. Bess let out an audible sigh. Barton snapped his paddle as the ball came toward him. On the other side of the table, Linda prepared to return the shot. She slammed the ball so hard it went speeding out at an angle, bouncing at the very corner of Barton's side of the table. He took a wild swing and missed.

"Game," said Linda, tossing her curly dark hair.

There was a smattering of applause from the rest of the band members. Mark Bailey, the other guitarist, was sitting in an armchair; Jim Parker, the keyboard player, was on the couch.

"Nice shot." Barton wiped his forehead. Then he looked toward the door for the first time. His expression lightened up. "Hey, gang, we've got guests. Hiya."

"Guys," Roger said, "this is Nancy Drew. I was telling you about her. And these are her friends, Bess, Alan, and Georgia."

"George," she corrected.

"Sorry." Roger grinned. "So, all of you, say hello to Mark, Jim, Linda, and Barton." Roger pointed to each person, but Nancy had studied Fender's album covers enough to know the band members instantly.

"Thanks for inviting us to come tonight," Nancy said to them.

"The pleasure's ours," Barton replied gallantly. "We get to

have the hottest detective around at our show tonight."

Nancy could feel heat rising to her cheeks. Barton's face had been on the cover of *Rolling Stone, Time, People,* and half a dozen other major magazines, and he was complimenting *her.* "I am beginning to make a name for myself," she said humbly.

"Beginning? From what I hear, you've done it." He looked at Nancy. "If you don't mind, I'd like to talk to you after we're finished playing tonight." Nancy cocked her head. Did she detect a note of urgency in Barton's voice?

"I'd be glad to," she said, trying to read his expression. But if he was worried about something, he gave no further clue. Instead he joined in the enthusiasm of her friends.

"This is a dream come true for me," Alan blurted. "I'm Fender's biggest fan. And I've learned a lot by listening to you," he said to Barton.

"You play guitar?"

Alan nodded. "I mean, I'm no—well, no Barton Novak." He grinned. "But I'm getting better all the time."

"Do you play in a band?" Jim Parker wanted to know.

"The Mud Castles," Alan answered. "We've been getting gigs in some clubs and bars around River Heights."

"The Mud Castles?" Roger turned to Alan and studied his face closely. "Hey, you know, I think I heard you when I was visiting my old man a few months ago. Did you play a bar over in the South End—Puffy's or Puffer's or something?"

"Puffin's. Yeah, that was us. But how come we didn't recognize you?"

"I had on dark glasses and a hat," Roger said, almost apologetically. "It's nice to be able to go out like a regular guy once in a while, have a couple of beers. But I had to leave when someone at a table near the bar started giving me funny looks. I just didn't want to hassle with anyone figuring out who I was."

Nancy tried to picture Roger in her hometown bar, rubbing elbows with people she'd known all her life.

"Yeah, I like that little place," he went on. "And Alan, your band was terrific. You play lead, right?"

Alan nodded.

Roger turned to his fellow band members. "This kid is okay." He jabbed his finger in Alan's direction. "More than okay. Someday he'll put us out of business if we're not careful!"

The smile on Alan's face could have lit up the entire room. Nancy flashed Bess a thumbs-up sign.

"We'll be out of business sooner than you think," Linda interjected, "if we're not on stage in half an hour." She looked at Nancy and the others. "Make yourselves comfortable. Play some Ping-Pong or something while we get ready."

"We'll be back soon," Barton Novak broke in, "and then we'll take you out to the wings to watch the show."

Nancy grinned. She sensed that this night—this rock concert—would be special.

George was going for the game point twenty minutes later when the lounge door burst open. The ball flew by unheeded as Roger Gold appeared in the doorway.

"Showtime?" Nancy asked excitedly, putting down her Ping-Pong paddle. Then she saw the worried expression on Roger's face as his eyes darted around the room.

"Barton's not here?" Roger was trying to sound calm, but Nancy could hear the edge of panic in his voice. His hands were clenched, knuckles white, on the door frame.

"What's wrong, Roger?" she asked.

"Barton's disappeared. I've looked all over the building, and he's gone."

"Disappeared?" George finally caught the bouncing Ping-Pong ball. "Maybe he just went out to get some air."

"Five minutes before we go on? No way!" Roger took a deep breath. "I've got a bad feeling about this. Real bad."

CHAPTER TWO

Nancy stood in Barton's dressing room with her friends and the rest of Bent Fender. On the vanity lay uncapped tubes and containers of stage makeup. An open can of soda was almost full. A guitar was leaned up in the corner of the room, next to a portable amplifier.

"It looks like he was right in the middle of getting ready," Nancy said. "Not like he planned on going anywhere."

"You're sure?" Roger asked.

"There's no question about it," Nancy replied grimly, bending down to look under the vanity. A pair of cowboy boots—the ones the rock star always wore on stage—sat on the floor.

"Barton had these on when we were introduced to him before. That means—"

"—that wherever he is, he's barefoot," George finished.

"Exactly. That's why I don't think he intended to leave this room."

"You mean he was just sitting here, and then . . ." Bess's voice trailed off.

"*Something* happened. Maybe someone knocked on his door and he got up to answer it." Nancy thought out loud, trying to piece the puzzle together. She felt herself switching gears, the excitement she'd experienced at meeting her rock idols melting into the clear, quick thinking that had earned her her reputation as a detective.

She pulled open the door to the little dressing room, just as Barton might have done. Across the corridor was a rehearsal studio for the Rockettes, who danced in special shows at Radio City Music Hall. Lights from the street washed through the room, glinting off the mirrors lining one wall. The hallway between the two rooms was littered with stage props and lighting equipment.

Nancy stepped out of the room to inspect the jumble of boxes, painted scenery, and other theater paraphernalia. "Hey, you guys, come look at this." A few yards down the hall, the contents of a box of lighting gels were scattered every which way. A papier-mâché tree trunk nearby was broken in half. "Looks like a scuffle," Nancy noted.

"Here's something else," Bess observed. A broken lamp lay on the floor down the hall.

"Wow. There's a whole trail of things," Nancy said.

"I don't know, Nancy," Linda Ferrare spoke up. "We've performed in a lot of places, and it's not that unusual for the backstage or storage areas to be a jumble of stuff like this." She paused, and her voice dropped. "Besides, I think there's something you ought to know. It's been kept quiet because we don't want the press to find out. But this isn't the first time."

"I don't understand." Nancy surveyed the trail of clues. "Has Barton vanished before?"

"Not exactly," Mark Bailey said. "A few years back—twice—he just took off. We were scared stiff at first because he didn't tell anyone anything, but both times it turned out that he just couldn't cope with the pressure of being a super-celebrity. The first time he flew off to some island in the Mediterranean and rented himself a house on the beach for a few weeks. The second time he spent the weekend with some friends in the country."

"Yeah, but Mark, don't forget, that was two years ago," Roger said, "when we were just starting to make it big. Barton's gotten much better about dealing with his fame." A worried look crossed his face. "I just don't have the same feeling about this."

"Why not?"

"Look," Roger said, "this whole Rock for Relief thing was his idea. I know he's pretty quiet about his sister, but he's totally devoted to her. You know that. He wouldn't let her down."

"What does his sister have to do with it?" Nancy asked.

"She's been in a wheelchair all her life," Roger explained. "That's one of the reasons Barton got the idea for these shows. I'm positive that he wouldn't run out on us now. Besides, if he were planning on going, he wouldn't have left all that stuff in his dressing room. Even his guitar is there."

Jim Parker ran a nervous hand through his short dark hair. "But he's got two other guitars, Roger. I don't know. Barton's done some crazy things."

Nancy listened carefully. Barton was beginning to be a real human being to her, with fears and weaknesses like any person.

If he had chosen to vanish before, she had to consider the possibility that he might do it again. On the other hand, there was evidence to the contrary.

Nancy sighed. "I can't begin to make guesses about someone I've just met, but I'm inclined to agree with Roger. Vanishing just before a big show like this doesn't make sense and isn't going to be overlooked by the press. If Barton wanted to get away from it all, he couldn't have picked a worse moment to do it."

"Look, everything you're saying sounds reasonable," Linda volunteered, "and it's true that Barton's become more comfortable being famous, but just recently he's been a lot more like the old Barton. I don't know, he seems really uptight about something."

Nancy couldn't help thinking about the urgency she'd sensed when Barton had asked about her detective work. "Linda, do you have any idea what was bothering him?"

Linda shrugged. "Beats me. But he's been acting weird for the past couple of weeks. Ever since . . ."

"Ever since what?"

"Ever since we started talking about our new contract." Linda's olive complexion went pale. She glanced from one member of Bent Fender to the next. "You don't think he's going to leave the band, do you?"

"No way, Lin," Roger reassured her. "Look at the way he's been going at the songs he's writing for the new album. He's totally into the music we're making now." Roger paused. "But he has been tense about the contract." He turned to Nancy to explain. "He thinks we're not getting all the royalties we're entitled to. He started fighting with our agent and our producer. That's why we called your father. We decided to bring in a lawyer."

Nancy nodded. But before she could ask more questions, the telephone in Barton's dressing room rang shrilly.

Mark grabbed the receiver. "Yes?" Pause. "Hey, thanks for calling. Have you found him yet?" His expression darkened, and Nancy held her breath. "Right. Okay, I understand."

"That was the stage manager," Mark said when he hung up. "No trace of Barton, and the audience is getting pretty rowdy. They want to know why we're not on stage. What do we do?"

Jim shook his head thoughtfully. "Whew. All those kids are out there. We can't let them down."

"Yeah, but how are we supposed to play without the main attraction?" Linda asked, her tough tone barely hiding the concern in her voice. "Boy, if this is Barton's fault, I'm going to make him disappear for good."

"I could cover the leads," Mark said, "but can you imagine doing 'Fever' with one guitar?"

"'Fever'? What a great tune. I can play every riff in that song," Alan said.

Roger spun around and looked him squarely in the eye.

"Hey, I'm sorry." Alan looked at the ground, embarrassed. "At a time like this I guess no one wants to hear me go on about playing your music."

"No, maybe we do," Roger said, studying Alan intently. "Can you play all our tunes?"

"Well, yeah."

"Really well," Bess added proudly. "He has a great voice, too."

Roger grabbed Barton's guitar from the corner of the room and fiddled with the knobs and dials on the amp. "Try the fast middle section on 'Fever.'" He pressed the guitar into Alan's hands.

Astonishment filled Alan's brown eyes. Roger flashed him a smile of encouragement. "Go ahead," he said.

Nancy listened as Alan tuned the guitar strings and, after taking a long, deep breath, sang the familiar Fender music in a clear, confident voice.

"Not bad." Linda's face was serious, her eyes appraising. "What else can you do?"

"How about 'Little Brother'?" Jim asked, as Alan finished up on "Fever." "Do you know that one?"

Alan's brow crinkled in concentration. "That's an oldie," he said, "but I think I can do it." Once again, music filled the room as Alan broke into a slow, dreamy number from Bent Fender's first album.

"What do you say?" Roger addressed his fellow band members. One by one, Nancy saw them signal their approval.

"Champ," Roger said, putting his hand on Alan's shoulder, "how would you like to be our pinch hitter tonight?"

As if in a fog, Alan put down the guitar. "Me? You want *me* to play with Bent Fender? *Here*?"

"We need your help," Roger said.

"We'll pull you through the rough spots," Mark promised.

Nancy watched as Alan's angular features reflected a rainbow of emotions from doubt to dazed happiness. Then the smile left his face. "What about Barton?" he asked suddenly. "Are you going to call the police?"

"They wouldn't take this seriously," Roger replied gloomily. "Not after the other two times. Barton's earned himself quite a reputation."

"But you can't just do nothing," George said.

Nancy cleared her throat. Despite seeing her dreams of vacation vanishing as rapidly as Barton had, she said, "Look, maybe I could—"

"Nancy, *would* you?" Roger didn't even wait for her to finish her sentence. "I can't tell you how grateful I'd be."

Linda, Jim, and Mark echoed his sentiments.

"Nancy Drew can't turn down a chance to do some sleuthing," George said. "It's in her blood to track down clues."

Nancy had to admit that George was right. Nothing was more of a challenge than solving a mystery. But just then, the tingle of enthusiasm that she usually felt at the beginning of a case was overshadowed by her worries about Barton. Maybe he *was* running away again, but if not, she couldn't lose any time. He might be in terrible danger.

As she combed the halls of the renowned Radio City Music Hall, Nancy could hear strains of the concert coming from the direction of the stage. Alan's playing wasn't as slick or polished as Barton's, but from what Nancy could hear, his fingers were really flying over Barton's guitar. The rest of the band was helping Alan out by covering more of the leads themselves and taking more solos. Still, Alan was winging it like a true pro.

Nancy wished she could be in the wings watching, but finding Barton came first. Bess and George had offered to help her, but she insisted they enjoy the show, telling them she would come get them if she needed their help. Bess, in particular, had looked relieved, obviously not wanting to miss a single note of Alan's performance.

The sounds of the concert grew clearer as Nancy entered an elevator, pressing the button for the street level. When the elevator door slid open and she headed for the guards' booth, the music grew faint again.

The guards and some of Fender's roadies were playing cards. But the bearded guard she had met before looked up from his hand when Nancy asked about Barton. "Novak hasn't shown yet," he said.

"And you haven't seen anyone back here besides the people with the band?"

"The only folks I let in, besides you and your friends, were these guys here"—he pointed to the three card-playing roadies—"the gal running the lights, the guy at the sound board, the stage manager, and the two who were unloading equipment before the show."

"What two?" One of the roadies, a lanky, fair-haired young

man, put down a can of beer and shot the guard a puzzled look. "We unloaded all the equipment this morning."

The guard frowned. "You're off the wall," he snapped. "Those guys had passes, and they were carrying boxes and stuff."

"They weren't with *us*," another roadie declared.

Nancy drew in her breath. "Sounds like trouble." She opened her shoulder bag and took out a felt-tipped pen and the tiny notebook she always carried with her. "Tell me everything you can remember about those guys," she said.

"One of 'em was real big—tall with brown hair," said the bearded guard. "How was I supposed to know they didn't belong here? And those boxes—they looked like they had instruments in them, you know—"

"Guitar cases?"

"Yeah, I guess. And they had a huge brown box, too, looked like the kind that refrigerators are packed in. Actually, they left with that one. Said they were taking out a broken speaker."

Nancy's heart sank, a terrible thought occurring to her. "Was that box large enough to hold a person?"

"I don't believe it!" exclaimed the blond-haired roadie, throwing down his cards. "Did you let someone carry Barton out of here in a box?"

"Please!" Nancy shouted. She got the group calmed down and continued to pump the guards for information about the two unknown men. "Was the tall man's hair straight?" she prodded. "Curly?"

"Straight. Not too much of it, I don't think. I sort of remember

DEADLY INTENT

a bald spot. And he was a heavy fellow. Dressed in jeans and a jean jacket."

"What about the other one?" Nancy said.

"Younger. Your age, maybe. Shorter, but he looked strong. Dark wavy hair. Longish. Parted on the side. He had on slacks."

"Gray ones, I think," put in the other guard. "And a button-down shirt. Oh, and he had on a heavy gold chain and a gold ring. I noticed the ring when he showed us their passes. Real different looking, like a sea serpent or something, and it had little red jewels for eyes."

"That's terrific," Nancy said. "Thank you. Anything else you can think of that might help me?"

"Well," one of the guards said slowly, "we *have* had a little trouble around here lately—break-ins, equipment missing, that sort of thing. But I don't see what that would have to do with Barton."

"All right," said Nancy. "Well, you've been a big help."

"Now what are you going to do?" the roadie asked.

"I want to take one more look around and make sure I didn't miss anything."

Nancy didn't discover anything more in the basement or on the street level. The rehearsal studios were dead ends. But as she poked around near Barton's dressing room, she spotted two black instrument cases. She'd seen the cases earlier and thought nothing of them, but because of her talk with the security guards, she raced over and unlatched them. Empty. They'd probably been carried in just so the two mysterious men would look as if they belonged backstage.

153

Nancy poked at one of them. It moved slightly, and she noticed something new—a fat wallet. She picked it up, turning it over in her hand. The wallet was made of soft, top-quality leather, decorated on one side with a tooled design of a dragon, its tail curled into the letter L. It was bulging with money.

Nancy ran her finger over the raised leather. Suddenly she remembered the guard's description of the gold ring one man was wearing. He had said it was shaped like a sea serpent—but couldn't the sea serpent have been a dragon?

Eagerly, Nancy opened the wallet to see what other clues she could find, but just as she did she heard a noise behind her. She whipped around and felt a dull thud on her head. It was the last thing she remembered before everything went black.

CHAPTER THREE

The back of Nancy's head ached when she woke up. Her fingers discovered a large bump, and she rubbed at the soreness. It was then that she recalled being struck. She blinked hard, pulling herself to her feet. The walls around her seemed to spin, and she put her hand out to steady herself.

From the direction of the concert hall came the sound of applause, stamping feet, and cheering fans. Was the show already over? That would mean she'd been out for at least an hour. Taking a few deep breaths, she tried to clear her head. Then she remembered the wallet.

She looked on the floor, under the instrument cases, behind pieces of scenery, inside boxes of props. The wallet was gone. "What on earth is going on?" she whispered in frustration.

"Nan? Did you say something?" George appeared around the corner, followed by Bess, Alan, and the members of Bent Fender.

"Did you find out anything about Barton?" Roger called to her.

"Did you hear Alan? Wasn't he incredible?" That was Bess.

"Did you miss the whole concert, Nancy?" asked Linda.

"Hey, one person at a time," Nancy replied weakly. Her friends' faces looked blurry.

"Nancy, are you okay? Is something the matter?" George asked. She and Bess rushed to Nancy's side.

"I'm not sure. I found something—that much I know. A wallet. But just as I was taking a look at it, someone hit me over the head, and I blacked out. When I came to, the wallet was gone."

"Someone knocked you out?" Bess's voice was a frightened whisper. "Do you know who did it?"

Nancy shook her head. "Maybe the same people who have Barton. Or maybe just some creep who wanted the wallet. It was full of money, and the guard said there have been some break-ins recently."

"But you said somebody might have taken Barton." Roger Gold's voice trembled.

"Well, I think so. Two men were back here before the show . . ." Nancy told them everything she had found out. "I want to look around a little more," she said, finishing up. "Maybe that wallet wasn't the only thing around that might tell us something. *Ouch*." She put her hand to her aching head.

"You're not looking for another thing tonight," George told her firmly. "You've got some bump there. We're putting you right to bed and getting you an ice pack."

"But George . . ."

"Your friends are right," Linda said. "In fact, it might be a good idea to have a doctor take a look at you."

"I'm all right, really," Nancy insisted, but as she spoke, the hall began to spin and she felt her knees weaken. She reached out to lean on Bess's shoulder.

"Nancy, the doctor is a good idea," Bess said.

"But if there are other clues . . ."

Roger spoke up. "We'll have the security guards search every inch of this place and report back to you if they find anything out of the ordinary."

"Well, okay," Nancy agreed grudgingly. She did feel awfully woozy.

She let the band members put her and her friends in a taxi to the hotel, but not before promising them that she would be back on the case first thing in the morning.

At the hotel, the house physician gave Nancy a clean bill of health, much to everyone's relief.

Carson Drew had arrived home from the opera to find his daughter in bed in the luxurious suite they were sharing. An ice pack rested on her head, and Dr. Harris was bending over her.

"Dad, you should be getting used to my misadventures by now," Nancy joked weakly.

But the tight lines around Carson Drew's mouth did not soften even after the doctor announced that his daughter was going to be as good as new in the morning. Nancy knew that her father worried about her.

"You go right to sleep and get a solid night's rest," Dr. Harris told Nancy. "That's my prescription."

Nancy nodded sleepily. Once she was alone—her friends in their own suite, her father in the next room—she tried to go over the evening's events in her mind. But she was thoroughly exhausted. Try as she might to stay awake for just a few minutes longer, she felt herself drifting into a deep, dreamless sleep.

"Sleeping beauty," Bess giggled.

"Shh. You'll wake her up," George whispered. "Let's just leave the tray."

"But the omelet will get cold," Bess protested.

"Bess, you know Dr. Harris said she needs rest."

Nancy rolled over and pulled at the quilt that covered her. She opened one eye. Her friends were setting a breakfast tray on the table in the corner of the room. "S'all right, you guys," she mumbled, still half asleep. "I'm getting up."

"Nan! Good morning, sleepyhead." Bess flounced down on the edge of the bed. "How are you feeling?"

Nancy pulled herself into a sitting position, leaning against the backboard of the king-size bed. She checked the bump on her head and found that the swelling had gone down. "Pretty good." She looked around the hotel room. "Hey, it's nice in here, huh?" She hadn't had a chance to look around much when they'd checked in, and after the concert nothing could have been farther from her mind than the hotel room.

"Yeah, and get a load of the view," George said, pulling open the curtains to reveal the skyline of New York's Midtown, sparkling in the early-autumn morning sunshine.

"The Empire State Building!" Nancy noted enthusiastically.

"And that other one is the Chrysler Building," Bess informed her. "One of the bellhops told us all about it. Boy, you should have seen him. He was really cute!"

"Bess, honestly," Nancy kidded. "I thought Alan was enough for you."

"Well, I only noticed 'cause I thought maybe George—"

"Thank you very much, cousin dear, but I think I can take care of myself," George interrupted her.

"You guys . . ." Nancy laughed. "Hey, what's on the tray? I'm starved. Whoever gave me that smack on the head did me out of an after-the-show supper."

"Nancy, that's not funny," George said. "You could have really been hurt."

"George, I'm fine. If you should worry about anyone, it's Barton Novak." Nancy grew serious. "Speaking of whom, is there anything new on him?"

George held up a newspaper. Four-inch headlines were splashed all over the front page. Nancy could read them from across the room. ROCK STAR VANISHES, the headlines screamed. "That's the latest," George said. "He still hasn't turned up, and nobody's heard from him."

Nancy pushed off the covers and jumped out of bed. "Time to do some investigating."

"Wait," George protested. "Aren't you even going to have breakfast? We brought it up here for you, and you said you were starved."

"This is more important."

"Nan, I really think you should eat something. You can't

miss meals if you're going to start running around the way you do on cases." She brought the breakfast tray to Nancy's night table.

Bess looked longingly at the scalloped potatoes and cheese omelet. "I wish I could put away dairy like that and not feel sick," she said. "You don't know how lucky you are, Nancy."

Nancy sat back down on the bed and took a big bite of a croissant. "All right. You two win." She ate quickly, not tasting much, wanting to get to work as soon as possible. "By the way, where's my dad?"

"He went out jogging. The woman at the front desk told him about a trail in Central Park. He looked in on you before he left, but you were sound asleep. He told us to keep an eye on you." George joined Bess at the edge of Nancy's bed.

"Oh." Nancy wolfed down a few bites of omelet. "I was hoping he could take me over to meet Bent Fender's agent. I know he was planning to see her about their contract this morning."

"Well, he ought to be back soon," Bess said. "But what do you want to talk to that agent for? You think she knows something about Barton?"

"Roger said Barton was fighting with her about their royalties. And with their producer, too. I think that's where I have to start." Nancy took a last swig of orange juice and pushed her tray away.

"Finished?" asked Bess, helping herself to the remaining half a croissant.

At that moment, the door to the hotel suite opened, and Carson Drew stepped in, wearing a navy blue jogging suit and running shoes, his salt-and-pepper hair pushed away from his face with a sweatband.

"Hi, Dad. Did you have a good run?"

"Very nice. Lots of company. I think half the city must be out jogging in the park this morning. How are *you*?" he asked, planting a sweaty kiss on Nancy's forehead.

"Raring to go." Nancy got out of bed and opened her suitcase, taking out her favorite black jeans and a hot pink oversized shirt. "In fact, I wondered if you would mind bringing me with you to Bent Fender's agent this morning. I'm hoping she might be able to give me some information about Barton. Did you see the headlines about him?" She held the newspaper out for her father to look at.

Carson Drew nodded. "I read the article. The media really have a field day when something happens to a big star. They didn't have anything substantial to report, though. Well, perhaps Ann Nordquist can help. I'm meeting her"—Carson Drew checked his watch—"in forty-five minutes," he said as he headed for his room.

Nancy showered and got dressed quickly. "Do you guys want to meet me for lunch later?" she asked Bess and George. She was whisking on a light dusting of blush and pulling a brush through her hair.

"Sounds good," George said. "How about you, Bess?"

"Can't." Bess shook her head. "I told Alan I'd meet him at the record producers'. Then we'll go out for lunch, just the two of us."

"The same producers who handle Fender?" Nancy shot Bess a quizzical look.

"Yeah. Alan's gone to talk to them about getting a recording contract." Bess was almost exploding with joy. "Nancy," she said, "I know you didn't get to hear him last night. He was incredible! This is the start of something really big. I can just picture screaming fans all around, begging for Alan's autograph, trying to get a glimpse of him, to see him smile—and he'll wade through the crowd and climb into the limousine that's waiting for him." Bess smiled impishly. "Of course, I'll be in the back seat." Bess opened up the locket she always wore around her neck and studied Alan's photograph.

"Don't you think you might be getting the teensiest bit carried away?" Nancy asked gently, trying to avoid jolting Bess out of her fantasy. "I know Alan's got a lot of talent, but only the biggest groups record on the World label. They don't go with unknowns."

"Nan, after last night, Alan is *not* an unknown. They even mentioned him in that newspaper article."

"Okay, Bess, but don't be disappointed if they don't sign him right up. Remember, last night was his first major show, and his job was really to imitate Barton's playing as closely as possible."

"I'm not worried."

George caught Nancy's glance and arched a troubled eyebrow.

"Ready, Nancy?" Carson Drew called.

"Ready," Nancy replied distractedly, her mind on Bess and Alan. She slung her bag over her shoulder. "See you guys," she said, taking one last worried look at her friend as she left. When, she wondered, would Bess's bubble burst?

CHAPTER FOUR

Nancy and her father entered the twenty-third-floor office of Ann Nordquist's agency. The walls were papered with posters of foreign places.

"I love to travel," Ms. Nordquist explained, after Carson Drew had introduced her to Nancy and explained that Nancy wanted to speak to her for a few minutes. She ran a perfectly manicured hand through her pale blond hair. "I just got back from a tour of mainland China. And the first thing that happens is—that." Ann gestured to the day's newspaper Nancy had brought along. "It's awful, isn't it?"

"Yes, it is," replied Nancy. "In fact, that's why I'm here. Ms. Nordquist, Roger Gold told me that you and Barton had been, well, quite frankly, having some problems working together. Something about royalty money."

A tiny frown appeared on Ann's forehead. "I wouldn't exactly say we were having problems. You have to understand that royalty revenue is a complicated business. It goes through many channels and often takes some time before it ends up in the artist's pocket. I don't think Barton quite understood that. He felt he was getting shortchanged."

"And he wasn't?"

"I don't think so, not unless something irregular is going on at World."

"They're my next stop," Nancy said. "Maybe you could tell me the names of the people there who handle Barton and Bent Fender."

"Certainly. In fact, I'll make a list for you." The agent reached for a piece of paper, and Nancy studied the attractive woman as she wrote. She had a pleasant, straightforward manner, and she seemed open enough. But Nancy wondered whether there was more to her disagreement with Barton than she'd let on.

"Here you are." Ann pushed the list toward Nancy, a half-dozen names written out in her neat, round handwriting. "I ought to warn you about Harold Marshall. He's not the easiest man to deal with."

"Well, I'll try my best," Nancy said. She and Ann chatted with Carson Drew for a few minutes, Ann confirming some of the things the members of Bent Fender had said about Barton—that he tended to be publicity shy, and that he had indeed picked himself up and vanished on two occasions without telling a soul.

"That makes finding him all the more difficult," Nancy told her, "because if he has been kidnapped, there are going to be plenty of people who won't believe it."

"Like the little boy who cried wolf," Carson Drew supplied.

"Exactly." Nancy stood up to go. "Well, I'll leave you two to do your business. Ms. Nordquist, thank you for your time."

"You're welcome. I hope you can track Barton down quickly. We're all awfully worried about him." Ann extended her hand to Nancy. "I hope next time we'll meet under more pleasant circumstances."

"I do too. By the way, would any of the people on this list fit these descriptions? A tall, heavyset man with straight dark hair, but balding slightly. Or a shorter man with dark wavy hair, possibly wearing a gold ring in the shape of a dragon or sea monster?" Nancy looked up from her notes on the two men who had been seen backstage.

Ann thought for a few seconds. "I don't believe so. No." She shook her head.

"Okay. Well, thanks again." Nancy said goodbye and walked the ten blocks to World Communications' offices. Normally, she would have been thrilled to be on the streets of New York, watching the stream of people and window shopping, but that day she walked quickly, her mind on Barton Novak as she weaved through the crowds. Had he been kidnapped, as Roger Gold suspected, or had he gone on his own, as the rest of the band seemed to think?

Soon, World Communications loomed up in front of her, an imposing steel-and-glass tower with uniformed guards at the door. Not again, Nancy thought, recalling the guards at Radio City Music Hall. She prepared a little speech, but was surprised when the guards let her in with no trouble. In fact, though she found out no new information about Barton, the people at the company were happy to answer her questions. That is, until she got to the last person on the list Ann Nordquist had given her — Harold Marshall.

She opened the door with his name on it and found herself standing before a stylish, sharp-featured young woman of about her own age. The woman's dark hair gleamed with henna-red highlights, and her blue sweater was cut low in the front.

"Yes?" The woman looked up from her desk.

"I'd like to see Mr. Marshall, please." Nancy smiled.

The young woman did not smile back. "Do you have an appointment?"

"No, but I'd like to speak with him about Barton Novak."

"Barton?"

"I'm investigating his disappearance."

"Mr. Marshall is a very busy man, Miss—"

"Drew. Nancy Drew." Nancy extended her hand.

The young woman barely touched it. "I'm afraid he's all booked up today."

"Could it be that he has something to hide?" Nancy suggested, surprised at her own brazenness. When she got no response, she moved toward the inner door and pushed it open.

"Hey, what are you doing? You can't go in there!" the secretary announced, following behind.

"I've already done it," Nancy replied. She found herself facing a small, wiry man with a brown mustache and glasses, who was sitting behind an enormous desk. "Hello, Mr. Marshall."

"Who are you?" He released a cloud of noxious cigar smoke

as he spoke. "Vivian, what's she doing here? I gave specific instructions that—"

"I'm sorry, Mr. Marshall," Vivian said, her voice taking on a honey-sweet tone, "but she barged right in here. I couldn't stop her. Please don't be angry."

Harold Marshall's expression softened for a split second. "Oh, Vivian, of course it's not your fault. I didn't mean to snap at you." Nancy watched him. "But as for you—Miss Drew, did you say?" His expression changed to a sneer as he turned back to Nancy. "What is so important that you felt you could waltz right in here? First, my office is invaded by a wannabe who thinks that just because he banged out a couple of Barton Novak's riffs last night we must be dying to cut a record—"

"Alan?" Nancy groaned out loud. So poor Alan, filled with dreams of glory, had come face-to-face with Harold Marshall. Nancy's heart went out to him and to Bess.

"You're a friend of his? Look, I told him no dice, and I mean it. Now, if you'll excuse me . . ." Marshall swiveled around in his chair.

"I am a friend of Alan's, but that's not why I'm here. I'm a detective, and I must ask you a few questions about Barton Novak. Ann Nordquist said you handle his band."

Marshall spun back around, puffing on his cigar. "Ann Nordquist is pushy."

"You mean you don't handle Bent Fender?" Nancy asked.

"I didn't say that. Oh, all right. Go ahead and ask your questions. But be quick about it. I have more important things to do than chat away the morning with someone who calls herself a detective."

Nancy felt her face flush with anger, but she tried to stay calm. "Mr. Marshall, suppose you tell me everything you can about Barton's disappearance."

"Disappearance! Hah!" he snorted. "I hate to disappoint you, Miss Drew. I know how excited you must be about solving this mystery." His voice oozed sarcasm. "But Barton Novak is safe and sound."

"He is?" Nancy's emotions were a confused jumble of astonishment, relief, and disbelief. "What do you mean?"

"Publicity." Harold Marshall pronounced the word as if it were an explanation in itself.

"I don't understand."

"It's a publicity gimmick. News like this is certain to boost sales on Fender's most recent album. It's been done plenty of times before. Remember the rumor after the Beatles released *Abbey Road*? That Paul McCartney had died? No, you kids don't appreciate the Beatles."

"I *do* know what you're talking about," Nancy countered. She couldn't imagine a rock-and-roll fan who hadn't just about memorized the history of the band. "The record buyers kept thinking they saw clues about it on the album cover and in the lyrics to the songs, isn't that right?"

"The girl detective gets an A plus," Marshall said snidely.

"So you mean Barton's disappearance was engineered?" Nancy shook the newspaper in anger, the realization of what

Marshall had done washing over her like a tidal wave. "Why didn't you tell anyone? The rest of the band members are either furious or scared stiff about him."

"Hey," Harold Marshall drawled. "That anger and fear bought us four-inch headlines. If we'd told them, their reactions wouldn't have been so . . . real." He allowed himself a satisfied smile.

"That's a rotten, inhuman trick," Nancy exclaimed.

"Kid, this is business. What counts is what sells records." Marshall shrugged. "Those fans are going to go wild when they think Barton's gone. They'll start looking for clues in the records, the rock videos. . . . All teens think they're detectives, as you well understand," he added condescendingly.

Nancy bristled. "What I understand is that you think it's good business to lie to Bent Fender's fans. Either that, or to lie to me."

"Look, Miss Drew, if you don't believe what I've told you about Barton, that's your problem. Anybody find a ransom note?"

"No," admitted Nancy, fighting back the urge to grab the mug of coffee on his desk and fling it in his face. "But couldn't you tell the rest of Bent Fender where Barton is, just for their own peace of mind?"

"Let's get something straight." Harold Marshall's lips thinned. "We're sitting on a publicity gold mine here. I only told you what's really happening so you'd stop wasting my time. If you go to the press with anything I said, I'll deny it. Who do you think they'll believe—me, or some kid playing detective?"

He stared at Nancy, challenging her. "As for Barton, he's a big boy. He could call the band members to tell them he's okay—if he wanted. Maybe he wants some privacy. Think of this as kind of a vacation for him. And do us both a favor. Keep your mouth shut about this whole business."

Nancy didn't like Harold Marshall's tone, but she had to admit to herself that what he was saying jibed with everything she'd heard about Barton's thirst for privacy. "Maybe," she said. "But wasn't it strange to pull off this stunt right before the biggest of the Rock for Relief concerts?"

"More publicity that way. Now, if we're all finished here, you can show yourself out."

Nancy took a few steps toward the door, where Vivian, who had stood there all the time, put an insistent hand on Nancy's arm. The interview was clearly over.

"Oh, just one more thing, Mr. Marshall." Nancy turned in the doorway. She asked if he'd ever seen the two men described to her by the Radio City guard.

Marshall shrugged. "How am I supposed to keep track of everyone who goes in and out of this place?"

Did I expect any other answer? Nancy asked herself, leaving Harold Marshall's office without further conversation. She found her way back to the elevator banks, rode down to the main floor, and walked past the indoor fountain and the greenery that adorned the lobby, into the crisp midday sunshine.

Her head swam with conflicting thoughts as she made her

way back to the hotel to meet George for lunch. Harold Marshall was one of the rudest, most self-important people she had ever met. But he was just the kind of person to cook up a sneaky publicity trick like the one he'd described. And the fact that no ransom note had been received would suggest that Barton hadn't been kidnapped.

But what about the two mysterious men at the Music Hall and all the clues Nancy had discovered outside Barton's dressing room? Marshall's publicity scheme didn't explain them.

And it didn't explain something else, Nancy thought. That attack on me last night was no stunt. It was serious—deadly serious.

CHAPTER FIVE

Georffe, can you think of any reason why Harold Marshall would want his biggest star out of the way?" Nancy asked, helping herself to a breadstick.

"How do you know he's not telling the truth?" George held down her napkin as a breeze drifted across the outdoor table at the café where the two girls were having lunch.

"I *don't* know. That's the trouble. It's so confusing. But George, even if Barton isn't in trouble, I'm absolutely convinced that something fishy is going on." Nancy rubbed the back of her head as proof. "But how am I supposed to know where to look when I don't even know what I'm looking for?"

"You tell me, Nan. You're the detective."

"All I do know is that Harold Marshall is creepy. Poor Alan, getting his dream shattered by that goon."

"Well, someone was going to do it sooner or later. That concert last night really put stars in his eyes. I mean, he's acting totally blind as far as realistic expectations go." George leaned over sideways to allow the waiter to put down a bacon cheeseburger in front of each girl and a basket of french fries between them. "Thank you," George said, reaching for a fry. "Anyway," she continued, "Bess isn't helping matters. The way she's been talking, you'd think Alan was going to be the next Bruce Springsteen."

"Well, it's pretty obvious that Harold Marshall cleared up that misconception quickly."

"Mind if we join you?" Nancy heard a familiar voice behind her. She turned around to find Bess and Alan, both smiling broadly.

"Hi! What are you guys doing here? Bess, you said you and Alan were going to have lunch together somewhere."

"We were, but we stopped off at the hotel first and got the most incredible news. We just had to tell you. The hotel manager said he'd recommended this place." Bess plopped down in an empty seat beside Nancy. Alan sat next to George.

"So what's happening?" Nancy asked, noting the looks of pure happiness on their faces. She was more than ready to hear some good news.

"They've decided that—" Bess and Alan both began speaking at once.

Bess laughed. "You go ahead and tell them, Alan. It's your news."

"Well, Vivian from the record company called," Alan said breathlessly, "and they've decided they want me to cut an album for them!"

"What?" Nancy couldn't believe what she was hearing. "But I saw Harold Marshall after you did and he said . . ." Her voice trailed off. There was no point in repeating what would only hurt Alan.

"I know what he said." Alan nodded. "But he must have changed his mind. There was a message from Vivian waiting for us when we got back to the hotel. I returned her call, and she told me to come right over to World Communications. Mr. Marshall wanted to congratulate me in person!"

"What made him change his mind?" Nancy could picture the sneer on Harold Marshall's lips as he mentioned Alan. She wouldn't have expected him to change his mind for all the gold in Fort Knox.

"I think it had something to do with Barton," Alan said.

"Barton!" Nancy sat straight up in her chair.

"Yeah, that's the other piece of great news," Bess put in. "Alan saw him!"

"When? Where?" Nancy's head swam.

"Right after I went back to Marshall's office. Barton wanted to thank me for filling in for him, and he asked me to do his next couple of gigs while he stays out of the public eye for a while."

"You're kidding," Nancy said.

"Nope. He was hanging around, waiting for a limo to take him to his beach house, that purple bandanna around his neck, sitting in an armchair drinking a beer and watching some movie." Alan leaned back in his chair with a happy sigh. "I guess he sort of coaxed Marshall into signing me on. And to think that until yesterday Barton was just someone I dreamed about meeting!"

"Nan, George, isn't it unbelievable?" Bess leaned over and grabbed Nancy's arm.

"Unbelievable," Nancy echoed, meaning it more literally than Bess had. Was she to believe that Harold Marshall had so completely changed his mind about Alan? Or that the only person Barton Novak had asked to see was not a member of his own band, not a close friend or relative, but a fan he'd spoken with for no more than a few minutes?

"Alan, are you *sure* about this?" she asked.

"Sure I'm sure." Alan grinned, his brown eyes shining. "Bess and I are going over to get a tour of the recording studios later this afternoon, and Marshall's having Vivian draw the contracts up this week. So let's celebrate! Lunch is on me!"

The food was wonderful, and the weather at the outdoor patio was perfect, but throughout the rest of the meal, Nancy's thoughts spun. If Barton was fine, there was no mystery at all, was there? But what about the wallet and the two mysterious men? And what about Harold Marshall's offer to Alan? Just that morning, Marshall was calling Alan an idiot who "banged out a couple of Barton Novak's riffs." Now he was signing a record contract with him.

Nancy had an uncomfortable feeling in the pit of her stomach. Something was very wrong. But she kept her thoughts to herself until after Bess and Alan had left for World Communications. It wasn't until she and George were on their way back to the hotel that she confided her feelings.

"George, don't you think Alan's announcement was kind of, well, weird?"

"What do you mean, Nancy?"

"I mean, everything's happening so fast. One day Alan's taking guitar lessons in River Heights, and the next day he's signing a solo recording contract with one of the biggest labels in the business. George, we both know Alan's got a lot of talent, but this is just a little too much for me to believe."

"What's not to believe? By the end of the week, Alan's going to have a World Communications recording contract in his hands!" George was matter-of-fact. "I mean, it is pretty wild, but it's true."

"I don't know. What if Harold Marshall is stringing Alan along? I don't like that man."

"You think he might not come through?" George asked. "Then why would he make the offer in the first place?"

"I wish I could tell you." Nancy flung her hands up in despair. "I keep trying to get answers on this case, but all I get are more questions."

"And what about Barton?" George voiced one more of those questions as they rounded a corner and came to their hotel.

"Barton—a guy who agrees to disappear right before a concert he's spent months planning. It doesn't figure." Nancy pressed her lips together.

"Well, what do you intend to do?" George asked.

The doorman opened the hotel door, and Nancy and George started toward the elevators but were waved over to the front desk by the clerk on duty.

He handed Nancy and George a slip of paper with a telephone message on it. *Carl Rutland, security guard at Radio*

City Music Hall, it said. *Found something you might want to know about*. A telephone number was written at the bottom.

"This might answer your question," Nancy told George. "Come on. Let's go up to my room and find out what Mr. Carl Rutland has to say."

As Nancy fitted her key in the lock, she heard the room phone ringing. "Maybe that's him calling back," she said to George. She pushed the door open and reached for the phone. "Hello?"

"Hi, beautiful," a male voice said.

"Ned! Hi!" Nancy felt herself smile at the sound of Ned Nickerson's mellow baritone. "How are you?"

"Curious, actually. I read in today's paper that Barton Novak vanished right before his concert, and I was wondering what happened. Weren't you supposed to hear Bent Fender play?"

Nancy walked over and eased herself onto the edge of the bed. "It's a pretty strange story. At first I was sure Barton had been kidnapped, but now it turns out that it's really just a publicity gimmick. I think. I mean, I don't know what to think. Ned, I don't know if I've got a mystery to solve or not." Nancy's words came out in a fast, nervous rush.

"Nan," Ned said slowly, "slow down and tell me all about it."

Nancy took a deep breath and recounted everything that had happened since her arrival in New York.

When she was done, Ned let out a long, low whistle. "Sounds like you've run into some people who play awfully rough. That blow on the head is serious. I don't like it at all," he said, worry rising with his voice.

"Ned, I'm fine," Nancy assured him. "The worst part isn't the bump on my head. It's that I don't know if the wallet has anything to do with Barton or the two men backstage, or anything. I'm so keyed up. I don't know whether to forget this business or what."

"Well, how about a consultation?" Ned suggested. "Say, in about two hours? I can get on the road right away."

"You're coming up from school to spend some time with me in New York? Oh, Ned, that sounds great! I'm sure you can share Alan's room with him."

"Alan? You mean Bess's new superstar? The one who was offered the recording contract?"

Nancy frowned. "Yeah, Bess's superstar. And Ned, maybe you can help me figure out what's going on here."

"I'll do everything I can," Ned promised. "And if anyone tries to knock you over the head again, I'll give them a taste of their own medicine."

"My hero," Nancy giggled. "But don't forget, I'm the one with the brown belt in karate."

"Do you have to remind me?" Ned said, groaning.

"Well, I won't try any of my new moves on you this time," Nancy said solemnly. "Except maybe on the dance floor. Roger Gold is taking us to a wild new club tonight."

"Sounds great."

"Good. It's a date." Before saying goodbye, Nancy gave Ned the address of the hotel. "There's an indoor parking lot right across the street," she added.

"Well, you look a little happier than you did a few minutes ago," George observed from the couch. "Love is the miracle drug," she sang teasingly. It was the refrain of one of Bent Fender's new songs.

"George, do you think Ned's ready to forget about Daryl?" Nancy felt herself blush.

"I don't know, Nan, but a few days together in the most exciting city in the world ought to do *something* for the two of you."

"Hmm. You know, this might turn out to be a good vacation after all. If I could just stop worrying about Barton, and Alan's record contract . . ." Nancy felt herself coming down to earth. "Speaking of which, I better call that security guard back."

She dialed the number on the message sheet. "Hello, is this Carl Rutland?" she asked the man who answered the telephone.

"Speaking."

"Hi, this is Nancy Drew. From the concert last night."

"Oh, Miss Drew. Yes. Hello."

"You said you found something?"

"That's right. Well, first of all, whoever gave you that knock on the head came in and out by the fire escape, off one of the dance studios. When I checked the windows leading out to it, I found that one of the latches had been forced open, and we always keep them locked."

"Mr. Rutland, do you think someone would go through all

the trouble of climbing the fire escape and breaking in just to steal a wallet?" Nancy asked.

"Maybe. But it would be very risky. There are too many people around the Music Hall when there's a rock concert. You know, fans come without tickets and try to scalp them or just sneak in, and they wind up hanging around outside. Anyway, there'd be too good a chance of being caught."

"Then," Nancy mused aloud, "there must have been something worth far more than money in that wallet. Well, thank you for the information, Mr. Rutland."

"Wait, that's not the only thing I wanted to tell you," Carl Rutland said. "I found something outside Barton Novak's dressing room, near all those boxes and things."

"You did?" Nancy was alert.

"Yeah. A scarf. A violet-colored scarf with designs on it."

"Mr. Rutland," Nancy said hoarsely, in a flash of understanding, "you mean you found a purple bandanna—a square of heavy cotton, with a sort of leafy pattern stitched on it in green?"

"Yeah, that's it. Is it yours?"

"No. No, it's Barton Novak's, sort of his good luck charm," Nancy said, "and one of a kind. His sister did the embroidery." Nancy remembered reading that in several articles about Barton. "He never plays a concert without it. Um, Mr. Rutland, when did you say you found the bandanna?"

"Last night, after they took you home. I've got it right here in my pocket."

"Last night?" Nancy's brain was working overtime. "Well, just hold on to it. I'll make arrangements to get it from you." Nancy thanked the man again and got off the phone in a hurry, her hand trembling as she hung up the receiver.

"Nancy, what's the matter? You look like that security guard has been telling you ghost stories or something," George said.

"No, not ghost stories. Something much more real and much more frightening. It's Alan, George. He's been lying to us."

CHAPTER SIX

George's eyes widened. "What do you mean?"

"That guard found Barton's bandanna," Nancy explained.

"So? Maybe he dropped it without realizing."

"But don't you see?" Nancy felt sick at the realization. "Just this morning, Alan told us he saw Barton. And he said that Barton was wearing that bandanna!"

George began to look sick too. "Oh no."

"Even if he was a little flaky, I always thought I could trust Alan," Nancy said. "But now I don't know *what* he's gotten into—except that it's really dangerous." She got up and headed for the door.

"Hey, where are we going?" George grabbed a sweater from the bed.

"To find Alan." Nancy slipped on her jean jacket and took the room key. "He and Bess must be getting their tour of the World recording studios right now." She put an insistent hand on George's back and moved her toward the door.

"Wouldn't it be easier to call him there?" George suggested.

Nancy shook her head vigorously. "No way. What if they wind up putting us through to Vivian or Mr. Marshall's office?

I don't want them to know anything about this. I want to get Alan alone. Besides, I need to see the expression on his face when we confront him with his lie." Nancy stepped out of the room.

George followed, a worried look in her brown eyes. "Nancy, do you think Bess knows Alan's lying? I mean, it seems so impossible—"

"I know. Bess has never been anything less than a hundred percent straight with us. I'm sure she wouldn't hold anything back. One thing really scares me, though. If Alan isn't the kind of guy we think he is, Bess could be in trouble." Nancy locked the room and headed for the elevator, with George a few steps behind her.

"But, Nancy, it's so obvious that the guy cares about Bess. And don't forget, he helped us solve your last mystery."

"I know. I only hope he's got a good explanation for this."

Finding Alan turned out to be easier said than done. When Nancy and George arrived at World Communications, the receptionist told them that the recording facilities were not housed in the same building as the executive offices. "Our recording is done by an independent company. Oraye Sound." She wrote down Oraye's address.

"Is it far from here?" Nancy asked.

"All the way downtown."

Nancy took that to mean yes. "Come on, George. It looks like you and I are going for a little cab ride."

They raced outside and hailed a taxi. "205 East Fourth Street,"

Nancy told the driver. "And go whatever way's the fastest. It's important."

"Lady, it's always important. Everyone in this town is always in a hurry," the taxi driver responded. "But I'll do my best. Of course, going through Midtown this time of day, there's always traffic."

"Isn't there some way to avoid it?" George asked. "This really is an emergency."

"Then you shoulda chartered a helicopter." The driver swung out into the flow of cars, inches in front of a gray hatchback. The driver of the gray car let out an angry blast of his horn.

"Oh brother," grumbled Nancy a few minutes later, looking nervously at her watch. "We could walk faster than this." She pulled several crinkled dollar bills out of her jacket pocket. "We'll get out here," she announced, before they had reached their destination. She pushed the money through the opening in the Plexiglas shield that separated the driver from his passengers. "Keep the change."

The taxi came to a halt, and she jumped out. "Come on, George. Maybe we can still make it down there before Bess and Alan leave."

The girls reached East Fourth Street in record time. "We should have recruited you for girls' track in high school," George panted.

Nancy wiped her forehead. "Let's see," she said, trying to catch her breath, "194, 196 . . . It must be on the other side of the street. 201. Yeah, there it is, 205."

Nancy rang the buzzer for Oraye Sound, Inc., and she and George entered the building and headed for the fifth floor. The elevator opened on a large area divided into a number of work spaces by movable partitions. Several halls branched off in different directions from the central space. People rushed back and forth busily, and the hum of voices filled the room. In one corner was a large desk that was not hidden behind any of the dividers; a young man sat behind it, typing.

Nancy and George approached him, and Nancy cleared her throat. He looked up from his computer. "Hi, are you with the NYU group?" he asked. "You're late," he continued, without waiting for an answer. "The tour's started already. They're down that way, in one of the editing rooms."

"NYU?" Nancy asked.

"Yes. New York University. Aren't you film students?"

Nancy shook her head. "Actually, we're here looking for our friends Alan Wales and Bess Marvin."

"Who?"

"They should have come in early this afternoon. He's medium height with frizzy brown hair. She has blond hair a little past her shoulders, and she's on the short side," George supplied.

The man thought for a moment. "Oh, you mean the two Harold Marshall sent over."

Nancy's brow furrowed at Mr. Marshall's name. "Yes. That's right."

"Oh, you just missed them. They were talking about going out to celebrate something."

Nancy felt thoroughly frustrated as she and George started back across the large room. "George," she said, in what was for her a down voice. "What's going on with this case? I feel as if I'm following shadows, not leads." Now she wouldn't be able to get hold of Alan until their rendezvous at the club that evening. She'd lose several hours of sleuthing time—hours that could be critical to Barton Novak.

Before George could reply, Nancy saw something that made her pulse speed up. Moving as quickly as she could, she pulled George into an unoccupied work space. "It's Vivian!" she whispered, peeking out from around the partition.

"Who?"

"Harold Marshall's secretary." Nancy watched as Vivian emerged from the stairwell carrying a bulky package under her arm. The woman glanced around furtively and slipped down one of the hallways. The young man at the corner desk, his back to the work spaces and network of halls, continued to type, and Vivian passed by unnoticed.

"Looks to me like she's sneaking around," George said.

"Come on," Nancy urged. "Maybe the trip down here won't be a waste after all." She grabbed George's elbow, and silently, keeping a safe distance behind her, the girls followed Vivian down the hall.

Vivian seemed to know exactly where she was going. After proceeding along a maze of corridors past numerous doors, she stopped abruptly in front of one of them. Second-guessing the next move, Nancy pulled George back around the last corner in the corridor—and not a second too soon. Nancy edged around the corner just in time to see Vivian whipping her head around, clearly checking to make sure she was alone. Then she entered the room she had stopped in front of.

"Now what?" George hissed as they both breathed a sigh of relief.

"Well, we can't follow her in there," Nancy thought out loud, "so we'll have to wait until she leaves. Then we can see what's in that room. But let's get out of here. She's going to come back this way, and besides, someone might see us."

"Maybe there's a ladies' room around here," George suggested. "We could hide in there until she leaves."

The girls found one a few doors down and entered cautiously, making sure it was unoccupied. Then Nancy posted herself by the door, leaving it open a finger's width so she could peer out.

Vivian didn't take long. Only a few minutes later, Nancy heard the clicking of her high-heeled black pumps on the tiled hallway floor and noticed that Vivian no longer carried the package that had been under her arm. "She must have dropped something off," Nancy said, pulling the restroom door shut as Vivian walked by.

Nancy waited until the footsteps faded. Then she peeked out again. The corridor was empty. "Okay, *now!*" she instructed George. The two friends made a dash for the room Vivian had entered and let themselves inside, the door opening and closing with a faint squeak.

The walls of the small room were lined, floor to ceiling, with cabinets, and in the middle of the room were low, free-standing, enclosed bins.

"It's some kind of storeroom," Nancy observed.

She pulled at the handle of one of the cabinets—labeled A THROUGH C—and found it locked. She tried one on the adjacent wall. The typed sticker on the door read G THROUGH K. It didn't open either.

George was walking around, fiddling with the cabinet doors. "These are locked too," she said, her words colored with annoyance. Then she called out softly, "Nancy, come look at this."

When Nancy joined her, the young detective took a look at a list George had been studying. It was taped to the wall. The page was divided into columns headed *name, title of master, date borrowed, date returned.*

"Masters. So that's why all these drawers are locked so securely. George, this is where they keep all the original recordings."

"Right," George said, "I remember back when we were sophomores, this store in Mount Harmon was closed down because the owner was selling albums that had been made illegally. I'm not sure of the details, but he was buying the albums for way under the normal costs, selling them for the retail prices, and raking in a fortune."

Nancy nodded. "Right. If these masters get into the wrong hands, they can be used to make a lot of illegal money."

As Nancy talked, she skimmed the list in front of her for Vivian's name. It wasn't there. What was Vivian up to? she wondered. She guessed that the parcel contained masters Vivian had sneaked out and then sneaked back in. Was Vivian getting them for Harold Marshall so he could illegally sell music? If so, then Barton was right to wonder about Bent Fender's royalties. They wouldn't earn money on copies sold illegally.

Nancy pondered that, continuing to study the list. Suddenly a familiar name near the bottom of the page caught her eye. "George!" she gasped, pointing to the bold script.

George's gaze followed Nancy's finger. "Oh wow! Barton Novak!"

"And he was here just a few days ago!" Nancy added. "George, I bet Barton came here and discovered something. Maybe he found out that some of the masters were missing!"

"And then someone found out that Barton knew, and had to make sure he didn't tell anyone."

Nancy nodded, her face taut. "That's a really strong motive. Now I'm sure Barton didn't disappear on his own. He must have been kidnapped."

CHAPTER SEVEN

The pieces of the puzzle were finally beginning to fall into place. "This explains why there was no ransom note," Nancy continued. "Barton's kidnappers weren't interested in getting money, just in keeping him from spilling the beans. I bet all this has something to do with his wanting to talk to me after the concert." Nancy leaned back against one of the cabinets, digesting the implications of the new discovery.

Suddenly, a thought occurred to her that made her blood go colder than an arctic ice floe. "George," she said, "if Barton's kidnappers don't want a ransom for him, maybe they don't intend to free him at all."

George's ruddy complexion drained to pale.

The two girls stood in silence, the horrible realization sinking in until the stillness in the room was shattered by the soft but unmistakable squeal of the door opening. Nancy gasped.

A sandy-haired man with a mustache stepped inside. There was no place to escape his gaze in the small room. "Who are you?" he asked gruffly. "No unauthorized personnel allowed in here."

Nancy thought quickly. "We, um . . . we're with the NYU group."

"Film students," George added, backing up Nancy's story.

"Oh. Well, what are you kids doing in here? Your group is over in one of the editing rooms." He motioned for them to leave. "Down this hall and to the left."

For a moment, Nancy was flooded with a sense of relief. "Oh. Thank you, sir." She and George moved toward the door.

But as soon as they were safely out of Oraye Sound and outside again, Nancy's relief dissolved in a flood of nerves. What if she couldn't locate Barton before it was too late? Or was it already too late? Who was at the bottom of the sordid mess, and how much did Alan know about it? How safe was Bess if she inadvertently had been caught smack in the middle of a music industry conspiracy?

Stop! Nancy admonished herself. Standing in the middle of a busy New York street thinking about all this wasn't going to get her any closer to answering the questions that were gnawing at her. She took several breaths, taking the air deep into her body and breathing from her stomach, the way she'd been taught in karate class.

"Okay," she told George, "the first thing to do is to find out which people have access to the room with the masters in it, and then find out what they know." She decided to give Roger Gold a call.

Answer. Please answer, she thought.

"Hello?" Roger answered.

"Roger. It's Nancy Drew. Thank goodness you're there."

"Nancy, what's wrong? Is it about Barton? Do you know where he is?"

"Not yet," Nancy replied, trying to keep from sounding frightened, "but I think I've got my first solid lead."

"Was he kidnapped?" Roger sounded nervous.

"Yes, I think so."

"I knew it! No way did Barton go off on his own. He was too involved in those concerts." Roger paused. "So what do you think's going on?"

"I think someone's pirating Bent Fender's music. And probably other groups' too."

"Pirating our albums?" A string of angry words streamed out of Roger Gold's normally soft-speaking mouth. Nancy waited for him to calm down. "I'm sorry," he said finally. "Listening to me get mad isn't going to help Barton, is it?"

"That's okay, Roger. I'm not exactly a bearer of good tidings. But there is something you can tell me that will help get to the bottom of this."

"Anything."

"Who has access to the cabinets in the masters room at Oraye Sound?"

"Well, all the techies—the recording technicians—at Oraye, for starters. And they usually give a key to the musicians who record there."

"Like you and Barton and the rest of the band?"

"Right. I mean, we do most of our work at our own private studios, but we do some mixing and stuff there sometimes. Yeah."

"Anyone else?" Nancy asked.

"The top executives at World," Roger said.

"Harold Marshall?"

A moment of silence, then Roger exploded. "Is that creep in on Barton's disappearance?"

"Well, he has an interesting reason for why Barton didn't make the concert."

"I don't buy it," Roger said firmly, after hearing Harold Marshall's story. "Barton would want the sales of our albums to center around our music, not around gossip about where he is. Besides, he doesn't like the idea of people poking around in his private life. Nope. Marshall's story just doesn't make sense."

Nancy wasn't surprised by Roger's opinion. Marshall's story had too many holes in it for her to swallow it completely. "Roger, thank you. You've been a big help. Oh, and one more thing. How does Harold Marshall get along with his secretary?"

"Vivian? They're a perfect team. The witch and the warlock. Marshall thinks she's the greatest thing since stereophonic sound. The rat has had his eye on her since the day she came to work for him. And she'll do anything he asks. And I mean anything."

"Roger, would Vivian do Marshall's dirty work?" Nancy pictured Vivian sneaking into the masters room.

"Sure."

"And would Marshall be low enough to betray his own company and pocket the profit?"

"He is low enough to do anything," Roger answered.

"You know, it's possible that we might have our man," Nancy

said. "But we have to catch him in the act to make sure."

"You just tell me what I have to do to help," Roger offered. "I'd be only too happy to nail that guy."

"The best thing you can do is act as if nothing's happened. Meet us at the club tonight, work on your new songs, do whatever you would normally do. We don't want Marshall to think we're onto him." Nancy inhaled sharply. "Because if Barton's disappearance is any indication, what we know could be hazardous to our health!"

She hung up the phone and looked at George. "Come on. We've got to find out a lot more before we crack this case."

"Action!" George rubbed her hands together. "This is the part I like the best."

Nancy shook her head. "I'm not so sure this is action you'll enjoy . . ."

"Ugh. I feel like I'm back in school again," George moaned.

"School was never a life-or-death situation," Nancy responded gravely. "Now read."

The girls were seated in the research room of the Jefferson Market Library, a brisk walk from the studios of Oraye Sound. Books and back copies of magazines were piled next to them on the old wooden tables.

Nancy skimmed through an article in *Allegro*, the monthly newspaper of the musicians' union. "George, listen to this." She read out loud, keeping her voice low, so as not to disturb the people around her. "'One billion dollars per year are lost in residuals due to pirated sound and video recordings in the United States and abroad.' One billion dollars' worth of royalty money! Can you believe that? No revenue from these sales goes to the artist or company that holds the copyright," she exclaimed. "Wow, I had no idea what a huge black market there is for pirated recordings. There's certainly enough money at stake to make some crook want to get rid of anyone in the way."

Nancy's stomach did a slow somersault as she thought about Barton's safety.

George's brown-eyed gaze glided across the page as she summarized another article. "A whole bunch of countries have copyright laws—the U.S., Russia, China—but apparently enforcement can be lax."

"China!" A bell went off in Nancy's head. "George, that wallet I found backstage during the concert—it had a dragon on it—a Chinese dragon!" Nancy rested her elbow on the table and propped her chin on the palm of her hand.

"Do you think Harold Marshall might have some connection to the Chinese?" George asked. "Or Vivian? Somehow, I can't imagine her teetering around anywhere outside New York in those high-heeled shoes." George let out a giggle, despite the severity of the situation. Then she clapped a hand over her mouth. "Sorry, Nan."

But Nancy wasn't at all annoyed with George. "You're a genius!" she said excitedly, trying at the same time to keep her voice down. "Maybe not Vivian, but I know someone who likes to travel."

"Nancy, what are you talking about?"

"That picture you had of Vivian reminded me of a poster I saw just this morning . . . hanging on the wall in Ann Nordquist's office!" Nancy grabbed George's arm. "Ann is Bent Fender's agent. And she just came back from China. She was telling my dad and me about her trip." Nancy's pulse was racing. "What if that wallet belongs to her? And what if she wasn't just sightseeing?"

"But what about Mr. Marshall?" George reminded her.

"Yes, then there's Harold Marshall." Nancy pondered that for a few moments. "You know, he and Ann Nordquist both made a point of telling me how much they disliked each other. But what if they did that just to throw me off the track? It's possible they're working together."

"But Nancy, you told me that Ann Nordquist seemed like a nice woman."

"She did. I mean, she does. I liked her. And I don't see why she would own a wallet with the initial L. Still, I don't think we can rule her out entirely. You can never be too sure."

"I guess not. We thought Alan was playing straight with us, and look what happened. If he drags Bess into this, he's going to be really sorry."

Nancy nodded. "Speaking of which, let's get back to the hotel. I want to pick up Ned and get to the club. Bess's wonder boy and I are in for a little heart-to-heart." She gathered up the books and bound volumes of magazines and began replacing them on the shelves. "And," she added, "I think I ought to do a little checking up on Ms. Ann Nordquist."

"Yeah," George said. "Maybe she got tired of earning her ten percent and decided to make a real killing."

"I hope it hasn't gone that far. . . ." Nancy hesitated before going on. "As far as murder."

CHAPTER EIGHT

Ned!" Nancy threw her arms around the tall, broad-shouldered young man. "Sorry to keep you waiting. Have you been here long?" Nancy had found Ned sitting on the plush velvet sofa in the hotel lobby.

"Got here just about five minutes ago," Ned said, bending down to give her a powerful hug. A lock of thick dark hair fell forward over his eye, and Nancy brushed it away.

"I want you to know," she said, her mind still reeling from her frenzied afternoon, "your visit is the one bright spot in this entire trip."

"Uh-oh. Sounds like my favorite detective is wrapped up in a tough case. What's happened since we talked on the phone?"

Nancy let out a sigh. "First I had so few real clues that I didn't even know if I had a mystery or not. Now, all of a sudden, there are all sorts of leads . . . and I don't know which ones to follow first." Nancy could see George coming across the lobby. "Listen, why don't you come upstairs, and I'll tell you everything?"

A few minutes later, the three friends were seated around the table in the main room of the suite, drinking the milkshakes they had ordered from room service. Nancy and George recounted the day's events, from the newspaper headlines about Barton to their library research.

Ned looked thoughtful. "So you think the trail of evidence could lead to that record producer—"

"Harold Marshall," George supplied.

"Right, or the Nordquist woman, or even Alan?" Ned's voice dropped as he uttered Bess's boyfriend's name. "So, I'm sharing a room with one of your suspects, Nancy?"

Nancy shrugged. "I haven't even seen Alan since you called, so I haven't had a chance to ask him about sharing his room. And once I confront him about his lie, I'm not sure how generous he's going to feel about doing any favors for my friends." Nancy twisted a strand of hair around her index finger. "But don't worry. There's a couch in Dad's room. I'm sure he wouldn't mind having you stay with us."

As if on cue, the door to the suite opened, and Carson Drew stepped inside. "Ned! Well, hello. I thought I heard your voice. It's good to see you again."

Ned stood up, and they shook hands. "Good to be here, Mr. Drew."

"So." Carson Drew turned toward his daughter and George. "Anything new on the case?"

"As a matter of fact, Dad, yes. I was wondering if you could arrange another meeting between me and Ann Nordquist. I need to talk to her."

"I'm sure she'd be happy to. In fact, I'll ask her tonight at dinner."

"You mean you're having another business meeting?" Nancy wondered if she should tell her father that Ann Nordquist was on her list of suspects. No, she decided. She'd keep it to herself until she had more information.

Carson Drew liked to tease his daughter, to remind her that her detective's methods were a direct contrast to his own lawyer's procedure.

"Not exactly," he replied. "Actually, I asked her to dine with me more for pleasure."

Nancy felt a chill race through her. "For pleasure?" she echoed dully. Normally she would have been happy that her father had a dinner date. Her mother had died when she was a little girl, and she felt it was time for her father to be open to love again. He dated occasionally, but for the most part, when he had free time, he threw himself into extra work projects. But Ann Nordquist? The woman had seemed nice, but Nancy couldn't get the China connection out of her mind.

"Yes, for pleasure." Carson Drew chuckled. "Your old father deserves to enjoy himself occasionally. And I find Ann Nordquist a very attractive, highly intelligent woman."

Nancy swallowed hard. "Oh," she said, exchanging looks with George and Ned. "Well, I—I hope you have fun." Her voice came out in a high, tight squeak. What if her father were going out with one of Barton Novak's kidnappers?

"Psycho killer . . ." Vintage rock blared from the speakers, and dancers spun beneath the ultraviolet lights. The club was a study in downtown funk. A stage had been set up at the front, and the people milling around in the crowded room ranged from the utmost in fashionable to the totally outrageous.

"Wow! Check *that* getup," Ned said, tapping Nancy on the arm.

A girl with a rainbow-colored bristle of hair walked by the table where they sat, her slender body draped in black satin and lace.

"What? Oh, yeah, I see her," Nancy replied, glancing at the girl for only a brief second. Quickly, she turned her attention back to the entrance of the club, which was visible from her balcony perch. The second Alan and Bess walked through that doorway, she wanted to know about it.

"Nan, they'll be here soon," Ned assured her gently. "Meanwhile, you might as well enjoy yourself. How often do you get to come to a place like this?" He reached out and trailed his fingers up her back.

Nancy could feel the electric tingle of his touch. She inched her chair closer to his and rested her head on his shoulder, the softness of his sweater caressing her cheek. "Oh, Ned, I'm sorry. I guess I'm distracted."

"You're the best. I just wish I could do something to cheer you up."

"Ned, sometimes I think I don't deserve you. You come all the way from school to be with me, and I'm so wrapped up in this case I'm no fun at all."

"Hey, it's okay. This is me, remember? I've stuck by you during lots of tough cases. I know what you're going through."

Nancy lifted her head and looked into Ned's brown eyes, her gaze holding his. "You're not mad at me, are you, about what happened on the last case?"

She couldn't quite bring herself to pronounce Daryl's name. Sure, she'd been a willing victim of Daryl's beautiful eyes and magnetic personality, but it had been Ned who'd bailed her out of a dangerous situation during that case, and Ned who had been there for her once the criminals were safely behind bars.

Ned cupped her face in his large hands. "It hurt, sure. I mean, if it hadn't, I'd have to start wondering how much I really love you. And Nancy, I do love you."

Nancy held her breath, afraid to break the spell of the moment. But when Ned's tender gaze left her face, she followed his glance.

"Alan!" She was on her feet, the tough detective back in top form. "Let's go!"

Nancy and Ned flew down the back staircase and caught up with Alan and Bess at the coat checkroom. The attendant was already hanging up George's coat. She must have gone ahead to check out the dance floor.

"Nan! Hi. And Ned!" Bess gave him an exuberant hug while Alan greeted Nancy easily. "Hi. How're you doing?"

Nancy steeled herself. "I'd be a lot better if I could figure out why you lied to me about seeing Barton Novak."

Bess spun around, looking like she'd just been slapped. "What do you mean?" Her voice rose. "Alan wouldn't lie, would you?" she asked, moving quickly to his side.

Alan looked from Nancy to Bess, and then back to Nancy. "I, ah—"

Bess was gazing up at Alan, who met her eyes and held her glance for a moment that seemed to go on forever. Nancy watched nervously. She couldn't imagine anything worse than getting caught between them.

"No," Alan said finally, his voice stronger, "of course I wouldn't lie."

"You told me you saw Barton wearing his purple bandanna," Nancy said accusingly.

"That's right."

"Alan, the security guard at Radio City Music Hall found Barton's bandanna last night after we left. He's had it ever since."

Alan's cheeks blazed under the colored lights. "Well, maybe . . . maybe there are two bandannas."

Nancy felt a rush of annoyance. Why was Alan playing games with her? "You know as well as I do that it's a one-of-a-kind good luck charm. Every article written about Barton mentions that."

Alan shifted from one foot to the other. Bess's gaze was still frozen on him. "So, um, suppose I remembered wrong. Suppose he wasn't wearing the bandanna. What's the big deal?" He raised his eyes and looked at Bess, a note of pleading in his voice. "You believe I saw him, don't you?"

"Of course I do," Bess responded. She whirled to face Nancy. "What's gotten into you?" she snapped.

Bess's angry tone stung Nancy like a bitter wind. "Bess, I don't mean to hurt you, but I don't think Alan is telling the truth. Doesn't it strike you as a little weird that in the last two days, one of the few people to have any contact with Barton Novak is someone who barely knows him? Not even Barton's sister or his best friends have heard from him."

"Why would I lie?" Alan said after what felt like an interminable pause. "I feel kind of like Barton's my brother. I mean, I learned all about rock and roll from listening to him. Now we're even recording on the same label."

"That's just it! Frankly, Alan, your instant success hasn't felt right to me since the second you told me. We all know how good you are, but you're not a professional. Not yet. And World is a label for professionals. You know what I think? I think Harold Marshall offered you that contract in return for throwing me off the scent."

Nancy waited for Alan's response, but it was Bess who jumped forward, her face inches from Nancy's, her hands clenched. "*Nancy Drew!* I thought you were one of my very best friends. What a jerk I was. Alan got that contract on talent. Pure talent. And if you can't realize that, at least you ought to keep your opinions to yourself!" She spun on her heels, grabbing Alan's arm and maneuvering him away. "We don't need to waste our time with people like that," Nancy heard her say.

"Wait, Bess!" Nancy called out frantically. She started after her friend, but Ned put out a restraining hand.

"Nancy, why don't you wait until she's cooled off."

"She's never going to cool off, Ned. Bess is going to hate me forever." Nancy watched her friend storm off, rigid with fury, never once looking back.

CHAPTER NINE

George whirled around the dance floor with one partner after another—first Linda Ferrare's cousin, then Jim Parker, and finally a friend Jim had brought with him. Across the room, Bess was also dancing, laughing and clearly making a show of having a wonderful time.

But Nancy's feet seemed to stick to the floor. Her body barely swayed to the song pulsing through the room.

"Nancy, maybe we ought to call it a night," Ned shouted over the loud music.

Nodding her head wearily, Nancy stopped dancing. Ned put his arm around her shoulders and guided her off the floor. "I'll bet Bess doesn't stay mad at you for more than a few hours," he consoled her.

Nancy's glance strayed to Bess and Alan, who were dancing to an old Rolling Stones tune. As if sensing that she was being watched, Bess turned and shot icy daggers with her glance across the crowded room. Then she guided Alan around, leaving Nancy to stare at her back. "I don't know," Nancy said glumly. "Besides, it's not just Bess. It's Barton and the pirating and my father going out with Ann Nordquist . . ."

"Look, at this point, you don't know if Ann Nordquist is anything more than an enthusiastic tourist, right?" Ned asked. "She might not have anything to do with the pirating at all."

"Maybe not. I mean, she did seem really sweet when I met her, but the Chinese connection is the only plausible link I've been able to turn up so far between that wallet I found and the scam."

"The key words are 'so far,' Nan. You don't know anything for certain yet. So how about if we head back to the hotel and you try to relax and get a good night's rest. Tomorrow you'll have lots of energy. Maybe you'll be able to crack this case once and for all."

The corners of Nancy's mouth turned up for the first time all evening. "Okay, Mom."

"Just giving you good, sensible advice, my dear," teased Ned.

They got their coats and said their goodbyes, making plans to have breakfast with George the next morning.

"See you in the hotel dining room," George said as Nancy and Ned were leaving. "And Nancy, don't get freaked out about Bess. She'll come around. She loves you to pieces, just like I do."

Nancy gave George a big hug. "Thanks. You're the best."

"Yeah, you're a good friend," Ned agreed, giving George an affectionate pat on the back.

"Hey, hey, please. You don't want me to get a swollen ego, do you?" George winked.

Nancy and Ned headed for the exit. Cool, crisp air greeted

Nancy as she stepped outside. She inhaled the night, savoring the relative quiet after the pulsing music and din of voices in the club. The street was dark. Except for a streetlamp down the block, the only source of light was the club's marquee.

"Something catch your eye?" Ned asked.

"No. Just thinking what this street must look like in the daytime. Pretty dingy, I guess." Nancy's eyes slowly gazed up and down the street.

"Yeah, there's some difference between the junk piled out here and the way the club's fixed up." Ned's hand gently took hold of Nancy's. "Do you want to walk for a while? It may be seedy down here, but I don't think it's dangerous."

Nancy smiled. Maybe now was a good time for them to work on their relationship. "I'd love a walk with you, Ned. Dangerous or not."

Ned could feel the sincerity in her words. Slowly he leaned forward to kiss her.

"Ned? Ned Nickerson?" The mood was broken by a short young man who was leaving the club behind them. He rushed up to them, brushing his wavy brown hair out of one eye.

Ned took a hard look at him. "Dave, isn't it?"

"Yeah. Dave Peck. Long time no see, buddy." Dave stuck out a leather-gloved hand, and Nancy could see a thick gold chain bracelet studded with gems that sparkled under the streetlights.

Ned grasped Dave's hand in his. "Yes . . . a long time. I guess I didn't recognize you all . . . all dressed up."

"Yup. Great new threads, don't you think?" Dave patted his

leather jacket, which was decorated with tucks and folds and numerous zippers. He wore it open, revealing a short, muscular body in a pair of beige slacks and a silk shirt, several of the top buttons open to show off more gold jewelry. On his feet were a pair of green snakeskin cowboy boots.

"Oh, Nancy, this is Dave Peck. We know each other from school. Dave, my girlfriend, Nancy."

"Hello," Nancy said, trying to imagine Dave at Emerson College. Somehow she couldn't quite picture him spending hours in the library.

As Dave turned toward her, the smile on his face slipped away. He stared at her with his mouth open, his eyes wide, as if she were a frightening vision from the past.

"Is something wrong?" Nancy asked.

Dave gave his head a hard shake. "Oh . . . no. No, I'm happy to meet you." He grasped her hand, and through his tight gloves Nancy could feel a large ring on one finger. "Any friend of Nickerson's is a friend of mine." He turned his attention back to Ned. "So, what's happening?"

"The usual," Ned responded politely. "Studying, going to classes. Midterms are coming up in a few weeks."

"So, you're just in town for a vacation?"

Ned nodded. "We had Friday off because Emerson is hosting an education conference. I decided to spend the three-day weekend here with Nancy. How about you? What are you doing these days?"

Clearly that was the question Dave had been waiting for.

"Man, I've got to tell you, dropping out of school was the best thing I ever did."

So that's his story, Nancy thought.

"Life is great," Dave went on. "Couldn't be better. No more forcing myself to get up in the morning and go to classes. No more tests or papers. I do what I want. Lots of money, lots of chicks." He gave a lewd laugh and flashed Ned a thumbs-up sign. "No offense to the little lady," he added to Nancy.

Nancy gritted her teeth.

"Yup. This is a great town if you're into success. Got myself a great little business."

"You've got your own business?" Ned blurted out.

"Well, actually I've got a—sort of a partner," Dave hedged.

Nancy found herself betting anything that Dave's so-called partner was, in truth, his boss. She could tell that Ned didn't quite buy his story either. Though whatever Dave was doing, it was plain that he did have money to throw around.

"So, what is it you do?" Ned asked, as if reading Nancy's mind. "I wouldn't mind a little extra pocket money," he kidded.

"A little of this, a little of that," Dave replied vaguely. "But I still like to keep up with the rock scene. No better place for it in the world than right here in this city."

"I guess not," Ned said. "Well, it was nice talking to you, Dave. We'd better get going."

"Sure. There's my limo anyhow." Dave pointed to a black stretch limo pulling around the corner and stopping across the street from the club.

"Wow, that's some car." Ned couldn't hide his astonishment.

"She's a beaut, huh?" Dave said smugly. "Well, good bumping into you. Nice to meet you, Nancy." His words were cordial, but Nancy caught the peculiar look in his eye again as he addressed her.

"Bye, Dave." Nancy watched him go, stepping into the street. She gave a little shudder. Dave was definitely not her idea of a nice guy. And she seemed to make him uncomfortable, too.

"What is it about him?" she said to Ned. "He gives me the creeps."

"Yeah, he's pretty weird. Truth is, he didn't drop out of school; he got kicked out. Never did a bit of work. I don't know why he was there in the first place. The only thing he seemed at all into was his part-time job at the local radio station. But there was some problem there too. I have the feeling he got fired. Pretty soon after that, I stopped seeing him around campus at all."

"He worked in music, Ned?" Nancy asked, a funny feeling in the pit of her stomach. "Isn't it a little weird, all this music stuff?" Nancy watched Dave climb into the back of the limo. Then the thought hit like a cyclone. "Oh no, Ned!" Her voice was low. "He fits the exact description."

"What description? What are you saying?"

"I think Dave might have been one of the guys backstage the

night Barton disappeared! He could even have been the one who hit me over the head. Maybe that's why he kept giving me such funny looks!"

Nancy darted from the club entrance into the street, determined to make out the license plate before the limo vanished. But just as she passed a pile of crates, Ned cried, "Nancy, look out!" Nancy had never heard such panic in his voice. She turned suddenly, looking back at him, but lost her balance.

As she fell, her eyes caught the glint of something metallic cutting through the air and heading straight for her. Her body slammed onto the sidewalk as a knife jammed into a crate just inches away. It quivered there, giving its serpentine handle the illusion of movement.

Ned was by her side in seconds, but Nancy was already on her feet, running down the street as the limo pulled around a corner. "It stopped for a moment," she said, "as if they were waiting to see what would happen."

The limo was too far ahead to catch, but she did see the license plate. The numbers were caked with mud, but the decoration on the right side was clearly visible: a dragon with its tail curved into an L! Then it turned the corner and sped off into the night.

"Did you see the dragon?" Nancy asked breathlessly.

"Yeah, I saw it. Nancy, are you all right?"

"I guess so." She trembled at the thought of her near brush with death. "The fall didn't hurt much, but that knife came pretty close. Come on, let's get it. Someone has finally given us our first real clue!"

Cautiously they ran to the pile of crates where Nancy had fallen. "The police might be able to lift some—" She came to a sudden stop and stared in amazement at the crate. "It's gone! The knife is *gone!*"

CHAPTER TEN

Then we flagged a cab and tried to follow him, but he was too far ahead of us. We couldn't find him," Nancy told George, spearing a french fry and popping it into her mouth.

"So first thing this morning we called the radio station Dave worked for." Ned picked up where Nancy had left off. "It turns out that Dave Peck was fired for selling cheap pirated music on the side. Music people take that seriously."

"You're kidding!" George put down her coffee cup with a chink. "Wow! That sleazy guy could play a really important part in this mystery, huh?"

"You know it." Nancy finally felt she was on the trail that would crack this case. "I bet anything Dave's ring has a dragon on it," she went on, "and his ring and license plate match the wallet I found at the Music Hall. If the wallet belongs to Dave, maybe Ann Nordquist is in the clear."

"A good thing, since she and your dad are spending the day together," Ned remarked. "I think he really likes her."

"Hmm, I can't say I'm entirely comfortable with that," Nancy admitted. "And I won't be until I know what's going on."

George nodded. "Well, one way or the other, the truth will

come out, as they say. So, anyhow, what'd you do next?"

"Well, the radio station didn't know where to get in touch with him, so Ned called up the Emerson College registrar's office. His roommate works there a few hours a day, and Ned talked him into looking up Dave's mother's telephone number. The problem is she doesn't answer. We're going to try her again after breakfast."

George nodded. "Well, if there's anything I can do . . ."

"Thanks. I'll definitely let you know," Nancy said. "So, now that we've told you about the rest of our night, how was yours?"

"Pretty good. They played some really hot dancing music. But we didn't stay all that long after you guys left. Everyone was kind of keyed up about Barton. Roger especially."

"I can understand that," Nancy said. "What are he and the rest of the band going to do about tonight's performance if Barton's still a no-show by concert time?"

"Alan," George said simply.

Nancy groaned. "I was afraid of that. You know, if Alan keeps getting to fill in on these gigs, he's never going to come clean with what he knows about Barton. I mean, why should he? As long as Barton's not around, Alan's a star."

"And is he playing the part," George added. "He took Bess over to the Hard Rock Cafe for late-night snacks after we left the club. He said all the biggest names in the music world hang out there. I think he was counting himself as one of them."

Nancy's expression grew dark. "I can't believe Bess. She's

buying in to Alan's fantasy without stopping to consider how much harm he might be doing."

"So you really think Alan's hiding something? I mean, I know he's on another planet these days, but do you really think he'd put Barton's life in danger?"

"The only way to answer that question is to get to the bottom of whatever's going on," Nancy said. "Speaking of which, we'd better start calling Dave's mother again." She finished up her eggs and pushed her plate away. "Ready?" She stood up.

"Reporting for duty, Detective Drew," Ned replied, and they all got up.

Several hours later, in the Drews' suite, they still were having no luck. Ned dialed Mrs. Peck's number for what seemed to Nancy like the thousandth time, and Nancy and George held their breath. "One ring," Ned announced. "Two. Three."

Nancy rolled her eyes in frustration.

"Hello? Is this Mrs. Peck?"

Ned began talking, and Nancy sat up straight and hung on to his every word.

"Mrs. Peck, my name is Ned Nickerson. I'm a—a friend of Dave's," Ned lied, looking slightly sheepish.

"We went to school together, Mrs. Peck," Ned went on. "Yes, as a matter of fact, I saw him just last night." Ned seemed relieved to be saying something truthful. "But he forgot to give me his address. That's why I'm calling, actually." Ned paused, his brow furrowed. "You don't?" He rolled his eyes. "If you will excuse my saying so, that's—well, that's a little surprising to me."

"George," Nancy exclaimed. "How can a man's own mother not have his address? There is definitely something weird going on."

"Yes, I see," Ned said, signaling for quiet. "Then, do you know who his partner is? Oh, his boss—okay. His name is Lee? But you don't know how to contact him either?" Nancy's heart sank.

"Whew!" Ned sighed when he finally hung up the phone. "If I hadn't said I had to go, she would have gone on all day."

"So tell," Nancy demanded, a touch impatiently.

"Oh, sorry, Nan. Well, Dave's mother obviously thinks Dave's the greatest thing since sliced bread, even though she's disappointed he left school."

"But she doesn't know where he is half the time," Nancy put in.

"She told me his work takes him to so many places he can't have a permanent address. But she sure was quick to add that he calls her every week."

"To keep up the image of the perfect son," George observed.

"Except that he lives out of a suitcase," Nancy said. "All set to pick up and move if anyone's on his tail."

Ned agreed. "That business Dave's involved in can't be aboveboard. Anyway, his mother said his boss is a guy named Lee. James Lee. She started telling me how this Lee took her and 'her Davey' out to some restaurant in New York that Lee's brother owns. She would have told me what they had eaten, too, if I'd let her." He shook his head. "You know, I felt bad misleading her about Dave and me. She seemed kind of lonely."

"Poor woman. She probably deserves a lot better than Dave," Nancy said sympathetically. "When I get my hands on him . . ."

"But Nan, he doesn't have an address," George reminded her friend. "How are you going to find him?"

Nancy was silent for several minutes, contemplating. "Listen, Dave said he likes to keep up with the music scene, right?"

"Right," Ned affirmed.

"Well, isn't tonight's concert the most talked-about show around? Bent Fender plays Rock for Relief at the Rotunda," Nancy said, paraphrasing a radio advertisement, "the nightspot everyone wants to be seen at."

"Yeah, Roger was telling us last night that there will be huge crowds of people outside the Rotunda begging the doormen to let them pay their hundred-dollar admission charge and come inside," George injected. "Doesn't that sound nuts?"

"When you're hot, you're hot," Ned said, grinning. "But I see what you're getting at, Nancy. This is just the kind of scene a guy like Dave wouldn't miss."

"Exactly. So all we have to do is show up—and keep our fingers crossed that Dave will too."

"Wow! Look at all those people," Nancy exclaimed as she, Ned, and George arrived at the Rotunda later that evening. "How're they all going to fit inside?"

"A lot of them aren't," Ned replied. "That's part of the gimmick. If you keep a huge crowd of people standing outside your club, dying to get in, everyone will think it's popular, the place to be. And everyone who gets in will feel extra special about being there—you know, a member of the elite."

"Yuck. I'd have too much pride to stand out here praying the doormen would pick me out of the crowd." George wrinkled her nose in disgust.

"I'm with you," agreed Nancy. "It's a good thing we're on the guest list." They walked around to a lane cordoned off for guests of the club and people with free passes.

"You're on my list too," Ned whispered in Nancy's ear, his lips grazing her cheek.

Nancy almost melted. "And you're on mine," she said. Ned looked so handsome in his jeans and black pullover sweater. But despite her confident manner, Nancy still wondered about their relationship. The two of them needed time to relax together, time to really laugh and let loose and put their problems in the past, where they belonged. Until the mystery was solved, that would be impossible.

Once they were inside the club, Nancy's thoughts turned to Dave Peck. Determined to hunt him down, she and Ned split up and swept through the rooms of each of the three levels of the elegant club, searching every corner. Nancy was impressed by the vastness and extravagance.

Nancy looked at each person there, her search for Dave dead-ending in an upstairs room that was lined with televisions all tuned to MTV. Ned was waiting for her there, and it was plain from his expression that he'd had no more luck than she had.

"No sign of him?" Nancy said.

Ned shook his head no.

"I saw a few people I knew, but not Dave. Vivian, Mr. Marshall's secretary, was down by the stage. And I saw Bess with Alan, not that she would talk to me." Nancy slumped down in an armchair and stared blankly at the checkerboard of television screens.

Ned sat down next to her. A heavy bass beat filled the room as a wild music video came to life on all the screens simultaneously.

The song faded, and a familiar Bent Fender tune came on. Nancy watched the screen a bit more attentively. The video cut from one scene to another, a collage of different shots. As Barton launched into the chorus of the song, a crowd scene came on, men and women emerging from a subway station. In the crowd were the members of Bent Fender themselves and several other people Nancy recognized. Linda Ferrare's cousin was there—the boy George had been dancing with the night before—and a woman who was the female lookalike of Mark Bailey, the guitarist. His sister, Nancy surmised.

Fender had chosen to use people they knew, rather than using actors to fill out the crowd. Nancy spotted Ann Nordquist, and her stomach did a nervous flip-flop. Her father and Ann were out again this evening.

But she forgot about them, her eyes suddenly glued to a television screen. Coming up the staircase on screen was a couple, kissing. The man was short. He had longish wavy brown hair and a familiar-looking, stocky, muscular physique. In amazement Nancy stepped up to the television screens.

"Ned, you won't believe this," she said slowly.

"What?"

"In a way . . . we did find Dave." Nancy pointed at the screen and at the same time tried to figure out who Dave was with. The girl's face was mostly hidden, but when the twosome reached the top of the staircase and pulled apart, Nancy let out a gasp. "I can't believe it! Ned, *look*! It's *Vivian*! What if she and Dave are a number off the screen as well as on!"

Instantly, Nancy was running. "Come on, Ned. Vivian was just downstairs. We have to find her."

Down the two flights of stairs Nancy flew, around the side of the dance floor and toward the stage where she had last seen Vivian. Ned was right behind her.

She scanned the mass of people, picking out the back of Vivian's jet-black coif. Marshall's secretary was in the wings to one side of the stage, talking to someone. The person leaned forward, into the light, and Nancy saw his scowling face. *Alan.* He moved his hands wildly, saying something Nancy couldn't hear.

Moving in closer, Nancy motioned to Ned to stay down below stage level where they wouldn't be seen. The dance music stopped. Linda Ferrare was tuning her bass. Mark Bailey was adjusting one of his guitar strings. A surge of excitement raced through the crowd as they waited for the band.

But Alan and Vivian continued to face off. "No!" Alan said furiously. Nancy and Ned were close enough now to make out what he was saying. "It's gotten totally out of control! I had no idea—"

"Save it," Vivian interrupted. "You'll come around. I'm going to make absolutely sure of it."

"No way, Vivian. As soon as the concert is over, I'm going to tell Nancy everything.

"And what's more, I'm going to tell Bess, too." Alan looked behind him. Nancy couldn't see through the dark curtain at the edge of the stage, but it was clear that Bess was back there, probably standing just out of earshot.

"But Alan," Vivian singsonged nastily, "if you tell Bess what you know, you'll have to admit that you lied about seeing Barton."

"I knew it!" Nancy exclaimed under her breath.

"Your precious angel won't like that one little bit," Vivian mocked.

"I can only hope she'll understand," Alan said. "I never should have believed your stories in the first place."

Nancy and Ned exchanged glances.

"The second I finish my last note, Vivian, you're through." Nancy could hear Alan's footsteps as he stormed away and took his place on stage.

"Don't count on it!" Vivian called out, her voice following him, and she let out a frightening laugh.

"What do you suppose she means by that?" Ned asked.

"I don't know, but I don't like the sound of it."

Nancy and Ned made their way to a table when they were out of Vivian's field of vision. By then the band had assembled on stage, their instruments fully tuned, their sound levels set.

Alan was watching Jim Parker, seated behind his keyboard console. Jim gave an almost imperceptible nod, and the band let their first chords wail.

They were halfway into their second number when Alan's amp began crackling with ear-piercing static. He stopped playing immediately and fiddled with some dials on the equipment. Suddenly, sparks spewed from one of the wires. Someone in the audience screamed. Then the equipment went dead—and the club was plunged into total darkness.

CHAPTER ELEVEN

W hat's happening?" A girl shrieked. "Is it a holdup or something?"

"No," someone else shouted. "It's a fire!"

"Fire?" a man yelled fearfully.

Mass confusion broke loose.

Separated from Ned, Nancy was jostled from two sides as she inched in what she hoped was the direction of the closest wall. She waved her arms in front of her until her hands found the smooth, solid plaster. Turning, she pressed her back to it, squeezing out of the way of the hordes of people making blind, panicked dashes in every direction.

"Simon? Simon, where are you?" a woman near Nancy was screaming, her voice filled with terror. "Simon, are you all right?"

"Stay calm!" Nancy called out to her. "The lights will be back on in a few minutes."

"Simon!" the woman kept shrieking.

"Ladies and gentlemen, please do not panic." A new voice filled the air, loud and hollow. Someone was speaking through a megaphone. "The electrical short on stage caused a temporary power outage, but the electricity should be restored in a matter of minutes. Please stay where you are. I repeat, stay where you are."

Nancy eased herself into a sitting position on the floor to wait. She could hear others do the same. But as the panic subsided, her own fears began to blossom in the overwhelming blackness. Had the power outage been an accident? Or was it perhaps a little too convenient, coming as it did on the heels of Vivian's threat to Alan?

The minutes ticked away. Nancy prayed to herself that this would be no rerun of the night Barton disappeared. Then, suddenly, the power came flooding back on. Nancy blinked, needing to adjust her eyes even to the subdued lighting of the club. The band stood on stage, checking their instruments and amplifiers now that the electricity was working again. But one person was missing. Where was Alan?

Nancy felt panic rising in her throat. Then she noticed that the curtain shielding the backstage area from the audience had been pulled down, a casualty of the frenzied rush of people immediately following the blackout. She let out a noisy sigh of relief as she saw Alan standing off to one side, staring at a sheet of paper.

Ned was still more or less where he had been before the power had blown. As he looked around, Nancy waved to him. He caught sight of her, his face softening with relief, and made his way across the room. Nancy kissed him quickly.

"Listen, Ned," she said. "I'm going to go talk to Alan and

see what he wanted to tell me. Maybe you should go look for George and make sure she's okay."

"What about Bess?" Ned wanted to know. "I don't see her back there." He looked behind the stage.

"I'll ask Alan about her."

"Meet you back here?" Ned asked.

"In ten minutes." Nancy hoisted herself onto the stage and headed straight for Alan. She wasn't bothered by any guards. They were trying to restore order in the club. The concert evening was over.

Alan stood rooted to the stage floor. He was staring blankly ahead of him, his cheeks pale, his eyes glazed. His right hand shook violently as he clutched his guitar.

"Hey," Nancy called out gently. "Alan."

He whipped his head around in her direction. "What?" he said, his voice as tight as a rubber band at the point of snapping.

"What's wrong?" Nancy moved to his side and touched his arm. The hollow look in his eyes made her almost afraid to hear his answer.

"Wrong? Why should anything be wrong?"

"I heard you arguing with Vivian."

Alan inhaled sharply but said nothing.

"I know you didn't really see Barton," Nancy prodded, "so why don't you tell me the rest?"

Alan shook his head back and forth, never lifting his eyes to meet Nancy's. "No. No, I can't. You wouldn't understand." Nancy sensed the terror behind the stubborn words.

"How am I supposed to understand if you don't tell me?" she asked. Only a short time before he had seemed so determined to let her in on whatever he knew. What horrible thing had happened while the lights were out to make him change his mind so completely?

"Alan," Nancy persisted, "that blackout happened for a reason, didn't it?"

"Please," Alan begged, "I said I'm not talking."

"Okay. I can't force you. But at least tell me where Bess is. I thought she was back here."

Alan bit down hard on his lower lip, and Nancy could see it tremble.

"Oh, *Alan!*" Nancy cried. "It isn't Bess, is it?" She held her breath. Alan didn't utter a sound. "Alan!"

"She's fine," he whispered hoarsely. "Bess is fine."

"Where is she?" Nancy felt like a five-gear car being forced to run in first.

"She's sick. She went back to the hotel."

"Alone?"

"She took a taxi."

"How'd she get out of here so fast? The lights just came back on. Besides, I saw her when I got here, and she looked fine." Nancy reached for Alan's shoulders and started shaking him. "What's wrong with her? Tell me!"

"Hey, give me a break," he protested weakly, stepping back. "She left by the back door—had a cold or the flu or something, and she specifically asked that no one disturb her later tonight."

Nancy listened to Alan's story gain momentum. "She went back to the hotel to take some cold medicine and go to sleep, okay? Are you finished giving me the third degree?"

Nancy let her arms drop. "You mean Bess went home to take her Motocillan?"

"Motocillan. That's right."

"Are you sure?"

"Of course I'm sure."

Nancy shivered, despite the warm air inside the club. "Alan," she said coldly, "if Bess ever took Motocillan, she could die. She's allergic to it. Now tell me the truth."

The guitar slid out of Alan's hand. His knees gave out, and he slumped to the floor.

"I can't. I can't. If I tell, they'll . . ."

"Who's they?" Nancy fought to stay calm. "Is there anyone here you're afraid of?" She motioned to the members of Bent Fender, who had gathered around nervously when they'd seen Alan collapse.

Alan shook his head.

"Then how is anyone going to know you told us?" Nancy asked softly.

"Because you'll try to find her . . ."

"Bess? Then she's not back at the hotel." Nancy's voice hardened. "Alan, what's going on?"

Alan's words came out in a jumbled rush. "You can't go after her—the shipment—they'll hurt her if the shipment doesn't go out tonight. Please, just let them get it out . . ."

"What shipment? Alan, I swear, I'd never do anything to harm Bess. You've got to believe me.

Alan sighed deeply. "They grabbed her," he rasped, "during the blackout so I wouldn't tell you what I heard. I don't know where they took her."

"Who's they? Vivian? Mr. Marshall?"

"Marshall?" Puzzled, Alan looked up. "No, not him."

"You mean Vivian's in on this, but Harold Marshall isn't?"

"Vivian," Alan said through clenched teeth. "Everyone thinks Marshall is the boss, but Vivian's got him running around in circles, and he's too stupid and egotistical to realize it. He's like a marionette, and she's pulling all the strings."

"Of course!" Nancy nodded grimly. "How could we have been so blind? Roger, remember you said Vivian would do anything for Marshall? She buttered him up until she had complete control over him. Marshall's huge ego made him take credit for all the ideas she fed him, which was exactly what Vivian wanted. That way, if anyone caught on to what she was doing, her boss would shoulder the blame. I almost fell for it too."

"It's an easy mistake to make," Roger said. "Marshall's personality doesn't exactly make you want to give him the benefit of the doubt." His mouth settled into a tight line. "Although he did offer you that record contract, didn't he?" Roger turned to Alan.

Alan hesitated.

"You promise that nothing will happen to Bess if I tell you?" Alan asked again.

"Alan, we're all Bess's friends," Nancy assured him. "I know she and I had that fight, but I love Bess. If anything happens to her—"

"Okay. You were right to think that Marshall offered me the contract just to get me to tell you I'd seen Barton. But I didn't think about that, just like I didn't realize that Marshall's offer was *Vivian's* idea. I didn't see anything I didn't want to see. I was so wrapped up in the idea of being famous . . ." Alan pounded his fist against the floor. "This whole thing is my fault. If I hadn't been so convinced I was star material, Bess would be safe right now."

"Alan, this is no time to start blaming yourself," Nancy said firmly. "You have to tell us what you know so we can figure out what to do about it."

"I really believed them. I thought they wanted me to record because they thought I was good. And when Marshall told me that Barton's disappearance was a publicity stunt, I believed that, too. I mean, I *wanted* to believe it. As long as he was all right, but out of the picture, he was my ticket to success. So when Harold Marshall asked me to tell you I saw Barton, I agreed. Don't get me wrong. I really believed Barton was fine."

"But Alan, I thought you said Marshall didn't have anything to do with whatever is going on," said Nancy, confused.

"That's right. He didn't. Vivian planted the publicity idea in his head and then told him she'd take care of the details. So when you started asking questions, Nancy, he thought you were nosing in where you didn't belong. Vivian convinced him to offer me a contract in exchange for getting you off his back.

Of course, neither of them ever expected to let me go through with the recording." Alan toyed with a strand of dark curly hair. "I guess I was a fool."

"Alan," Nancy asked impatiently, "how do you know all this?"

"I'm getting to that. See, I had convinced myself that my lie about Barton wouldn't hurt anyone, but when you and Bess had that fight, I saw that something was wrong. To make things worse, Bess was defending me when I didn't even deserve it."

"Why didn't you level with her right then and there? And with me?" Nancy bent down to look Alan in the eye.

"I wanted to. But I was so afraid Bess would hate me for it. I just didn't have the guts to confess." Regret was etched on his face, and Nancy felt her anger toward him soften a bit.

"So I stuck to my lie," Alan went on, "but I just didn't feel right about it after that. You started me worrying about whether Barton really was all right, and I realized that if anything happened to him, it would be partially my fault. I still couldn't bring myself to tell Bess then, but I decided that, at the very least, I ought to go to Mr. Marshall and insist that I see Barton in person. Just to know for sure." Alan took a breath.

"Anyhow, I went over to his office late this afternoon, while Bess was out jogging. He wasn't there, but Vivian was. She was sitting in his office using the phone, and the door was open a crack. I could hear everything she said, and it was what I just told you about the publicity story and my record contract."

"And something about a shipment of some sort?" Nancy asked, recalling his earlier words.

"Yeah. I don't know what kind of shipment, but she told whoever she was talking to that it was going out tonight."

"The bootleg copies," Nancy said. "Did she say where they were being shipped to?"

"Heading east, that's all."

"Weird," Roger said. "I thought New York was as far east as you could get. Maybe she meant the east side of town."

"Or maybe she wasn't talking about this country at all," Nancy said. "Maybe by east she meant the eastern hemisphere."

"Like China?" Roger asked.

"Exactly," Nancy sighed. Her hunch could very well play out. But that didn't make her feel any better. It meant that Ann Nordquist might not be off the hook after all.

However, any further thoughts about China and Ann Nordquist ceased when Alan began talking again. "I don't know if the destination is going to matter much when you hear the rest of Vivian's conversation," he said.

"Oh no." Nancy steeled herself for what was next.

"Vivian said that there was a body going out with the shipment."

"Barton!" Roger Gold exclaimed in horror.

"Tell me Vivian's exact words," Nancy instructed Alan, her heart filling with dread.

Alan tensed. "Like I said, 'one body going out with the shipment,' was the way she put it. Then the person on the other end of the phone must have said something. Vivian answered, 'No, we're going to do it right before we ship him out—silence him for good.'" Alan's voice was shaking again. "The last thing I heard was, 'Yeah, pick up at the duck house, as usual. Ten-thirty. Right.' Then Vivian hung up."

Nancy glanced at her watch. Nine o'clock. "What happened next?" she said, her own voice trembling. If she couldn't find Barton in an hour and a half, she might never find him *alive*—or find Bess either!

"I tried to sneak out," Alan said, "but I was so freaked out about what I'd overheard that I knocked something over as I was leaving the outer office—a chair, I think. After that, I just ran as fast as I could, down the stairs and out of the building. I went to the hotel and got Bess and brought her here to the club. I thought I got away clean."

"But you didn't tell Bess what you'd heard?" Nancy asked.

Alan shook his head. "I knew I had to tell you everything—tonight, I thought, here at the club—so I figured I'd level with Bess at the same time. Besides, I guess I wanted to put that part off as long as possible, having Bess find out she'd fallen for a jerk."

"But how did Vivian find out you knew?" Nancy asked.

Alan reddened. "Vivian looked out the window and saw me leaving. She knew she'd find me here at the concert."

"So she arranged the power outage and had Bess kidnapped to keep you from talking?" Nancy asked, beginning to put all the pieces together.

Alan stood up, reached into the back pocket of his leather

pants, and pulled out a crinkled piece of yellow lined paper. Silently, he handed it to Nancy.

She smoothed it out and read the words printed in bold, box letters. *DO NOT SAY A WORD TO ANYONE IF YOU WANT TO SEE YOUR GIRLFRIEND AGAIN*, the note read.

CHAPTER TWELVE

Who gave this to you?" Nancy demanded, waving the note.

"Someone pulled me off stage and pressed it into my hand while the lights were out," Alan explained.

"What I don't get is why they didn't just take Alan," Roger said.

"I think they realized that if Alan vanished before this show, like Barton did before the last one, it was going to look pretty suspicious. And they wouldn't have such an easy time explaining it the second time around."

"I wish they *had* taken me," Alan said. "I didn't mean for anyone to get hurt. I was so busy dreaming about how famous I'd be. If anything happens to Bess—or Barton—"

"We've got to find out where they're shipping from," Nancy put in, "and get there fast!"

"But you can't look for her!" Alan's voice rang out. "You promised. If they realize you're coming after them, who knows what they'll do to Bess!"

"Alan, think about it," Nancy said, barely able to face the facts herself. "We don't have any choice. You heard Vivian's plans for Barton. If we don't go after them, there may be two bodies going out with the albums."

"What are we going to do?" Anguish was written all over Alan's face.

"We're going to get ourselves out of this madness," Nancy said, determined. "And then we're going to find that duck house Vivian mentioned."

A few moments later, Nancy was running her index finger down the listings in a telephone book. "Duck House. Let's see. D-U-B, D-U-C . . . Duck. The Duck's Back, Duck Floor Coverings, Duck Sport and Leisure Shop. No Duck House." She slammed the heavy book shut. "Any luck, George?"

George shook her head. She was bent over the yellow pages. "No pet stores with that name. Maybe duck house isn't the *name* of the place, just a place that has ducks."

"How about stores that specialize in aquariums and water habitats?" Alan suggested.

"You'd be more likely to find goldfish there," Nancy said.

"There are tons of pet stores listed that specialize in birds," George said. "Not that we'd have any idea which ones to go to first."

"Maybe we should divide up," Roger Gold suggested. "There are enough of us to cover a pretty big area."

With the concert postponed, the members of Bent Fender had gathered with Nancy, Alan, Ned, and George in the private office of the club manager to try to come up with a rescue plan.

"Well, it's true, there are plenty of us," Nancy said, "but if we split up, I don't see how one or two of us is going to be much of a match for a gang of killers. Besides, like George said, who knows if 'the duck house' has anything to do with pet shops at all? It's just a shot in the dark."

"But it's the only shot we've come up with so far," Alan reminded her anxiously. "Listen, there's 'Jungle Paradise,' 'Birds of a Feather,' 'Hot House Exotic Birds' . . ."

"Somehow, I don't exactly think a duck is considered an exotic bird." Nancy's mouth settled into a grim line.

"Or even a pet, really," Linda Ferrare spoke up.

"The truth is, I kind of think of it as something to eat. You know, like Peking duck," Roger Gold put in. "What a time to be thinking about food," he said with a rueful smile.

"Roger!" Nancy jumped out of the lounge chair she had been sitting in. "Say that again."

"What? What a time to be thinking about food?"

"No, before that."

"Peking duck?"

"That's it! Why didn't I think of it right away?"

Ned put a hand on Nancy's shoulder. "You want to let the rest of us in on it, Nan?"

"The Duck House, the dragon, James Lee." Nancy reeled off a list of clues.

"James Lee. You mean Dave Peck's boss?" Ned asked. "I still don't get it."

"Don't you see? Mrs. Peck said James Lee had taken her and Dave to a restaurant his brother owned, right? What if 'Lee' is the Chinese last name. It could even be 'Li.' Remember, we've never seen it spelled."

"You mean Dave's boss might be the connection to China. And Ann Nordquist isn't mixed up in all of this?" Ned asked.

"Exactly," Nancy affirmed. "China just might be his native country, and the place where he still has black-market contacts." She grabbed the yellow pages and thumbed through them. "All right! Roger, you did it! You hit the nail on the head! Here it is! Li's Duck House in Chinatown!" She clapped triumphantly. "Bess and Barton, here we come!"

Nancy got out of the cab that had sped her to the restaurant. Ned, George, and Alan got out too. Another taxi behind them dropped off Roger, Linda, Jim, and Mark.

Across the street was a four-story building. The windows of the top two floors were boarded up. The two lower floors were bright with lighted windows, through which Nancy could see diners seated at tables laden with tureens and platters of food. A deep red facade decorated the lower level, with a sign above the entrance spelling out "Li's Duck House." Sure enough, the *L* of *Li's* was formed from the tail of an ornate dragon.

"That cinches it!" Nancy announced, pointing to the sign. "That *L* on the dragon, it must be a sort of calling card for Li and everybody who works for him. I'm sure the limo Dave was in belongs to him, too."

She strode toward the curb. But Ned followed and caught hold of her arm. "Nan, the people who have Bess and Barton aren't playing games. Don't you think we should wait for the police to get here? Sergeant Wald said—"

Nancy had telephoned the police just before leaving the club and arranged for them to meet her at Li's Duck House. She could still hear Sergeant Wald's words ringing in her ears. "The Li gang is involved in everything from gambling to smuggling. Watch out, kid. They're dangerous."

"No," Nancy answered firmly. "We have to get Bess and Barton out of there! The sergeant and his officers will be our backup."

"But we can't very well waltz into that restaurant and ask them to turn Bess and Barton over," George said sensibly.

"That's why the rest of you are going to wait here while I go scout out the building."

"Nancy," Ned said sternly, "remember what you said earlier. If it comes down to one of us against a whole gang of them, it won't be much of a match."

"It won't come down to that."

"At least let me come with you," Alan spoke up. "I was the one who got us into this mess, at least in part, so let me help you get us out."

"Well, okay. Maybe it would be safer for two of us to go in."

Once inside the restaurant, Nancy breathed in the warm, spicy-smelling odor, then gave a quick but thorough look around. Most of the dozen tables were occupied by diners. In the rear, the kitchen was partially visible through the windows of swinging metal doors. To one side was a flight of stairs going up and another flight going down. A sign for the restrooms and telephones hung over an arrow pointing downstairs.

"Two for dinner?" A woman approached Nancy and Alan, holding out menus.

"Oh, ah, would you mind if I used your restroom?" Nancy asked politely.

The woman frowned. "Customers only," she said coldly.

"My uncle eats here every week," Nancy lied. Her blood was running cold, but she flashed her warmest smile. "A tall man, gray hair and a mustache. I was here with him just last Sunday."

The woman stood aside. "All right," she said grudgingly, "go ahead."

Nancy glanced at the clock located over the metal swinging doors. It was already a quarter to ten, and she had only until ten-thirty to find Bess. That left only forty-five minutes—and time was running out fast!

CHAPTER THIRTEEN

The hostess turned away, and Nancy tugged at Alan's sleeve. "We've got to hurry! When no one's looking, go up to the next floor and see what you can find. Look for another staircase. I'm going to check out the downstairs, but so many people have access to it, I think the top floors are our best bet."

Alan grabbed Nancy's hand and squeezed it warmly. When the coast was clear, he headed for the stairs.

In the basement, Nancy found an open space with two wall telephones and a shabby sofa. Off this area were two tiny restrooms and a closed door. The door opened easily. Behind it was a large boiler, water pipes, a central heating unit, old kitchenware, and a walk-in refrigerator. Wall shelves were lined with cans of Chinese ingredients. But there was no sign of either the two prisoners or a bootleg shipment.

Nancy raced back up the steps. Then, unnoticed, she went up the next flight. She found Alan standing at the edge of the second-floor dining room. "No luck" was the meaning of the look they gave each other.

Waiters were carrying food to the customers from a dumb-waiter that was positioned on one wall. The staircase Nancy had come up ended there, and she saw no exits that could have led to the third floor. She surveyed the ceiling, looking for a trapdoor.

Nothing.

Alan gave her a helpless shrug. "Maybe people going upstairs use *that*." He pointed to the dumbwaiter, half-concealed by a partition.

Nancy gave him a look. "I suppose, if you're prepared to tie yourself up like a pretzel."

"Sorry. It was a dumb suggestion." Alan sighed. "But how else do you get to those top floors?"

"There's got to be a way. They can't possibly move heavy loads of albums down on a dumbwaiter." Not to mention moving down a body—or two bodies.

Don't think of Barton and Bess as "bodies," Nancy scolded herself, but she sensed Alan was thinking the same thing. She glanced at her watch. It was coming on to ten o'clock, scarcely more than half an hour before pickup. If nothing had gone wrong, Bess and Barton were alive and somewhere in the building. But where?

Nancy looked around once more at the people enjoying their dinners under a tapestry depicting a serene waterfall. It hurt her to watch life going on as usual while Bess's and Barton's lives were still at stake.

The tapestry! Suddenly Nancy realized what she'd missed on her first look around the room. "Follow me," she whispered urgently to Alan. She moved toward the tapestry, which decorated the wall opposite the windows she'd seen when she'd gotten out of the taxi. As she and Alan crossed the room she discreetly put a hand to her left ear and removed one of her blue teardrop earrings, which she then dropped into her shirt pocket.

"Excuse me," she said to a couple at one of the tables beneath the woven wall hanging, then gestured toward Alan. "My friend and I had dinner at this table earlier in the evening, and I think I might have dropped an earring. Do you mind if I take a look?"

"Go right ahead," said a silver-haired man, getting up from his chair to allow Nancy to look behind the table.

Quickly, she bent down and grasped one of the bottom corners of the tapestry. When she lifted it up, she saw a window. That was it! The rear of the building faced the next street. There was probably a second entrance at the back. All she had to do was go around to the next block to find the door to the top two floors.

"What are you doing?" the man asked. "How could your earring possibly get behind the tapestry?"

"I'm sorry. No time to explain." Nancy took Alan's arm and tore down the stairs and out of the building, leaving the man to stare after them.

The plain brown truck sat outside the other side of the building, the cab doors open. "All ready to load in the albums," George hissed to Nancy as she and the others peered around the corner of the block.

"Not just the albums," Nancy said with grave apprehension. "We can't wait for the police any longer. We've got to move in right now."

"But what about that heavyset man at the door?" Roger said. "He might be armed."

At that moment, the guard stubbed out the end of the cigarette he'd been smoking and pulled open the door he had been standing in front of. A short man in dark clothes came out carrying a large crate.

"Dave!" Nancy whispered. "With a load of albums!"

"But they're early. They weren't supposed to start until tenthirty," Alan said.

"I know," Nancy replied grimly. "We've got even less time than we thought. Where on earth is Sergeant Wald? When Dave brings down the last box, Bess and Barton are through." Dave put the crate into the truck. Behind him, a taller heavyset man came out with another crate, and then a third man emerged. The tall man fit the description the Radio City Music Hall guards had given of the man who had been Dave's partner.

"Okay, guys, listen up," Nancy said, gathering everyone around. "We have to put Dave and his pals out of commission for a while. There are more of us than them, so if we take them by surprise, it shouldn't be too tough. Once we're inside, we'll break into groups to look for Bess and Barton."

"What if more of those creeps are inside?" Mark Bailey asked.

"Then we'd better pray their hands are full of crates and that we're faster than they are," Nancy replied uneasily. "Now, I'm going to go ask Mr. Muscles over there for a cigarette." She pointed toward the guard. "While he's holding the match for me, I'm going to practice a new move we learned in karate."

Nancy rounded the corner, walking slowly toward the guarded door.

The guard watched Nancy's progress down the narrow, empty side street. He shifted uneasily when she made eye contact and gave him a tentative smile.

"Can you spare a smoke?" she asked, hoping her voice sounded normal.

Arching a bushy eyebrow, the guard looked down the block, which was home to a handful of grocery stores that were closed for the night. Then he put a hand into his jacket pocket and pulled out a red-and-white box. After giving Nancy a cigarette, he fished around in another pocket for a book of matches.

Nancy was close enough to make out the L-tailed dragon on the matchbook. James Li again. She put the cigarette in her mouth. The guard held a lit match with one hand, cupping the other around the flame as Nancy bent forward and edged the tip of the cigarette toward the light. Then, in one brisk, split-second movement, she smashed the heel of her hand into the guard's chin. He didn't even have a chance to shout before he fell to the pavement.

"Ned, Roger," she called out. "Quick. Give me a hand." They hoisted the unconscious guard into the back of the truck. Then they waited behind the door to the building. When Dave and his cohorts reappeared, they jumped them.

Dave fought free from the surprise attack. Nancy brought her right arm up for a blow, but he caught hold and pinned it behind her back, twisting painfully. By then, though, the others had appeared. George and Alan helped Nancy overpower Dave, while Linda, Mark, and Jim gave Roger and Ned a hand in carrying the other two, still kicking and fighting, into the back of the truck.

They finally shoved Dave in too and slammed the back door shut. With her left arm, Nancy snapped closed several padlocks that were attached to it, imprisoning the four men in their own vehicle. "There. That ought to hold them for a while." Nancy allowed herself a second to inspect her twisted right shoulder. She could hardly lift her arm, and she massaged the soreness with her other hand.

"Nancy, you're hurt!" George observed anxiously.

"It's not that bad." Nancy said, steeling herself against the pain.

"Are you sure?"

Nancy managed a stiff smile in spite of the throbbing in her shoulder. "Okay," she said, "someone better wait down here for the police while we go in. Alan, will you volunteer?"

"I'll do whatever you say."

"Good. If you have any trouble, yell. The rest of you, follow me."

Inside, they groped their way up two dark, narrow flights of stairs and then split up, Ned and George exploring the third floor with Nancy, the musicians taking the top level.

"What a place to get stuck in without a flashlight," George muttered as their group inched forward blindly.

With Ned and George behind her, Nancy guided herself along the wall of what apparently was a narrow hallway. Suddenly her hand slid around a corner. The hallway had ended. "I think we're in a big room," Nancy whispered. "There's got to be a light switch somewhere near here."

"Pay dirt!" came Ned's voice, as fluorescent overhead lamps illuminated a huge loft space.

"Wow!" Nancy looked around her in amazement. The loft was filled with the best, most modern recording equipment available.

"Nancy! Ned! George!" It was Roger calling from above them down the staircase. "We found them! Hurry!"

The recording equipment forgotten, the three friends followed Roger's voice, racing upstairs and through another loft littered with cartons like the ones Dave and his cohorts had been carrying.

"In here!" Roger peered out from a smaller room partitioned off at the very back of the loft.

"Nancy!" cried Bess as Linda, Mark, and Jim finished untying the ropes that had bound her and Barton. "George! Ned!" Bess was on her feet, hugging them all at once. "I can't believe you found us! I thought I was never going to see any of you again!"

Nancy pulled Bess close with her left arm, warm tears of relief trickling down both friends' cheeks. Nancy squeezed her as hard as she could. "Oh, Bess, thank goodness we got here in time!"

"I'll say," Barton Novak agreed tremulously. The members of Bent Fender were having their own reunion.

"Barton, are you okay? Did they hurt you?" Linda asked.

"Well, spending two days tied to a chair isn't my idea of a vacation." Barton grinned.

Bess was less ready to laugh off their near brush with death. "Oh, Nan, to think I didn't believe a single word you told me," she cried. "Barton was in this awful place, just like you said, and they were going to kill us . . ." Her sentence dissolved into sobs.

"It's okay, Bess," Nancy consoled her. "Everything's going to be fine."

"No it's not. I was so rotten to you. How can you ever forgive me? I apologize a million, trillion times."

"Hey, no need."

"Boy, just wait until I get my hands on Alan Wales."

"Wait a minute, Bess," Nancy said, surprising herself. "Don't be so hard on the guy. His biggest crime was just being swept away by his dreams."

"I don't know, Nancy. Those dreams almost got Barton and me murdered!" Bess paused. "So where is the rat, anyway?"

"Downstairs waiting for the police."

"You're very much mistaken," an unfamiliar male voice boomed out behind Nancy. "The police are downstairs in the basement, locked to the pipes with their own handcuffs."

Nancy whirled around to see a small man dressed in a neat

gray suit, with a dark hat pulled low over his face. He held a gun. And the gun was pointed directly at Nancy.

The man smiled a bone-chilling, evil smile. "James Li at your service," he announced. "The next person who moves is dead."

CHAPTER FOURTEEN

May I extend my congratulations, Miss Drew? You almost put a damper on my little party. Almost, but not quite." James Li gave a demonic laugh. "It is Miss Drew, isn't it?" He touched the tip of her nose with the cold, hard barrel of his gun.

The tap of high-heeled shoes sounded on the bare floor behind James Li. "That's Nancy Drew all right." Vivian stepped out of the shadows, Dave by her side. "This'll teach you to go poking around in business that doesn't concern you," she said.

Nancy remained silent, not giving Vivian the satisfaction of an answer.

"It's a pity my little warning the other night failed to scare you off," Li offered,

"That knife-throwing act was yours?" Nancy asked, an edge of bitterness to her voice.

"Through one of my boys."

"Lucky for me he missed."

"Lucky, Miss Drew? I told you it was just a warning. Otherwise . . ." The look in James Li's cold dark eyes more than finished the sentence. Nancy knew this man played for keeps. "Alas, it seems only the inevitable was delayed." Li smiled. "Did you really think you could stop us? I knew something was wrong tonight as soon as I saw your budding rock-and-roll star standing at the entrance instead of my guard, Petey. When Vivian told me who the young man was, we realized you must have traced us here. But no matter. I let my boys out of the truck, they told us the police were on their way, and we simply waited inside the entrance for your friend Sergeant Wald and his brave men in blue."

"But what did you do to Alan?" Bess demanded. "Not that I really care," she added unconvincingly.

James Li frowned. "A minor setback. He managed to get away while we were attending to the officers. But some of my boys went after him. He won't get far. As for the rest of you, I'll give you a chance to say your goodbyes to each other."

"How nice of you," muttered George.

"Once the truck is loaded," Li continued, "we're going to send you on a one-way trip."

Bess let out a choked cry.

"Don't worry, he won't get away with this," Nancy said.

"I wouldn't place any bets on that, Miss Drew. Dave, tie them up."

One by one, Dave pushed the prisoners down into hard, straight-back chairs, bound their wrists and ankles, and secured them to the chairs with more rope. He saved Nancy for last, pulling the rope extra tight. A shooting pain seared through her injured arm.

"That's for practicing your karate moves on me," he said, sneering.

"It evens the score," Nancy said through gritted teeth, "for that rap on the head at the concert. You were the one who hit me, weren't you, Dave?" She tried to keep a hard look on her face in spite of the burning pain in her shoulder. Ned also eyed Dave angrily. If he got the chance, he'd pay Dave back for hurting Nancy.

Nancy could hear the sounds of boxes being carried down the stairs. When the boxes were gone, it would be all over.

Li fired off more orders. "Okay, Dave, you help the boys finish loading up. Vivian, you take this gun and keep it pointed at our guests. If they so much as breathe too loudly, let them have it. I'm going down to the ship to tell them to start the motors."

"The ship that's going to carry the albums?" Nancy asked.

"And Vivian and my boys and me." James Li smiled. "There isn't a thing you can do to stop us. I'm not thrilled about leaving the States, but once Mr. Novak here caught on to what we were doing, things got a little too hot to handle. I decided to make one more big shipment and then leave the country until things cooled off. It was unfortunate that I had to wait until tonight before doing away with him, but I couldn't risk having his body found before I was safely aboard ship."

"Then Alan found out about your plans right before the final shipment," Nancy said. "But you were afraid the disappearance of a second Fender guitarist would attract too much attention right before the critical night."

"Very perceptive of you, Miss Drew. We didn't want the police alerted."

"But we were able to coax the story out of Alan . . . and contact the police. You didn't count on that."

"No," Li agreed. "But it didn't pose much of a problem in the end, did it?" His mouth spread in a frightening smile. "And now, ladies and gentlemen, it's time for me to say good night." He tipped his hat. "Dave, you know what to do once the truck is loaded." He looked back at Nancy. "You see, there's going to be a tragic fire in this warehouse. But then, I'm sure my brother won't mind collecting insurance on the building while we're out of the country, lying low. And the diners downstairs will certainly leave at the first sign of smoke. It's just a shame you people on the upper floor will be trapped." Li laughed cruelly. "All right, go ahead, Dave. I'll meet you at the ship when you're through."

"You're leaving *now*?" Confusion registered on Dave's face. "But we had a deal. I'd take care of the shipment. You'd take care of the people."

"Correct. That was our arrangement. But I'm changing the deal. I don't like dirty work, and I want to be far away while it's being done. Do you understand?"

"But I can't. I've never . . . I mean, I know this guy." Dave pointed to Ned, horrified as he realized what Li expected him to do. "He was my friend, kind of."

"Dave, I am going down to the dock. We'll be pulling anchor in twenty minutes, shipment or no shipment. The police will be looking for their men as soon as they discover they're missing. If you want to stay around and visit the prison wards, fine. If you want passage on my ship for yourself and your girlfriend"—he looked at Vivian—"you'd better do as I say." James Li turned on his heel. But heading out the door, he was intercepted by Petey, the guard Nancy had asked for the light.

"Hey, boss?" Petey said. "We got a problem. It's that kid. We looked everywhere for him. I don't know how he got away so quick. It's like he just vanished or something."

Li tapped his pistol nervously against his palm. "Well then, you'd better hurry with those albums. He might get to the cops."

Petey nodded.

"You too, Dave," Li commanded. "Get to work."

"But—"

"That's the end of the discussion." Li headed out.

Dave looked around at Nancy and the others. "Viv, what do you think?"

"You mean about them? I think we better do what Li says," Vivian told him. "I don't have any intention of winding up in jail."

"I guess." Dave handed her his gun (with some reluctance, Nancy thought), and went into the next room to move the crates of albums.

"Vivian, you're not really going to listen to James Li, are you?" With her hands tied behind her back, Nancy had no option other than to try to talk Vivian out of the drastic plan. She suspected that Vivian was the person to convince. Dave was clearly shaken up at the thought of being responsible for so much bloodshed. If Vivian changed her mind, Nancy was certain that Dave would go along with her. "You wouldn't really set that fire," Nancy said.

"A lot you know," Vivian replied roughly. "Before Dave introduced me to Jimmy Li, every nickel I earned from my lousy job went toward the rent on a one-room dump. I never had fancy clothes or went to nice restaurants or owned real jewelry."

"And now you have it all?"

"These aren't rhinestones on my finger, sweetheart." Vivian flashed a sparkling ring of gold and diamonds.

"But are all those luxuries worth having murder on your conscience for the rest of your life? Think about it. We're talking about human lives."

"I know what we're talking about." Vivian's voice was deadly cold.

"Look, it's no longer just a question of stealing masters or illegally copying recordings or even knocking me out backstage at the Music Hall," Nancy said desperately. "You must be pretty loyal to James Li to kill for him."

"He takes good care of Dave and me."

"Vivian, how long have you known him?"

"Dave introduced me to him a few months ago, when he needed to get on the inside at World Communications. But I don't see what difference that makes."

"And Dave hasn't worked for him very long, either."

"They started doing business back when Dave was in college."

"That was less than a year ago," Ned put in.

"And you're ready to put yourself entirely in the hands of

someone you've known for such a short time?" Nancy asked. "A man who makes deals and then 'changes' them as it suits him? Vivian, you and Dave are planning on escaping to a country where you don't know a soul except Mr. Li. You don't speak the language, you don't know any of the customs. Without that man, you're lost. And he's ready to let you carry out murder, so that he isn't responsible for it."

Vivian seemed to be considering Nancy's words. But then her face hardened. "You don't really care what happens to Dave and me. You're just pleading for your own lives. Well, you all deserve exactly what you get. We had a great thing going, and you came along and messed it up."

Dave poked his head into the room. "We're about to bring the last load down."

Nancy drew in a sharp, frightened breath. This was it.

"Good," Vivian said. "The sooner we get this over with, the better."

"Vivian, please," Nancy begged as Dave headed down the stairs with the crate. *"Please . . ."*

"Save it for the guy at the pearly gates." Vivian waved her gun menacingly.

"I guess this is goodbye," George managed to choke out. Nancy had never seen steely-nerved George shed a tear. She dropped her head, expecting the gunshot. But instead, she heard an ear-shattering scream!

CHAPTER FIFTEEN

Nancy jerked her head up to see Vivian drenched in a steaming liquid. And wrestling the gun from her hand was . . .

"Alan!" Nancy cried out. "How on earth?"

Alan stood behind Vivian, holding her gun in one hand and a huge bowl in the other. "Hot egg drop soup," he grinned. Working swiftly, he untied his friends. "I figured the last place those muscle-brains would look for me was in their own building. I sneaked back in through the restaurant side and came up the dumbwaiter. You were right, Nancy. It was *not* the most comfortable ride." Alan unknotted the last bonds.

"Alan," Nancy said gratefully, "without you, we'd—"

"—never have gotten into this mess in the first place. The least I could do was save you."

Before Nancy could reply, footsteps on the stairs signaled Dave's return. "Okay, guys," she whispered. "You're going to have to take Li's henchmen on your own. I'm afraid my shoulder's given out on me."

"I thought you said it was fine," George scolded her.

"So I lied. I don't think I'm up for any fancy karate moves."

"It's all right, Nancy," said Roger Gold. "Even without you, it's nine of us against four of them."

Suddenly, Dave appeared in the room along with Li's other bullies. "Hey, what's going on? Viv, what are you doing on the fl—"

Dave caught a right to his jaw before the word was out of his mouth. The small room reverberated with sounds of punches, kicks, and heated exclamations.

It didn't take long for Nancy's friends to overpower Li's cohorts. "Good job," Nancy said breathlessly. "Alan, go down and see about those policemen. Take Vivian's gun, just in case."

Alan left the room and a few seconds later reappeared with four men in blue uniforms.

"Sergeant Wald," Nancy said, pointing to Dave, Vivian, and the other three men, "we have a little present for you. But there's one more. The boss, James Li. He's trying to escape on a ship that's about to pull anchor. Li told his boys he'd leave without the merchandise if he had to. Do you think we can stop him?"

"That should be easy." Sergeant Wald stepped forward. "Just tell us what dock he's leaving from, and we can radio headquarters. They'll have cars and a special navy unit over there in no time."

Nancy turned toward Li's little gang, now securely tied with the ropes that had held her and her friends just moments earlier. "Okay, which one of you wants to tell me where your boss is leaving from?"

Dave and the others remained silent.

"Do you think he'd do the same for you?" Nancy asked. "No way. He wouldn't stick his neck out one fraction of an inch. In fact, he's getting ready to leave without you right this second."

No answer.

"Dave, think about what James Li left you to do. He didn't want to do it himself, so who did he stick with it?"

Dave scowled.

"Come on, tell us," Nancy urged. She'd learned in karate class that a chain was most easily broken at its weakest link. "Maybe if you cooperate, they'll let you off with a lighter sentence."

"Don't listen to her," Vivian commanded.

Dave looked from his girlfriend to Nancy, and back to his girlfriend.

"You know, your mother would be heartbroken to see her son locked away forever," Nancy said, trying a different tack.

"How do you know what my mother would think?" Dave shouted.

"Ned had a little chat with her," Nancy replied calmly. "We were trying to track you down."

Dave's face went from furious to panicked. The chain snapped. "All right, you win. I'll tell you where he is."

Nancy allowed herself a long overdue sigh of relief.

She was safe. Bess and Barton were fine. And Li's gang was about to be put away. It was true that her shoulder ached, that her wrists and ankles were sore where Dave had tied them, and that her head was still bruised from where he had hit her the first night. But she had never in her life felt happier or more alive.

That happy feeling was still with Nancy the next morning as she flounced down on the edge of Bess's bed. She steadied herself with her left arm, since her right one was still sore from the previous night. "Come on, lazybones! Do you want to sleep through your last day in New York?"

Bess groaned and pulled the covers over her head.

"Bess!" Nancy jostled her friend's leg through the blanket. "It's almost eleven o'clock."

Bess peeked one half-open eye out from her cocoon. "Nan, don't you know that people who've been through traumas need lots of rest?" She rolled over on her stomach.

"You seemed just fine at our midnight celebration supper. Remember putting away all those spare ribs?"

George came out of the bathroom, a towel wrapped like a turban around her wet hair. "Don't even mention spare ribs. I ate enough last night for the rest of the week."

"And you're going to eat even more this afternoon at that luncheon the Chinatown Neighborhood Association is giving for us," Nancy reminded her. "Mrs. Chen—she's president of the association—told me that the community is incredibly grateful to all of us for helping to put James Li behind bars. What a bully! It wasn't enough for him to pirate music and run all those other big-time illegal operations the police told us he had going. No, he had to muscle in on the small businesses in Chinatown, too."

"Yeah, I can certainly understand why the community is so glad to see him go," George said. "And it's really nice of them to give us an honorary luncheon. But I don't know if I'm going to be able to touch it." She patted her stomach.

"Don't worry. I'll help you out." Bess finally sat up in bed and stretched her arms over her head.

George rolled her eyes. "Well, look who finally rises at the mention of her favorite sport—eating."

"Oh, come on, give me a break. How often do you get some of the best Chinese chefs this side of the Pacific to make a special meal just for you?"

"Not too often," George answered. "And speaking of not too often, there's something I've been wanting to ask you, Bess."

"Yeah?"

"Alan said he went down to World Communications yesterday while you were out jogging. Since when have you turned into a jock?"

Bess made a face. "We-e-ell . . . I sort of ended up doing more shopping than jogging . . ."

"Figures," George said. "So how much did that little jog cost you?"

Bess cringed. "I don't think I should say."

"Come on, spill it. What'd you blow?"

Bess pouted. "George, don't tell me you've never gone out on a spur-of-the-moment shopping spree. How about that time you bought all those weights from the sports shop to use at home, and then you joined the gym, so you don't even *need* your own weights?"

George frowned. "Well, at least I don't go out running with a shopping bag and my wallet."

Nancy sighed. "Okay, you two. No more arguing. From now on, this vacation's going to be fun, fun, fun."

"Famous last words," George said.

Nancy shot George a mock glare. "Don't even think it," she said. "It *is* going to be a vacation. Even if it's for just one more day."

"Yeah, I wouldn't mind some fun today either," Bess agreed. "I think I deserve it after yesterday. Now I know where the expression 'scared to death' comes from. I honestly believed I was going to die of fright before those thugs even did anything to me."

Nancy leaned over and tugged on Bess's blond hair. "I know. It was a nightmare. But it's all over."

"Is it?" Bess punched her pillow, her expression sober. "Maybe for you, but I've got some serious thinking to do."

"Alan?" Nancy asked softly.

Bess nodded. "He told lies to get what he wanted. I didn't realize the boy I fell in love with would do something like that."

George pulled a chair up next to the bed. "But he also saved our lives. Bess, your boyfriend's a hero."

"Maybe."

"Barton and Roger sure seem to think so," Nancy put in.

"They wouldn't have offered to help him out otherwise."

"Yeah, just think of it, Bess. He might get his dream one day, after all," George remarked.

"I'm thinking of it. But I'm also thinking that I want to take it more slowly with him. What happened made me realize that there's a lot about Alan Wales I don't know."

"But you still feel something for him, don't you?" Nancy asked.

"Well, when the chemistry's right . . ." Bess's face grew pink.

"Good. Because I told Mrs. Chen to seat you two next to each other," Nancy said with a laugh. "Oh, did I tell you that my dad's bringing Ann Nordquist to the luncheon?"

George's brown eyes opened wide. "Talk about chemistry!"

"Yeah. Dad's really enjoying her company." Nancy sighed. "I can't tell you how glad I am to have a suspect turn out innocent."

"And speaking of couples," George said, giving Nancy a poke, "how are you and Ned doing?"

"I think we're going to be all right." Nancy smiled brightly. "As a matter of fact, this afternoon he's taking me on a very special boat ride to a tiny island!" She raised her eyebrows suggestively. "It's a start."

"Sounds romantic," Bess sighed.

Nancy giggled. "Yeah, it's called the ferry to the Statue of Liberty! Now how about getting up, Bess, or the guests of honor are going to miss their own luncheon."

"And don't take too long putting on your makeup," George added.

"Okay, okay." Bess climbed out of bed. "Are Barton and Roger and all the Fenders going to be there?"

"Absolutely," Nancy replied. "Hey, did you know that Barton told me he's going to write a song about us and the whole mystery? He's going to call it 'Scared to Death.'"

"Wow! You mean every time we turn on our radios in River Heights we're going to hear about ourselves?" Bess asked.

"An instant souvenir," Nancy answered.

"Maybe they'll even make it into a video," George said hopefully.

"That would be neat," Nancy agreed. "And I know just the threesome to play the detective and her two friends. . . ."

MURDER
ON
ICE

CHAPTER ONE

A light snow was falling from the overcast February sky as Nancy Drew steered her Mustang expertly along the twisting Vermont road. More snow meant even better skiing! Nancy's blue eyes sparkled at the thought.

Nancy, George Fayne, and Bess Marvin, her two best friends, were looking forward to a really fabulous ski trip. And having Ned Nickerson along would make the vacation just perfect.

"Sorry you decided to come along?" Nancy asked Ned. "The only guy with three girls?"

"You've got to be kidding!" George spoke up before Ned could answer. "Ned knows I'll be hitting the slopes every minute I can, and Bess will have guys falling all over themselves to impress her. And there isn't a mystery in sight! You and Ned will have plenty of time for snuggling by the fire."

"Really?" Nancy answered innocently. "I thought we were here for skiing."

"How would you like some snow down your neck?" Ned teased.

"Hey," interrupted Bess, "aren't we looking for Webb Cove Road? You just passed it!"

Nancy slowed the blue Mustang and made a careful three-point turn, her reddish blond hair bouncing as she turned her head to check the side-view mirror. She pulled onto the narrow road Bess indicated and proceeded smoothly through the snow. Soon a rustic sign appeared on the left: Webb Cove Road. "Okay, everybody, watch for the sign to the lodge," Nancy said.

Bess's blue eyes met Nancy's in the rearview mirror, and she shook her blond head. "I've heard about snow blindness, but it looks like Nancy's got a bad case of Ned blindness. Pay attention, Nan, and you won't miss any more turns."

"Hah! Look who's talking about boy blindness!" dark-haired George retorted. She and Bess were cousins, but they couldn't have been more different. George, a top athlete, was shy with boys. Bess's favorite sports were shopping and men, not necessarily in that order.

"Okay," Ned exclaimed as Nancy steered around a curve and heavy stone gateposts loomed before them. "This is the place. Webb Cove Lodge!"

Nancy swung through the open gates and pulled up before a heavy, dark red door. The lodge was long and low, snuggled into a fold of the hill. Its peaked roof looked vaguely alpine, and the overcast skies made the weathered boards seem very dark—like something out of a ghost story, Nancy thought. Then she smiled to herself, realizing that she was automatically seeing things as mysterious.

She parked the car in a small lot and she and her friends piled out.

"All right! The sun's out!" George cried happily. She and Nancy took their skis off the roof carrier and pulled boots out of the backseat. Bess and Ned would have to rent ski equipment. "Let's get checked in and hit the slopes fast!" George said enthusiastically.

As Nancy and the others stepped into the lodge's cozy office, lugging bags and skis, a sturdy, cheerful young woman in jeans and a plaid wool shirt looked up from behind the registration desk. "Welcome to Webb Cove," she said. "You must be the group from River Heights. Come on in. Which one of you is Nancy Drew? Since you made the reservations, you might as well sign in for everybody."

Bess read over Nancy's shoulder as she filled in the registration form. "Name, address, phone and credit card numbers, license plate number . . . hey, you forgot to fill in the blank for occupation. Put down, 'Nancy Drew, Notorious Girl Detective'!"

"Knock it off," Nancy muttered. She hated it when Bess said things like that in front of people she didn't know. Nancy was always modest, even though her detective work had earned her an international reputation.

Nancy left the occupation line blank. "Here you are," she said, handing the registration form back to the woman behind the desk. "Nancy Drew, George Fayne, Bess Marvin, and Ned Nickerson, all present and accounted for."

"Thanks. I'm Liz Whitcomb. I run this place. Best way I know to make a living and still be a ski bum." Liz grinned.

"Leave your skis and boots in the entryway. I'll show you to your bunks.

"I'm afraid we don't have porters or the rest of the fancy trimmings you'd have if you stayed up the road at the Overlook—the big resort hotel. But then, most people don't bring many clothes along," she added dryly, watching Bess struggle with her two suitcases. "By the way, if any of you need to rent skis from us, you'd better do it quickly. We have a lot of guests this week so we're short on rentals."

Liz led Nancy and her friends through a large, wood-paneled sitting room. Comfortable sofas covered in red wool plaid were gathered around a big stone fireplace. Sheepskin rugs dotted the slate floors, and sports magazines were piled haphazardly on the tables. At one end of the room, swinging doors led to what sounded like the kitchen. Liz led them through a rustic door at the opposite end of the room that opened onto a corridor.

"As you probably know, this place is dormitory-style," she explained. "Most of our guests are college students and hostelers from overseas. The guys' room is on the left, gals' on the right.

"The ski area, Big Birch, is on the other side of the mountain. An old chairlift will take you to the top. You can connect into the main trails easily there. The schedules for meals and ski classes with our resident instructor are posted in the dorms."

Ned nodded. "The lodge has its own ski instructor?" he asked.

"Not always. Instructors come and go. But we have a good one right now—Luke Ericsen. He showed up a few weeks ago, looking for work. He's a ski bum like me," Liz said, laughing, "and a fantastic athlete and teacher."

She opened the door to the women's bunk room. "Here you are, girls. You'll be able to tell which bunks aren't taken. Let me know if there's anything you need."

Ned caught the sleeve of Nancy's down jacket. "See you on the slopes in a little while, okay? I have to see about renting skis." He waved to the others and followed Liz toward the men's bunk room.

The girls' room was simple but attractive, even if it wasn't, as George remarked, fancy enough to suit Bess's taste. The bunks were built of dark-stained wood and covered with comforters in bright patchwork patterns.

Nancy dropped her suitcase onto the bunk by the back window and sat down beside it, yawning. "Whew! Driving in that snow really tired me out."

"I could go for a nap by the fire in the lounge. If only I had somebody cute to curl up with," Bess added wistfully.

Her friends grinned. "Bess, a couple of days from now you'll have boys falling at your feet, just as George said," Nancy reassured her.

"Who wants to wait?" Bess said with a sigh. "It's easy for you to talk, Nancy. Your tall-dark-and-handsome's here with you."

"Face it, Bess, you have a one-track mind," George told her bluntly. "Nancy'd have a good time even if Ned weren't here.

Nancy," she added significantly, "likes skiing. A little fresh air wouldn't hurt you any."

Bess groaned. "I'd rather be shopping."

Nancy and George exchanged amused glances. "Maybe you should hunt up that ski instructor," Nancy suggested. "What was his name? Luke something?"

"Ericsen," Bess said promptly.

"Did you take notes, Bess?" George asked, giggling.

Bess grinned. "No, but a handsome ski instructor isn't such a bad idea." She began brushing her long blond hair. "Although he'd probably be more interested in a skiing ace like George."

"For all we know, the guy's middle-aged and has a wife and sixteen kids," George returned, blushing.

Bess gestured for quiet, and they heard a deep voice in the next room.

"Hear that?" Bess's eyes sparkled. "Boys. Hmmm . . . I think I'll wear my new blue ski sweater."

"Happy hunting!" Nancy exclaimed. "I'm going skiing!" She zipped up her jacket, grabbed her mittens, and tramped out the door.

Liz was sitting behind the registration desk as Nancy passed the open door to the office. She rose so quickly that Nancy realized Liz had been waiting for her. "May I speak to you a minute?" she asked quietly. "In private."

"Of course," Nancy said. She stepped into Liz's office. To her surprise, Liz closed the door, then locked it. She turned to Nancy, her face serious.

"Is it true, what your friend said? You're a detective?"

Nancy nodded. "Yes. Why?"

Liz didn't answer at once. A draft of cold air sliced through the cracks around the windows. Something—a tree branch, probably—scratched against the windowpane. It was a faint sound, but Liz jumped as if it were a thunderclap. She whirled around, her face drained of color.

"Liz," Nancy cried, "what is it? There's nothing there."

"I know," Liz answered shakily. "I guess it was just a tree branch."

"But that's not what frightened you, is it? Please tell me," Nancy urged gently.

Liz swallowed and forced a smile. "Look at me, jumping out of my skin like that! A week ago, I'd have said I was never afraid of anything."

"But now you are afraid. Has something happened?"

Liz looked nervously at Nancy. "It started last week," she began. "I came down here to get something in the middle of the night, and I saw a face staring through that window. It was a monster's face—no body, no nose or mouth—a face that could scare you to death!"

CHAPTER TWO

W hat?" Nancy exclaimed. "How could that be?"

"Well," Liz said, "that's just the way it looked at first. The guy had his face pressed against the glass, so his features were all distorted. And he was probably wearing dark clothes, which was why he seemed to have no body."

"He?" Nancy asked. "How do you know it was a man?"

Liz flushed. "Oh, his . . . his size," she said uncomfortably. "It's a high window."

Nancy frowned. Liz seemed terribly flustered. "Did you notice anything else about him?" she asked.

"Yes. I could see that he had blue eyes and blond hair."

"You're sure? You could tell that in the dark?"

"Oh." Liz cleared her throat. "Yes, well . . . pretty sure."

"All right. That should help me," said Nancy.

"But, Nancy," Liz went on, sounding frightened, "he was trying to get inside!"

Nancy felt a shiver run up her spine, but she made her voice matter-of-fact. "What did you do?"

"I went straight to the back door," Liz answered grimly. "By the time I unlocked it and opened it, there was no one outside!

But there were ski tracks in the snow beneath the window, and nobody has any reason to be messing around that part of the yard on skis!"

"Could it have been somebody from another lodge just checking the place out?" Nancy suggested.

"In the middle of the night?" Liz sighed dramatically. "Nancy, I'm frightened. I don't like the idea of somebody poking around here. Aside from the Overlook, which is about two miles away, at the bottom of the Big Birch chairlift, we're very isolated here."

"It's creepy, for sure," Nancy said in a calm tone of voice, "but it doesn't sound too dangerous. I mean, that guy didn't actually do anything and he hasn't come back . . . has he?"

"That's just it. He has!" Liz shot an apprehensive look toward the door. "Last night—late—I saw a figure skiing away from the lodge. And this morning, it looked to me like the lock to the kitchen door had been tampered with.

"There's something else, too. I've received two phone calls in the last three days asking for somebody named John. The first time, I said we had nobody here by that name, and the caller became very angry, almost violent-sounding. The next time, he hung up on me."

"Let's go back to those ski tracks you found. Where did they come from?" Nancy asked. "Did you follow them?"

"Yes," replied Liz. "They came from the little trail that connects us with the Big Birch ski area and the Overlook Hotel. Those tracks had to have been made after the snowstorm stopped—and that was after two a.m." Liz looked at Nancy. "You're a detective, you tell me. What was somebody doing prowling around here at that time of night? I can't think of any pleasant reason."

Nancy nodded soberly. If someone wanted to get inside Webb Cove Lodge, it would probably be fairly easy . . . and that meant danger!

"I don't scare easily," Liz said, "but that face at the window was terrifying."

Nancy knew what was coming. "And you're asking me to do some detecting for you."

"Yes!" Liz replied emphatically. "I want to hire you, but I want you to keep a low profile. I'm not going to the police unless I have to. Rumors about a prowler won't do my lodge any good."

"This prowler doesn't sound like a regular thief," Nancy said slowly. "Liz, why do *you* think he was trying to get in here?"

"I haven't the faintest idea," Liz answered. "If he just wanted to steal, the Overlook Hotel has a lot more guests, and richer ones. It doesn't make sense."

"Well, I'll be glad to do what I can," Nancy said.

"Thank you very much." Liz unlocked the door. "Now, go hit the slopes. After last night's snowstorm, the skiing should be great."

Nancy stepped into the entryway where she and George had left their ski things. She buckled herself into her clunky ski boots, then grabbed her skis and poles and hurried outside into the dazzling sunlight.

As she fumbled for her sun goggles, Nancy caught sight of a male figure in a blue ski suit silhouetted against the sun. I might as well get acquainted, Nancy decided, especially now that I'm supposed to be checking things out. She walked over to the guy and stood her skis in the snow. "Hi," she said. "My name's Nancy."

He turned to face her. He had blond hair and piercing blue eyes. "Hello," he replied. "I'm Luke Ericsen, the ski instructor here."

"Oh," Nancy exclaimed, "I've heard about you. Liz told me you're very good."

"I am."

That brought the conversation to a crashing halt. Luke neither spoke again nor moved. You may be a good skier, Nancy thought, but you're a real snob. She glanced back at the lodge, then toward the trail leading to the ski lift, hoping to catch sight of Ned.

Nancy waited for several minutes, but Ned didn't appear. Finally, she laid her skis on the snow and snapped her boots into them. "I guess I'll head for the chairlift," she declared, half to Luke, half to herself.

"No!" the ski instructor barked. "I have to check it to make sure it's working all right."

"Is something wrong with it?" Nancy asked.

"No, but it's my responsibility to check it each week and make sure it's safe. You'll have to wait until I'm done before you go skiing."

Nancy looked down at her skis and made a face. This guy was definitely a pain. "Isn't there another lift around here? I'm dying to hit the slopes."

"There's a rickety old rope tow I use when I'm checking the chairlift," Luke admitted, gesturing toward a small clearing nearby. "But it's a very steep trail and I'm not letting anybody except an expert mess around on it."

"What makes you think I'm not an expert?" Nancy said hotly, but Luke turned away without answering.

At that moment, Ned stepped out of the lodge. "Hey, Nancy," he called, hurrying up to her. Then he turned to the ski instructor. "I'm Ned Nickerson," he said with a smile. "Are you Luke Ericsen?"

"That's right," Luke replied briefly.

"I was planning to rent some equipment, but Liz told me you have an old pair of skis and boots you're looking to sell. If the boots fit me and I like the way the skis feel, I might be interested in buying them. How about letting me try them out for the day?"

Luke just nodded and strode back into the lodge.

Ned whistled. "Obviously a man of few words."

"The fewer the better, if you ask me," Nancy answered. "Why don't you go get the skis? I'll meet you at the top of the mountain in half an hour." She was determined to go skiing right away. She'd just take the old rope tow. She was a good skier. And after all, Luke was planning to take the rope tow himself.

As Ned followed Luke into the lodge, Nancy picked up her poles and headed for the tow.

She found the start button, pushed it, and watched the tow line begin to move smoothly up the mountain. Placing her skis in the faint tracks in the snow, Nancy grabbed the rope and let herself be pulled swiftly up, her skis sliding easily across the packed powder. It had been years since she'd been on a rope tow, and she'd forgotten that it was kind of fun skiing uphill. But it brought back another vague memory—of something not very pleasant. . . .

All at once, Nancy saw a blue-suited skier farther up the slope, waving wildly. Smiling, Nancy lifted one hand off the tow rope and waved back. Bess should be here, she thought.

Then she frowned. It wasn't a friendly wave. The man began skiing swiftly down the gorge. He executed a complicated maneuver, jerked to a stop, and shouted something frantically to Nancy.

But what? He was too far away for her to make out what he was saying.

All at once, Nancy realized what the feel of the rope tow reminded her of. The memory was from years ago, when she was a kid . . . ice skating, playing crack the whip, holding on to a chain of other skaters . . . then suddenly being whipped off that human rope, hard and fast. The wind stung Nancy's face, and the sun goggles impeded her vision. She jerked one hand out of its mitten and pulled the goggles off. Then, squinting with concentration, she scanned every inch of the tow line that she could see and slid her cold fingers along the rope.

Then Nancy caught her breath. Just beyond her reach she could see a spot that was definitely thinner than the rest of the rope. Several strands had parted and now, because of her weight, the rest of them were beginning to fray.

All right, thought Nancy, all I have to do is let go of the rope and stop moving. She loosened her grip.

But at that very moment, the rope broke with a sickening snap. The force whipped her through the air like a rag doll, throwing her toward a massive birch tree.

In a kaleidoscope of confused, blurred images, Nancy saw the frozen slope rise up to meet her.

The rest was darkness.

CHAPTER THREE

Nancy was someplace dark, cold, and lonely. The wind whistled, and a shower of ice stung her face as she struggled back to consciousness. She lay half buried in the drifts of snow. *Ned*, she thought achingly.

But Nancy wasn't alone. Gradually she realized that someone was bending over her, urging her to wake up. It was a man's voice, but it wasn't Ned's.

"Come on, *fight!*" Two hands shook her shoulders roughly. Nancy tried to wrench herself away, but the hands still held her. Then the voice spoke again, but it sounded different—concerned and anxious. "Open your eyes. Come on," it said gently.

Nancy's eyelids felt as if they'd frozen together. She was cold, so cold. She drew her breath in. Slowly, she forced her eyes open and looked toward the bright sky.

Between her face and the light was a dark blur that, as her vision cleared, became the face of an unfamiliar young man. It was a handsome face, with blue eyes the same color as his sleek ski suit and topped with a mop of curly blond hair.

"Are you all right?" asked the young man.

"I think so," Nancy murmured. She moved her head tentatively, and it pounded painfully. Then a wave of nausea swept over her, and the blackness threatened to close in again.

Nancy wasn't completely unconscious, though, and she could dimly make out voices through the haze.

"Haven't seen you since the Broken Leg Café," a second male voice was saying. Even in her stupor, Nancy was sure she knew that voice. After a few moments of confusion, she realized it belonged to Luke Ericsen, the ski instructor.

Nancy felt the stranger's grip on her shoulders slacken. Slowly, painfully, she opened her eyes just enough to peek through her lashes. Luke Ericsen was standing over her, looking directly at the stranger with the curly hair.

There was an alarmed expression on the stranger's face—more alarmed, even, than when he had looked at Nancy a moment ago. Then her vision blurred and once again she sank back into darkness.

The next thing Nancy felt was a cold, tingling sensation on her face. Her eyes opened more easily this time. Luke was kneeling beside her, rubbing snow into her face.

Nancy jerked her head away to avoid the next dose. As she did so, pain exploded in starbursts behind her eyes.

"Don't move like that until you're sure nothing's broken," Luke said sharply.

"I think I'm all right," Nancy said weakly.

"Move your legs slowly, one at a time."

Nancy moved her right one, then her left, and groaned.

"Hurts, doesn't it?" Luke said brusquely. "That's what you get for not listening to me."

Nancy let Luke's comment pass. "Where did your friend go?" she asked.

There was a split second of silence. "What friend?" Luke asked blankly.

Too blankly, Nancy decided. "The guy who saw the rope breaking and warned me," Nancy said deliberately. Then another question occurred to her. The stranger had been farther up the slope, far enough away so that Nancy couldn't understand his words when he shouted to her. How could he *possibly* have seen the rope fraying from that distance?

There was another silence. Then Luke said, "There was nobody else here. You really must have hit your head hard."

Her head was definitely throbbing. Nancy explored it with her fingers and found a bump—and agonizing pain. Could I have imagined that man? she wondered. Then a shout broke into her thoughts.

"Nancy!"

Ned's familiar yell. Nancy sat up painfully to see Ned, George, and Bess running up the mountain toward her.

In another minute, Ned was right by her side, his arms around her in a concerned hug. "Are you okay?" he demanded huskily.

"Mmmm," Nancy murmured. "Luckily, I know that the best

thing to do when you're falling is just to go limp. I only wish I hadn't hit my head in the process!"

"Good thing you knew what you were doing," George said seriously.

"Knew what she was doing?" Luke cut in. "If your friend here really knew what she was doing, she wouldn't have been on that tow in the first place! I told her not to take it."

"Oh." George frowned slightly at Nancy. Then she turned to Luke and threw him a shy smile.

The young ski instructor glanced quickly at George. "I'm glad *you* understand what I'm talking about. Maybe you can talk some sense into your friend here." He shot Nancy a disgusted look, as he hurriedly put on his skis. Then, abruptly, he turned and headed down the slope.

"Now, why is he going in that direction?" Nancy said thoughtfully, as Ned and George helped her to her feet. "I thought he had to check the chairlift. Maybe he's going after that other guy."

"What other guy?" Bess asked.

Quickly, Nancy told her friends about the man who had warned her. "I don't care what Luke says," she finished up. "There was someone else here, and he was the one who saved me."

"Luke claimed there *wasn't* anyone else?" Ned asked thoughtfully.

"Right." Nancy rubbed her head. Suddenly her hand froze. Her conversation with Liz came rushing back to her. . . . A stranger at the lodge, trying to get inside.

Suddenly alert, Nancy thought, *two* blond, blue-eyed strangers appearing out of nowhere at the lodge—that's just one coincidence too many for me. I'll lay odds that the stranger who scared Liz and the one who saved me are the same guy. But, Nancy realized, now I'm not sure if that stranger is someone to be afraid of.

"Listen, everyone," Nancy suddenly exclaimed. "Something funny is going on here." She told them about Liz's prowler and how the lock had been tampered with. "I don't know what it's all about, but I think it has something to do with the man who saved me and that awful Luke Ericsen. Luke's acted a little oddly, don't you think?"

Just then, Nancy and her friends were interrupted by a shout.

"Hello there!" a young man called out, making his way toward them on cross-country skis. Liz skied up behind him.

"Gunther!" Ned waved. He turned to the others. "I met him in the dorm," he explained. "He's from Germany, and he's taking a semester off from school to travel through the United States."

Gunther and Liz glided to a stop beside them, and general introductions followed.

"Why don't you rent some cross-country skis and join us?" Gunther asked. He had brown hair and warm brown eyes that were already, Nancy noticed with amusement, fixed on Bess.

Bess, the dedicated nonathlete, beamed back. "Maybe I'll try it . . . ," she said.

Nancy saw Liz stifle a smile.

"You can borrow my skis," Liz offered. "Gunther would be a great teacher for you, Bess. He's fantastic on both downhill and cross-country skis. He's part of an alpine rescue team back in Germany."

"Borrow Liz's skis, and I will show you what a pleasure outdoor sports can be," Gunther urged.

"Well . . ." Bess's dimples started to show.

"Why don't we all go back to the lodge first?" Ned interrupted. "Nancy just had a bad fall."

Alarm leaped into Liz's eyes. "Are you all right? What happened?"

"The rope tow broke," Ned said grimly.

"Oh, no!" Liz gasped. She shot Nancy a questioning look. "Do you think this has anything to do with . . ."

Nancy answered with a faint shrug that made her shoulder throb. "I'll explain later," she said quietly, not wanting to discuss the strange incident in front of Gunther.

"Come back to the lodge," Liz said, concerned. "Some hot chocolate would do you good."

Ned helped Nancy down the hill and into the lounge, and then he and Gunther went off to find an ice pack and make some cocoa. While they were gone, George, Bess, and Liz helped Nancy out of her ski boots as she lay down on one of the couches.

"Okay," Liz said, firmly closing the door. "I want to know exactly what went on out there."

"First of all," said Nancy, "you should know that I already

told Bess, George, and Ned what you told me in the office. Oh, it's all right," she rushed on, seeing the look of alarm on Liz's face. "They help me with all my cases."

Liz relaxed and Nancy continued, "Anyway, I'm not quite sure what happened on the slope. The rope must just have been worn through."

"How awful!" Liz exclaimed.

"Fortunately, that man somehow saw that the line was frayed and gave me some warning."

"What man?" Liz asked, then caught her breath. "The prowler?"

"I don't know," Nancy replied. "But if so, we could certainly use more prowlers like him. If the rope had snapped before I was prepared, I could have been badly hurt. . . . And he was very concerned after I hit my head."

"I can't say as much for that ski instructor," Bess put in indignantly. "He was so rude! And he didn't even act worried! Who *is* that creep, anyway? If he's such a hotshot skier, why isn't he hitting the big-time competitions?"

A strange, startled look sprang onto George's face.

"Luke's a good skier and a good instructor," Liz said, as if trying to be fair. "He's very careful, too. That's why it's hard for me to understand why he didn't see that frayed rope before we had an accident!"

"I really don't understand you, Bess!" George exclaimed. "When you're in a position of responsibility like Luke is, you have to set down rules."

She turned to Nancy. "No wonder he was mad! How could he know that you're a great skier and that you're used to handling dangerous situations? Besides, he was right, Nancy. You *should* have waited to use the chairlift. If you *had* been badly hurt, he would have been responsible—"

George broke off abruptly. The others were staring at her, openmouthed. George turned scarlet. "I . . . I'll be back later," she muttered. She hurried out, banging the door behind her.

"What's with *her*?" Bess asked in amazement.

"If you ask me," Nancy said, "George has fallen for our bad-natured ski instructor, and fallen hard. Didn't you see the way she was looking at him on the slope?"

Bess looked bewildered. "But George never gets crushes."

"There's always a first time," Liz said with a grin. "Nancy, I'll go get you some aspirin. Be back in a minute." She left the lounge.

Nancy pressed her hands against her temples, trying desperately to make her head stop pounding. She needed to think—about Liz's prowler, the broken tow rope, Luke, and her mysterious rescuer. And now George.

Ned and Gunther came in with the cocoa and an ice pack just as Liz was returning with the aspirin. "About your friend George," Liz said, "I saw her going up the chairlift with Luke just now. . . . I have some work to do—see you later. Let me know if you need anything else." She disappeared into the passageway.

Nancy groaned. "Wouldn't you know that when George

finally does fall in love, she does it in a big way. And with Luke Ericsen, of all people!"

"Don't jump to conclusions," Ned said with a laugh. He handed Nancy the ice pack. "George is an athlete. Luke is an athlete. She just understands where he's coming from, that's all."

"You're an athlete. How do you feel about Luke?"

"Hmmm." Ned bit his lip thoughtfully.

"Let's hit the slopes and look for them," Nancy suggested between sips of hot chocolate.

Ned hesitated. "Are you sure you're up to it?"

"I'm okay," Nancy lied. She knew if she told Ned how she really felt, he'd never let her go investigating the mysterious Luke Ericsen.

"Bess and I could meet you later," Gunther suggested. "I want to give her some cross-country skiing lessons."

"Great!" Bess flashed Gunther a dazzling smile.

"Excellent! I will go find the skis Liz promised you." Gunther took off across the lounge, whistling.

Ned looked at Nancy. "Did my ears deceive me? Bess actually said 'great' to going out in the cold and exercising? You don't suppose she *likes* Gunther?"

"Not so loud!" Bess protested, giggling. Then her face sobered. "I don't know if I should *let* myself like him. He's going back to Germany at the end of the semester."

"Since when has Bess Marvin stayed in love with the same guy for a whole semester anyway?" Nancy asked, amused.

"True," Bess admitted. "But I never plan it that way."

Nancy buckled her boots on once again and went outside to put on her skis while Ned snapped his boots into the skis he'd borrowed from Luke.

"Well," said Nancy, as she and Ned headed slowly for the lift, "obviously Luke has finished checking the chairlift if he and George already took it up the mountain. I hope we run into those two," she added.

Nancy and Ned took the next chair up and sat quietly for a moment, watching the snow-covered trees move past them. The cold air helped to clear Nancy's head, and soon she was enjoying the feeling of whizzing down the slopes. But even though Nancy and Ned skied the entire afternoon, they never ran into George and Luke.

"They're probably hot-dogging down the hardest slope on the mountain," Ned commented.

"It doesn't matter," Nancy said. "We'll catch up with them back at the lodge."

But when Nancy and Ned returned to Webb Cove Lodge, George was nowhere to be found. In fact, she didn't appear until everyone had gathered around the long table in the lounge for dinner. Then she marched in, her color high, and spent the entire meal ignoring Nancy and talking to the other guests at the lodge, most of whom were college students.

She's mad at me, Nancy realized dully, because she knows I'm suspicious of Luke. Nancy chewed her food without really tasting it, feeling slighted and unhappy.

Only later, as she lay sleeplessly in her bed, did Nancy manage to push thoughts of George out of her mind. Unfortunately, those thoughts were replaced with even more troublesome ones. Liz's description of the hideous face pressed against the office window came back to her vividly.

If the prowler really was the same person who had saved her, she was inclined to trust him. After all, he'd warned her about the breaking rope.

And if he really wanted to get into the lodge, he probably could have done so already. Liz's locks, Nancy had noticed, wouldn't be hard to pick. Maybe he had a good reason for looking around Webb Cove . . . and maybe that reason was Luke Ericsen!

They know each other, Nancy thought, that is, if the blond stranger really is Liz's prowler. But Luke hadn't wanted her to realize that. Why?

Nancy lay very still, her head still aching a little from her fall. There were no sounds except the steady breathing of the sleepers in the other bunks. Then Nancy's sharp ears detected a faint crackling sound outside.

A shiver ran down her back as a current of cold air eddied through the cracks in the window frame.

Nancy turned toward the window—and froze. The shade wasn't pulled down all the way . . . and she could see someone at the window. Then, as quickly and silently as it had come, the figure slipped away.

Nancy rose to her knees on the bed. Cautiously, she peeped outside.

No one was there.

There was only wind, moonlight, and snow—and scarring the snow, as if etched by a giant's finger, were letters a yard long. They spelled: MURDERER.

CHAPTER FOUR

The message in the snow was the first thing Nancy remembered the next morning. She knelt on her bed and looked out the window, but the letters were gone, perhaps swept away by the wind.

What had it meant? Could someone at Webb Cove really be a murderer? Just as important, who had written the letters in the snow, and why?

Nancy didn't have any answers, so she decided not to say anything about what had happened until she could talk to Liz and Ned alone. She showered, dressed, and went to breakfast.

The guests sat around the table in the lounge, eating and talking so excitedly about getting in a good day of skiing that Nancy couldn't help but feel a little better. Glasses clinked, silverware rattled, and the enormous piles of pancakes disappeared rapidly.

"These are great," Ned exclaimed as Liz came in from the kitchen with another platter.

"Good! Have some more!" Liz said cheerfully. She caught Nancy's eye. "How are you feeling after your fall?"

"Fine, except for a few aching muscles. I'd like to speak to you in a little while, though."

"Sure. Right after breakfast." Liz set the pancake platter in front of Bess, who eyed it despairingly.

"If I eat another helping, I'm going to have to ski all day just to work it off," she moaned.

"I'll be glad to give you some more lessons," Gunther said gallantly.

Ned choked on his own second helping and Nancy kicked his ankle warningly. Then she sent a mischievous glance toward George. To her dismay, George turned away and asked loudly, "Is Luke teaching any advanced classes today?"

A prickle ran down Nancy's spine. So George was still giving her the cold shoulder.

"Sure," Liz answered. "He's out fixing that broken rope tow. Why don't you hunt him up?"

"I think I will." George pushed her chair back and got up to leave.

"Why don't you wait for us?" Nancy called.

"You go ahead and finish your breakfast. I'll see you around," George replied abruptly, and walked out.

Suddenly Nancy wasn't interested in her breakfast anymore. But she was definitely interested in the mysterious Luke Ericsen. "Does Luke stay here at the lodge?" she asked casually.

Liz nodded. "He has a room upstairs."

"Oh. Where's he from?"

"He told me he's from some little town up in Maine. And that," Liz said frankly, "is about all anybody knows. But it's been a big help having him around. Less work for me. At least he doesn't hang around the Overlook all the time, the way most of the ski bums do!" She disappeared into the kitchen.

"What's that place like, anyway?" Bess asked. "I hear it's got a great nightclub."

"Perhaps we could—how do you say, 'check it out'?—some evening," Gunther said quickly. He looked at Ned. "Maybe you and Nancy would like to come, too?"

"Definitely," Ned agreed.

Nancy nodded. She wanted to look around the hotel to see if she could get a lead on the tall blond stranger. And maybe learn some more about Luke.

Out loud, she said, "Come on, Ned, help me clear some of the dishes." She stacked the empty plates, and she and Ned took them to Liz in the kitchen.

"What's up?" Liz asked. "Shall we talk in my office?"

"That might be a good idea," Nancy replied. She and Ned followed Liz into her office.

When they were settled with the door shut, Nancy said, "You two better steel yourselves, because this is a real shocker. The prowler came back last night and he left a message in the snow. It said—get this—MURDERER."

"Wow," Ned said softly.

"That's crazy!" Liz exploded—a bit too loudly, Nancy thought. "How could there be a murderer at Webb Cove—at *my* lodge! There haven't been any murders around here—"

"Calm down, Liz," Nancy said. "I wouldn't put much stock in some weird message left in the snow in the middle of the night. But I do intend to find out what's going on here."

"Have you got any ideas yet?" Ned asked.

"Maybe," Nancy replied. "I can't help feeling that the blond guy who warned me about the rope was your prowler. That little ski trail he was on leads only to Webb Cove Lodge, and we know he's not staying here."

"Why do you think he left the message?" Liz wondered.

"Well," Nancy began slowly, "he warned me once—about the tow—so maybe he's trying to warn me, or all of us, about someone he thinks is dangerous."

"And could that someone just possibly be Luke Ericsen?" Ned asked. "You said he deliberately denied knowing our mystery man."

Nancy was silent for a moment. "We don't know much about Luke. I'd certainly hate to accuse him of anything before we have proof. After all, we don't even know if a murder really has been committed! I would say, though, that we should keep an eye on him."

"Both eyes," Ned agreed.

"Maybe I should fire him," Liz said slowly. "Just to get him out of here. . . ."

Nancy frowned. Why would Liz suggest something so drastic? But all she said was, "No, then we'd never solve the mystery. Besides, we don't *know* that he's done anything. And you don't have any cause to fire him."

Ned smiled faintly. "Nancy, you're becoming obsessed with yet another case. Do you think we'll *ever* go on a vacation without having to share it with thieves, kidnappers, or murderers?"

Nancy sighed. Ned was trying to be good-natured, but she got the message. He was tired of coming second to every mystery that came along. She couldn't blame him for feeling like that. But how could she sit still if there might really be a murderer in the lodge?

"Someday, we'll have a real vacation, I promise," Nancy said. "But for now, we have a ski instructor to follow. And on the slopes, that's not going to be easy."

Ned grinned. "Well, let's hit the mountain."

"Liz, don't worry. We'll get to the bottom of this," Nancy promised as she and Ned left the office and headed for the bunk rooms.

When Nancy reached the women's dorm, she found Bess eyeing several combinations of pants, sweaters, and vests, which she had spread out on her bunk. "Don't tell me you're changing again!" Nancy groaned.

"I think I ate too many pancakes for these pants," Bess said ruefully, looking down at her tight violet corduroys. "And this sweater doesn't really go with any other pants."

"Forget clothes for a minute. I need to talk to you about something serious." Nancy sat down on her bed. Swiftly she outlined everything that had happened, from the message in the snow to her conversation with Liz and Ned. "Keep quiet about it," she finished. "Liz doesn't want rumors getting out."

"You're going to tell George, aren't you?" Bess asked.

"I don't know," Nancy answered, and sighed. "George gets

defensive the minute any of us says a word about Luke. Besides, she's already mad at me."

"She's flipped over him," Bess said bluntly.

"And I don't like it." Nancy's eyes darkened. "Bess, keep an eye on her, will you?"

Bess nodded as she chose a new outfit. "You can count on it."

Nancy and Bess met Ned outside. "I have to wait for Gunther," Bess said. "He's going to give me my first downhill ski lesson."

"Okay," Nancy said with a smile. "Have fun! Ned and I are going to take the chairlift up to Big Birch."

"Remember," Ned added wickedly, "that is your left ski. This is your right ski. This is a pole . . ."

"How can you *stand* him?" Bess complained to Nancy.

Nancy laughed. "Oh, I manage—but just barely!"

Bess shook her head and went back inside to look for Gunther.

Ned looked at Nancy in mock anger. "You just barely manage, huh?"

"Well, a little more than barely," Nancy conceded, laughing. "Come on, let's go." She started toward the lift.

The chairlift ride to Big Birch was so beautiful that Nancy almost felt sad. It would have been so much fun for her and Ned to be at Webb Cove without a mystery hanging over them!

The lift neared the top of the mountain, and traveled smoothly over one of Big Birch's expert slopes.

"Hey, look over there," Ned cried, pointing. "Luke seems to be holding a private little advanced technique class down there. Very exclusive."

Nancy glanced down at the slope. There were George and Luke, obviously as engrossed in each other as they were in skiing. "Terrific," she muttered, squinting. "We'll have to move fast to catch them. Think you can keep up with me, Ned? This is one of the toughest trails," she teased.

"Don't get cute!" Ned retorted. "Remember, I beat you the last time we raced!"

"The *only* time we raced," Nancy answered.

"Then how about a rematch?" Ned said promptly. "Since you're feeling so cocky. I think I can handle the trail."

"If that's a challenge, you're on!"

The chairlift reached the top of the mountain, and Nancy and Ned got off. The slopes were growing crowded as the morning sun turned the hills a dazzling white.

Ned skied over to the side of the slope and adjusted his boot buckles. "How do you like Luke's ski equipment?" Nancy asked. "It's really top quality."

"It feels good to me. I just might end up buying it from him."

"Isn't it a little unusual for a ski bum to have not one, but two pairs of first-rate professional skis?" Nancy asked.

Ned laughed. "Clickety-click," he said, tapping Nancy's forehead with his index finger. "Your wheels are always turning."

Nancy smiled, batting away Ned's arm. "Well, *don't* you think so?" she persisted. "I mean, Luke's obviously a terrific skier, but

I've watched him and his movements are kind of quirky. I think he favors his right leg a little."

Ned nodded. "I noticed that, too. Could be from an old ski accident."

"Ned, think about this picture for a moment and see if it fits Luke. A guy loves skiing, but an injury keeps him from becoming a real pro. He doesn't want to admit it, though, so he keeps himself supplied with the best ski equipment available and acts like a big cheese."

"Makes sense," Ned admitted. "And George is falling for his delusions of grandeur. You'd think she had more sense than that."

"Love sure *is* blind sometimes," Nancy murmured.

"Now what does *that* mean?" Ned demanded teasingly.

"Oh . . . nothing! Hey, slowpoke, better ski fast if you want to catch me!" And with that, Nancy pushed off, heading down the slope in a flurry of glittering snow.

Behind her she heard Ned let out a surprised bellow, and then he was after her. Nancy shot a glance over her shoulder just in time to see him swoop down and pass her with only inches to spare. He shot ahead, zooming through a couple of quick turns before coming to a perfect parallel stop a little farther down the slope.

Nancy waved one of her ski poles as she shot by him. She could feel him racing after her.

Ned put on a burst of speed and shot past Nancy again. She could tell that he was determined to win the race. Nancy watched the taut lines of his body as he skipped from mogul to mogul.

But suddenly, with a cry of pain, Ned flipped face forward into the snow. He tumbled down the hill, one ski coming off and then the other flying after him.

Horror-struck, Nancy streaked down to where Ned was lying and pulled to a stop. She heard no sound except the whistling of the wind. Ned was absolutely silent, his eyes shut. He was as still as death.

CHAPTER FIVE

Ned lay motionless, one leg bent unnaturally beneath his body, his face frozen in a grimace of pain. Frantic, Nancy unsnapped her skis and dropped to her knees beside him. "*Ned,*" she called sharply. There was no response.

Nancy refused to consider her worst fear. She scooped up a handful of snow and rubbed it against Ned's face. Luke had brought her back to consciousness that way after the rope tow accident. Maybe it would help Ned.

She leaned over him, so close their faces almost touched, her ears straining for the sound of breathing. After a moment, she detected a faint groan.

"Ned!" Nancy was almost sobbing. Her eyes scanned his face for any sign of a response. To her relief, Ned's eyelids twitched and then opened slightly.

"Ned," Nancy called again. "Can you hear me?"

Ned's faint voice cut her off. "I must be dead . . . there's an angel rubbing noses with me."

"Ned!" Nancy scolded, relief washing over her.

"Going to kiss me to make it better?" Ned joked weakly.

The kiss that followed was anything but a joke. When Nancy

drew back at last, she knew her heart was in her eyes. But her loving expression quickly turned to alarm as she watched Ned, his teeth gritted, slowly try to straighten his bent leg.

"Don't! Don't move at all until you're sure it's not broken!" Nancy gasped.

"I'm pretty sure it isn't," Ned said, wincing. "Have a look, will you?"

Nancy unfastened his boot and eased it off. Then she explored his leg carefully with her fingers, trying not to hurt him. "I think you're okay," she said finally.

"Good. Put my boot back on and help me get to my feet."

"No way! This leg is bad news—your ankle's already swelling."

"I've been hurt worse playing football."

All at once Nancy and Ned heard someone call to them from farther up the slope. George and Luke were silhouetted against the shining snow.

"Fantastic," Ned said. "They must have taken the lift back up the mountain while we were skiing down."

"Come give us a hand!" Nancy shouted.

George swooped toward them, with Luke following close behind. "Everything all right?" she called. "We saw you—" Then she got a good look at Ned's leg, and whistled. "How did *that* happen?"

"I don't know," Ned replied. "One minute I was doing fine. The next, my boot was out of the ski and I was rolling down the mountain like an out-of-control snowball."

Luke bent down to check Ned's leg. "It looks like nothing's broken, but you could damage the ligaments seriously if you try to use it and you fall again. I'll ski down and get a carrier." Luke sped away.

"I don't need a carrier!" Ned shouted after him, but Luke was already too far off to hear.

"For Pete's sake, stop showing off about how brave you are," George scolded.

"Look who's trying to give lessons in good sense," Ned muttered.

George straightened up angrily. "What's that supposed to mean?"

Ned and Nancy exchanged glances. "Nothing," Ned said in a gentler tone. "I'm just furious with myself for falling. And I'm worried about how I may have messed up my leg for the baseball season. I'm sorry."

George looked dubious, but accepted the apology.

Soon after, Luke reappeared, pulling a stretcher behind him. Nancy and George helped him load Ned onto the stretcher. Luke laid Ned's skis, poles, and the boot Nancy had taken off next to him.

Then he strapped Ned in, picked up the stretcher's handles, and began a slow, careful snowplow down the treacherous slope. Nancy and George skied anxiously behind.

"Can't we stop for a rest?" Nancy called when they were halfway down. She could tell from Ned's face that, although

Luke was trying to be gentle, the ride down was very painful.

"I know he's hurting," Luke said over his shoulder, continuing his snowplow, "but the sooner we get to the bottom, the better he'll feel." Nancy sighed. She knew Luke was right, so she and George skied on.

At last the foursome reached the bottom of the steep slope. Luke pulled the stretcher up to the doors of the first-aid station. "Here we are," he said, unstrapping Ned and helping him to stand on his good leg. He supported most of Ned's weight as Ned limped into the infirmary.

When at last he was lying on a nice, motionless bed, Ned drew in a ragged breath. Luke looked at him with a faint smile. "You're a lot like me, aren't you? You don't like anybody to tell you what you can do or can't do. But let me give you one piece of advice, okay? *Don't* ski on a trail until you're ready for it."

"I know. But I have this daredevil girlfriend . . ." Ned gave Nancy a secret smile.

Suddenly Luke turned on Nancy, his face darkening. "What? On the most dangerous slope we have? Are you crazy? If you want to take your own life in your hands like you did yesterday, that's one thing! But I *will not* allow you to go around here daring other people to kill themselves!"

"She *didn't*," Ned said with all the force he could muster. "The race was my idea."

"Was it?" Luke demanded harshly. "You don't strike me as the kind of guy who'd do something that stupid unless you had a pretty good reason. Maybe that reason was impressing Nancy Drew."

All at once Luke was shouting at Nancy. "You've got to be more careful! *Do you have any idea at all what it's like to be responsible for someone else's tragedy?*" He stopped, mid-breath, suddenly realizing that the others were staring at him. His eyes locked with George's.

George's face went from white to scarlet and back to white. With a choking sound, Luke wrenched around and ran out of the first-aid station.

There was a moment of stunned silence. Then George ran after him.

Ned managed a whistle. "Man, that guy's *weird*!"

"Something's weird all right," Nancy said, "and George knows it."

"What set Luke off like that, anyway?" Ned asked.

"I don't know." Yet, Nancy added to herself. "It sounds as if Luke was responsible for an accident. Maybe that's why he's such a dictator about safety." She frowned. "Although that doesn't explain everything." But before she could continue, the infirmary attendants came in.

After Ned's ankle had been examined and wrapped in an ice pack, one of the first-aid attendants drove Nancy and Ned back to Webb Cove Lodge. Luke and George were standing on the front porch of the lodge when the medical van arrived. They stepped aside as Nancy helped Ned up the steps. Clearly, they were embarrassed about what had happened in the infirmary, but didn't want to talk about it.

"I hope you're feeling a little better now," Luke said quietly as Ned and Nancy passed him.

George retrieved Ned's skis, boots, and poles from the van. "Thanks for bringing my friend home," she told the driver.

"Get better soon," the attendant called to Ned as he headed back toward Big Birch. Then the uncomfortable silence closed in on the foursome again.

The front door opened, and Liz's voice interrupted the awkward moment. "Lunch in five min—oh, no!" She stepped outside quickly. "What happened, Ned?"

"Bobcat Trail was too much for him," Luke said briefly. "He sprained his ankle."

Liz shot an alarmed look at Nancy. "Another accident?" she asked. Then she shook her head. "It doesn't matter right now, anyway. First thing we have to do is to get Ned inside where he can lie down." She looked at Nancy with concern. "You take it easy young lady. You look as though you've had the stuffing knocked out of you, too."

"I'm okay," Nancy replied, picking up Ned's borrowed ski boots and collecting the skis. She looked at them absently.

Then she looked at the skis again, hard, and dropped the boots with a thud.

"It wasn't the trail that caused Ned's fall," she burst out, "or our racing! The binding on this ski has come loose—one of the screws came out."

There was a chorus of shocked exclamations. Nancy cut through them sharply.

"Look at this!" She pointed. "This screw hole's a lot bigger than it ought to be. Somebody enlarged the hole so the screw wouldn't hold! This wasn't an accident—it was caused deliberately! And it nearly killed Ned!"

CHAPTER SIX

Give me that!" Luke said sharply. He snatched the ski from Nancy's hand and examined the binding in silence. "This screw hole wasn't shaved down," he said finally. "It *wore* down. That's why the screw came out. It could happen at any time."

Luke seemed calmer, but his hands still trembled. He paused and inhaled deeply. "Ned, I'm terribly sorry. I haven't used these skis lately. I should have inspected them before I lent them to you."

"It's not your fault," Ned said after a moment. "Let's just forget it, all right?"

Nancy took the ski back from Luke. "It can happen at any time?" she asked skeptically. She wondered why Luke, who was such a fanatic about safety, *hadn't* inspected his equipment before lending it to somebody.

"On gear that gets hard use, yes." Luke stepped to Ned's side. "We'd better get you inside and lying down." He helped Ned hobble into the lodge and over to the couch in front of the fire. Nancy followed them, frowning and thinking that Luke was showing an awful lot of concern.

"It may be just a sprain—but if the swelling doesn't go down by morning, I'm going to drive you to the hospital to get an X-ray," Liz told Ned. "I'll bring you an ice pack," she added, heading for the kitchen.

Nancy followed her. When they were alone, Nancy asked, "Liz, have you ever heard of a binding coming loose and leaving a hole like that?"

"It's possible. But it's definitely not common!" Liz's eyes narrowed. "You really think somebody deliberately tried to kill Ned? Who would have a motive for doing that?"

"You *have* had a prowler," Nancy pointed out. "Somebody looking in windows and writing MURDERER in the snow. None of that's very rational."

Nancy swallowed hard. Then suddenly she burst out, "Wait a minute! Those were *Luke's* skis!"

"Luke's skis," Liz repeated. "And he gave them to Ned." She paled. "Do you think he's to blame for Ned's accident?"

"An awful lot of accidents seem to happen around Luke," Nancy said thoughtfully. "These skis. The tow rope. It's just that . . ."

"What?" Liz demanded.

"Someone else could have seen Luke's skis and not realized that Ned would be using them. Same thing with the rope tow. The traps could have been set *for* Luke, not *by* him!" Frustrated, Nancy paced around the room. "I need a good motive, or even better, some useful evidence."

"This is really turning into a nightmare," Liz said, shuddering dramatically.

"Just stay calm," Nancy cautioned. "And let's keep this conversation between the two of us, okay?" She gave Liz's hand a squeeze and then hurried back out to Ned.

Nancy hadn't planned on a quiet afternoon with Ned, but she decided that the idea suited her just fine. However, they didn't spend it by the fire. With the aid of a pair of crutches that Liz kept on hand for such emergencies, Ned was able to limp out to the small lake beside the lodge. It was cleared for skating, and that's just what Nancy did. Ned sat and watched from a wooden bench, his leg propped up on a log.

Nancy was an excellent skater, and she found the rhythm of the sport soothing. She was glad to have a chance to mull over what had been happening. Writing didn't just appear in the snow, and bindings on skis didn't just wear down! As Luke well knows, Nancy told herself. Somebody had deliberately sabotaged those skis!

The problem was, who? And why? And who was the intended victim? Liz had jumped to the conclusion that Luke had done it. Maybe he had, maybe not. Even if he hadn't, he apparently knew or suspected the answers to those questions. What exactly was he trying to cover up?

Much as Nancy loved solving mysteries, this one was causing some trouble.

She felt—lonely. The case had already come between her and George. And she could see it creating problems between her and Ned. Who's next? she wondered. Will Bess get angry at me? She skated over to sit with Ned for a while.

They returned to the lodge as the shadows started falling.

Keeping his leg up all afternoon had done Ned's ankle good. The swelling had gone down a bit. As the aromas of chili and baking apples wafted into the lounge from the kitchen, the other guests began straggling in from the slopes.

Bess and Gunther appeared first. "We heard about your ankle, Ned. How are you feeling?" Bess said. "You missed some great skiing!" she called as she headed toward the dorm.

"You say that like a confirmed athlete!" Ned called back, grinning. Bess stuck her tongue out at him before disappearing. A group of college students appeared next and then, last of all, Luke and George.

Luke went directly upstairs without speaking to Nancy or Ned, but George came over to them right away. "How's the ankle?" she asked. Nancy noted that George's voice sounded strained.

"Hanging in there," Ned said lightly.

Nancy smiled at George. "How was the skiing?"

For a moment, George's eyes were radiant. "Oh, I had a great time!" she replied. Then her smile stiffened, and the light faded from her eyes. "Well, I'd better get ready for dinner." As she left the lounge, Nancy watched her thoughtfully.

Luke joined the guests for dinner that night, but he took a seat at the far end of the table near Liz. Ned hobbled over to the closer end, on his crutches, and Nancy, Bess, and Gunther joined him.

Soon, George returned. She had changed into dark red stretch pants and a Norwegian sweater, adding small gold earrings. She looked, Nancy thought, absolutely gorgeous. George hesitated for a moment, looking the table over, and then sat with Luke.

Luke didn't act like his usual aloof self at dinner. He actually relaxed and smiled, talking with George, the two of them in their own private world. They even joined the others after dinner, toasting marshmallows around the fire.

"How's the ankle doing?" Luke asked Ned.

"Pretty good. I guess it'll be okay by baseball season." He smiled and went on, trying to sound casual. "We've sure had a lot of accidents lately. Whatever happened to that old towline?"

"I threw it out," Luke replied shortly. He looked as if he was about to get up and leave, until he caught George's eye. "Not much skiing, I guess, where you come from?"

"Nope," Ned answered.

"How about *your* hometown, Luke?" Nancy put in. "Lots of skiing there?"

Luke's face tightened. He looked as if he was quite alarmed, but was trying not to appear so. "Little town in Maine," he said, and immediately turned back to Ned. "Do any competitive skiing?"

Ned shook his head. "If I had, would *this* have happened?" He laughed. "After this accident, I guess it's obvious that I'm no Olympic star."

Suddenly Luke seemed very, very uncomfortable. He tried to laugh with Ned, but the sound that came out of his throat was more like a croak. Nancy glanced at George and realized with a shock that George wasn't smiling, either.

Ned hit a nerve, Nancy thought. I'd better follow it up. "Is that something you'd like to do, Luke?" she asked. "Ski in the Olympics?"

"No," Luke replied shortly.

"Why not?" Nancy asked casually. "You're quite a skier."

"Leave it." George cut Nancy off abruptly. "He said no."

By now Gunther and Bess were looking at them strangely. Nancy signaled Bess with her eyes, and Bess jumped into the awkward pause with a giggle.

"What are we playing here, Twenty Questions?" she asked. Deliberately, she steered the conversation back to Nancy's line of questioning. "What competitive sports are you interested in?"

"I'm not. Competition can be destructive if people care too much—or if they don't know what they're doing." Luke looked straight at Nancy. "You shouldn't go taking risks. Mountains have no mercy."

Nancy narrowed her eyes. "Some risks are worth taking . . . as long as they don't endanger other people."

Luke's fair skin flushed dark red. "One kind of sport I don't like is answering nosy questions. Excuse me." And with that, he stormed off.

As soon as he was out of the room, George jumped up. "For once in your life, can't you be something other than Nancy Drew, girl detective? Do you always have to go poking into people's private lives?"

"George—"

"Just forget it!" George cried. Then she stalked off after Luke.

Ned whistled. "I hope that risk was worth taking."

"It better be." Nancy's eyes followed George. "I hope I didn't hurt her too much."

"I'll see what I can find out," Bess said. She ran after George and Luke.

It wasn't until bedtime that Nancy met Bess in the dorm room and was able to ask her what had happened.

"Shh." Bess glanced significantly toward the door. "These walls are paper-thin," she whispered. "I could hear George and Luke from out in the hall, but all I could make out were a few words. Luke said, 'police,' and then 'investigation . . . broken leg.'"

"Broken leg." Nancy frowned. "They couldn't have been talking about Ned. I'm sure Luke broke his leg once, and badly, because of the stiffness in his one when he skis. But what do the police and an investigation have to do with that? . . . Wait— *broken leg*!" Nancy exclaimed suddenly. "Bess, have you ever heard of the Broken Leg Café?"

Bess just stared at Nancy. "The what?"

"'Haven't seen you since the Broken Leg Café'!" Nancy quoted. "That's what Luke said to the man who rescued me yesterday!"

Bess shook her head confusedly. "It doesn't make sense."

"We know one thing," Nancy said. "Luke talks to George in private about things he doesn't want the rest of us to hear."

At that moment, George walked in. She looked bemused, as though she'd just been kissed. But she did not look happy. She undressed and climbed into her bunk without a word. Bess and Nancy silently followed her example.

But long after all the others in the room were sleeping soundly, Nancy lay awake, arms locked behind her head, thinking. Finally she slid out from beneath the covers, put on her warm bathrobe, and tiptoed out to the lounge.

The fire had died down, but red embers still glowed in the darkness. Nancy lay down on the couch and stared at the coals, her thoughts tangled.

Suddenly she heard sounds overhead. A door opened somewhere, then closed. Footsteps quietly approached the head of the stairs, then started down cautiously.

Nancy gripped the arm of the couch. Its high back would conceal her, but it also blocked her own view.

Someone, heard but unseen, was moving across the room toward the front door. The door creaked open and then there was silence. Nancy got up and crept to the window.

Moonlight, reflecting off the snow, showed a figure crouching on the porch. A small pool of light from a flashlight illuminated a pair of shiny skis. They were Luke's skis, the ones Ned had worn earlier.

The flashlight beam jerked upward for a fraction of a second, just long enough for Nancy to see the figure's face—Luke's face. He was checking out the skis he had insisted so emphatically had been *worn down*. And while looks might not kill, there was murder in his eyes.

CHAPTER SEVEN

Nancy's heart skipped a beat. What was Luke doing with those skis in the middle of the night? She had to know. Despite the fact that she was wearing only her bathrobe, she tiptoed to the door. Without a sound her fingers turned the knob. Then all at once, she yanked the door open.

Luke sprang up, the ski and the flashlight clattering to the porch floor. Even without the light, there was no mistaking the panic in Luke's eyes. He snatched the flashlight up again and shined it full in Nancy's face.

"*You!*" he hissed. "What are you doing sneaking around?"

"I could ask you the same thing," Nancy retorted. "I couldn't sleep, so I decided to sit by the fireplace for a while. The next thing I knew, somebody was prowling around out here. I thought I'd better check it out."

"You aren't afraid of anything, are you?" Luke said with grudging respect. He forced a soft laugh. "We must be having an insomnia epidemic around here. I couldn't sleep either, so I figured I might as well work on my skis."

"So why were you tiptoeing around out here like a thief?" Nancy asked.

"Look who's talking," Luke countered.

Nancy ignored his sarcasm. "Think you can fix them?"

"Why not? It takes more than a missing screw to ruin a good pair of racers."

Nancy sat down on the porch bench. "You don't mind if I watch you work, do you?"

Luke stood the ski back against the wall. "No. But I've changed my mind. The light's not good enough to work out here. And I don't want to wake the guests by working inside. By the way, don't go spreading around stories about your boyfriend's accident. You'll start a panic among the snow bunnies." Luke opened the door and pointedly waited for Nancy to go in first.

Nancy murmured a good night and went straight to the dorm. Whatever Luke was up to, he wasn't going to finish it that night.

Late as it had been when she fell asleep, Nancy woke very early. The other girls in the room were still sleeping soundly as she slipped on her black ski pants.

The sky was gray and the woods looked bleak as Nancy let herself out onto the porch. The skis still leaned against the wall, exactly as Luke had placed them a few hours before. Nancy picked up the defective one and, holding the ski so that the early morning light hit it, examined it carefully.

Everything about the binding seemed normal except for the missing screw. The hole was definitely larger than the others, but now Nancy noticed something else, too. She could see knife marks, and traces of a grayish substance in the hole.

Nancy pulled her Swiss army knife from her coat pocket and pried some of the gray stuff out with her knife blade. She rolled it between her fingers. It was soft and malleable, like non-hardening putty or children's modeling clay.

And somebody, Nancy thought grimly, had deliberately put the clay there after enlarging the hole and then stuck the screw in it, so that it would pop out under the stress of skiing. Some accident! Just like my "accident"!

Nancy stood the ski carefully back in place and went inside. As she had hoped, Liz was now awake and working in the kitchen. Nancy greeted her, then turned immediately to the problem at hand.

"Liz, what happened to the rope Luke removed from the tow after I fell?" Nancy didn't mention that Luke had said he'd thrown it away.

"It's out back in the shed with the emergency generator," Liz replied. "You can go in if you want to. The door's unlocked."

The shed was a small building half hidden by a rise of ground. Nancy stepped in and flicked on the light. The generator was purring away quietly in a corner. On the floor were several large coils of rope. Then Nancy saw a smaller one. She could tell by the markings on it that it was the old rope from the tow.

Nancy felt all along the rope. At the end, her fingers stiffened. It had been cut three-quarters of the way through. The rest of the rope was frayed, as though a break had been carefully, maliciously arranged.

Suddenly a voice spoke from behind Nancy. "Don't you ever mind your own business?" It was Luke.

"Why did you lie to me about the rope?" Nancy demanded.

"Because Liz insisted we keep it, and it isn't safe to use! Now, listen, little Miss Detective—"

"Liz said I could come out here," Nancy cut in.

"Maybe she did. But *I'm* the one she'll hold responsible if any more accidents happen. This place is off-limits to lodge guests." Luke took the rope from Nancy. Then, to her surprise, he smiled. "Anyway, breakfast's ready. Liz made apple pancakes with sour cream. And your boyfriend's looking for you."

It was so odd. Sometimes Nancy actually thought there was a nice guy underneath Luke's nasty exterior. She left the shed quickly and went in to breakfast. But she sneaked back afterward with Ned. She simply made sure that Luke wasn't around.

They went by a circuitous route, partly to find the easiest going for Ned's crutches, partly to avoid running into anyone. But when they reached the shed, Nancy stopped short in dismay. "Oh *no!*" In the short time since she'd left before breakfast, the door had been padlocked.

"Now what?" Ned wanted to know.

Nancy laughed. "Easy. I'll pick the lock." Once again, she pulled out her Swiss army knife. She began removing the screws that held the door latch in place. "This wasn't here an hour and a half ago," she commented. "Luke must have installed it."

"Or Liz," Ned suggested softly. "Even if she did say it was okay to come and look."

Nancy nodded. "I know. I have only Liz's word about the prowler and the phone calls."

Ned blinked. "Do you really think Liz is behind all this?"

"Stranger things have happened. Maybe she'd cash in on a lot of insurance money if this place went out of business. Who knows?" Nancy remembered what Liz had said the day they arrived—that she was just a ski bum. "She seems so nervous sometimes. On the other hand, maybe she's just the hysterical type."

The door latch came off in Nancy's hand. Inside, the generator still hummed quietly, but the coils of rope were gone.

Nancy and Ned searched every corner, but found nothing. At last they gave up. They left the shed, and Nancy screwed the door latch and padlock back in place.

"Okay," Nancy said as they headed for the lake, "it's pretty clear that none of these 'accidents' have been accidental. But the question is, why? I haven't come up with a good motive."

"I have," Ned said quietly. "Maybe someone is afraid of Nancy Drew, detective. Someone who, as the writing in the snow said, is a murderer. . . ."

Their eyes met. Nancy was more shaken than she wanted Ned to see. His theory was very possible. After all, the first "accident" had happened to her. Anyone could have heard Bess telling Liz that she was a sleuth.

Ned leaned toward Nancy. "Don't worry," he whispered against her hair. "Bad ankle or not, the next time anyone tries anything, I'll be there."

Nancy was shocked to discover how matter-of-factly they were both accepting that there would be a next time. But who would the victim be?

Nancy's troubled thoughts kept returning to Luke. He was so guarded about his past. And he'd lied about the damaged ski and the rope tow. Luke—was he the criminal or the target?

Face it, Nancy told herself. All I have so far is circumstantial evidence, but that evidence points to Luke Ericsen. Means, method, opportunity. I don't know what the motive is yet, but I'm sure all I have to do is dig deeper and I'll figure it out.

Then, with horror, Nancy realized something else. George— one of my best friends—may have fallen in love with a murderer.

CHAPTER EIGHT

I've got to warn George about Luke, whether she wants to hear it or not!" Nancy exclaimed.

Ned nodded. "Even if Luke isn't responsible for what's happened to us, he's definitely involved in some way. And we know he's hiding something."

"So's George! I'm sure of it," Nancy said apprehensively. "I've got to find out what it is. Otherwise I may never get to the bottom of what's going on around here."

Nancy's last words hung in the air ominously.

Ned looked at his watch. "You may still be able to catch her before she heads over to Big Birch."

Nancy caught her breath. "Can you make it back to the lodge alone?"

"Yes," Ned replied.

"Great!" And with that, Nancy took off running.

Nancy found George standing in front of the chairlift, snapped into her skis and ready to go. "Hey," Nancy said casually, "how about a race this morning?"

"Sorry, I'm busy now." George glanced at Luke, who was telling a few of the other guests about the schedule for ski lessons.

"George, I *have* to talk to you," said Nancy. "You've been avoiding me ever since we got here. I know it's because of Luke, and it makes me feel just awful."

"I never thought a guy would come between us," George admitted.

Nancy laid one mittened hand on George's arm. "I'm worried about you. Right now, I don't even know how to talk to you without hurting you. We've been friends for so long, but now you're a million miles away from me."

George sighed. "I'm just not sure I can trust you," she said. "You're saying all these horrible things about Luke, and you don't even know him!"

"Aren't you at least going to let me explain why? I think there are things you'd better know about Luke," Nancy said seriously.

George shot her a frightened glance. "Like what?"

"Like he may be connected with Ned's accident—and mine, too."

"Oh, come *on*, Nancy!" George exclaimed.

"George," Nancy pleaded, "you know something about Luke, and you've got to share it. Before someone else gets hurt."

"Listen, Nancy," said George quietly. "I've helped you on a lot of cases, but no way am I going to help you investigate *me*!"

Nancy paused to think. At last she said earnestly, "Look, if Luke's such a great guy, then convince me! Tell me what you know about him."

George's eyes dropped.

"You can't, can you?" Nancy persisted. "Because you know something about Luke's past, and it's not good."

"You don't know what you're talking about!" George cried.

"It has something to do with a place called the Broken Leg Café, doesn't it?"

Suddenly, uncharacteristically, George began to cry. With a burst of energy, she skied quickly away.

Nancy closed her eyes despairingly. What am I going to do with her? she thought. She resisted the temptation to run after George. She knew she'd blown it with her; she just hoped she hadn't blown the whole case, because now she was sure that one of her best friends was intimately involved.

Nancy walked slowly back to the lodge and found Ned alone in the lounge. "How did you make out?" he asked.

Nancy's shoulders sagged. "I couldn't have done worse. George thinks I'm against Luke for no reason, and she's ready to defend him to her dying breath."

"Let's hope not literally," Ned said.

Nancy winced. "I did find out one thing, though," she added. "George jumped when I mentioned the Broken Leg Café."

"So you are getting somewhere." Ned limped over to Nancy and gave her a reassuring hug.

Nancy smiled. "You're not doing too badly with that ankle."

"It doesn't hurt much." Ned grinned. "If I stay off it today, I think I'll be able to ski tomorrow."

Nancy returned his hug. "So what are you going to do about skis? Liz says every pair is rented now."

"That's all taken care of," Ned replied smugly. "I phoned Big Birch and arranged to rent a pair there. We can drive over in the morning and pick them up. Maybe we should stop off at the Overlook Hotel while we're at it. I hear they've got a huge hot tub."

Bess and Gunther walked into the lounge just in time to hear Ned's last comment. "We're going dancing at the hotel tonight," Bess chimed in. "Why don't you come along? You'll have fun even if you can't dance."

Ned looked at Nancy. "You want to?"

"Sure! We deserve to have a little fun on this vacation!" Then Nancy's face became more serious. "Have you two seen George?"

Gunther and Bess nodded. "We just passed her," Gunther said. "She was looking for Luke and she seemed very upset. Is something wrong?"

Nancy hesitated. "I had a talk with her about Luke. She thinks I'm picking on him."

"Oh." Gunther nodded. "I begin to understand. Our ski instructor is a bit of a mystery, yes? Perhaps not so good for your friend."

Before Nancy could ask Gunther what he meant, George herself walked in. She looked quite calm, though slightly red-eyed. "How's the ankle?" she asked Ned, obviously trying to act as though everything were normal.

Bess and Nancy exchanged glances. "We've just been talking about going to the Overlook tonight to do some dancing," Bess replied brightly. "Ned is much better. You and Luke want to come?"

George looked grateful. "Sounds good to me. I don't know what Luke's plans are, though."

"We can all ride over in my car," Nancy offered. At least that way everybody will be safe, she added mentally.

In order to keep an eye on Luke, Nancy took an advanced class with him that afternoon. He was a good teacher and an excellent skier, even if he did favor his right leg slightly. Nancy noticed that it didn't bend well at times. Had Luke damaged his leg in a skiing accident or some other kind of accident? Nancy wondered.

Luke did not show up at the lodge for dinner. Nancy preferred it that way, except that George looked so unhappy. Immediately after dinner, she scooped up a pile of ski magazines from the lounge and headed for the dorm.

Bess made an exasperated sound. "This has gone far enough. Come on," she said to Nancy. The girls went to the bunk room and cornered George. "Are you coming dancing with us?" Bess demanded.

George didn't look up. "I don't know. I told Luke you guys were going, but he wasn't too thrilled with the idea."

"Well, *you're* coming," Bess ordered. She pulled George to her feet. "You're already dressed for it, anyway," she commented, surveying George's tight gray pants and oversized turquoise sweater.

"If Luke wants to find you, he'll know where to look," she went on. "It's a good idea not to let guys think you're just sitting around waiting for them. Trust me." George allowed herself to be led out of the room.

The girls found Ned and Gunther and piled into Nancy's car for the two-mile drive to the Overlook Hotel.

The first sight of its ornate wrought-iron gates produced a squeal of delight from Bess. The hotel looked like a French château and was surrounded by trees decorated with little white lights.

The hotel's dance club was spacious and elegant. The band was playing a Stones classic, and the dance floor was already crowded. To one side, glass doors led to an indoor swimming pool complete with Jacuzzi.

Ned and Nancy found an unoccupied table as the others made their way to the dance floor. "This is a good spot to watch from," Nancy said. She smiled at Ned. "This is fun!"

Ned smiled back and took her hand. "You'd have more fun if you were dancing."

"We agreed you'd stay off the ankle today, remember?"

"That's no reason for you to stay off yours."

"I've done enough tearing around the mountain today. I'd rather sit the night out with you." Nancy meant it, but she found it hard to keep still while listening to the music.

After a while, Bess, Gunther, and George returned to the table. Gunther politely asked Nancy to dance.

"Go! I'll talk to George while you're gone," Ned whispered.

Nancy smiled and got up. Maybe George would listen to Ned more easily than to her. She followed Gunther to the dance floor and started moving to the bass beat.

Ned was right, it felt great to dance, even though the floor was crowded. It was impossible to avoid colliding with other people. Nancy felt her elbow connect with someone behind her. "Sorry!" she exclaimed, laughing, and turned around apologetically.

A deep voice said, "It's perfectly all right." She looked up at a tall, blond man with a deeply tanned face and vivid blue eyes. "I've already clobbered a few people that way myself," the young man said, smiling.

There was something oddly familiar about him, but Nancy couldn't quite place his face. "I really am sorry," she said again, turning back to Gunther.

"Are *you* all right?" the stranger's voice continued.

Those words! That voice! Nancy was sure she'd heard them before. She spun back around. The young man was looking at her with an odd expression in his eyes.

Nancy gasped. "It was you!"

CHAPTER NINE

For a moment Nancy and the blond man stood staring at each other. "*It was you!*" she cried. "*You're* the one who rescued me when the tow rope broke!"

The stranger's blue eyes crinkled into an admiring smile. "You must be quite a skier. You reacted so fast once you realized the danger, and you knew exactly how to fall."

"Not well enough to keep from getting knocked out!" Nancy laughed breathlessly. "I'm so glad to see you again! I was beginning to think I'd imagined you, and I never did get a chance to thank you."

"That doesn't matter. I didn't want to leave while you were out like that, but your boyfriend came up and took over. Pretty abruptly. Who is the guy, anyway?"

"Luke Ericsen," Nancy replied as the music ended. "And he isn't my boyfriend. Ned Nickerson is. Over there." She indicated the table where Ned was sitting. "Luke's the ski instructor at Webb Cove Lodge, where we're staying. This is my friend Gunther."

Gunther and the man shook hands, then Gunther excused himself and threaded his way through the crowd to Bess. You and Luke know each other, Nancy thought, looking at her rescuer. You were talking about being together at a Broken Leg Café. "I still don't know who *you* are," she said aloud.

"Michael Price," the young man introduced himself with another dazzling smile. "I'm a freelance writer, mainly sports. Right now, I'm researching ski resorts in New England."

"I'm Nancy Drew."

"What do you do?" Michael asked.

Nancy decided not to tell Michael she was a detective. "Right now, I dance," she replied demurely. The crowd around them had started rocking to a new song, and Michael grinned.

"We do seem to be blocking traffic." Michael began moving to the music, and Nancy fell into sync with him. "Doesn't your boyfriend dance?" he asked.

"He loves to, but I won't let him tonight—he's banged up his ankle."

As Nancy told Michael about Ned's accident, he frowned and asked, "So this Luke lent him damaged skis?" He pursed his lips, thinking. "That sounds pretty irresponsible to me."

Nancy looked up into Michael's face. All of a sudden, she couldn't stand it anymore. Why was Michael pretending he didn't know Luke, when Nancy had heard them talking together? She *had* to find out from him what was going on!

"Michael!" Nancy exclaimed. "I'm going to be honest with you, and I hope you'll be honest with me. I don't trust Luke, and I need to find out more about him for the sake of a friend. I know you know him . . . so why don't you tell me whatever you know?"

A peculiar expression crossed Michael's face, but Nancy couldn't read it. Then he replied, "All right, I think I can be open with you. I said Luke sounded irresponsible to me. Well, there's more to it than just a hunch.

"You're right, I *have* met Luke before. He lent some equipment to someone I knew. And guess what—that guy had an accident, too. Only he wasn't as lucky as your boyfriend. He hit his head, went into a coma, and three days later, he was dead."

Nancy gasped. Luke really *could* be a murderer!

"Remember," Michael said, "I'm not telling you he did it on purpose. Maybe it was just carelessness. But that doesn't bring my friend back to life."

Suddenly the words Luke had shouted at her after Ned's accident reverberated through Nancy's head. "Do you have any idea at all what it's like to be responsible for someone else's tragedy?" he'd said.

Nancy shuddered. "How awful." George really may be in love with a murderer! she thought. And what can I do?

Suddenly, inspiration struck Nancy like a lightning bolt. It would be a whole lot easier to get George's mind off Luke if somebody else fell for her. Someone handsome and charming . . . "Why don't you come on back to our table and meet the rest of my friends?" Nancy suggested.

Michael shook his head. "Thanks, but I'd rather dance."

"I'd like you to meet George Fayne. She's a fantastic skier. She followed every minute of the last Olympic competitions on TV. I'll go get her. I really think you two have a lot in common."

Nancy started back to the table. This is great, she thought. Michael should be the perfect antidote to Luke.

Nancy found George and Ned alone at the table, both looking blue. Apparently Bess and Gunther were dancing again. Quickly, Nancy explained that she wanted to introduce George to a friend.

George studied Nancy for a moment. "I never thought I'd see you stoop so low as to fix me up with a blind date," she said. "Bess, yes, but not you, Nancy."

"Oh, come on. A blind date isn't stooping low! Don't make such a big deal out of it," Nancy said. "He's a nice guy."

"Look," George replied firmly, "I like Luke, even if you don't, and some good-looking, empty-headed skier isn't going to change that."

"He's not empty-headed," Nancy said. "Besides, this is more for him than for you. I think he's really lonely." So she'd lied. If her plan worked, that wouldn't matter.

"Oh, all right," George said, groaning, "but only because I know you won't leave me alone until I go with you."

But when the girls reached the spot where Nancy had left Michael Price, he was nowhere to be seen.

"Oh, well," Nancy said, "you can meet him some other time. Maybe he's just shy—like you," she added artfully.

Nancy and George went back to the table to find Bess and Gunther sitting with Ned and a few new acquaintances. Everyone was chattering about the various ski slopes, but Ned was unusually quiet.

Nancy put her hand over his. "Ankle bothering you?"

"It's fine," Ned said briefly.

Bess glanced from Nancy to Ned and back again. "If you guys are getting tired," she offered, "we can get a ride back to the lodge with somebody else."

There were immediate offers of rides from their new friends. "I don't want to drag Nancy away this early," Ned protested.

"I'd *like* to go. Really! We have things to talk about, anyway," Nancy said, thinking of Michael Price. "I'll go get the car and pick you up at the door."

"I think I can make it to the parking lot," Ned said with a laugh.

George shook her finger at Ned. "Look, super-jock, we all know you don't let sports injuries get you down. Just think of it as saving your ankle for the baseball season." She yawned. "I'm tired, too. I think I'll go home with you."

So Nancy didn't get a chance to discuss Michael with Ned as they drove home after all. But she definitely thought about him. How frustrating it was that he had disappeared before she'd gotten a chance to talk to him more.

He was my big chance to get information and clues, she told herself miserably as she lay in her bunk a little while later. And I let him slip away, trying to set him up with George. She looked over at her sleeping friend. Time to stop worrying about her and start solving this case.

Where did Michael fit in? Why had he been at the rope tow?

Nancy felt a chill in spite of the thick comforter on her bed. *Could* Michael be the midnight prowler?

Nancy closed her eyes. Nothing made sense. But it will before I'm through, she swore. I'll track Michael down. And I'll find out why he and Luke pretended not to know each other. I'll get the answers—before somebody else gets killed.

CHAPTER TEN

When Nancy woke up the next morning, George was already gone. "She had an early ski date with Luke," Bess said darkly. "I couldn't talk her out of it."

"We've got to get her to listen to us, and fast!" Nancy told Bess about her conversation with Michael Price, and Bess looked shocked. "Luke *could* have killed Michael's friend on purpose—but maybe he didn't," Nancy continued. "What matters is that his carelessness is causing dangerous accidents, so George's life could be on the line right this minute!"

"George is planning to help Luke give some of the ski lessons today," Bess told Nancy. "There are a lot of opportunities for accidents on the slopes, aren't there?" She rubbed her aching legs. "Well, I guess Gunther and I had better sign up for those classes," she said bravely. "That way I can watch Luke and keep my eye on things for you."

Nancy nodded. "This is creepy, though, Bess. Michael might give Luke the benefit of the doubt, but after what happened to Ned and me, I wouldn't call what's going on here just coincidences. Three accidents, one of them fatal—and Luke involved in all of them. He's *got* to be doing it on purpose."

Bess looked at Nancy, frowning. "But what's Luke's motive?"

"That's what I have to find out. Ned and I are going over to the hotel again today to look for Michael and to see if we hear anybody talking about Luke Ericsen. How long did Liz say he's been here? A few weeks? That's long enough for people to have started noticing anything odd."

As soon as breakfast was over, Nancy and Ned decided to head for the Overlook. But when Nancy turned the key in the ignition of her car, the engine wouldn't turn over.

"Maybe it's just too cold," Ned suggested.

"I don't know. It was colder last night than it is now, and the car was running fine then." Nancy tried the engine several more times but got no response.

"Want me to call a service station?" Ned asked.

Nancy shook her head. "Let me talk to Liz first."

When Nancy found Liz in the office and explained her predicament, Liz promptly took a key ring from a wall hook and tossed it to her. "Take Luke's old Jeep," she suggested. "He won't be using it until late this afternoon because of classes, and he leaves the keys here in case someone needs emergency transportation."

Nancy thanked Liz. "We'll take good care of it," she said. Then she and Ned were soon on their way.

At the Overlook, Nancy and Ned found the hotel's indoor swimming pool empty of swimmers, with no one around except a bored lifeguard. "We'll check the Jacuzzi out later," Nancy said with an enticing smile, "but right now, we've got work to do."

"How about this?" Ned suggested. "You check the hotel for Michael. I'll go spread my charm around the lobby and try to get the story on Luke. If he has such a bad reputation, then people should have something to say about him. We can meet in the coffee shop at noon."

"Okay," Nancy agreed. "Good luck."

Nancy started her search by asking for Michael at the front desk. He was registered, but the clerk wouldn't give Nancy his room number. She tried calling him on the house phone, but there was no answer. She checked the bar, the coffee shop, and the main dining room, all without success. Then she headed for the skating rink.

The rink, like the rest of the hotel, was plush. The roof was open to the icy sky, but walls of tinted glass held off the wind. There were lots of spectators, and Nancy guessed that many of the Overlook guests passed by just to watch.

She leaned against the rail and studied the skaters for a moment. With a start, she realized that one of them was Michael. An idea popped into her mind, and without a second thought, she rented a pair of skates herself.

Nancy laced them up, stepped onto the ice, and began a few warm-up tricks. She liked the music that was playing. It had a beautiful Latin beat to it. Gradually, Nancy added a few spins and easy jumps to her graceful movements.

Pretty soon a small group was watching Nancy and applauding. But all she saw was another skater at the far end of the rink—Michael Price.

As if feeling Nancy's eyes on him, Michael looked up. Then he bowed, his eyes glinting with mischief, and skated smoothly over to her.

"Shall we dance?" he inquired.

"Sure. How do you feel about talking after we skate?"

"What do you want to talk about?"

"Luke Ericsen."

"Okay," Michael said. "But I've already told you what I know about him."

Nancy had to admit that skating with Michael was great fun. He had a natural sense of grace and ease, and he knew a lot of tricks. But she was much more interested in getting some answers.

After a few minutes, she took Michael's hand and skated over to the railing. "So let's talk," she said.

"What do you want to know?" Michael asked.

"Well, for starters, why have you and Luke been pretending you don't know each other?"

Michael grimaced. "Quite frankly, after what happened with my friend, Luke and I can't stand the sight of each other. Neither one of us ever wants to see the other again, and I guess we both feel the less said, the better."

Nancy nodded. "Okay, I'll buy that. But there's something else. We've had a prowler around our lodge, a prowler who leaves some very frightening messages in the snow. . . . You wouldn't happen to know anything about that, would you?"

Michael coughed. "I—I don't know what you're talking about, Nancy."

There was a moment of awkward silence. Nancy could tell by the look in his eyes that Michael was lying. She understood why. Creeping around someone's yard in the middle of the night wasn't the kind of thing you'd want to own up to. What puzzled Nancy was why, if neither Luke nor Michael ever wanted to see each other again, Michael had gone to all the trouble of leaving that message. What did he hope to gain by it?

Nancy was beginning to get the feeling that Luke and Michael's history was just a bit more complicated than Michael was letting on.

Nancy saw Michael glance over her shoulder. "Speak of the devil," he said, "here's Luke now."

Luke marched up to the railing, his face grim. "You have some nerve helping yourself to my Jeep," he said tersely to Nancy. "It's meant for emergencies only. Coming over here doesn't count as one, so hand back the keys!"

"I don't have them," Nancy said hastily. "I left them with Ned. I think he's in the coffee shop."

"Fine. I'll get them. I do not want you driving the Jeep back to the lodge." Luke swung around.

"Just a minute," Michael called. An odd smile touched his mouth. "Luke—Ericsen, is it?"

Luke turned back and fixed his eyes on Michael. A peculiar expression was on his face. Hostile? Not exactly. It was more like . . . confusion, as if he were looking beyond Michael, seeing someone else.

Nancy felt confused as well. She had been certain that

Michael and Luke already knew each other, but they were acting like virtual strangers.

"We used to have a mutual friend," Michael continued. "Dieter Mueller. Remember him?"

Luke just stood there, unmoving; but slowly, in a delayed reaction, his eyes began to bulge and his face went white. Nancy decided he looked completely terrified, as if he were watching his own funeral.

Then, all at once, Luke was running as fast as he could away from the skating rink, away from Michael—or from his own past?

As Nancy watched Luke racing across the snow, she turned to Michael—and found that his face had paled, too.

"You came over here in his Jeep? The old, beat-up one with the ripped top I saw parked out back in the lot?" he asked.

Nancy nodded. "We didn't realize he'd mind."

"I'm glad you won't be going back in it," Michael said. "And I'd advise you to stay away from anything else belonging to that guy. You saw what happened when your boyfriend used his skis!"

"Michael," Nancy asked bluntly, "who was Dieter Mueller?" She had to be sure.

For a minute, silence hung between them. "Can't you guess?" Michael said finally. "He was my friend, the one who borrowed Luke's skis."

"Michael, I'm sorry," Nancy said comfortingly.

"Yeah. Me, too," Michael replied. "Hey, are those people over there friends of yours?"

Nancy turned to see Bess and Gunther waving to her from across the rink. She and Michael skated over. "Where's George?" Nancy asked.

Bess shrugged. "She told me to get lost, in so many words. She's probably waiting for Luke back at the lodge. Or working off some emotion on the ski jumps!" She shook her head. "They had a date to go for a ride. Luke absolutely hit the roof when he found the Jeep was gone!"

Michael frowned. "That sounds very dangerous."

"Oh, George knows what she's doing where *sports* are concerned!" Bess said, laughing. "I think she could be an Olympic contender if she wanted to. Sometimes, I actually think she's going to go for it—she keeps such a close eye on all the tryouts.

"Besides," she went on with a grin, "if there *is* any danger, she has the perfect bodyguard—Nancy Drew, the fabulous detective!"

Everybody laughed. But underneath the laughter Nancy felt a tenseness. The sensation lasted for only an instant. Almost immediately, Michael and Gunther were laughing at Bess's teasing. When Nancy looked at Michael, his eyes were warm with admiration. "I *thought* you were more than just a tourist! You're here on a case, aren't you?"

"No way!" Nancy exclaimed and laughed gaily. She managed to send Bess a warning glance as she went on smoothly. "I've ruined too many vacations that way."

Nancy glanced at her watch. It was just past noon. "Speaking of which, I'd better go find Ned. Now that I know where you're staying and you know where I am, let's keep in touch. Skating was fun. I'd really like to see you again."

Nancy's last comment was no lie. Michael was the only one around who seemed to know anything about her prime suspect. She *had* to see him again.

"You can bet you'll be seeing more of me," Michael said as Nancy stepped from the rink.

"He skates well," Gunther said, watching Michael glide across the ice as Nancy unlaced her skates and returned them. Then she, Bess, and Gunther headed for the coffee shop.

"What was going on out there?" Bess asked.

Nancy sighed. "I wish I knew. It was weird, though, that's for sure!" She turned to Bess and smiled wearily. "Listen, I'll have to explain all this another time. Right now, I think Ned and I need to be alone."

"Say no more," Bess replied promptly. "Gunther and I will make ourselves scarce."

"Thanks," Nancy said.

"Bye." Bess waved. "Take it easy."

Nancy found Ned drinking hot chocolate in a secluded booth in the back of the Overlook's coffee shop. "How are you doing?" he asked as she made her way toward him.

"I have definitely been better," Nancy said. She dropped into the seat across from him.

"Maybe we should forget this case," Ned said, a smile playing at the corners of his mouth, "and go on a ski vacation."

"That would be very funny if I weren't so upset," Nancy

replied. She signaled to the waitress to bring her a hot chocolate, too. "By the way, did Luke get those car keys from you?"

Ned looked up, surprised. "No. I haven't seen him."

"I guess after what Michael said to him he was too angry to come and find you." Nancy quickly related the story to Ned.

"Wow, that's bizarre." Ned's face was serious when Nancy had finished.

"And Luke obviously feels very guilty about the accident," Nancy added.

"Yeah," Ned replied. "Michael really pushed a button in him, bringing the whole thing up like that.

"Oh, well. Since Luke didn't catch up with us, I guess we can take the Jeep home," Ned went on. "It would have been a real pain to walk all the way back to the lodge on this ankle — and I mean that literally."

The waitress brought Nancy her cocoa and she began to sip it slowly. "So, did you find out anything about Luke?" she asked.

Ned drained the last of his hot chocolate. "Not much. He's new to this area, just arrived during the past couple of months. Two college girls who work here part-time were definitely interested in him, but he wasn't interested in them.

"You know," he added, "whether the guy's a creep or a crackpot or a menace to society, I think he really does care for George."

"I don't know whether that makes the situation better or worse," Nancy said darkly.

"Anyway, the opinion of the athletes around here is that

Luke's a very experienced skier. They say he's obviously had some serious racing training and that he's good enough to win medals in lower-ranked races—his bad leg would slow him down too much for the high-ranked ones. But he completely avoids all ski competitions, won't even watch them.

"Hey," Ned said suddenly, glancing out the coffee shop's large windows, "it looks like a storm is on the way. Maybe we ought to get going."

By the time Ned and Nancy had paid their bill and hurried out of the coffee shop, the sky was leaden, the air heavy and damp. Ned handed Nancy the keys to the Jeep, and she turned on the ignition. Soon they were speeding down the drive.

The approaching storm made the wrought-iron gates to the Overlook appear more ominous than glamorous. As the Jeep neared them, two enormous yellow snowplows came rumbling through, heading toward the hotel. Nancy had to jerk the Jeep to the right to avoid them.

"Close call," Ned commented.

"I know. I haven't got the hang of this thing yet."

They passed through the open gateway and out onto the mountain road. The wind whipped through the ripped canvas top. Wet snow began to drift down. "Hang on!" Ned shouted.

"*What?*" Nancy shouted back, her eyes intent upon the twisting road.

"I said—" The rest of Ned's words were lost in the roar of the wind.

Nancy shot a glance at him out of the corner of her eye.

Then the steering wheel gave a convulsive jerk in her hands, and she turned her attention strictly to her driving. They whizzed around a loop in the twisting road, and she brought her right boot down on the brake.

It did not respond.

Was the road slippery? Or was it something worse? With a burning sensation in her throat, Nancy pumped the brake pedal again, negotiating a sharp curve as she did so. The pedal offered no resistance, and the Jeep didn't slow down even a fraction.

The brakes were gone.

Nancy yanked at the gearshift, trying to put the Jeep into a lower gear, but she couldn't manage to do it.

Ned poked her sharply. "*Slow down!*" he yelled.

"*I'm trying to!*" Nancy shouted back. The Jeep kept gaining speed. "*I can't stop this thing!*"

They careened around another curve, and suddenly the road dropped off sharply into a deep gully on the right side. On the left rose a cliff face, a wall of rock.

"*Keep left!*" Ned yelled, gesturing wildly. "*Stay by the rock wall.*"

"I can't!" Nancy screamed. "*We'll be killed if there's a car coming toward us!*"

They roared around another bend, and the road disappeared into an impossibly tight hairpin turn. In front of them, the gully yawned, a bottomless empty space . . . and they were headed right for it!

"*Jump!*" Ned screamed. He tried to pull himself to his feet as the Jeep hurtled toward the gully beyond the curve.

In that instant, the one thought that leaped into Nancy's mind was of Ned's leg. It wasn't completely healed—he'd never make the jump. No way would she abandon him. She *had* to make that hairpin turn. Nancy gripped the steering wheel tightly and stuck to the road like glue.

Miraculously, she negotiated the turn. Then she scrutinized the road ahead for any possibility of escaping their situation. All at once, Nancy saw her chance!

The road, for a very short stretch, opened out a bit, climbing uphill. There were trees on either side. And a fallen trunk lay against the cliff face.

Nancy could do one thing, and one thing only. She could try to slow the Jeep and get it under control on that short uphill stretch, then use the tree trunk to stop it completely—before it slammed into the rock wall beyond.

Deliberately, Nancy yanked the wheel left and sent the Jeep heading straight toward the granite cliff.

CHAPTER ELEVEN

The jeep catapulted toward the granite face of the cliff. As it shot ahead, Nancy yanked at the steering wheel with both hands. But her arms weren't quite strong enough.

Then Ned's hands closed over Nancy's with such strength that they crushed her fingers. Together, in unspoken agreement, they forced the Jeep to do her bidding, but they came so close to the cliff that the side of the vehicle scraped against the granite with an ear-piercing shriek.

The Jeep sped up the hill, slowing almost imperceptibly. Then it screeched up onto the fallen tree trunk, recoiled, tipped over, and came to rest on its left side at the edge of the road.

Nancy became aware of Ned's voice almost sobbing out her name. She was trapped inside the overturned vehicle, but Ned had somehow pulled himself loose. He was kneeling over her, brushing back her hair.

Nancy struggled to get her hand free. She locked it tightly with his. For several seconds they stayed like that, motionless, Nancy inside the Jeep, Ned outside. Then Ned spoke hoarsely. "If you hadn't tried that, we both would have been killed—"

"Let's not think about it. Please." Nancy shut her eyes.

Ned's fingers tightened on hers, but he spoke with deliberate calm. "We can't stay here. It's a bad curve. If a car comes around it fast, we could be in trouble again. How badly are you hurt?"

Nancy fought back an insane impulse to giggle. "It seems to me I've been through this before, after the rope tow broke," she murmured. She flexed her arms and legs, one at a time. "I'm all right. I'll probably be a mass of bruises tomorrow, but I landed on snow and nothing's broken."

"Then hold my hands and see if you can wriggle out." Ned braced himself against the fallen tree trunk.

Carefully, cautiously, Nancy twisted one way, then the other. It was like trying to get a cork out of a bottle. Slowly and painfully, she emerged. When she was finally free, she and Ned fell into each other's arms.

"I'm afraid we'll have to walk to shelter," Ned said finally. "It's starting to grow dark, and the storm's getting worse. We can't stay on this road!" He thought for a second. "We must have come more than halfway. Our best bet is to head for Webb Cove."

"You can't walk on that ankle—"

"If you're going to suggest that I let you go alone," Ned interrupted, "don't bother. Don't even think it! If I thought I was going to be able to ski today, surely I can take a short walk." Ned retrieved his crutches from where they had fallen in the road and he and Nancy, both still dazed, started slowly toward the lodge.

All at once Nancy began to laugh. Ned looked at her in alarm. "What are you giggling about? Are you sure you didn't break something in that beautiful head of yours?"

Nancy shook her head. "I was just thinking—if Luke looked murderous before, think what his face will be like when he finds out what we've done to his precious Jeep!"

"I'm thinking," Ned said grimly, "but I'm not laughing."

"I know," Nancy commented. "This time he's *really* going to kill us!" As soon as the words were out of her mouth, Nancy wished she could take them back. They'd come out sounding much more sinister than she'd meant. "Hey, what do you think, Ned? Could this be one more of Luke's planned 'accidents'?"

Ned groaned. "I bet you're right. Brakes don't usually just fail like that."

"And Luke's the most obvious person, isn't he? I mean, he's always involved somehow—his skis, his Jeep, the rope tow he was supposed to take care of— Wait, I hear something," Nancy exclaimed excitedly.

Behind them a motor sounded faintly. It grew louder, and then headlights swept around the curve. Nancy and Ned jumped out of the road, then started waving madly at the driver. The car slowed to a stop.

"Don't tell me you two tried to *walk*," Michael's voice said. Then he added in a shocked tone, "Was that *your* wreck I just passed? What happened?"

Nancy shook her head. "Something went wrong with the brakes." She shuddered.

"How did you get the thing to stop?" Michael asked gently.

"Nancy ran it up on a fallen tree," Ned said proudly. "If it weren't for that, neither one of us would be alive."

Michael frowned. "I thought Luke was going to take the Jeep back from you."

"He never found Ned," Nancy explained. "I think when you mentioned Dieter Mueller, he just got too upset to worry about it." She waited curiously for Michael's reaction.

Michael gave a short, mirthless laugh. "This is exactly the kind of thing I tried to warn you about, Nancy."

Ned's eyes narrowed. "Suppose you spell it out."

"Carelessness with his equipment—or dangerous jokes. Especially to get even with people who annoy him. People who take his wheels without asking, for instance."

"Some joke," Ned said.

Hmm, Nancy thought, something funny is going on here. Michael didn't mention dangerous pranks before. . . .

"Maybe it wasn't a joke," Michael said. He turned to Nancy. "Your friend said you're a detective. How much digging around into Ericsen's past have you been doing?"

"All I know is what you've told me," Nancy said evasively. "I certainly didn't come to Webb Cove to find Luke, if that's what you're suggesting. I came to ski."

Michael looked sternly at Nancy for a moment. Then he broke into a charming grin. "What I really should suggest is that you two get out of this wind before the snow gets any worse. Come on. Hop in the car and I'll drive you to the lodge."

"Fantastic," Nancy said gratefully, pushing Luke's "accidents" and Michael's changing story about them to the back of her mind.

"Thanks," Ned added as they piled into the car.

By the time they reached Webb Cove, the blizzard had begun in earnest—with the promise of much, much more snow to come.

Lights glowed from every window of the lodge as they approached it, and two cars loaded with luggage, skis, and people were pulling out.

Ned stepped out of the car slowly, wincing as he put his weight on his bad ankle. "This is already beginning to swell up again," he said. "I'd better get off it." He leaned over and gave Nancy a kiss before hobbling inside.

Nancy eased herself out of the car. She had a lot of questions to ask Michael, but she didn't know how to put them into words. He was so nice and straightforward, yet she couldn't help but realize that there was something strange—and maybe a little ominous—about his relationship to Luke.

Michael got out of the car. "It's really beginning to come down, isn't it?" he said, flashing Nancy one of his heartwarming smiles and motioning to the whirling snow around them.

"Should mean good skiing," Nancy replied, grinning.

"Sure, when it stops in a few days and the sun comes out."

Nancy's grin vanished. "But until then, we'll probably be stuck here—snowed in. No one will be able to get in to us, and we won't be able to get out."

Nancy took a deep breath. "And the way you've been talking, it sounds like you think Luke is . . . dangerous. So before we get stuck in the lodge with him, I want you to stop hinting around about him and tell me straight."

"I have no proof, Nancy, but I'm worried," Michael said soberly. "Maybe you and your friends should get out of here before the storm closes down the roads. You saw those people leaving just now. They've got sense.

"People from out of state usually think being in Vermont during a blizzard will be great. But if the power lines go down and you have no electricity—which also means no ski lifts—it's just awful."

"It seems crazy to leave a ski area in the middle of a huge snowstorm," Nancy commented.

"Well, why don't you talk to the others about it?" Michael said.

"I will," Nancy told him. "And why don't you come in and wait for a break in the snow before you drive back to the Overlook?" Michael smiled and followed Nancy inside.

The lodge was warm and cheerful. A huge fire roared up the chimney in the lounge, and as they entered, George and Luke came through the back door carrying armloads of logs.

"About time you brought my Jeep back," Luke said curtly. He noticed Michael. Nancy saw him swallow hard, then make the difficult decision to ignore him totally.

Michael raised an eyebrow. "They didn't—"

Nancy brought her heel down on Michael's toe. "We didn't

mean to be so late," she finished smoothly. "Did we, Ned?"

Luke wasn't paying attention. He dropped his load of logs on the hearth and strode back out again without a word.

"George," Nancy said hastily, "this is the guy who rescued me when I fell, the one I wanted you to meet last night. Michael, meet George."

Michael came forward at once with his hand out, smiling. "I hear we have a lot in common! Bess says you're practically an Olympic skier. I'd be glad to show you some of the trickier runs around here."

"No, thank you," George replied coolly. Her face had taken on a closed, shuttered look that Nancy knew only too well.

"Hey, give him a chance, George," Ned said easily. "We all know Luke's monopolizing your time, but—"

George shrugged. She turned to Michael. "I apologize for what my *friends* have tried to rope you into, but Luke told me what you said this afternoon, and I just don't think we'd get along very well."

"Hey, now, wait a minute!" Michael said quickly. "First of all, I don't get pushed into doing things I don't want to do. Second, I never could turn my back on a beautiful woman in trouble." His voice changed from flirty to serious. "You are, you know."

Something in Michael's voice stopped George cold. "Are what?" she asked suspiciously.

"Both. Beautiful and in trouble."

George's face went tight. "I don't want to hear this. If you'll excuse me, I'm going to go help Luke. We want to get the pre-blizzard chores done. There's supposed to be a lull in the storm this evening, and we plan to go night skiing at Lookout Ledge." She turned on her heel.

But Nancy wasn't about to let her friend run off that easily. She stepped in front of her and took her by the shoulders. "You are going to listen to me whether you want to or not," she said. "There's been another 'accident,' this time in Luke's Jeep."

Quickly she described what had happened. Bess and Gunther arrived in the middle of her story and stood listening.

George's face went white. "Are you trying to tell me Luke's carelessness is responsible for almost killing you and Ned?"

"It might have been carelessness," Michael cut in. "It could have been planned. There have been too many 'accidents' around Luke lately."

George stared at Michael for a moment, her eyes beginning to blaze. "Apparently Nancy didn't tell you that I'm loyal to my friends," she said fiercely. "And I don't pay attention to people who are prejudiced against them. So why don't you just take yourself back to your fancy hotel, Mr. Price! You've done enough to poison things around here."

Michael gave Nancy a helpless shrug. "I tried," he said as he walked back out to his car.

George turned on the others, tears in her eyes. "I'm surprised at you, I really am! I thought you guys would have more faith in me."

Nancy felt frightened and helpless. George was determined

to stick by Luke no matter how many people suspected him. What Nancy needed, she decided, was concrete proof, or George would never give him up.

"George, listen," Nancy said as persuasively as possible. "Even if the guy is a saint—don't go skiing with him tonight, not with a storm coming. He might be a good skier, but he does have a bad leg."

"Oh, come on!" George was indignant. "Why, in the last Olympic trials—" She suddenly stopped dead, as if she'd just bitten into an apple and discovered a worm in it. Then she turned and bolted toward the door.

Nancy's mind was churning. George had mentioned the Olympic trials. Had Luke been in them? If he had, then there were sure to be newspaper articles about him—and maybe even about poor Dieter Mueller's death.

There have got to be copies of old ski magazines in the public library in town, Nancy told herself. They just might hold the key to the Luke Ericsen mystery. All of a sudden, Nancy felt sure that she would crack the case soon.

But the question was, could she do it before the blizzard trapped her and her friends in the lodge with her prime suspect?

CHAPTER TWELVE

Y ou've got an important decision to make," Liz said to Nancy, Ned, Bess, and Gunther as they sat in front of the fireplace. "The blizzard has started. We have plenty of supplies and our own generator, but you could get snowed in here, perhaps for days. Are you going to stay or leave? All the other guests have checked out."

"What do you think we should do?" Nancy asked.

Liz spread her hands. "I don't like the idea of being snowed in alone with the prowler on the loose. On the other hand, I don't want you to be marooned here, too, out of a sense of duty."

"You won't like what I've got to say," Ned said, his face serious. "But I think we should leave—for George's sake."

Nancy shook her head. "You don't really think George would come home with us now, do you? She'd insist on taking the bus home by herself at the end of the week, and staying here with Liz and Luke. We can't leave her."

Liz shook her head. "I feel sorry for that girl."

Nancy sucked in her breath. "Then you think Luke's guilty?"

Liz blushed. "Oh," she stammered, "I don't know. I—I guess

if I really thought so, I would have fired him already. No, I feel the way George does—I want proof."

"Against Luke?" Nancy asked.

"Yes! No . . . I mean, against whoever's guilty. It's the—the not knowing I can't stand," Liz told her. "Anyway," she rushed on, "I think you should talk to George about leaving. The storm isn't supposed to get really bad until tomorrow, so you've got the evening to figure out what you want to do."

Dinner that night was strange with only six people at the long table. Luke had decided to skip the meal. George picked at her food, looking angry and miserable and doing her best to avoid talking to the others. At last Nancy broached the subject of leaving Webb Cove early.

"Are you kidding?" George exclaimed. "Leave Vermont in the middle of this gorgeous snowstorm? Miss all the great ski conditions? No way!"

"But, George—" Nancy began.

"Oh, no," George cut in. "If you want to go, then go ahead. I'm staying no matter what you decide."

Nothing any of the others said could convince George to change her mind. When the conversation turned to other subjects, she just moped again. She perked up, however, when Luke came in later. He and George spent the evening playing cards and laughing together while the others watched TV.

"At least she's here with the rest of us, instead of out skiing in the dark with Luke!" Nancy whispered to Ned.

During the evening, the electricity flickered several times.

When it went out completely for a minute, Liz groaned. "That means the county power lines are in trouble. I'll have to go switch over to our generator."

Luke stood up promptly. "You stay put. George and I will do it." They pulled on their ski jackets and went out.

But they were gone fifteen, twenty, then thirty minutes. Nancy began to get worried. Murmuring an excuse, she sauntered toward the door. Ned followed. "You want to go find George?" he asked quietly.

"You know me too well," Nancy replied. "That's exactly what I want to do."

"My ankle's feeling better. Let's both go looking," Ned said promptly. They pulled on their jackets and, steeling themselves against the snow, plunged into the night.

Ned touched her shoulder. "Look." He pointed in the direction of the generator shed. A faint glow shone in the darkness.

Oblivious to the rapidly growing snowdrifts, Nancy and Ned hurried toward the shed. Ned wiped some snow from a lower pane, and Nancy raised herself on tiptoe to look in.

George and Luke were sitting facing each other on a wooden bench, polishing their skis and talking earnestly. Or rather, Luke was talking, and George was listening.

All at once, George leaned forward to kiss him tenderly. In the next second they were locked in each other's arms. Nancy and Ned turned and made their way back to the lodge in silence, feeling a little embarrassed at having spied on them.

Later that night, as Nancy lay in the dark trying to sleep,

she went over the strange collection of facts, rumors, and suspicions. They were like the pieces to a jigsaw puzzle. But somehow, when Nancy tried to put them all together, they just didn't fit. What was she missing?

Then Nancy had an odd thought. If Luke were the one causing all the 'accidents,' he'd done a great job of messing up his own belongings. Skis, a Jeep—they cost a lot of money. And he was making himself look awfully guilty. Would Luke really risk that just to get at Nancy and Ned?

Nancy stared into the darkness. The case seemed to revolve around Luke, but as possible killer—or intended victim? Had someone thought that Luke, not Nancy and Ned, would be using the Jeep and skis and rope tow? Then there was Liz. Nancy couldn't discount her suspicions about insurance money. And Liz seemed unnecessarily nervous at times.

Nancy shifted uncomfortably on the bed. Every time she looked at the case from a different angle, it came apart. If only she could get a line on Luke! At least she had another clue there—George's slip about the Olympic trials.

I've got to go to the library tomorrow, Nancy told herself, blizzard or no blizzard. If Luke was an Olympic hopeful, any scandal connected with him would show up in the ski magazines. That's where I'll find clues—I just have to!

By morning, the snow still hadn't stopped. Nancy decided to skip breakfast and go right to the library, before they got snowed in. She asked Liz if she could borrow her cross-country skis.

With her car out of commission and the roads dangerous and icy, and especially after the "accident" the day before, Nancy thought she would be safer just skiing the two and a half miles to town.

By the time Nancy reached the library, the sky was white with snow and the wind was fierce. The library was deserted except for a middle-aged librarian standing behind the check-out desk. She looked up, frowning, as Nancy entered. "We're closing early because of the storm."

"There's something I have to find. It's urgent!" Nancy gasped, out of breath from her trek. "But I'll be quick. How long will you be here?"

"I'd better leave in ten minutes." The woman glanced worriedly out the window. "Can I help you?"

"I need information on the last Winter Olympics trials," Nancy said. "Magazine articles about accidents or scandals connected with them or with any of the competitors."

The librarian stared at Nancy. "You call that urgent?" she asked.

Nancy nodded. She didn't care what the librarian thought. The woman disappeared into the back room and returned with several magazines. "You can't take these out. But you can have a few minutes to make copies, if you want." She pointed to the machine in a back corner.

Nancy ran rapidly through the tables of contents in the magazines. All covered the Olympics, and she put several aside to study later. Then she came to an issue of a skiing magazine with an article titled "Scandal on the Slopes."

Nancy began reading feverishly.

> *On the last night of the tryouts, the American bronze runner-up, Jon Berntsen, challenged a young German Olympic hopeful, Dieter Mueller, to a dangerous night race. It was a grudge match, fueled by an intense personal antipathy . . .*

Nancy's heart leaped when she saw Dieter Mueller's name. But who was Jon Berntsen?

Suddenly the librarian was standing right beside Nancy. Nancy flushed and closed the magazine quickly. She'd been caught reading when she should have just photocopied the story and left. "Here's another article," the librarian was saying. "If you're going to copy anything, please do it fast."

"Thanks. And could you please reserve these for me? My name's Nancy Drew." Nancy hurried over to the photocopying machine. As she copied the scandal article, her eyes scanned the other periodical the librarian had produced.

It, too, dealt with the Mueller accident.

> *. . . both lost—Dieter Mueller, his life, in a fatal fall, and Jon Berntsen, the chance to become an Olympic winner. Berntsen's crash left him with leg injuries and a concussion. When he came to,*

Berntsen claimed to have amnesia, and no memory of anything just prior to the race.

However, sympathy for the young athlete quickly turned to suspicion when Mueller's bindings showed evidence of tampering. Berntsen disappeared before he could be charged, which has been generally regarded as proof of his guilt. Mueller's cousin, Gerhardt Mueller, also a member of the German ski team, vowed to make Berntsen pay for what he had done.

The librarian was putting on her coat, and she looked impatient. "I'm ready to leave," she called.

Quickly Nancy copied the second article. As she picked up the copies, she noticed a photograph of the American ski team.

Berntsen. The name leaped out at her from the caption. Third from left, last row. Nancy looked intently, and her heart turned over.

It was a picture of Luke Ericsen!

CHAPTER THIRTEEN

Nancy didn't have time to study either the original magazine picture or the copy she'd made of it. The librarian was at her elbow, visibly annoyed. "Young lady, please. We must close now!"

"I'm coming!" Nancy said hastily. She thrust the photocopies inside her jacket and hurried to the door. "I'm really sorry to have kept you, but it *was* important."

The librarian sighed. "It's all right, but now I hope you'll get back to your hotel as fast as you can. *Tourists!*" she added under her breath as Nancy passed her.

The wind was howling and whipping the snow into the air. Stores and businesses were closed in anticipation of the storm as Nancy skied through the center of town, her mind whirling.

According to Michael, Luke had loaned Mueller some defective ski equipment, which had caused the accident. But the magazine article said something completely different, that Luke—or Jon Berntsen—had challenged Mueller to a dangerous nighttime race which had resulted in his death.

Why had Michael changed the story? And why hadn't he called Luke by his real name? Was he trying to help Luke keep his awful secret? He certainly didn't act as if he wanted to do him any favors.

But even with her new information, one thing didn't change. Luke most likely was still guilty of manslaughter, if not murder! Could he have heard Bess mentioning that Nancy was a detective? That would explain those "accidents"—he'd be trying to get rid of Nancy and Ned so they wouldn't find out about his past.

But what about the letters in the snow? They made no sense. Unless . . . Nancy caught her breath. One of the articles had mentioned Dieter Mueller's vengeful cousin. Maybe *he* was after Luke (or Jon Berntsen). Maybe *he* was responsible for everything that had been going on at Webb Cove.

Nancy thought hard. Who around Webb Cove could be Mueller's relative? Michael? He was involved in the case somehow, and he certainly didn't like Luke. But he wasn't German.

Wait a minute, Nancy told herself sharply. *Gunther* is German. And he was at the lodge when the prowler episodes began. It would have been the easiest thing in the world for him to sneak out of the lodge at night and leave the message in the snow or damage the rope tow and the skis.

Nancy's jumbled thoughts began to take shape. Gunther had plenty of skiing know-how, from his experience on the German alpine rescue team. And he'd been cozying up to Bess since the very beginning, possibly to keep Nancy from suspecting him. He'd definitely put himself in a position where he found out much of what Nancy did or discovered. Nancy hadn't been very candid with Gunther, but Bess undoubtedly had.

Oh, great! Nancy thought, aghast. Either way, one of my best friends ends up falling for a killer. The only saving grace is that if Gunther is a Mueller, he'd have no reason to attack anyone but Luke.

Unless someone else became a threat.

Nancy reached the edge of the town and began cutting through the fields. Her eyes scanned the snow carefully, watching for obstacles. At the same time, her mind raced.

Luke as the target of a killer made more sense than Luke as a killer himself. Unfortunately, the killer was very reckless, and didn't care who else got caught in the traps he set.

The thought that Ned could have met Dieter Mueller's fate sent a shudder through Nancy. She stopped and leaned against a tree for a minute before going on. She was very conscious of how alone and unprotected she was there in the woods, in semidarkness.

The snow was whirling wildly, but through it, Nancy could make out a crossroads not far ahead. She had reached the bottom of Webb Cove Road. The slope would be murder to climb. She glanced around. Suddenly, she caught sight of a figure in a red-and-blue ski jacket some distance behind her. Whoever it was apparently hadn't seen her yet.

Acting on instinct, Nancy pulled herself behind a large fir tree and crouched down. She waited, concealed by the woods and the snow, as the figure approached and passed. It was Luke, also on cross-country skis. When he was a few yards past her, she cautiously pulled herself upright and began to follow him.

Luke made no attempt to ski along the road. He was heading toward the lodge, but by a circuitous route, one that was easier than heading straight up the hill. Luke reached the crest of the last rise before the lodge and then disappeared behind the hill. Panting, Nancy reached the top a few moments later. She skied down the incline after Luke.

He was not heading for the lodge after all, she realized then, but toward the shed that housed Liz's electric generator. What's he up to? Nancy asked herself, frowning.

She decided on a bold move. Giving him just time enough to get inside but not, she hoped, time to lock the door, she skied straight to the building.

She was in luck. The door was not locked, and she pushed it open. Luke was bent over the generator, and as he felt the rush of cold air he straightened quickly. "What are *you* doing here?" he demanded.

"I was just about to ask you the same thing."

"I went to town to get parts for Liz's shortwave radio, if you must know," Luke said coldly. "It's not working right, and we'll need it if the telephone lines go down. And since there's a major blizzard in progress, it did occur to me to check the generator to make sure it's working properly! What were *you* sneaking around the woods for?"

"I went to the library to get some books to read," Nancy said primly.

Luke gave a harsh laugh. "Well, you can't read them here!

Go back to the lodge and curl up by the fire with your boyfriend. You'll get yourself in a lot less trouble that way!" He waited pointedly for her to leave, then followed, locking the shed door behind them. "And don't come back here."

Luke didn't accompany her in the direction of the lodge, but took off as soon as he had snapped on his skis. He went by a path Nancy had not noticed before. After giving him a few moments' head start, Nancy followed.

She kept her eyes glued to Luke. Where was he going in the middle of the storm, anyway? Nancy couldn't tell where the path was leading. But she did see something else.

Barely visible in the thickening blizzard was a rope strung across the trail at neck height. Anyone skiing quickly down that path would be caught right across the throat. Nancy watched in horror as Luke headed toward it. He was skiing swiftly into a death trap.

CHAPTER FOURTEEN

Look out!" Nancy screamed. *"Luke!"*

Luke reacted an instant too late. He carved a tight turn and tried to brake, but the rope caught him squarely across the forehead and he was thrown to the ground. At least he wasn't badly hurt. Immediately, he pulled himself up to a sitting position and groaned, rubbing his head.

"Are you all right?" Nancy called, skiing over and kneeling beside him. He nodded vaguely.

"Don't try to talk." Nancy pulled off his cap. She noticed that it was actually a blue-and-white ski mask with the lower part rolled into a cuff. "If you'd kept this pulled down over your face, you'd have made out better," Nancy said, looking at the broad rope burn Luke had received above the eyebrows.

"What hit me, anyway?" Luke muttered.

"There's a rope strung across the path. If you hadn't ducked, it would have caught you right across the throat." Nancy squinted down the path. "Where does this trail lead, anyway?"

"To Liz's storage shed. I needed to get some storm supplies."

"Who knew you were coming here?" Nancy demanded.

"I don't know. Nobody. Anybody." Luke pulled himself to

his feet. "Liz and I are the only ones who use this trail."

"Luke, who's trying to harm you?" Nancy asked gently. "Please tell me. I can help."

Luke turned and looked straight at her, his face deeply troubled. "There's only one way you can help. Clear out. All of you! Before the blizzard shuts you in."

"*All* of us? Including George?"

"Especially George! She's terrific, and I don't want her getting hurt." Abruptly, Luke turned and pushed off into the woods.

Nancy headed for the lodge, thinking hard. Now I know where Luke fits in—as prospective victim. And he knows who's trying to kill him, she decided, but he's been trying to keep me from finding out because then he'd have to tell me the whole story. Luke doesn't want anyone to know he's Berntsen, because Dieter Mueller's suspicious death is still hanging over his head!

That was the only logical explanation for the way Luke had been acting—and the way George had been acting, too. George must have recognized Luke as Jon Berntsen from all the Olympic coverage she'd watched on TV. It was just like George to protect and defend him, if she believed he'd been accused unjustly of Dieter Mueller's death.

But someone else at Webb Cove didn't believe that accusation was unjust. That person could be Dieter Mueller's good friend Michael Price. Or he could be a relative of Dieter Mueller—Gunther?

When Nancy reached the lodge she leaned her skis against

the porch wall and hurried into the lounge without even taking off her jacket. Everything in the lodge seemed incongruously calm. A fire burned as always, Ned and George were playing Monopoly, and Gunther and Bess were snuggling by the fire. They all turned and looked at Nancy as she entered.

"You look like you've seen a ghost, Nancy," Bess said, giggling at her snow-covered friend. "In fact, you look like a ghost yourself!"

"We almost *did* have a ghost," Nancy said bluntly. "Luke almost got killed."

George gasped and immediately started for the door.

"Sit down!" Nancy said firmly. "He's all right, and he's gone off somewhere. Besides, for your own protection, he doesn't want you with him." She turned to Ned. "We need to talk. Alone. Now."

"But what happened to Luke?" George cried.

"I'll tell you the whole story later," Nancy replied, taking Ned's hand and leading him toward the kitchen.

Nancy pulled up two chairs and, in a low voice, told him about her morning and her suspicion about Gunther.

"Here." Nancy pulled the two articles out of her jacket. "Read these."

"Luke's Berntsen, all right," Ned said when he'd finished reading and had examined the picture. "If Gunther *is* out to get him, I don't want George caught in the cross fire."

"Me neither," Nancy said. "But we can't get George to leave."

"Look," Ned said, "I'll try to convince her to go. Maybe she'll listen to me."

"It's worth a try," Nancy said.

They went back to the lounge and found that Gunther was gone. I hope Luke's keeping his eyes open for trouble, Nancy thought anxiously, but there was nothing she could do to help him.

Ned immediately took George off alone. When they came back, she said to the others, "You guys go pack. I," she added defiantly, "am going to tell Luke we're leaving, even if I have to ski this whole mountain range to do it."

Nancy and Bess headed for the bunk room and started throwing their clothes quickly into their bags. We'll head straight for the police, Nancy thought. I bet we can wrap up the case in no time flat.

"It's too bad we're leaving early," Bess said, "but I won't mind so much if Gunther decides to come with us."

Nancy looked at her friend sympathetically. "I don't know how to tell you this, Bess," she said, "but I don't think he will." She gave a rapid summary of her suspicions about Gunther. "If he's the one who's after Luke, I'm sure he'll stay for the storm and try to finish him off. And if that's so, I just hope we can get the police out here before that happens."

Bess's face was flushed. "Gunther isn't out to kill Luke," she said steadily. "I *know* him."

"We've all been fooled by people who seemed nice," Nancy said.

Bess frowned at her. "Think what you want, but you'll find out you're wrong. Anyway, the thing that matters most is getting out of here. After all, somebody around here is a potential killer, and I don't want to be around if and when he succeeds. Come on, let's finish packing. I'll get George's stuff for her."

Within an hour they were loading Nancy's car. Ned got the battery recharged, so there were no start-up problems. The power lines were down and Liz was using candles, firewood, and the generator out back to run the lodge. Gunther, as Nancy had predicted, had decided to stay on. George was close-mouthed and somber, standing mournfully beside Luke.

The snow was coming down much harder. The lodge looked like something from a dark fairy tale, with lights burning only in the windows of the lounge. For a moment, that picture crystallized in Nancy's mind—the dark lodge; Luke deeply anxious and frightened; George, also frightened but defiant; Liz trying to be strong.

Then the image was broken by a voice calling cheerfully, "Hey, there."

It was Michael Price on cross-country skis, coming from the direction of the Overlook and carrying a loaded backpack. "Where are you people going?" he asked.

"Someplace safe," Luke replied stiffly. "Why are you here?"

Michael stared at Luke for a moment with a decidedly unfriendly air. Then he turned to Nancy. "I'm sorry you waited so long to leave. There's no point in trying to get out now. I heard at the hotel that the fallen power lines have blocked the roads to the highway. That's why I'm here—I brought you some supplies." He pointed to his backpack.

"We have enough, but thanks for the thought," Liz said quietly. "Why don't you all come back in?"

Michael set his backpack on the porch and helped Luke unload the luggage from the car. Suddenly Luke turned angrily away.

"I'm going to ski over to the hotel to see if I can get a two-way radio from somebody there," he said. "Ours is out of commission. I can't get it to work at all."

"Wait, Luke. I'll go with you," George cried.

Luke turned, a gentle smile lighting his face as he looked at George. "No," he told her. "You stay here for now. But I'll meet you up at Lookout Ledge at nine o'clock, okay?" He turned to Michael. "I hope you're gone by the time I get back." With that, he stalked away.

"There's that temper," Michael said to Nancy, shaking his head. "See what I mean?"

But George overheard the comment. "If Luke's furious, you made him that way," she snapped.

"Now, wait a minute—"

"No! You wait! I know exactly what you're up to, and I think you're disgusting! You're deliberately loading a guilt trip on him—" George broke off, her eyes blazing, and stormed into the lodge.

"What did I do?" Michael asked.

"You set that up," Nancy answered absently. But her mind was on other things. In a way, she decided, she was glad they were staying on at the lodge. Now she would have to solve the mystery herself.

The rest of the time before dinner passed uncomfortably. Bess remembered that she had a small pocket radio somewhere in her luggage, and she dug it out. It produced mostly static, but provided a much-needed distraction.

Gunther asked her to dance to some barely audible rock music. From a news bulletin on the radio, they heard that, although the snow had stopped momentarily, the worst of the blizzard was yet to hit.

At last Liz brought in a huge pot of stew and set it on the table. "Dinner!" she announced.

Bess left to get George but came back to report that George wasn't eating.

"Oh, yes, she is," Liz said grimly. "I'm sick and tired of all the emotional carrying on around here!" She stalked off in the direction of the dorm and reappeared with an angry-looking George in tow.

"I'd better beat the second onslaught of the storm," Michael said. "Wish I could stay for dinner, but I don't think it's such a great idea."

"Thanks for the provisions. I hope you get home safely," Liz said.

The others, except for George, said good-bye, and then they all sat down to dinner. They were just finishing when the old wall clock began chiming the half-hour—eight-thirty.

George rose from the table and strode to the door. "I'm going to meet Luke at the ledge," she said, as if daring her friends to try to stop her. She quickly put on her outdoor clothes, then stepped out into the storm.

Nancy stood up. "I'm going to follow her."

Ned rose too. "I'll go with you."

"What about your ankle?" Nancy asked.

"It'll hold me. If you're going, I'm going."

"Okay. Bess and Gunther, you stay here," Nancy said. The last thing she needed was Gunther out at Lookout Ledge with Luke in the darkness. "Liz," she continued, "we'll need directions to the ledge."

"No problem," Liz said.

A few minutes later, Ned and Nancy were pulling on their heavy outdoor clothing. Once outside, they stepped into cross-country skis. Nancy stood for a moment, looking out into the dark forest. How still the night seemed. Every sound was strangely muffled by the falling snow.

Nancy shuddered. Somewhere in the silent night a killer lurked.

Ned reached out and squeezed Nancy's hand.

"I'm so glad you came," she whispered.

"I would never have let you go out on this one alone," Ned said. He kissed her softly, and they started off toward the ledge, searching the hillsides for some sign of George or Luke.

But when Nancy and Ned reached the ledge, there was no sign of them. "Where are they?" Nancy asked anxiously. She glanced at her watch. "It's ten after nine."

"Maybe they've already met and have gone off together," suggested Ned.

"Could be," Nancy replied. "With this snow coming down, there's no way to tell whether there were tracks here ten minutes ago. Or else—" Nancy's words were cut off by a scream. "It's George!" she cried.

Nancy and Ned stood silently, listening. It was hard to tell which direction the scream had come from. The snow muffled and distorted all sounds.

Ned gripped Nancy's arm. "I could swear it came from right over there, through that clump of trees," he whispered.

Then it came again, a loud, desperate scream, and the sounds of a struggle.

Nancy pushed off, skiing with all her strength and speed. Ned was right behind her. They burst into a clearing and jerked to a stop, horror-struck.

On a narrow ledge, two figures were locked in a death struggle. George had been forced into a kneeling position on the cliff edge. Her back was arched and her hands scrabbled desperately to pull a masked figure's hands from around her throat. But that blue-and-white ski mask was distinctive—it was Luke Ericsen's.

CHAPTER FIFTEEN

George struggled with all her might, but the attacker—Luke?—was too strong. Luckily, at that moment, Ned shot forward. He grabbed Luke's arms from behind, wrestling him backward. At the same time, Nancy flung herself across George's legs and hung on. They were so near the edge of the cliff that one false move could send them over.

In the split second that Luke was thrown off-guard, George's hands grabbed his wrists and jerked them up and out. His hold broke and George fell backward, saved from the cliff edge only by Nancy's grip.

Ned battled Luke, throwing a punch into his masked face that rocked him back on his skis. Luke snatched up his ski pole and sent it whistling toward Ned's head, but Ned blocked it, moving in for another punch. Suddenly, Luke kicked out viciously, his ski slamming into Ned's injured ankle. As Ned fell, he tried to tackle Luke.

Nancy looked up just in time to see Luke deftly sidestep Ned, then sweep up his other ski pole. Pushing off with his right leg, then his left, he vanished from sight around a curve in the path.

For a moment everyone remained frozen with shock. Then Ned scrambled to his feet and started after Luke.

"*Not now!*" Nancy shouted. "We can get him later." George needed them more. She was gasping for breath and sobbing as Nancy held her in a warm hug. There were bruises across her throat, and her hat and scarf were gone, pulled off in the struggle. And Luke never even lost his ski mask, Nancy thought with anger.

"Don't try to talk," she murmured as George struggled to make herself understood. "Does anything feel as if it's been torn or broken?" George shook her head. Clearly she was hurt, but it didn't seem as if anything serious was wrong.

"What happened?" Ned asked.

"I don't know," George whispered.

Nancy and Ned exchanged glances. They had never seen George so shaken before. It was going to be a while before she could begin to explain anything. "It's all right . . . it's all right," Nancy soothed her. "You're safe now." She only hoped she sounded more convinced of that than she felt. They had scared Luke off, but there was no knowing what he would do next.

What mattered was getting George back to the lodge. "Can you walk?" Ned asked.

George nodded and started to pull herself to a standing position. Then her eyes, staring past the others, grew wide with fear. Nancy and Ned turned in the direction of her gaze.

A figure on skis had come soundlessly around the curve—a figure in a too familiar red-and-blue ski jacket and a ski mask rolled up into a cap. Luke had come back. He stopped short, looking at them blankly.

"What's going on?" Luke's face changed as George turned away from him, and he caught sight of her bruised neck. "*George, are you hurt?*" He started forward. George shrank away with a cry and Ned shot forward to fend Luke off.

"That's a strange question," Nancy said, just barely controlling her fury.

Luke's eyes snapped from one figure to another. "What's happened? George, why didn't you show up at the hotel?"

Nancy stared at Luke. "What do you mean, at the hotel? You told her to meet you at Lookout Ledge. We all heard you!"

"Yes, but when I was at the h-hotel t-trying to borrow a short-wave radio," Luke stammered, "the clerk said she had a message for me. She said George Fayne had called to say I should meet her at the hotel."

He turned to George. "I waited and waited. Finally I got worried and came looking for you. Now, will somebody *please* tell me what's happened?"

"You creep!" Ned burst out. "You *know* what happened. You just tried to strangle George and throw her over the ledge!"

Luke's jaw dropped. "How can you say that?" he cried. "I wasn't here! It wasn't me! And I swear, I'll kill whoever tried to hurt you!"

He reached out and touched her gently. George jerked away, trembling violently.

Nancy studied Luke's strained face. If Luke was acting, he

was doing it very well. She turned to George. "Did you ever see your attacker's face? Was he wearing the ski mask the whole time?"

George shivered. "I—can't remember."

"George, it wasn't me!" Luke cried. He gave her an aching look. She didn't answer, and he turned to Nancy. "Is she hurt? We've got to get her back to the lodge."

"We'll take care of that," Ned said tightly. "You get lost."

"Tell me one thing. The attacker—which way did he go?" Ned jerked his head down the trail. Luke gave George one last troubled glance and then, without a word, skied off in the direction Ned had indicated.

Nancy watched him, noticing again that he skied with most of his weight on his good left leg, dragging his right one a bit. Suddenly, it hit her. How could this be the same man who'd hurried away moments before? With his injured right leg, Luke would never have been able to push off the way the other had.

But who else could it have been? The mysterious man had worn the same mask and the same jacket as Luke. Nancy didn't know the answer to her question, but she knew that she'd have to wait until later to figure it out. They had to get George back to the lodge.

"George, let's go home," Nancy said gently.

Back at the lodge, Nancy and Bess helped George into bed. Then Nancy locked the door and said, kindly but firmly, "Okay, George, now talk. You know you need to, and it's important."

"I . . . I just don't know what to say!" Tears welled in George's eyes. "I met Luke where we were supposed to. He didn't say anything, just motioned for me to follow him. It was like . . . like he wanted to show me someplace really special. I was really happy, you know? And then—then we got to that ledge—" She broke off, sobbing.

"What did he do?" Nancy asked calmly.

"He just came after me, and grabbed me."

"Like somebody straight out of one of those cheap horror movies!" Bess exclaimed. "Why on earth would Luke do that to George?"

"It wasn't Luke. I could tell from the way he skied," Nancy said abruptly, searching George's face for a reaction. Even though she thought Luke had betrayed her, George was still holding back information.

Nancy took hold of George's hands. "It wasn't Luke," she repeated more gently. "Or should I say, it wasn't Jon Berntsen?"

George gasped. "How long have you known?"

"Just since this morning."

George drew in a ragged breath. "And I thought I was being so smart, hiding the *Sports Illustrated* issues that told about the scandal. I guess Liz never read them, or she'd have known, too."

Maybe she did read them, Nancy thought.

"Will somebody," Bess asked plaintively, "please tell me what's going on? Who's Jon Berntsen?"

Nancy explained the scandal to her. Bess's eyes grew very dark. "Then Luke *is* a killer."

"No, he's not!" George cried passionately. She gripped Nancy's hands. "Luke didn't kill Dieter Mueller! I know he didn't. No one has treated him fairly."

"George, has Luke admitted to you that he's Berntsen?" Nancy asked.

George nodded. "But I'd already guessed. His face was familiar—and then when I saw his skiing style, I knew for sure."

"Does *he* say he was responsible for Dieter Mueller's death?" Nancy probed.

"He's sure he wasn't. At least, he *says* he's sure. But he can't remember anything that happened right before and right after the race."

Nancy could see the pain and exhaustion in George's eyes. "Don't think about it now. Things will look better in the morning," she said soothingly.

She sat holding her friend's hand until George fell asleep. When her breathing had settled into a steady rhythm, Nancy slipped away from the bed.

All she wanted was a nice, long shower to wash the day's terrible events away.

But Bess had other things on her mind. "Nancy, I've got to talk to you," she whispered urgently.

Nancy realized that Bess had looked troubled ever since she and Ned had brought George back.

"It's about Gunther," Bess said shakily. "I—I don't know how to say this, and I didn't want to say anything in front of George because she's so upset, but . . . well, it's just that as soon as you and Ned went out to find George, Gunther left, too. He didn't say where he was going, but I saw him putting on his cross-country skis."

Nancy gasped. "If he skied really fast—and we know he can— then he could have gotten to George before we did and . . ."

Bess let out a little cry. "Nancy, what are we going to do?"

Nancy wrapped her arms around Bess. "We can't let on that we know," she told her, "not until we have proof that we can take to the police—and until we're no longer stranded with him!"

"I don't think I can do that," Bess said in a small voice.

"You have to," Nancy told her earnestly, "no matter what it takes. Now I'm going to tell Liz and Ned what we know about Luke. Then I hope we can sleep. We're going to need a lot of rest if we're going to make it through tomorrow alive."

By morning, conditions at the lodge had worsened. The girls awoke to bitter cold. When they entered the lounge, they found Ned and Gunther helping Liz cook breakfast in the fireplace.

"Bad news," she announced. "The generator's failed—and it looks like someone may have tampered with it. We've got no lights, no stove, no heat, and no running water. Luke's already skiing to the Overlook to get help."

Suddenly there was a startlingly loud pounding at the door. "That can't be Luke back already," Liz said as she went to open it.

Michael stamped in, bundled up against the storm. "I skied over from my hotel to see how you're doing. When I saw that there weren't any lights on, I got worried."

"Somebody sabotaged the generator," Ned said grimly.

Michael stared at him. "You're kidding!" Then he added, "You realize it must have been Luke who did it."

Suddenly Nancy had an idea. "You should see the stories I found at the library about the last Winter Olympics trials," she said. "They were all about Jon Berntsen and Dieter Mueller."

"Dieter Mueller!" Gunther exclaimed. "What does he have to do with all this?"

"Did you know him?" Nancy demanded.

Gunther nodded. "We were on the same junior racing team when we were quite young. What happened to him was tragic—but, of course, he shouldn't have taken a wild dare like that in the first place. I don't know Jon Berntsen, though."

"Do you know either of them?" Nancy continued, turning to Michael.

Michael's eyes were guarded, and he looked at Nancy strangely. "You know . . ."

Then George exploded into a torrent of words. "Oh, we know all right! You know who he is! You've been baiting him, poisoning people's minds, implying horrible things. . . . Luke wouldn't be in the mess he's in right now if it weren't for you."

But Liz cut her off. She was listening to something outside the window. "That's funny," she said, "I hear thunder on the mountain. That usually doesn't happen during a snowstorm."

A moment later, the sound came again. The lodge shook with vibrations, and a coffee cup fell off the table. "That's not thunder!" Liz exclaimed.

Everyone threw on ski jackets and hurried outside. About a mile down the road, a cascade of snow was tumbling down the mountainside, gathering a frightening amount of force with each second.

George gasped, ashen-faced. "An avalanche! And it's right on the trail Luke's taken!"

CHAPTER SIXTEEN

Snow rolled down the mountain as the lodge shook from the rumbling of the avalanche. The whole world appeared to be tumbling down the slope.

George grabbed frantically for her jacket and cross-country skis, and Nancy, Ned, Liz, and Gunther did likewise. "If Luke's trapped, we have to get to him as fast as we can," Liz said. "You can breathe for only so long under six feet of snow."

She looked at Bess. "You don't ski well enough, so just take care of things back here." Her face was serious. "We'd better be careful. There's no way of knowing how much more snow will fall. We could get trapped ourselves."

"That's one risk we'll just have to take," George said fiercely.

Then Michael spoke up quietly. "Maybe we shouldn't rush out there like this." He looked around at the others' stunned faces. "Are you sure you want to risk your lives to save a murderer who's already done his best to kill again?"

"*I'm sure!*" George cried. "And he's not a killer!"

"Whether he is or not, we can't abandon him under an avalanche. Now, let's get going!" Nancy said, and grabbed her ski poles and started after Liz.

"Be careful!" Bess called.

Nancy, Ned, Liz, Michael, and Gunther fought their way forward, the snow stinging their faces. "Are you sure Luke would have gone this way?" Nancy shouted to Liz.

"Absolutely! It's the fastest trail."

They searched for some sign of Luke, but the snow had already covered any tracks. Tears were freezing on George's face. Ned forged doggedly along beside Nancy. If his ankle hurt, he was not letting it hold him back.

Just when it seemed as if they were going to fight through the storm forever, Liz skied around a curve, and Nancy heard her cry out.

They shot ahead to find her staring at an immense pile of snow—the avalanche. "Spread out!" Liz ordered, "and keep your eyes peeled!"

Silently, they obeyed, although the sky was almost as dark as it was at twilight. Michael, ignoring Liz's instructions, skied ahead and then doubled back.

"I've been all the way to the other side of the avalanche, and I didn't see a thing. We might as well give up. I think I heard more rumbling."

But at that moment, George let out a yelp. She tore past Michael and fell to the ground, clawing frantically at the snow. As Nancy rushed to join her, she saw the tip of a ski protruding from the snow. "That must be him!" she cried, dropping down at George's side.

Feverishly, they all dug around the ski until Luke's leg

appeared, then his torso, and then his whole body. He was icy cold, and a dark trickle of frozen blood came from his nose. George ripped Luke's ski jacket open and pressed her ear against his chest. "He's breathing. Barely," she said hoarsely. "We have to get him back to the lodge, and fast!"

The trip back was ominously slow as they took turns supporting Luke's limp weight on a makeshift stretcher made of coats and ski poles. With what felt like a hundred stops and starts, they reached Webb Cove Lodge.

Bess had the fire roaring. They carried Luke in and laid him on a couch in front of it. George stayed by his side, chafing his hands. "All we can do is keep him warm," she finally said, a tremor in her voice. She swallowed hard and hid her face in her hands.

The others had seen Luke's twisted leg and the blood on his face, and knew what she wasn't saying. He could have broken bones, or worse.

"We can't just sit here and wait!" Nancy said fiercely. She jumped up. "I'm going for help."

"Not alone!" Ned said immediately.

"Two people should go," Michael suggested. "George should stay here with Luke. So how about you and me, Nancy?"

"Wait," Ned and Gunther both said at once. "I should go, too," Ned insisted.

"Not with your ankle," Nancy told him.

"What about me?" Gunther said.

Nancy thought for a moment. On the one hand, it might be

better to get Gunther as far away from Luke as possible. On the other hand, Gunther didn't know the area as well as Michael. If he got them lost, Luke was as good as dead.

"I think you should stay here, too," Nancy said. "If Michael and I aren't back in an hour, you and Liz can set out as a backup rescue team."

"We should head for the Overlook," Michael said. "The power's on there, and they can call for help. If we cut through the tall trees, we'll get some protection in case there's another avalanche."

Nancy and Michael stepped outside and snapped on their cross-country skis. They set off through the howling wind, Michael in the lead. He skied rapidly, so Nancy had to work hard to keep up with him. After fifteen minutes, Michael halted and turned to look at her. "How are you doing?" he called, smiling.

Nancy drew to a stop beside him. "All right."

"Just all right?" There was a teasing, admiring note in his voice. Michael's mood, considering the circumstances, seemed a bit too happy.

"What are you smiling about?" Nancy asked.

Michael laughed. "Oh, come on! The two of us alone together, speeding through the storm on a dangerous mission. What more could anyone want?"

"Maybe to have a friend survive," Nancy answered grimly.

Michael frowned. "Luke Ericsen, or whatever he says his name is, brought his fate on himself."

"If you mean Berntsen, say so."

"Funny your catching on to that." Michael pushed off expertly and skied quickly down a small slope.

Nancy caught up with him and stopped him. "I didn't have to catch on. He admitted everything to George."

"So his memory's coming back, is it?"

"How did you know he lost his memory?" Nancy asked, a chill running up her spine.

Instead of answering, Michael skied away, intent on reaching the top of the next rise. At its crest he balanced lightly and turned to wait for Nancy. "Look," he said as she joined him, sounding annoyed. "Just because we're being angels of mercy for the guy, do we have to talk about him? It's ruining the whole trip."

Nancy stared at Michael in disbelief. "You're really enjoying this, aren't you?" she asked incredulously.

"I always enjoy danger!" A glint of excitement danced in his eyes again. "Admit it, that's what real living is all about. Taking risks. Only the weak accept defeat!"

Nancy shuddered. What was going on with Michael? He was acting very strange, and she was scared to find out why. She dug her poles into the snow and, pushing off in a burst of speed, flew past Michael down the slope.

Immediately, Michael was after her. "Nancy!" he called. "You're not being logical. Luke tried to kill George! If he dies from the avalanche, it would spare everyone—including the two of them—the pain of a trial."

Nancy stopped suddenly. "How did you know what happened to George last night?" she asked.

"Liz told me." Michael sounded so cool, so honest.

But Nancy was afraid.

"I'll lead the way," Michael said. "We're getting to a dangerous part of the trail."

As they skied on, Nancy realized that they were headed in the same direction that she and Ned had taken the night before in search of George. Finally, she recognized the spot on Lookout Ledge where George and her masked attacker had struggled.

"Isn't there an easier way to go?" Nancy shouted.

"This is fastest," Michael shouted back. "It's risky, but we're both good skiers. We'll make it."

Nancy paused, eyeing the ledge uneasily.

Michael laughed. "You go first," he suggested. "Then I'll be able to help if you have trouble."

Cautiously, Nancy eased herself onto the narrow ledge. As she rounded a curve, a chunk of the ledge broke off beneath the tip of her ski and tumbled downward. She gasped and leaned back, her heart pounding. There was no choice but to go on, though. She pushed off again.

Nancy felt as if she'd skied Mount Everest when she finally got to the bottom of the slope. Turning to watch Michael flying gracefully down the path along the cliff face, Nancy was amazed at how easy he made it look. He passed her, stopped, and pushed off again. First his right leg, then his left, expertly zipping around a tree.

Suddenly Nancy froze. She'd seen that same fabulous technique before—when the masked stranger had escaped after the murderous attack on George.

As if he felt her eyes boring into him, Michael's perfect style wavered. Not much, but just enough to make him misjudge an overhanging branch in the gloomy light of the storm. He crashed into it and went sprawling.

As he climbed to his feet, muttering exasperatedly, a small black object fell out of his pocket. Not noticing, he brushed himself off and skied on.

Nancy skied over and picked it up. It was a little black box, a remote control device of the sort used in TV shows about spies and cops . . . *and bombs*.

Suddenly Nancy's breath caught in her throat. I've been so stupid, she chided herself. Michael's been right in front of my nose, and I've completely missed seeing the truth. *He's* the killer. And now I'm stuck alone with him, in a forest, in the middle of a blizzard.

CHAPTER SEVENTEEN

The edges of the little black box cut into Nancy's hand as she clutched it. A bomb control. Michael probably hadn't set a big bomb, just one large enough to cause a few tremors on the snow-covered mountain. Enough to send down an avalanche to bury Luke Ericsen (and Jon Berntsen) without a trace. Nancy thrust the box into her pocket and set off after Michael.

Michael was the prowler, the one setting the death traps around Webb Cove, the masked attacker who'd almost killed George.

The case ran through Nancy's mind. Everything was becoming crystal clear. Michael had been lying all along, and poor Luke had had to take the rap for him.

Nancy wasn't sure why Michael was determined to kill Luke, but she knew it must have to do with Dieter Mueller's death. Was he bent on revenge for his dead friend, as she had suspected earlier?

Nancy had the feeling it was much more sinister than that. Clearly, Michael had set the first few traps—the broken rope tow, the loose bindings, the Jeep crash—for Luke. He'd probably written the word MURDERER in the snow to scare Luke and to shake him up.

But then he'd turned on George, deliberately disguising himself as Luke and trying to strangle her. There could be just one reason—because she knew who Luke really was, and she realized that *Michael* was to blame for the "accidents." And if Michael realized that Nancy had figured that out, too, he'd turn on her next.

However, he'd then have to get rid of a whole lot of people—everyone who knew that Luke was Jon Berntsen—everyone at Webb Cove.

All at once, Nancy was terrified for her friends back at the lodge. Had Michael planned for something to happen to them after he'd left Webb Cove? She shivered.

Nancy's thoughts raced through her mind as she herself raced along on Michael's trail. She must not, *must not*, let him guess what she knew. Nancy kept on skiing expertly while one thought filled her mind. How was she going to get away from Michael Price? Her friends' lives—and her own—depended on it.

Nancy peered ahead. Oddly, nothing looked familiar. At last, mercifully, the trail widened for several yards. With a burst of speed, Nancy shot past Michael. She had to reach the hotel ahead of him! Desperately, using all her will, concentration, and skill, she skied as she'd never skied before.

But as good as Nancy was, Michael was better. He swooped after her. Nancy streaked through the storm, only too aware that Michael was right on her tail . . . and gaining.

The trail narrowed, corkscrewing into a curve. Nancy poled

around it—and a hideous realization struck her. Among all the little hills between Webb Cove and the Overlook Hotel, she had lost her way. But Michael hadn't. Using a circular route, he'd lured her back to Lookout Ledge, where an accident would be *so* plausible.

With a chill, Nancy imagined it all. Michael would reach the Overlook, distraught, claiming that Nancy had had a fatal accident.

There was no way for her to escape. She was at the edge of a precipice, with Michael blocking her path. He stood there smiling, slowly removing his ski goggles as if he had all the time in the world. "You passed the turnoff about a quarter of a mile back. Not surprising in this weather, but too bad."

For a moment their eyes met, and everything was very still.

"Why did you do it?" Nancy asked quietly.

Michael's eyes changed, as if he couldn't believe her stupidity. "For a gold medal, of course," he sneered. "I deserved to be on the U.S. ski team more than Berntsen did! But at least I was a runner-up. If he got hurt, or died . . . Then I heard him in the Broken Leg Café, challenging Dieter Mueller to that stupid night race. There was my chance."

Nancy never took her eyes off Michael's. "You mean *you* were trying to kill *Jon*? Then why did you rig Dieter's skis?"

Michael shrugged. "They were a similar model. It was dark, and I made a mistake. I watched the whole 'accident' from behind a tree on the slope. I didn't realize I'd rigged the wrong skis until I saw Dieter go down instead of Jon.

"But it turned out not to matter after all, because then I had the chance to kill *two* birds with one stone. I could take care of Berntsen, and eliminate some major Olympic competition at the same time. Too bad about Dieter. I didn't really mean to kill him—just disable him."

He shrugged again, as though the fatality didn't matter.

"How did you pull it off?" Nancy asked, trying to keep Michael talking.

"It was great!" Michael laughed. "Berntsen passed Mueller lying in the snow, so he put on the brakes and climbed back up to see if the guy was all right. I could tell from the look on Berntsen's face that he wasn't. Then Berntsen looked at Mueller's ski—"

Michael took a deep breath, almost in pride. "I knew I'd have to do something fast. I didn't know if Berntsen had seen me hiding in the woods, but I was sure he'd go for help. When he did, I was ready.

"He skied past where I was hiding, and I stuck out one of my poles and tripped him. While his face was in the snow, I hit his head with a stone."

Michael shook his head.

"I thought they were both dead—so it came as a nasty surprise to learn that Berntsen had survived. But he had amnesia. Then somebody started the rumor that Berntsen had rigged the race and the accident to eliminate Mueller as competition."

I'll bet you started it, Nancy thought, silently accusing Michael.

"It was perfect—except that the scandal wrecked the morale

of our team. I didn't even get a bronze," Michael said ruefully. "I told myself, so what? All I had to do was wait four more years for the next Olympics.

"Berntsen dropped out of sight. He had amnesia, anyway, so I didn't have to worry that he'd open his mouth about what had happened. Then I came here to do some skiing, and got the shock of my life when I spotted Berntsen on the slopes one day.

"I asked around, and learned that he was the new ski instructor at Webb Cove Lodge, except that he was using some other name. A little spying told me something else. Old Jon was beginning to get his memory back. I knew I had to get rid of him before he remembered what really happened in Colorado."

Nancy stood silently at the edge of the cliff. The more involved Michael became in his story, the less attention he was paying to Nancy. She hoped that would give her the opportunity she so desperately needed to escape.

Michael smiled crookedly. "So I rigged the rope tow," he continued, "and *you* got on it! I tried to be a hero, but rescuing you brought me face-to-face with Berntsen. And he mentioned the Broken Leg Café.

"That meant it was only a matter of time before he recovered from his amnesia. The worst thing, though, was that he started seeing George. She helped him remember more and more every day. I *had* to shut him up—and her, too, once she learned enough."

Michael sighed, the sound almost lost in the whistling wind. "I really did like you, Nancy. I'm sorry, but . . ."

Michael paused, gathering his strength. The next few seconds seemed to last an eternity. Then, as Nancy had known he would, Michael lunged toward her.

CHAPTER EIGHTEEN

As Michael moved, so did Nancy. She fell sideways, calling on her gymnastics skill to guide her away from the cliff edge. As she went down, one hand scooped up a handful of snow. The other went to her ski bindings, snapping one, then the second, free.

Michael was still hampered by his skis. Even so, his coordination was superb. He landed beside Nancy, righting himself swiftly.

But Nancy was a split second ahead of him. She flung the snowball in his face. As it hit, momentarily blinding him, she darted behind him and swung her ski pole across his throat, locking it against him in a choke hold.

Michael began to struggle. One of his hands flailed wildly, groping for her arm. But Nancy jerked the pole tighter. Michael made a muffled coughing sound, and then he sagged against her. Nancy held the viselike grip for a full minute, not daring to risk another of his tricks. Finally, she released the pressure. He slid to her feet in a heap.

Nancy leaned back against a tree, shaking with relief. She was still there moments later when she heard voices calling her name hollowly through the wind. "Here," she gasped hoarsely.

Within minutes, she was in Ned's arms. Liz was there, too, bending over Michael. Nancy was relieved that she could stop suspecting Liz. If Liz had behaved strangely, it must have been from tension. After all, prowlers and accidents and would-be murderers were not everyday happenings, and some people held up under strain better than other people did. She could stop suspecting Gunther, too. The only "evidence" against him had been circumstantial.

"Is he dead?" Nancy asked through cracked lips.

Liz shook her head. "He's alive but out cold. That must have been some stunt you pulled!"

"He was the one who tried to kill Luke . . . and then George, and me, too."

"Shh. We know," Ned whispered. He held her tightly, his lips pressed against her hair.

It was not until they were at the Overlook Hotel, waiting for the police to question Nancy and for rescue squads to attend to both Luke and Michael, that she was able to find out why Ned and Liz had come out in the forest looking for her.

Nancy and Ned were sitting in front of the hotel fireplace, their hands clasped gently, when she asked him about it.

"Luke regained consciousness," Ned said. "He hit his head during the avalanche, and somehow the blow jarred away his amnesia.

"He remembered all about Dieter Mueller's accident, how after Dieter fell he was hurt but still alive, how he'd discovered the missing screw in Dieter's bindings . . . and how he'd noticed Michael Price hiding in the trees farther down the slope. Of course, he didn't suspect that Michael would try to hurt him as he skied down to get help for Dieter. And he never remembered any of it—until today."

Nancy shuddered. "It's hard to believe anyone would do such horrible things."

"But Michael did," Ned exclaimed. "And when Liz and I realized that you were out there alone with a murderer, we took off after you."

"It was wonderful seeing you two come through those trees," Nancy said with a sigh.

"You managed to take pretty good care of Michael without our help, though," Ned said, smiling.

Soon after that, the police arrived to take Nancy's, Ned's, and Liz's statements. Afterward, an officer drove them to the county hospital, where George, Bess, and Gunther were keeping a vigil over Luke. Bess looked haggard, and Nancy knew that she felt both relieved at Gunther's innocence in the case, and guilty at having suspected him.

Michael had regained consciousness, but he wasn't talking. "And not just because of that bad sore throat you gave him," the police lieutenant said to Nancy. "We've been on the phone with the Colorado police and the German embassy. Price is going to need a very high-powered lawyer."

Luke was in surgery, having suffered not only a broken leg and a couple of crushed ribs, but internal injuries.

It wasn't until dawn that a nurse came into the visitors' lounge, smiling. "Mr. Berntsen's regained consciousness." She looked at Ned. "He's asking for someone named George."

George leaped up and rushed down the corridor with a cry of joy. The nurse, who'd obviously expected a boy to respond to Luke's call, was mildly astonished.

A few hours later, when the others were finally allowed into the room, George was still there, holding Luke's hand tightly. Luke looked haggard, but for the first time since they'd met him, he seemed at peace. His eyes lit up as Nancy came in.

"I guess I owe you a big apology for the way I've treated you," he said. "The first day, when I overheard that you were a detective, I—I just freaked out. The way you poked into things, I was sure that if you started investigating me, I'd end up in jail, even though I hadn't killed Dieter.

"But George tells me Price is going behind bars now, so I want to thank you, sincerely and deeply." Luke smiled almost shyly.

"You know, Luke," Nancy told him, "you're all right." Then she giggled. "I guess we'll have to get used to calling you Jon Berntsen, won't we? At least, if we're going to see any more of you."

"Oh, you'll see me," Luke assured her. He and George exchanged loving glances. Then George turned scarlet, and the others laughed.

"One more question, if you don't mind," Nancy said.

"Go ahead," Luke replied.

"Didn't you ever wonder if you might have been guilty? After all, you had amnesia and you couldn't remember what you'd done just before and during the race."

"No way," Luke said. "Dieter and I were friends, good friends, even if we were always competing with each other."

"You never suspected that anyone might get hurt in the night race?"

Luke sighed. "I should have. The other people at the Broken Leg thought I was crazy! The worst part was knowing that everyone else believed I'd killed Dieter—and not remembering enough to prove them wrong."

"I never thought you killed him," George cut in.

Luke smiled. "Yeah, but I think you and my mother are the only two people who can truly say that." He laughed. "Anyway, I was determined to remember. And it was starting to happen! Every once in a while I'd get a flash of memory. Nothing clear, just a feeling that when Mueller and I had had our accidents, somebody else had been there."

He turned to Nancy. "Then you had your 'accident' on the rope tow, and all of a sudden there were three people there, too—me, you, and Michael. It was like I was reliving a memory: seeing an unconscious body and then Michael. I had this flash, a picture of his face, smiling—sneering—at Dieter and me as we argued in the Broken Leg Cafe."

"So you asked him about it," Nancy prompted.

"And he denied it," Luke said. "But I kept getting more disturbing flashes. I felt sure that Price had more to do with what had happened to Mueller and me than he was saying. But I had no proof." His face softened. "And then George recognized me. And she believed in me."

"Why didn't you tell me?" Nancy exclaimed. "I could have helped! And we might have been able to wrap this case up before so many people got hurt!"

George just looked at Nancy. "You didn't like Luke, remember? Would you have trusted the word of someone accused of being a murderer? The only reason he wasn't prosecuted in Colorado was because the police didn't have proof, not because they didn't have suspicions!"

"And then he disappeared," Ned added. "That must have looked plenty suspicious!"

"All the same," Nancy said softly, "I wish you'd told me. I *trust* you."

"Do you?" George asked evenly. "You didn't tell me what you were finding out about Luke or the murderer. It sucked, not knowing."

"It sounds to me," Gunther said, "as if you two had a language gap, the way I did when I first came to this country. I had studied English, but I had—what do you call it?—a communications problem."

"That's it exactly," Nancy said ruefully. She smiled at George, and George smiled back.

"Hey," Ned said, rising and pulling Nancy up with him, "now that the storm's over and we can go out in the snow again, you people don't mind if we desert you, do you? We have things to do and places to go." He threw Nancy a teasing smile.

"Where?" Nancy asked, grinning.

"You'll see," Ned answered vaguely.

They went out into the early morning sun. The storm had ended and the trees, covered with glittering ice, shone silver in the light. Ned waited until they had reached the car to take Nancy in his arms and kiss her. "Come on!" he said exuberantly.

"Where?"

"Back to the hotel Jacuzzi! The rest of the gang won't think of it, so it's the one place we can count on being alone. We have," he added, kissing her again, "a lot of vacationing to catch up on."

TO SAVE THE WORLD, YOU NEED AN UNSTOPPABLE GIRL.

EBOOK EDITIONS ALSO AVAILABLE

Simon Pulse simonandschuster.com/teen